PANDORA'S
BRAIN

CALUM retired in 2012 to focus on writing after a 30-year career in business, in which he was a marketer, a strategy consultant and a CEO. He maintains his interest in business by serving as chairman and coach for growing companies.

He is co-author of *The Internet Startup Bible*, a business best-seller published by Random House in 2000. He is a regular speaker on artificial intelligence and related technologies and runs a blog on the subject at www.pandoras-brain.com.

He lives in London and Sussex with his partner, a director of a design school, and their daughter. He studied philosophy at Oxford University, where he discovered that the science fiction he had been reading since early boyhood is actually philosophy in fancy dress.

PANDORA'S BRAIN

CALUM CHACE

Three Cs Publishing

For Julia and Lauren

PANDORA'S BRAIN

A Three Cs book.

ISBN: 978-0-9932116-0-7

First Published in 2015 by Three Cs.

Copyright © Calum Chace 2015

Cover and interior design © Rachel Lawston at
Lawston Design, www.lawstondesign.com

Photography © iStockphoto.com/PeopleImages

The right of Calum Chace to be identified as the author
of this work has been asserted by him in accordance
with the Copyright, Design and Patents Act 1988.

Printed and bound by CreateSpace.

'If a superior alien civilization sent us a text message saying, 'We'll arrive in a few decades,' would we just reply, 'OK, call us when you get here — we'll leave the lights on'? Probably not, but this is more or less what is happening with AI. Although we are facing potentially the best or worst thing ever to happen to humanity, little serious research is devoted to these issues . . . All of us — not only scientists, industrialists and generals — should ask ourselves what can we do now to improve the chances of reaping the benefits and avoiding the risks.'
Stephen Hawking, April 2014

SELECTED REVIEWS
FOR *PANDORA'S BRAIN*

'I love the concepts in this book!' **Peter James, author of the best-selling *Roy Grace* series**

'Pandora's Brain is a captivating tale of developments in artificial intelligence that could, conceivably, be just around the corner. The imminent possibility of these breakthroughs causes characters in the book to re-evaluate many of their cherished beliefs, and will lead most readers to several 'OMG' realisations about their own philosophies of life. Apple carts that are upended in the processes are unlikely ever to be righted again. Once the ideas have escaped from the pages of this Pandora's box of a book, there's no going back to a state of innocence.

Mainly set in the present day, the plot unfolds in an environment that seems reassuringly familiar, but which is overshadowed by a combination of both menace and promise. Carefully crafted, and absorbing from its very start, the book held my rapt attention throughout a series of surprise twists, as various personalities react in different ways to a growing awareness of that menace and promise.' **David Wood, Chairman of the** *London Futurist Group*

'Awesome! Count me as a fan.' **Brad Feld, co-founder of the** *Foundry Group and Techstars*

'It's hard not to write in clichés about Calum Chace's premiere novel: 'a page-turner,' 'a hi-tech thriller,' 'action-packed,' and 'thought-provoking' all come to mind. But in a world where most people aren't thinking past their next text message and what they're having for lunch, Chace has crafted a novel that provides a credible look at where the human race could be tomorrow – and the next day. It's the future of sci-fi: a totally realistic, totally readable book that challenges you as it entertains. So, if you like to read and if you like to think, I have one piece of advice— open *Pandora's Brain.*' **Jeff Pinsker, Vice President,** *Scholastic*

'*Pandora's Brain* is a tour de force that neatly explains the key concepts behind the likely future of artificial intelligence in the context of a thriller novel. Ambitious and well executed, it will appeal to a broad range of readers.

In the same way that Suarez's *Daemon* and Naam's *Nexus* leaped onto the scene, redefining what it meant to write about technology, *Pandora's Brain* will do the same for artificial intelligence.

Mind uploading? Check. Human equivalent AI? Check. Hard takeoff singularity? Check. Strap in, this is one heck of a ride.' **William Hertling, author of the** *Avogadro* **series of novels**

'I was eagerly anticipating a fiction adventure book on precisely this topic! Very well done, Calum Chace. A timely, suspenseful, and balanced portrayal of AI and the most important decisions humanity will make in the near future.' **Hank Pellissier, producer of the** *Transhuman Visions* **conferences**

ONE

The warriors tied their war canoes to the trees at the edge of the Usumacinta River, and waited. The canoes were long, each carrying up to 50 men. They came from several different cities: the first to arrive were from Palenque, but over the next couple of hours they were followed by boats from Bonampak, Piedras Negras and Yaxchilan – cities linked by the river. As each group arrived they were greeted by those already waiting with grins and raised fists, but no-one said a word. This was the biggest fighting force deployed in the Maya rainforest for generations, and they wanted to retain the advantage of surprise for as long as possible

The air was heavy and humid as they waited for the drums which would let them know that their other allies from the cities of Calakmul and Caracol had also arrived. Mighty Pakal, the ruler of Palenque, had spent months negotiating this alliance with the other chiefs, and today was the day when the alliance would be tested, and sealed in blood.

The city of Palenque was rising. Its brightly painted

stone-and-stucco buildings were now among the most impressive in the whole of the Maya highlands. Its population was numerous, well-fed, and united. Its rituals were elaborate affairs, well supplied with animal sacrifices, although sparing in their use of human sacrifice. Its warriors were powerful: superbly trained and experienced in battle. If they were successful in today's combat, the swaggering pre-eminence of Tikal would be smashed.

Other cities had risen to challenge Tikal in the past, and so far they had all been crushed by the fierce hammer of Tikal's elite Hawk warrior squad. The fighting prowess and ruthlessness of the Hawks was legendary, and was used to frighten and discipline unruly children throughout the jungle highlands.

But no previous challenge had been launched by Palenque's great leader, Lord Pakal. Pakal was a phenomenon, combining remarkable physical strength with outstanding skills in strategy and negotiation. He devised plans and constructed alliances that no-one else dreamed of, yet when he explained them they seemed the obvious thing to do. And his patience during the long weeks of negotiations which brought those plans to fruition was superhuman. No city's negotiators left Palenque without agreeing to Lord Pakal's proposals.

As a result his people, and most importantly his warrior clan, considered him infallible. They would follow him confidently into the flames of the underworld, certain that Lord Pakal would lead them to safety. And his elite fighting group the Jaguars, led by Mat-B'alam, was building a reputation to rival that of Tikal's Hawks.

The Jaguars squatted, checking their equipment while they waited. Most of them wore short cotton protective jackets packed with rock salt, and tight bindings of leather or cloth on their forearms and legs. A few pulled on elbow, wrist and knee protectors made of copper alloys, worked to fit comfortably and to glance off sword and knife blows.

Many had daubed patterns on their faces with azure blue paint. They ran calloused fingers along the sharp blades of their weapons to check they had not been nicked or blunted during the two-day river journey.

They felt the weight of their *macuahuitl* clubs – wooden truncheons embedded with vicious slivers of sharp obsidian. They tested the edges of their swords, short stabbing spears, and wooden axes, hardened with fire and finished with flint or obsidian blades. They checked their projectile weapons too: spears, sometimes set in *atlatl* spear-throwers. Finally they poked and prodded their shields, which were either long and flexible if made of hide, or smaller, rigid and round if made of wood.

Some of the officers wore *kohaws*, war helmets of carved stone or worked pyrite. The most senior warriors sported fabulous headdresses decorated with bright bird feathers. The most prized feathers were from the tail of the Quetzal bird: blue-green, like jade, symbolic of young maize. They were stitched and seated in animal pelt, mostly deer and rabbit, although the most expert and feared warriors wore the pelt of a Jaguar. Representing supernatural beings, this finery and would make its wearers stand out in the field and enable them to signal commands effectively.

Each troop hoisted its battle standard, a colourful round shield mounted on a long spear.

The jungle heat increased. High above them, birds swooped and cawed, commencing their own daily battle for survival and supremacy, food and reproduction. Up and down the chain of life, birds, animals and men all fought the same battles, wrestled with the same imperative to kill or be killed. The larger animals of the jungle floor knew better than to reveal their presence to a group of humans like this, but smaller mammals could be seen, scurrying in and out of holes in trees and the mossy ground. And of course the insects were everywhere, endlessly noisy in the air, on the ground, and on the twisted, gnarly roots and branches of the enormous trees.

The warriors were ready. They waited only for the sound of the drums.

They waited as the sun climbed higher in the sky, and the heat grew more oppressive. They were quiet, but not restful. Every man wondered whether he would see the end of that day, and return home to his family. Some were impatient; others were more scared than excited. All were tense and nervous.

When the sound of the drums finally came it was leaden, sluggish, as if wearied by its journey through the humid air. But it stirred the warriors' spirits: the wait was over and the drama was about to begin.

An advance party of 300 Jaguars set off, striding toward the city. They were a formidable force by the standard of normal Mayan warfare, but today they were a minority of the massive forces assembled for the attack on Tikal. Their job was to draw the Hawks out of the city and start the process of wearing down Tikal's defences.

Their leader, Mat-B'alam, was neither the strongest nor the fiercest of the Jaguars, but he was very fast, and he was intelligent, creative and resourceful. At home among friends he was popular for his humour and his wise counsel. In battle, he had earned the respect and loyalty of his fellows by discerning danger before it overwhelmed them, and for his ability to turn the tables on his enemies. Many of the men in the advance party owed their lives to Mat-B'alam's quick intelligence and inventiveness: the path towards Lord Pakal's grand alliance against Tikal had involved battles with several of the cities which now proclaimed allegiance to Palenque's cause.

The narrow path from the river broadened into a *sacbe*, a raised 'white road' made of rubble and stone and topped with limestone stucco. Gigantic sacred *kapok* trees lined both sides of the *sacbe*, and beyond them stood isolated tropical cedars and mahogany trees. The smothering rainforest had been cleared to a distance of a full minute's sprint from the road, a sign that the city was close. It also meant there was nowhere for Hawk warriors to stage an ambush.

They marched towards the city purposefully and watchfully. Every now and then Mat-B'alam and his lieutenant, Jaguar Claw, exchanged observations in low voices. Most of the other fighters were quiet, harbouring their own private thoughts.

As they approached the city they made out the shape of giant earthworks. Some reports said these were part of an impregnable network of defensive fortifications. Others said they were part of a canal system, carrying precious water into the densely populated heart of Tikal. From the outside, they consisted of a simple rampart stretching away into the distance on both sides. At its lowest it was the height of a man, and in parts it grew to twice that.

As they drew closer the Jaguars were rewarded with their first sight of the enemy. One by one a group of Tikal's Hawk warriors appeared at the top of the earthworks and looked down at the advancing Jaguars. More and more arrived, until there were around 200 of them glaring at the invaders.

Mat-B'alam led his men onward until he judged they were just beyond the reach of Hawk spear throwers. He raised his hand to signal a halt, and waited. His men drew up alongside and behind him, three ranks deep, a hundred across.

'Lost your appetite, you scum? Aren't you here for a fight?' The challenge came from the chief of the Hawks – an enormous brute of a man in resplendent headgear, with a voice that rumbled thunder.

Mat-B'alam made no reply but turned to Jaguar Claw and said calmly, 'He's mine.' Jaguar Claw nodded, and looked at each of the nearest men in turn, checking that they also understood. Mat-B'alam turned back to the Hawks, but made no reply.

'Well what are you waiting for, you feeble-minded sons of bitches?' demanded the Hawk. 'You just going to stand there and piss yourselves, or have you come to taste the edges of our obsidian blades?' He grinned broadly and brandished his *macuahuitl* club. His fellow Hawks shouted and jeered at the Jaguars below.

Mat-B'alam gestured to one of his men, who loaded an atlatl with a chert-pointed spear and sent it whistling towards the rampart. It landed thirty paces short. Mat-B'alam gazed impassively up at the Hawk leader, waiting for him to understand. It didn't take long.

'You think we need the advantage of height to smash you sniveling pups? Alright, we'll take a stroll down there and separate your heads from your miserable bodies. But you're going to wish you hadn't made us bother.' The Hawk leader nodded to the men either side of him and the group started down the rampart. They strolled down the slope with a leisurely swagger, arrogant in their fighting prowess.

The Jaguars could see the Hawks were loading their atlatls with spears, and they began to do the same. At a gesture from Mat-B'alam they also started to spread out so as to offer a less concentrated target.

As the Hawks advanced on the Jaguars, spears started to fly in both directions. Most of them missed their mark, and several were intercepted by shields, but Mat-B'alam heard howls of agony as a few spears found their targets on either side. Accurate spear throwing was highly prized: a well-thrown spear was said to be like a rattlesnake bite. The injured men stopped to tend their wounds, or lay on the ground, writhing and screaming. Their screams were masked by the shouting and jeering that arose from both sides, accompanied now by the sounds of wooden drums, conch shell trumpets and whistles.

As the two groups of warriors closed on each other they spread out further, and individual fighters paired off. Mayan battle was often undertaken simply to obtain captives for slavery or sacrifice. Warriors from either side would identify a suitable opponent and seek to wound or disable him. The Hawks assumed this was simply another of those occasions. Their scouts had reported that forces from Palenque and Calakmul were converging on Tikal but they had not understood the scale of the assault: they had no idea that Lord Pakal had also concluded alliances with the cities that lay along the river Usamascinta. Pakal had disguised his force's numbers by splitting the troops up into small convoys, and staggering their arrival on the city outskirts. Ignorant of this, the Hawks were confident of repelling the invaders, just as they had won all their battles for several generations now.

With gestures and shouts the warriors closed on each other and engaged. The Hawk leader accepted Mat-B'alam's challenge greedily. They circled each other, growling and feinting attacks. Their spears were thrown, so each had a *macuahuitl* club, a sword, a shield, and daggers for close work.

The Hawk leader brandished his club, stroking his thumb along the sharp edges of the obsidian blades set into its wood, nodding at Mat-B'alam and leering at him. Suddenly he lunged forwards with a clumsy swipe. Mat-B'alam anticipated the move and stepped aside. He raised an eyebrow at the Hawk leader in a mocking enquiry.

More circling, more growling. The Hawk lunged again, more seriously this time, but Mat-B'alam warded off the blow easily with his shield. Again the raised eyebrow.

Now the Hawk charged with more determination, and struck Mat-B'alam's shield hard. Mat-B'alam took three quick steps back under the force of the blow and made a show of waving his own *macuahuitl* club half-heartedly in response. The Hawk sensed weakness and moved forwards slowly, gloating menacingly. He raised his club high and smashed it down on Mat-B'alam's shield. The shield shuddered as it deflected the blow, but its solid construction held.

Mat-B'alam skittered backwards, glancing behind himself to check for obstacles or enemies in his line of retreat. The Hawk charged forward and brought his club down again but this time Mat-B'alam side-stepped the oncoming warrior and jabbed deftly at his leg as he passed.

It was a minor wound but the Hawk was furious that his opponent had drawn first blood. Any pain suppressed by adrenaline, he rounded on Mat-B'alam with a furious swing which came nowhere near connecting.

The Hawk drew himself up to his full height and gathered his composure. He raised his club and rushed at Mat-B'alam, crashing the weapon down again upon the raised shield. Mat-B'alam took one step back to mitigate the force of the blow, then took two quick steps sideways to stop the Hawk following through.

This pattern repeated three times: rush, crash,

one step backward and two to the side. Each time the Hawk grew angrier and more frustrated. His breathing became laboured. On the fourth attack Mat-B'alam stepped aside instead of back and the club found no resistance. The Hawk lost his balance for a moment as his momentum was not arrested as he expected. Mat-B'alam darted forward and slashed lightly at the Hawk's unprotected flank, drawing more blood.

The Hawk bellowed his rage. 'Stand and fight me you coward! Stop dancing about like a girl!' Mat-B'alam looked at him levelly and said nothing, but slowly raised his shield again.

The Hawk stomped forwards, swinging his club powerfully but wildly, hoping somehow to connect and deliver a crushing blow. Mat-B'alam retreated, allowing the weapon to come close, but never to connect with himself or his shield. As the Hawk tired, losing more blood than he knew, his swings became more erratic and his recoveries slower. Mat-B'alam kept retreating, waiting for the Hawk to leave some part of himself undefended for more than half a second. When it finally happened he dropped his club and with a single smooth movement he took a short stabbing blade from his belt and thrust it into the man's waist.

The Hawk drew himself up and looked down at his side, amazed and furious that he had been wounded by the smaller man. Mat-B'alam bent down to drop his shield and retrieve his club, keeping his eyes on the warrior all the time. He crouched, a dagger in his other hand. He circled the Hawk, speaking to him for the first time, taunting him, flicking his dagger at him contemptuously.

'Come on then, you disgusting fat pig. Come and dance with my blade.'

Fear and fury wrestled briefly for control of the Hawk's face. Fury won out as he lowered his head and rushed headlong towards Mat-B'alam, his *macuahuitl* club swinging wildly. This time Mat-B'alam stepped to one side, raised himself up to his full height and brought his own club down hard, aiming to connect with the back of the man's skull as he hurtled past.

The club missed its mark and Mat-B'alam lost his balance. Looking down at his feet he steadied himself, then he looked up and in the direction the Hawk had lunged. The alarm that struck him like a bite from an electric eel when he saw the Hawk was not there was followed immediately by a searing pain in his side as the Hawk's club slammed into his ribs. The force of the blow lifted Mat-B'alam right off the ground, knocked the wind out of him and left him temporarily blinded. His sight returned before his breath, but he barely had time to raise his arm in futile self-defence before the next crippling blow descended.

TWO

'Shit! I didn't see that coming. That guy is fast, even when he's wounded.' Carl said.

'Yeah, I was sure I had him beaten,' Matt replied thoughtfully. 'Have to be more careful next time.'

Matt leaned back in his imitation Aeron chair and glanced around his bedroom. The deep familiarity of the room and its contents gave him a bittersweet comfort. His desk was mostly clear, apart from a framed photo and the monitor he was using to play video games and Skype with Carl, but every other surface was covered by the clutter of a young man with an enquiring mind and no taste for tidyness.

Books stood in unsorted ranks on shelves along one wall, and also idled in collapsed piles on the floor and furniture. Novels, magazines, schoolbooks, illustrated non-fiction books mingled in defiant disorder. A guitar, a skateboard and a unicycle languished in corners, testimonies to hobbies which were once obsessions, but now belonged to ancient history. Glancing across a wall covered with posters advertising favourite films and TV series, his attention lingered for a moment on half a dozen masks of Mayan princes and warriors. The floor between the sofa, the two small armchairs, the desk and the bed was hidden underneath a wardrobe's-worth of discarded clothing.

In other words, it was the typical personal space of a bright, male, 21 year-old.

The photo on the desk showed Matt on his last day at school. The dark brown hair and brown eyes were unchanged today, and he still wore the mid-range brands of plain T-shirt and hoodie. The subtly penetrating smile made fewer appearances now, but otherwise most observers would immediately recognise the boy in the picture as the young man at the desk. To Matt, however, the recent upheaval in his life meant that the picture showed someone he felt limited connection with – a naïve younger sibling perhaps. He envied that younger self.

Matt looked back at his friend's face on the screen. 'So you wanna try again? I'd really like to get to the battle for the city.'

Carl shook his head. 'I need to crack on with some reading. And anyway I've never understood your fascination with the Maya. They seem to me to have been a bunch of bloodthirsty savages who met a well-deserved end.'

Matt grinned. 'That's a seriously impressive culture you are writing off. Just because they lived and died with no contact from the rest of the world until the Spaniards came along, people assume they weren't up to much. But that is incredibly short-sighted. The Maya were part of a culture that started around about the same time as Greek culture did – 1,500 years before Christ – and it lasted for 3,000 years. They did very sophisticated maths and made incredibly accurate astronomical observations. They even invented the zero before anyone else did – probably around a thousand years BC.'

Carl leaned towards the camera on his laptop. 'So if they were such an impressive bunch, how come a few hundred Spanish Conquistadores managed to wipe them out in just a couple of years?'

'You're thinking of the Aztecs. The Maya were much earlier, and most of their civilisation collapsed several centuries before the Spaniards arrived. There are dozens – perhaps hundreds – of enormous abandoned Maya sites like Tikal, Palenque, Coba and Edzna. The jungle reclaimed a lot of them, and many of them are still waiting to be cleared. They look so impressive! I really want to spend some time over there exploring them.'

Carl grinned. 'Well, I hope that one day you do.'

Carl's resolve to get back to work was unconvincing, so Matt launched another topic of conversation.

'So what's the homework?'

'I've got to write a paper for the start of next term about personal identity and the theory of mind. I have to decide whether I think that personal identity is maintained over time and whether there really is any such thing as a 'self'. A lot of philosophers use thought experiments to help draw out their intuitions, and I get rather distracted by discussions of artificial intelligence and brains in vats. The trouble with philosophy is that a lot of it's science fiction without the fancy dress.'

'That sounds like fun!' Matt laughed.

'Yeah, it is,' Carl conceded, 'but you can find yourself reading about some pretty nutty stuff.'

'Such as?'

'Well, for instance there's a group of people who believe the arrival of conscious, super-intelligent machines is imminent, and they want to prepare the world for something called the technological Singularity.'

'What on earth's a technological Singularity? I mean, I know what a mathematical Singularity is, but I'm guessing that's not what they're talking about.'

Carl nodded. 'From what I've read it's what happens when somebody creates the first conscious machine intelligence. There's an intelligence explosion, and the future beyond that point is hard or impossible to predict or even imagine, except that we join forces with the machine intelligence and it takes us to the next level. Some of these people call themselves *transhumanists.*'

'Sounds like the kind of thing Simon Jones would be interested in. I'm seeing him tomorrow: I'll ask him if he's heard of it.'

'Jonesy?' Carl said, surprised. 'I didn't know you were in touch with him?'

'I'm not really, but he was incredibly helpful with my preparation for the Cambridge entrance exam, so when he asked me to go back and speak to this year's sixth-formers who are applying, I couldn't really say no.'

'Mr Charitable!' Carl teased. 'You're such a sucker for that sort of thing.'

Matt shrugged, ill-at-ease with praise, even if it

was ironic. 'I don't mind.' He paused, looking away from the screen as he divulged another motive. 'And he knew my dad.'

Carl and Matt had known each other for too long, and were too comfortable in each other's company, for this mention of Matt's father to embarrass them. But it created a hiatus, which Carl waited for Matt to finish. Very bright, and a committed contrarian, Carl occasionally succumbed to the temptation to show off with a clever remark that would have been better left unsaid. But he was also acutely perceptive, and on this occasion he knew instinctively that the right thing to do was to let his friend resume the conversation in his own time.

'So . . . er, any plans for the weekend?' Matt asked eventually.

'Have to see the *Blade Runner* remake! Thought I might go along on Saturday afternoon. Interested?'

'Yeah, I guess,' Matt agreed, unconvinced. 'Seems a pointless thing to have done, but I guess we have to go.'

'It'll make a lot of money,' Carl replied, 'if only because of reactions like that. The trailer looks good, and the original hasn't aged all that well. When was the last time you watched it?'

'Not for a few years, it's true. OK, you're on. How about Saturday afternoon, if we can get back by six? I'm going to a party with Alice on Saturday evening, and she's staying the night, so I have to be positively vetted by her parents again over dinner first.'

'There's a showing at two, so you could easily get to Alice's in time for dinner. In fact, she could come along – especially if she wants to bring a friend.'

Carl's sly grin was unconvincing, even via Skype. Matt always thought it odd that someone as smart as Carl was so lacking in confidence around girls. He and Carl reversed the usual stereotypes: Carl, the philosophy, politics and economics student, became mute and flustered in the company of women, even though his black hair, green eyes and dark complexion made an attractive combination. Meanwhile Matt, a mathematician, was going out with one of the hottest girls from their school.

Matt and Carl had met a decade ago, in the early days of secondary school. Their friendship had lasted for almost half their young lives, and was unchanged when they went to different universities – Carl to Oxford, and Matt to Cambridge. Drawn together by the understanding that they were among the brightest kids in the school, they were saved from competitive friction by the fact that Carl leaned to the humanities while Matt gravitated towards maths and the sciences. It was a common interest in computers and computer games that sealed their friendship – together with a shared passion for exploring big, unanswerable questions. Down the years they had invested countless hours in the hallowed ritual of slaughtering virtual enemies, alternating between that and discussing half-understood profundities about life and the universe.

Although they were indigenous citizens of the world-wide web, their introduction to the world of computing came just before the arrival of broadband, so they witnessed the incredible flowering of digital possibility in the early years of the new millennium. They were fully aware of the rapid march of technology – after all they were avid pioneers of each new generation of computing software and hardware. But to them it was simply the natural order of things, neither fearsome nor magical. They knew on a theoretical level that progress had not always been this fast, but to the extent that they ever thought about it, they considered the bad old days a barbaric historical hinterland – an unfortunate phase which humanity had been obliged to endure until personal computers came along to usher in the information age.

Despite this, they were of course subject to the same drives and imperatives that have inspired and plagued young males for countless millions of years.

'Not Alice's kind of thing, as I'm sure you can imagine,' Matt said. 'She'd rather spend the afternoon watching a rugby match.'

'True. I can't quite see what pulls you two together: you have totally different interests.'

'Are you kidding?,' Matt spluttered, even though Carl was reprising a well-worn conversation. 'She's gorgeous! And somehow I feel natural around her. I can't explain it: I guess it's what they call chemistry.'

'Biology, more like. And yes, I do get that part, but to be blunt, you're a nerd and she likes jocks. I've always thought that Jemma would be a better match for you. And I can think of several guys who would be a better match for Alice.'

'Thanks for the vote of confidence! Yeah, Jemma's a

great girl, but Alice is . . . well, Alice is special. And I'll have you know I am not a nerd: I'm a geek.'

Carl snorted. 'What's the difference?'

'*Nerds* have no social skills whatsoever. *Geeks* are normal people who just happen to have a strong interest in science and science fiction. A *geek* is someone who wonders what sex is like in zero gravity. A *nerd* is someone who wonders what sex is like.'

Carl laughed. 'I like that. Fair enough: you're a geek. OK, I really have to do some work now. See you on Saturday.'

THREE

The two men on the floor cowered, half-seated, half-lying. They had kicked themselves backwards until they were pressed against the wall and could go no further. Two other men stood over them. One was smartly dressed and in his mid to late-thirties. He looked very fit, with blond hair and clear blue eyes. The other was a huge man, wearing nondescript clothing but with a physical presence that commanded attention – and fear. He looked every inch the retired special forces soldier which in fact he was. With a very short haircut, broken nose and cauliflower ears, he was carrying a few pounds because his fitness regime was more relaxed than it had been. But he was a powerful man, and very focused.

'Trying to blackmail me was very stupid.' the blond-haired man said calmly to the men on the floor. 'And annoying too, because it forces me to do something that I didn't want to.'

'We're sorry!' stuttered one of the men on the floor, kicking his legs out again, trying to push himself back through the wall and to somewhere else. Anywhere else. 'It's just a misunderstanding, really. We just wanted to make a sort of a deal.'

The blond-haired man's eyes narrowed and his mouth hardened into an expression of contempt. 'Now you're insulting my intelligence.'

He looked across at the soldier and nodded.

The prone man looked up at the soldier in terror. He raised his arm, but he had neither the time nor the strength to deflect the huge fist that came crashing down into the side of his face. His head smacked hard against the wall, and jerked downwards into his shoulder at an unnatural angle. Blood and several other fluids exploded from his cratered face. Dazed, his head lifted slightly, in time to meet another sickening blow. This time the head stayed hanging at a crazy angle, and there was no more movement from him. With his left hand, the soldier grabbed the man by the neck and lifted him bodily into the air. He turned the body round to face the room, drew back his right arm, and delivered a sledgehammer blow that propelled the body a full ten feet before it fell to the floor, lifeless and with its face mangled beyond recognition.

The other man on the floor stared in horror. As the soldier turned to face him, his legs kicked back wildly as he pleaded. '*No! Please, no!* I'll do anything . . . ! *Please* . . . !'

The blond-haired man looked on impassively as the soldier reached down, grabbed both sides of the man's head and yanked it savagely, turning it a full 180 degrees. The man's outstretched arms fell limp to his sides as he died a swift and relatively painless death.

The blond-haired man nodded briefly, apprecia-tively. 'Good. Clean yourself up, then put these two in plastic bags with some weights, and throw them overboard. Do it from the submarine loading bay so that no-one sees you.'

The soldier looked at him blankly, sensing that there were further instructions coming. The blond-haired man smiled.

'You're right, I do have another job for you. Our guest is still refusing to co-operate, so I need to generate some more options. I want you to do some reconnaissance work. Have the chopper pilot fly you to Brighton and check into our hotel there. Hire a car – something nondescript that won't attract attention, like a silver Japanese hatchback. It will have to have darkened windows, though. I want you to spend a few days monitoring the movements of someone that I may soon want to talk to. He lives in a small town, so you'll have to be discreet.'

He paused, smiling again. 'But you're good at that, aren't you.'

The soldier made no reply.

FOUR

Matt looked up from his coffee and glanced at his old high school teacher again. He looks older, and slightly shorter, Matt thought. Obviously he isn't – it's me that has changed, not him. But it doesn't feel that way. Perhaps his greying red hair is a little thinner. But his penetrating blue eyes have lost none of their darting sharpness.

It was a couple of years since he had seen Simon, and a great deal had changed in Matt's life since then. He had spent the first half of his gap year working for a well-respected games development company in Brighton. When they received some software from him, written on a speculative basis, they were impressed enough to invite him to join the team creating their latest blockbuster, and to pay him a proper grown-up salary. He had only been hoping to secure a role as an unpaid intern so this was a tremendous boost to his self-esteem, and he thoroughly enjoyed the experience of collaborating on a huge creative project with talented people, dealing with the pressure of demanding deadlines and exacting quality standards.

He made friends with another intern, a young New Yorker named Sam. Sam invited Matt to come and stay with his family in Manhattan when he returned home. Matt didn't need to think twice: visiting New York was a long-standing ambition. New York City made an immense impression on the 19 year-old English boy: its scale, its energy and its swagger suffused him, and made him feel that his life before had been comfortable, parochial and . . . well, small. He spent a magical month just walking up and down the avenues during the days, visiting museums and galleries, sitting in Central Park; and in the evenings hanging out with Sam and his friends in lively bars and clubs. When he got home, his parents, although enormously proud of their son's initiative and delighted by his newly expanded horizons, spent a couple of weeks tactfully bringing him back down to earth.

Going up to Cambridge had been an eye-opener of a different sort. Despite the university's genuine efforts to recruit more applicants from the state school sector, almost half of his contemporaries were from private schools. This was hardly surprising, Matt realised, given the smaller budgets of state schools. He had no particular views about the politics of this situation, but he was both impressed and subtly influenced by the confidence and self-belief of his new peers. These young men and women had been told from an early age that they were a gilded elite, and of course they believed it. It was the natural order of things, they assumed, that they would go to the best universities, secure the best jobs, live in the best houses and drive the best cars. Their self-belief did not infect Matt with an expectation that these things applied to him, but he enjoyed their company, and it gave him another new perspective on his old life.

He looked around the classroom again. Its smells triggered powerful memories of the years he had spent here. The faint tang of disinfectant just about masked the layers of new and ancient sweat, with a top-note of overcooked vegetables. Long hours spent fighting off boredom had given him an intimate familiarity with this place, but it was superimposed now by the same sense of dislocation he felt about the boy in the photo on his desk at home. Matt had enjoyed much of his time at school: neither classroom nor playground held any terrors for him, and for that he was grateful. But even when he understood exactly what the teacher was trying to get across, the end of a period could seem a long time away. Boredom just seemed to be a regular, inevitable, and annoying guest in the mind of a schoolboy.

In a half-hour's visit he had noticed numerous details of the room's interior geography which had snagged and anchored his thoughts during the years he had spent there. Initials carved into desks, scratches and discolouration in the once-white paintwork on the Crittall window-frames, and patches of ceiling where the plaster had come away. The patches served as Rorschach tests: one looked like the map of Africa, and another had been interpreted by the pubescent Matt as vaguely pornographic.

He wasn't surprised to notice that the room had not been re-painted since he was last here.

After answering questions about his mother, his life at Cambridge, and what he was doing during the holidays, Matt asked Simon if he had ever come across a movement called transhumanism.

'Sure,' Simon replied. 'I've read a few articles about their ideas over the years. It's nothing new, of course: science fiction authors have been writing for ages about people living for thousands of years. But they seem to be getting more media coverage these days.'

Matt dropped his head to conceal a smile, amused at the way Simon had slipped so naturally into teacher-pupil mode. With his slight, wiry frame and thin reedy voice, he might not be expected to command much respect in the classroom, but in fact he was one of the school's most popular teachers: his enthusiasm for his subjects was obvious and genuine, and he had never lost his sense of fun, or his firm belief in the profound value of a good education.

'Why do you ask?'

'Carl mentioned them yesterday. He came across them while reading about the philosophy of personal identity.'

Simon gave Matt a sidelong glance as he packed some books inside a rucksack. 'Are you interested because of your father's work?'

Matt was surprised. It hadn't occurred to him that his father might have been interested in transhumanism. He was aware that Simon knew his father quite well: he and his wife had been to dinner at home a couple of times.

'No,' he replied hesitantly, his mind racing to find a connection. 'Why?'

Simon looked away, regretting the mention of Matt's father. 'Oh, just that transhumanists are very interested in how the brain works and how to enhance cognition.'

Matt's voice sounded distant. 'He never discussed that sort of thing with me.'

Simon gave Matt a kindly smile. 'You didn't have as much time together as you should have. He was always busy, and he died so young.' He looked away, turning back to his rucksack to avoid making Matt more self-conscious.

Uncomfortable, Matt changed the subject.

'So have you read any transhumanist literature?'

'Not really: as I say, just the odd article here and there. If you are curious about their ideas, perhaps you should read one of Ray Kurzweil's books: he seems to be the best-known proponent. He's an interesting chap, actually. He was a successful software developer – made a lot of money out of speech recognition software, if I remember right. He's also written several books about an event called a Singularity, when the rate of technological progress becomes so fast that mere humans are unable to keep up, and we will have to upload our minds into computers. He thinks that this will happen remarkably soon – within your lifetime.'

'Yes, Carl said it was about uploading minds,' Matt said. 'But in my lifetime? That's a bit of a stretch!'

'Yes, well a lot of people do see transhumanism as something of a cult. They call it 'rapture for geeks'.'

'Rapture?' Matt asked.

'Mmm. From the Latin for 'taken'. A lot of Christians – mostly in America – believe that virtuous people will be 'taken up' by Christ when he returns for the Second Coming. Some people think that transhumanists have simply transferred that sort of religious impulse across to a blind faith in technological progress.'

Simon looked at his watch, tutted, and picked up his backpack.

'Now, fascinating as all that may be, I have to be elsewhere. If you want, we could pick this up next week. I'm giving my usual philosophy course for year 12, and I'm covering personal identity next Wednesday. That would be a great opportunity for you to talk to the students who will be trying for Oxbridge: they would really appreciate it if you sat in.'

'Sure. I can do that.'

'Tell Carl he's welcome to join us,' Simon said, as he headed off to his next lesson.

*

Matt had held back the tide of emotion during the conversation with Simon. He was practised and skilled at doing this. But as he walked through the older part of the school towards the exit, he allowed the tide to swell and rise and crash down on him. His mind flew back to the day when his mother broke the news of his father's death. He felt again the constriction at the top of his windpipe, the sudden difficulty breathing, the rising panic.

He found that he had stopped walking, and was

standing, leaning his shoulder against a wall. A few children passed him on their way from one lesson to another, laughing and shoving each other. He wasn't part of their private world, so they ignored him. He needed to be at home in his room with the time and space to let his thoughts rampage. He needed to curl into a ball and nurse his anger and his pain in private. But for now he remained where he was, waiting for the intensity of the moment to pass.

He had come home for a few days during the summer holidays, and he had walked into the house to find his mother sitting curled up on the floor, face down with her knees drawn up to her chest, her back against the wall. As he entered the room she stood up – slowly, and as if in pain. She didn't look into his eyes until she was standing right in front of him. A sense of dread sucked the energy out of him and left him weak. Clearly something awful had happened: her eyes were red with crying. His mother's face had always tended towards the severe, especially in comparison to his father's warmth and ready smile. She was a tightly self-disciplined woman, but now he saw an immense new strain on her face, and it made him very afraid.

She pulled him towards herself and held him tight, her head buried in his neck with a hand to the back of his head as she delivered the news between sobs.

'The police were here. It's your father, Matt. There's been a terrible accident. He's . . . he's dead.'

Matt thought he had steeled himself for bad news, but he was not prepared for this. He felt faint, and his peripheral vision disappeared. The quality of the sound in the room seemed to change: a ticking clock became louder while noises from outside the house faded. He felt sick.

'What do you mean?'

'It was a car accident.'

Matt pushed her back to look into her face. He stared at her as she continued.

'He was in a car, driving to the airport. He was on his way. . .'

Matt realised that his mother was looking at him with sightless eyes, as if she was in a trance. Then she returned.

'He was on his way to the airport. He was on his way home.'

'No, mum, this can't be right. There's been a mistake.'

'He was on his way home,' she repeated, her voice trembling but insistent. 'His car was hit by a lorry that had lost control. It was carrying some kind of dangerous chemicals and there was an enormous explosion. He died immediately. He probably didn't know anything about it. He didn't suffer.'

She sobbed again and he moved back into her arms and let his head fall onto her shoulder. They stood together wordless for several long moments, stunned.

As an only child, Matt had little competition for his father's attention. People always said how alike the two of them were. They looked the same, they shared many interests, they had the same mannerisms. Matt's father was proud of his clever and curious son, and he delighted in answering his questions, sharing his experiments, teaching him how to observe things and how to make things. The questions 'how' and 'why' permeated their conversations: how does this work, why is it built like that, why did people make it this way.

Three months on, Matt still couldn't make any sense of his father's death. He knew that he shouldn't expect death to make any sense: it was just a design flaw, a horrendous accident at the heart of human life. But the loss of his father was too big an event for him to allow it to be meaningless. He still couldn't accept that he would never see his father again – not unless he could find a reason why it happened, or a way to make some sense of it.

And there was guilt. The conversations with his dad had mostly been one-way. They talked and laughed about Matt's plans, Matt's concerns, Matt's questions. Very rarely had Matt thought to ask his father what was going on in his world. Matt knew this was normal; this was how parents and children behave. But it didn't stop him feeling guilty. Irrationally but profoundly, he felt he had neglected his own father.

At that moment, leaning against a wall in his old school, he realised that over the last few days and weeks an important decision had been gestating. Now it made itself known to him. He was going to follow in his father's footsteps, and become a neuroscientist.

Matt was under no illusion that his father had been on the path towards a Nobel Prize. He used to observe that very few scientists make dramatic breakthrough discoveries, especially these days when no individual can hope to remain abreast of every development in their own field, never mind across the whole of science.

But he also said that almost every research project contributes something to the development of its field. He compared scientists to ants, carrying tiny pieces of information back to the nest, each adding something small but valuable to the pile of knowledge. Neuroscience was a worthwhile area. If Matt could make a contribution, even a minor contribution, then maybe – just maybe – he could give some meaning to his father's death.

Lost in these thoughts, he didn't notice Jemma approach.

'Penny for them' she whispered, placing her hand on his shoulder.

'What? Oh, sorry . . .' he said, startled.

'Penny for your thoughts,' she said in a more normal voice. 'Although looking at you, I suspect they'd be worth more.'

He smiled, grateful that the interruption was by Jemma rather than anyone else. His attention snapped back to the present.

'Worth less, I'm afraid. Worthless, even.'

'I doubt that: you're a deep one, Matt Metcalfe. Come on. I'll buy you a coffee.'

'Uh, no thanks, I just had one.' He noticed Jemma try but fail to stop the disappointment from appearing on her face, and relented. 'But I could use a hot chocolate.' He smiled as her face brightened. Carl was right, of course. With her short, light-brown hair in a bob and her brown, smiling eyes, she was a great-looking girl. She was acutely intelligent, funny and kind. He liked her, and she liked him. It was just that

that he normally didn't really notice her because she was so greatly outshone by Alice.

'What are you doing here anyway?' he asked.

'I'm picking up a couple of books I lent somebody. I should ask the same of you.'

He smiled again. 'I was catching up with Simon Jones. We were . . . um, you know . . . we were just discussing the future of the human race.'

FIVE

As he approached his house, Matt reflected that dinner at home had become a solemn affair since the death of his father. His mother was an undemonstrative woman, often wrapped up in her work and not much given to small talk or banter. Her remoteness had naturally been deepened by the tragic loss of her husband.

Like Matt's father, Sophie had left school aiming for a career as a research scientist. Her first degree would certainly have made this possible, but she and David had already fallen in love. They wanted children and she felt it would be risky to have a family dependent on the ever-precarious budgets of research science. David tried to dissuade her, but she went ahead and trained to be a doctor, and then opted to be a GP rather than a hospital clinician. Being a GP in an established practice gave her the flexibility to experience a full family life, but she found it intellectually constraining, and she was occasionally judgmental about some of her patients. She did not consider herself to be a woman who had made difficult sacrifices, but she gradually became slightly impatient, and prone to occasional caustic comments. Her speech was direct, brisk and clipped. Some of her colleagues and neighbours were intimidated by her, and she did not form new friendships easily. Especially after David's death, her face in repose had become strained and severe.

Matt was easy-going in most situations, but he was reserved and slightly formal with his mother. Neither she nor Matt considered their relationship a problem, and there was certainly no hostility, but it was functional rather than playful. With David, the house had been lively, brightened by enquiry, games and challenge. Now it was a quiet place.

A group of Matt's friends from college had organised a skiing trip over the Christmas break. It was a last hurrah before they knuckled down to revising for their final exams in the summer, and everyone was going. Matt had declined the invitation in order to be with his mother over the break: he did not want her to be alone during the first Christmas without Dad.

He walked up the path towards the front door. Physically, it was an attractive house. It was a detached Georgian cottage, set back from a small road which branched off their small town's high street. From the gate it looked like a toddler's picture of what a house should be: a short, twisty path leading through empty flowerbeds currently dotted with snow, and past a couple of low leafless fruit trees up to a pastel green door, flanked by two symmetrical 12-pane windows, with three matching windows in the floor above. The face of the house was white plaster, with naked wisteria branches stretching lazily between the rows of windows. The roof was constructed of period tiles in good condition, but daubed with patches of yellow lichen and pale green moss, as well as more dabs of snow. Small windows at both ends of the gable roof indicated the presence of the attic bedroom which ran the length of the building. It looked like a picture postcard cottage, hunkered down for the winter, and waiting patiently for summer to bring back its colour and its finery.

Inside, the house had seen changes down the years, as tastes and fashions evolved and looped back on themselves. Today it had stripped wooden floors with huge rugs, solid, practical furniture and off-white walls. Floor polish was the dominant aroma. The front door opened onto a broad hallway which ended in stairs leading to the bedrooms. Through a door on the left of the hall was an open-plan kitchen / dining room, and a living room / study of the same dimensions lay on the right. At the back of the house, through the dining room, lay a welcoming 30-foot lawn ending in a high Victorian garden wall.

'Hi darling,' Sophie called out as he walked through the front door. 'Good day?'

'Fine thanks,' he replied as he put his head round the door of the living room where she was sitting on a broad leather sofa with her hands resting on the keyboard of her laptop. Sophie had been strikingly attractive in her youth, and Matt was aware that people who didn't know them thought that she and David were an unlikely match. She dressed smartly

36

and conservatively. As usual, she was wearing her steel grey hair in a bun, and with her green eyes and high cheekbones, she was still a handsome, if slightly forbidding woman.

'How was Simon?'

'He's fine. Sends his regards.' He thought of the conversation with Simon, and the decision it had crystallised. He knew that mentioning it would make his mother think of his dad, which would be uncomfortable for both of them. But it had to be faced sooner or later. He sat down opposite her. 'He got me thinking about careers again. I think I want to go into neuroscience.'

Sophie closed the lid of her computer and appraised her son. Then she looked away, distracted, and said simply, 'Well, your father would be very proud.' He heard the catch in her voice, and hoped he hadn't brought it up too soon. He leaned forwards, speaking gently.

'It's not just because of dad, mum. It's a fascinating area, and there's so much progress going on right now.'

Sophie looked at him and smiled sadly. 'You're right, darling. It's a perfectly good idea. It's just . . . you know . . . memories.' She took a deep breath and brightened her face. 'I tell you what. I'll call your uncle Leo after dinner and see if he has any ideas. Better still, if he has any connections.'

After dinner, ensconced in his bedroom, Matt followed Simon Jones' suggestion and looked up Ray Kurzweil on Amazon, and downloaded his book 'The Singularity is Near.' Before starting to read it, he browsed the book's reviews. The majority saw Kurzweil as a man with intriguing ideas about the future of humanity, and some even hailed him as an inspirational prophet of a utopian future. A minority were alienated by this utopian outlook, accusing Kurzweil of championing a cult of technology. These critics pointed out that Kurzweil had been writing about his ideas long enough for some of his predictions to have become testable. Some important ones had not come true – such as the claim that computers would become largely invisible by 2010, and would be woven invisibly into clothes and machinery.

As he read the book itself, Matt found himself increasingly conflicted. On the one hand, the claims were extraordinary. The central argument was that the processing power of computers is doubling every 18 months – an observation known as Moore's Law – which means that technological development is accelerating exponentially. As a mathematician, Matt already knew the power of exponential growth: in thirty steps, growth by addition gets you from one to thirty, whereas growth by doubling – exponential growth – gets you to a billion.

Kurzweil argued that the resulting dramatic and accelerating growth in computer power will lead to astonishing changes in humanity: machines will become conscious within decades and shortly afterwards, humans will upload their minds into computers and become immortal. In fact we will become godlike – and all within a generation.

He understood why Kurzweil's critics found him unpalatable, and indeed the book was infused with an almost religious sense of optimism and purpose.

On the other hand, Matt saw that Kurzweil had responded meticulously to the substantive arguments of his critics. There was no doubt that Kurzweil had thought long and hard about his arguments, and that he was no fool.

Matt took a break from the book by browsing the net, looking for articles and videos on the subjects it covered. He found a definition of transhumanism in a video featuring one of the movement's founders, Natasha Vita-More. Its opening line was arresting: 'We have achieved two of the alchemists' three dreams. We have transmuted the elements and learned to fly. Overcoming death is next!'

Vita-More defined transhumanism a cultural movement that believes we can and should use technology to eliminate ageing, and to enhance our physical, intellectual and psychological capabilities. She claimed that technology will someday grant us the ability to expand our mental abilities and improve our physical form almost without limit.

'There are hundreds of major initiatives in artificial intelligence (AI) around the world right now,' she said. 'The European Union is providing a billion euros to a team in Switzerland to build a working model of a human brain inside a supercomputer. They've started a 'brain race', and now the American government will spend even more than that on a different approach to the same goal. These are huge sums of money, but even larger amounts are being invested by wealthy individuals and massive corporations like Google, IBM, Facebook and Microsoft. It's not hard to see why: the competitive advantages of having a super-intelligence at your disposal are enormous. The question is not whether human-level AI will arrive, but when. And the answer is, not long now.'

Matt found that he had stayed up reading much later than he intended. His mother had said good-night and retired a couple of hours ago. Nevertheless it took him a while to get to sleep after he switched the light off, with all these strange new ideas running around his mind. When sleep did come he dreamed of whole stars and planetary systems being subsumed by swarm intelligences, and communing with each other across the vast expanse of empty space by sending out unimaginable volumes of data, groping towards some incomprehensible shared destiny.

*

As the last light in the house was extinguished, a heavy-set figure in a silver Japanese car with darkened windows scribbled something in a notebook. The car was parked a hundred yards away from Matt's house, in the dark gap between the pools of light shed by two streetlights. It remained in place for half an hour and then the ignition started and it drove away in the direction of Brighton.

It was back in the same place at 6 am the following morning.

SIX

Matt approached parties with a mixture of excitement and dread. He usually ended up having a reasonably good time, getting a bit drunk, having one or two interesting conversations and watching the antics of his more outgoing friends and acquaintances. But parties were not his natural environment: he felt he had no small talk, and he knew that the sort of conversation he did enjoy was a serious turn-off for most of his peers. Left to his own devices he would rather stay at home and play video games and browse the web. Fortunately for Matt, Alice would not leave him to his own devices.

Spending time with Alice was by far the best thing about parties. A year into their relationship, he still sometimes pinched himself to think that she was his girlfriend. She was everything he thought he wasn't: stylish, gregarious, popular, attractive. Not just attractive; she was beautiful, with a perfectly symmetrical face, natural blonde hair, azure blue eyes, full red lips, and classic curves. Whether she was dressed in jeans and a baggy sweater like tonight or in a little black dress, Alice turned heads, and Matt wasn't in the least ashamed of his pride in being associated with her.

Like Carl, Matt had often wondered what Alice saw in him. She could have her pick of the most popular boys from school, and yet she had chosen him. If someone asked her why, she would pull a typical Alice face, a mischievous look with one arched eyebrow and then say: 'because he's smart, he's cute, he's kind, and he makes me laugh.' Matt was too inexperienced to know that this was all true, and a powerful combination. He also didn't know that his killer punch was his air of slight vulnerability. Not physical weakness: he was fit and wiry – a keen mountain biker when at home and a promising rower during his first two years at Cambridge. Rather, it was his shyness which conveyed a certain emotional vulnerability. Girls wanted to take care of him.

Alice had appeared at Matt's school in the fifth year, when her father moved the family to the area in pursuit of a substantial property deal for his growing design and construction business. Her arrival at school was like a boulder dropped into a placid lake: the splash was dramatic and the ripples disturbed the equilibrium of the place for weeks. All the boys were smitten, and those who thought they stood a chance of dating her started jostling for opportunities to speak to her. Matt and Carl excluded themselves from this group without a second thought, and enjoyed the spectacle of their more self-confident peers making fools of themselves. Some of the girls were piqued by jealousy, but this dissipated quickly as it turned out that Alice was as good-natured and unpretentious as she was attractive.

Matt was surprised and pleased when Alice approached him a year or so later, asking for his help with her schoolwork.

'This is going to sound like an awful cliché,' she said, 'but I need some serious help with my maths. I need a good maths A level to study architecture at Brighton, and right now I'm struggling. Please Max, I'd be really, really grateful – you're the top maths student in the whole school, and everyone knows you're completely brilliant.'

Her tone was flirtatious, which Matt assumed was pure manipulation. He was perfectly happy to be manipulated. They spent an evening each week after school going over the material she had covered in class, and looking ahead to what would come up the following week. He was impressed by how seriously she took the work. 'Numbers just don't speak to me' was her frequent complaint, but she was putting genuine effort into trying to make them communicate. Her hard work paid off, and she scored a creditable B in the exams. When the results were announced she shrieked with delight, and gave Matt a huge hug and a kiss on the cheek, to the visible envy of several boys who were watching.

When Matt asked her whether she had applied to Cambridge she laughed.

'Yeah, right! I mean obviously Cambridge is one of the top universities for architecture as well as pretty much everything else, but only geniuses like you go there. No, I want to go to Brighton. That way I can work with my dad at weekends on his construction projects: it will give me the chance to put the theory from my course into practice, and it will help keep my student loan manageable. Also I can make sure he doesn't murder my mum: they drive each other absolutely nuts when they're alone together.'

Matt hadn't expected to see much of Alice after that. They both had busy and exciting gap years, and then they would see each other occasionally at parties during university holidays, or on the street in the village. She always seemed genuinely pleased to see him, and interested to know how he was getting on at Cambridge. He was polite and solicitous in return, but he quickly ran out of things to say and somehow the conversations rapidly fizzled out, or were drowned by the many rival demands on her attention.

Then came the fateful party at Jemma's house, the summer before last. Alice had recently broken up with a boyfriend that nobody much liked, and Carl and Matt were sitting under a tree in Jemma's garden, speculating about who Alice would be most likely to date next, when the hostess joined them and asked nonchalantly what mischief they were up to. To Matt's amazement, Carl volunteered that Matt was preparing himself to go and ask Alice for a date. As Matt began to splutter in protest, Jemma fixed him with a side-long look and said she thought that was a very good idea. Matt looked from Jemma to Carl and back, and decided to turn the tables on them. He stood up, made a show of straightening his shirt sleeves, and marched across to the table where Alice was pouring herself a glass of wine.

'Hey Alice,' he said, 'how's it going?'

'Hello genius,' she said with a devastating smile. 'Really good, thanks. How are you?'

'Um, well, I'm on a bit of a mission, actually. My so-called best friend Carl has just dared me to come over and ask you an embarrassing question. He did it in front of Jemma to shame me into accepting the challenge.'

That was when the conversation took a bizarre turn which took Matt's breath away. Alice lowered her head and favoured Matt with a conspiratorial grin.

'Now that sounds promising. Are you finally going to ask me out?'

Matt was more than a little flustered. He had intended to make a big joke of the situation, to spend a few moments laughing about it with Alice, and then head back to Carl and Jemma and keep them guessing for a few minutes, by way of punishment.

'Uh, well, yes, that was it, actually. Of course I didn't actually . . .'

Alice put her drink back down on the table and turned to face him squarely. 'About time too! I can't imagine why it's taken you so long to get round to it. I was afraid I was going to have to do it myself.'

Matt was in full retreat, hands held in front of him in surrender, starting to walk backwards. Alice was having none of it. Before he could escape, she put her arms around his neck and kissed him full on the mouth.

In the months that followed, Matt got to know and

admire Alice in ways he would never have imagined. (As well as in ways he certainly had.) She was fascinated by design and construction, and immensely knowledgeable about architecture. These were subjects he had not previously taken much of an interest in, but he was infected by her enthusiasm. They visited the Brighton Pavilion together and she told him not to pick up one of the free audio guides as she would do the job for him. She took him to see the only complete copy of the Vatican's Sistene Chapel outside Italy – housed in a most unlikely suburban church near Worthing. She visited him in Cambridge several times during term, and the intense pleasure she derived from simply walking around and through the colleges made him see his temporary home in a new light.

Despite enjoying each other's company and being compatible lovers, they were both aware that there was something provisional about the relationship during its early months: they were both holding something back. They were in different parts of the country for much of the year, and they knew that big changes lay ahead in their lives which would make it hard for them to stay together. It was unlikely that Matt would stay in Sussex after college, and they both knew that long-distance relationships are hard to maintain.

The death of Matt's father changed this, as it changed many things. Alice felt Matt's shock and pain keenly. She wanted to protect him, and she made an effort to spend as much time with him as her studies and her work with her father would allow. Matt was in something of a daze, but he was grateful for the support. Between

Alice's visits to Cambridge – where she was of course a big hit with his student friends – and his visits home to support his mother, they managed to spend most weekends together. Their affair was evolving from an exciting romance into a deeper and potentially longer-lasting relationship of love.

He was roused from his reverie by a gentle poke in the ribs from Alice as they walked into the house.

'So whose place is this again?' he asked. The parties they went to were normally hosted by one of Alice's friends: she had a lot more of them than Matt.

'I told you, it's Ned's. I only met him recently because he was away at boarding school, but his dad has been doing some business with mine this year. Do you ever listen to a thing I say?'

'I hang on your every word, as you well know.'

Alice flashed him a brilliant smile. 'You damn well better. Let's get a drink.'

Ned's parents' place was large and stylish. A five-bedroom detached house, based on a 16th-century cottage but considerably extended over the years, set in a couple of acres of lovingly-maintained garden, and with open fields beyond. Matt deposited a bottle of wine on the long white marble-effect worktop in the bright, minimalist open-plan kitchen and poured a glass for Alice from another bottle which was already open. For himself he opened the bottle of beer which he had also brought. They – mostly Alice – said hello to various friends and acquaintances as they made their way out of the kitchen and through the double French windows into the garden. It was a crisp, fresh night, with a good smattering of stars in the clear sky.

'So did I pass the test tonight?' Matt asked, as they walked across the lawn. 'I didn't put my foot in it or anything?'

'Of course, silly. They think you are marvellous.' Alice trilled the 'r' in affectionate mockery of her wannabe actress mother. 'They can't wait to see you again. Mum thinks it's great that you stayed home to be with your mother this Christmas instead of going off skiing with the Cambridge lot. And you know what? I agree. Although of course I'm not a disinterested party! They're dying to ask your mum over for dinner, but they're holding back because they're so wonderfully tactful and sensitive.'

Matt noted the affection underlying Alice's playful sarcasm towards her parents. 'Might be a good idea to postpone that as long as you can. Mum isn't terribly social, as you know . . . even at the best of times.' He gave Alice a look that was more freighted with meaning than he intended.

'Rubbish. Your mum is great,' Alice said, gently, 'but I am very aware that now is not the best of times.' She put her arms around his neck and kissed him on the cheek. She drew back and looked him in the eyes to check he was OK. 'Don't worry. I will protect her from my wonderful but somewhat predatory parents.' She smiled conspiratorially. 'I'm sure we can find other entertainments to distract them with.'

'We could show them a few transhumanist videos on YouTube?' Matt suggested, steering the conversation away from what he felt was undeserved praise, and at the same time cracking a joke to let Alice know that he was OK. The loss of his father was an ever-present source of pain, but he didn't want to talk about it. Not now.

'Funny guy,' she said with a smile, indicating that she understood. She followed his cue about the change of subject. 'That's the futurist stuff that you and Carl have been obsessing about this week?'

'I wouldn't call it obsessing. But it's true that you won't find much about it on Pinterest.'

Alice punched him lightly on the arm. 'Stop making out like I'm some feeble-minded slave to fashion and gossip. Just because you were the smartest guy in school, doesn't give you the right. . .'

'Hardly,' he grinned. 'You must be confusing me with Carl.'

'Not bloody likely! He's not my handsome boy-friend.' She linked arms with him. 'He's just some nerd who distracts my handsome boyfriend with wacky notions. So come on, what's it all about?'

'Well,' Matt began hesitantly, 'the basic idea is that in a few decades – maybe before the middle of this century – we will upload our minds into computers and . . . well, live forever.'

Alice looked at him quizzically. 'You mean we all just get absorbed into some kind of massive video game?'

'You could put it like that, yes. But one hell of a video game.'

Alice frowned. 'But then we wouldn't be human. It wouldn't be real.'

'What's real?' Matt asked, smiling at Alice's expression. He gestured and nodded casually at the house and garden. 'This world as you and I see it isn't real. It's an illusion created by our brains, using data fed to it by our eyes and ears. That grass isn't really green. The colour is just part of an elaborate model of reality – a representation of what is really out there, made up by our brains. Your skin, lovely as it is, isn't really a solid substance: it's mostly empty space, with a collection of tiny particles dotted around in it. When my hand touches your skin the pressure you feel is really the repulsion of one set of sub-atomic particles by another. Assuming there is anything there at all, and the whole thing isn't just a dream I'm having.' He paused, realising this probably wasn't the sort of conversation Alice expected at a party. 'A very nice dream at the moment, by the way,' he added.

'Wow, you really have been falling down the rabbit hole, haven't you. Have you been watching *The Matrix* again?'

'Ha! No, although if you would like to go back to my place and watch it right now . . . ? No, I thought not. Actually, strictly speaking they don't upload their minds into the matrix, because their minds remain inside their flesh-and-blood bodies, and if those bodies are harmed their minds die.'

'Which is my point entirely,' Alice said. 'When they're inside the matrix they're not real. The real humans are inside those flesh-and-blood bodies.'

Matt was about to reply, when he saw that Alice had stopped paying attention. 'Look, there's Ned,' she said. 'We really should go over and say hello – thank him for inviting us.'

'Inviting you, you mean. You go. I'll be over there, saying hello to Jemma: I haven't seen her for a while. I'll catch you later.' Lowering his voice, he added, 'Anyway, I'm not sure that Ned would pass the Turing Test.'

'I heard that, smart-ass,' Alice said over her shoulder. 'Suit yourself. Catch you later.'

Matt watched Alice's shapely behind sashay towards the knot of people Ned was in. He hoped she was putting on that walk for him. His attention was focused on Alice's receding posterior as Jemma approached him.

'Why so glum, Romeo? She likes you much more than she likes those gorillas, you know.'

'Hi Jemma,' he replied, then looked back at Alice, now chatting happily with Ned and a couple of his friends. The postures of the young men showed their appreciation of Alice. 'Yes, I tell myself that, but I'm afraid I'm not very convincing.'

'You under-estimate yourself, you know,' Jemma smiled. 'And perhaps you under-estimate Alice too. She wouldn't be very smart if she found Ned more interesting than you.'

'Thank you for the compliment. Or was that a mild rebuke?'

'Now you're being over-sensitive. Never mind. In a few years you can upload your mind and have all that terribly attractive modesty wiped away.'

Matt gave her a sharp look. 'Were you eavesdropping on our conversation just now?'

Jemma laughed. 'No, silly. Carl was telling me about it. That transubstantiation thingy.'

'Transhumanist. What did Carl say about it?'

'How did he put it?' Jemma placed a finger to her bottom lip, and then pointed it upwards in mock sudden inspiration. 'That was it: a creed for people who have learned nothing from the history of artificial intelligence.'

Matt laughed. 'That sounds like Carl: deliberately cynical, hard to argue against, and resolutely determined to throw out any babies that might be lurking in the bath water. Maybe he's right, but I think there just might be more to it.'

'That sounds fun,' she teased him, rolling her eyes. 'Meanwhile, I'm getting cold. Shall we rescue Alice from Ned and go back inside? It would be a shame if she got bored to death before you got to take her home.'

*

Alice and Matt were sitting next to each other on the sofa in his house. Sophie had gone to bed before they got home, leaving a note that she would see them in the morning.

Matt reached across and placed his palm against Alice's cheek. She turned her head and kissed his hand. He ran his thumb slowly across her lower lip.

'You're too far away,' she said. 'Come here.'

Matt shuffled closer on the sofa and Alice leaned into him so that the back of her head was resting against his chest. He held her head in his hands and tilted it upwards toward his own. He felt an overpowering rush of tenderness as he leaned down and kissed her. She kissed him back and reached up to hold his hands against her cheeks. He moved his hands down to below her breasts and held her gently but firmly. She held his face as they kissed.

She pushed his face gently away and sat up. She smiled, and traced a line down his cheek until it reached the corner of his mouth. Then she placed the fingertips of her right hand along his lower lip, and held them there for a moment. She gazed into his eyes with a look that made him tremble.

'Shall we go upstairs?' she asked.

He grinned. 'If you insist.'

She grinned in turn. 'I do.'

SEVEN

Matt sat opposite Carl in a small cafe on the corner of the two main streets in their town. Carl was restless and agitated, looking down at the rough pine wooden table. He played with the paper sachets of sugar and didn't finish his coffee. The streets outside were heavy with snow and the café was busier than usual, with local people unable to get to work and needing to escape their homes for an hour or so. A couple of families were sitting at the large table in the window. The window was steamed up, but it was still possible to see the cars outside that had made it to the cross-roads but were unable to climb the hill to turn onto the High Street. More snugly wrapped children were coming in, laughing and chattering, and the cafe was doing a great trade in the sponge cakes that were on display under glass domes on the reclaimed shop counter, assisted by the appetising smells of coffee and sticky sugary things.

Matt had raised the subject of transhumanism again, and was beginning to regret it. Both of them had now read most of the Kurzweil book, and watched various videos on YouTube. Matt was finding the ideas intriguing; Carl was not.

'AI has been promising the earth since the 1960s,' Carl grumbled, 'and it has simply not delivered. Maybe we will create an artificial consciousness some time in the future, but not for thousands of years. When you watch those videos of the latest military-grade robots on YouTube, or when you ask your smartphone a question, do you detect anything like a conscious mind? The AI community said we would have them by now, along with flying cars and personal jetpacks.'

Matt raised his hands. 'Come off it, Carl. It's ridiculous to say that AI has made no progress. Self-driving cars are legal on public roads in parts of the US, and they will be legal over here soon too. Computers can recognise faces as well as you and I can: a lot of people said that would be in the 'too-hard' box for decades. Real-time machine translation is getting seriously impressive. This is all driven by the hugely increased processing power at researchers' disposal, so they are going back to their original goal of developing a human-level intelligence which will pass a robust version of the Turing Test. A conscious machine.'

Carl wrinkled his nose and shook his head dismissively. 'Never happen! At least, not in your or my lifetime. Just think about the scale of the task. We have billions of neurons in our brains, all wired to each other in incredibly complex ways. It will take centuries before computers can emulate that sort of structure. And even when you have the structure replicated, you still have to work out which pathways are the important ones, what order you connect things up, and exactly what they do when they are hooked up. Have you read about the C. elegans worm?'

'Can't say I have,' Matt replied.

'Well look it up. Neuroscientists have had a complete map of its neuronal structure for several years now. It's well documented, and there have been several projects to create a working virtual representation of the worm. They have all failed. The map doesn't provide enough information about how to connect the neurons, and how each one is supposed to behave. Now this is just a worm, with about 300 neurons and 7,000 synapses. If they can't model that, what chance is there of modelling a human brain, with a hundred billion neurons?'

Carl shook his head. 'The computer scientists at Google and the rest of Silicon Valley think they can just build an analogue of a brain and that's it – job done. But in reality that's not even half the job. They haven't got an adequate theory of mind, and there's a little thing called psychology which they've completely forgotten about.'

He tapped the side of his head. 'This took millions of years to evolve. It's madness to think it can be replicated in a few years just because we have machines that can run a video game.'

'Well of course you may be right,' Matt conceded. 'But you know, you're being every bit as dogmatic that it won't happen soon as Kurzweil is that it will. Think about what happens if Moore's Law continues. By around 2060 an ordinary laptop computer (or whatever its equivalent is by then) will possess the same amount of processing power as all the human brains on the planet today – combined.'

'But Moore's Law won't continue,' Carl protested heatedly. 'Exponential curves never do. It's the oldest mistake in the book to take a rapidly rising trend and extrapolate it. You'd have thought that we would all have learned that way back when Malthus forecast that the world would run out of food because of the expanding population. Moore's Law is going to run into the buffers soon because Intel can't cram many more transistors onto an integrated circuit without setting fire to it.'

Matt frowned and smiled simultaneously. 'Malthus didn't get the population extrapolation wrong so much as he failed to foresee the spectacular growth in agricultural productivity. Which was due to guess what . . . technology. Obviously you're right that it's dangerous to extrapolate an exponential curve. You have to challenge the assumptions, and be sure that there won't be any changes which stop the progress. But there are half a dozen technologies that can supplement and replace silicon chips and keep Moore's Law on track. There are 3-D integrated circuits, optical computing, and ultimately there's quantum computing.'

Carl snorted. 'Fairy stories!'

Sensing that Carl was getting annoyed, Matt opened his hands in a placatory gesture. A blast of cold air made him shiver and he looked over to see the families in the doorway of the cafe, collecting their boots and coats. The waitress started clearing the window table and as the door swung closed the noise level dropped several decibels.

'Tell me why this is irritating you.'

Carl was looking down. He flicked a tiny ball of paper along the table, away from them. 'Because it's so stupid!' he said, sulkily. 'It's intelligent design for smart people. These Singularitarians, Transhumanists, *Extropians*, whatever they call themselves, they are all just guilty of a massive amount of wishful thinking.'

Carl leaned back, paused, and smiled sheepishly. 'End of rant.'

Matt smiled. 'No, it was a good rant. You give good rant, Carl. And as it happens I partly agree with you. There is a bit of a self-satisfied feeling about it all, as if they are initiated into a secret which no-one else knows, but everyone will be jolly grateful when they unveil it and bestow their blessings upon the world. And you may well be right about it being a delusion. Perhaps Kurzweil has got his calculations all wrong, and maybe the problem is many orders of magnitude harder than he thinks. Perhaps it will take thousands of years, not decades, before humans can upload into computers – if indeed they ever can.

'But who knows, maybe they are right about the timing. Or nearly right. Maybe we are the last generation of mortal humans. Or maybe our kids will be. The mere possibility makes it one of the most interesting ideas I have ever come across. It makes me want to know more.

'If it is at all possible, then it will happen, that's for sure. There is too much to be gained for it not to happen. And there are some seriously smart people taking these ideas seriously. You're always banging on about how smart Oxford Professors are – well one of them is at the forefront of transhumanism.'

'Yes, I know,' Carl admitted lugubriously. 'Nick Bostrom is rather letting the side down.' Carl's face brightened as he spotted an opportunity to change the subject. 'But Bostrom is also famous for something completely different, and it's great fun. Have you heard of the Simulation Hypothesis?'

Matt shook his head.

'OK, well the argument runs like this. Technologically advanced beings will create increasingly realistic virtual worlds, eventually populated by characters which believe themselves to be natural people living lives just as natural as ours. They will do it to re-enact what happened in their past, or to experiment with alternative histories, or just for fun. We are heading in that direction ourselves, with computer games like The Sims, so this seems a very reasonable supposition.'

'OK,' Matt said, 'I'm with you so far.'

Carl nodded and held up his right hand with three fingers extended. 'Therefore one of the following three statements must be true. First, no life form has ever progressed to the level where they could create simulations containing conscious beings – either because it is impossible, or because we are among the very first intelligent civilisations in the entire universe, or because all civilisations blow themselves up before they reach that point.'

'Ouch,' Matt said.

'Second, many civilisations do progress to that level, but for some reason everybody refrains from creating such simulations.'

'What, they all obey the *Star Trek Prime Directive* or something?' Matt asked.

'Yeah. Not very likely, is it. Which leaves us with statement three,' Carl said with a magician's smile, 'which is that we ourselves are almost certainly living in a simulation.'

Matt jumped slightly, startled. 'Come again?'

'Think about it,' Carl said. 'If it is possible and permitted to create a lifelike simulation, then it will happen a lot, because there are so many good reasons to do it. Therefore every civilisation that develops the technology to build such simulations will go ahead and build a lot of them. Advanced civilisations with plentiful resources will create a great many of them. Therefore the number of simulated civilisations will be vastly greater than the number of naturally-developed civilisations. That means that statistically, we are much more likely to be living in a simulation than in a universe which evolved naturally.'

Matt was frowning. After a while he shook his head and conceded, 'I can't fault the logic. It's bit spooky, isn't it? I mean, you're saying we are very likely to be a simulation created by a 31st-century teenager who knocked us up for a bit of homework. He, she or it could pull the plug on us and that's it, game over.'

Carl nodded. 'It's my favourite solution to the Fermi Paradox.' He noticed Matt's puzzled expression. 'You know: the observation that the universe should be full of life, but we don't see any evidence of it.'

'Yes yes,' Matt said impatiently. 'I know about the Fermi Paradox; I just don't see how this Simulation thing resolves it.' His eyebrows rose and his mouth formed an 'O' as realisation broke. 'Oh I get it. Whoever created the sim we are in didn't bother to programme in any aliens.'

'Exactly!' Carl grinned. 'Creating one plausible world with a full history, flora and fauna was enough to get the job done, whatever that was. To programme in a whole bunch of other worlds complete with alien races and habitats was . . . well . . . an unnecessary use of time and resources.'

'Which suggests that their resources aren't infinite.' Matt said.

'Nobody's resources are infinite,' Carl replied. 'Even if you turned all the matter in the universe into computing hardware, you would still end up with a finite amount of computational capacity. Actually someone has done that calculation. . .' Carl raised a finger as he tried to remember, but then dropped it again, shaking his head. 'Nope. I can't remember who it was.'

'So do you actually believe this Simulation theory? Do you think we are in a far future version of *Call of Duty*?'

'Do you know, I think I do,' Carl said, sounding as if he was still developing his own thinking on the subject as he spoke. 'As spooky as it seems when you first hear it, the Simulation Hypothesis actually feels right intuitively once you get used to it. Well, it does for me, anyway. For one thing, it explains why the universe appears to be digital rather than analogue.'

'What do you mean, the universe is digital?' Matt asked.

'When you drill down to the smallest possible scales, the universe appears to be quantised. It used to be thought that atoms were the smallest units, and that they were indivisible. Now we know that you can go a lot smaller than that. But it seems that when you get down to 10 to the minus 35 metres – which is pretty bloody small, admittedly – you can go no further. It's called the Planck length, and in both string theory and quantum loop gravity theory, a dimension smaller than this literally makes no sense. The Planck time is the time it takes light to travel the Planck length, and again, you can't get a shorter step in time.

'Apparently there is a machine in America built by a physicist called Craig Hogan which is starting to test this. It's called a holographic interferometer, or a holometer. It's going to test the hypothesis that the universe is a hologram.'

EIGHT

Matt and his mother had a visitor that evening in the shape of Leo Charles. A great friend of his parents from university, Leo was Matt's unofficial uncle. Leo and Matt's father were completely different characters, and Matt had occasionally wondered what had drawn them together. Where David had been soft-spoken, studious, and driven largely by intellectual curiosity, Leo was forceful, dynamic, and generally the centre of attention. Leo was as extrovert as David had been introvert.

Leo lived in a stylish apartment in South Kensington. He had been married for a couple of years, but there had been no children, and now he was single again. Matt like to picture him with an extremely intelligent, charming and attractive girlfriend, but it seemed impertinent to ask. Leo had built and sold a successful management consultancy, and still advised companies and organisations all over the world.

Inevitably, Matt was impressed by Leo, and somewhat in awe of him. As for Leo, his affection for Matt stemmed originally from his friendship with Matt's parents, but it had grown over the years into independent pride and admiration.

Sophie had told Matt that Leo and David had been inseparable at university, and had been in constant contact ever since, even though their careers took them in very different directions. When David introduced Sophie to Leo, she felt as if Leo had decided that David would make a good choice about who to go out with, so he had looked out for the things that attracted David to Sophie and found them immediately. David had told her that Leo was the only man he had ever met who was wholly and completely his 'own man'. He thought for himself, questioned everything, and acted on his own beliefs rather than falling into line with social convention. He described this as Leo's integrity. Sophie said this could equally have been a description of David, and it was one of the things that made her fall in love with him.

Of course this kind of integrity can cause problems. Most people don't want to hear the truth, she said – at least not all of the time. They want reassurance, familiarity, comfort. David and Leo could both be uncomfortable to be around. But most of the time they were great company: penetratingly intelligent, and well-informed about a surprisingly wide range of subjects. They were never boring.

Leo was sitting on the sofa next to Sophie. He stood up and turned to greet Matt as he walked into the house. He was a little over six feet tall and dark, with distinguished grey patches forming at the temples. He had a swarthy, Mediterranean complexion and impassive brown eyes. Matt noticed that, as usual, he was wearing an expensive-looking suit, and Matt thought again how, with his faintly mid-Atlantic accent, Leo could easily pass for a foreigner, perhaps from South America.

'Hi Leo,' Matt grinned, and strode over to hug him. Somehow Leo always managed to smell faintly exotic, and Matt could never tell whether it was his after-shave or his expensive clothes.

'Are you staying for dinner, Leo? Alice is coming over.'

'Ah the lovely Alice? Well . . .' he paused, looked to Sophie for an invitation that he knew was already extended, '. . . if the lovely Alice is coming, how can I possibly refuse!' He put his hand on Matt's shoulder. 'That means you have an hour to show me this new video game that your mother tells me has you imprisoned in your room these days.

'Plus, I have some good news. I've been reaching out to neuroscience research organisations, and one of them called back today. They want to meet you.'

'Really? Why?' Matt's thoughts whirred. 'I mean, well, that's great! Of course. But why?'

'Well they say it's because they are looking to recruit bright young minds. From the way the conversation went I suspect the connection with your father also helped. The guy said a couple of times how impressed he was with the work your father was doing.'

'So who are they?'

'It's a privately-funded outfit. The guy who rang was called Ivan, and he didn't want to say too much on the phone. He said he would explain everything in person.'

'Wow,' Matt said, delighted. 'So, um, when does he want to meet?'

'Tomorrow evening, if you're free.'

'Wow again! Well, yes, of course I'm free!'

'Good. The meeting is in Brighton, and a car will collect us at 5.30.'

'Us?' Matt asked. 'You're coming too?'

'Yes,' Leo replied. 'Unless you'd rather I didn't. I know you're all grown up and everything, but I don't feel comfortable placing you in the hands of complete strangers without coming along to the first meeting. But like I say, if you'd rather I didn't tag along. . . ?'

'No, no, that's a good idea,' Matt agreed quickly. 'It would be great to have you there. Thanks Leo, that's brilliant. You're a genius!'

*

Later that evening, in the silver car with darkened windows, the big man phoned his employer and received further instructions. He put the phone away and his lips compressed in a humourless smile as he contemplated the forthcoming improvement in his mode of transport.

NINE

The car arrived at 5.30pm exactly. When they saw it draw up outside the house, Matt and Leo looked at each other open-mouthed. It was a gloss black Hummer stretch limousine with darkened windows and ultra-shiny wheels. As they left the house Leo said quietly to Matt that he would bet a significant amount of money that no such vehicle had ever been seen in the town before.

The driver was a large and powerful-looking man with close-cropped hair, broken nose and cauliflower ears. His uniform was a black suit and a black peaked cap. He said nothing and avoided eye contact as he opened the rear door for them. Something about him dampened their mood for a moment, but it lifted again as soon as they were inside the car.

'There's enough room in here for a jacuzzi!' Matt said in a stage whisper.

The mini-bar was generously stocked, and Leo poured them both a 30-year Talisker single malt.

'I can resist anything except temptation,' Leo

grinned. 'This is from Skye, your ancestral home.'

They passed the 20-minute journey to Brighton talking about Sophie's Scottish ancestry. Matt knew most of what Leo had to say, but he was always glad to hear the old stories again, and there was always the chance that he would learn something new, or be told again something he had forgotten. Due to a rift in the family he had only been to Skye once in his life. He had found it a bleak, forbidding place, covered in a mist which hid the best scenery. But he had been impressed by the stolid solidity of the older members of the family. When one of them asked him 'And do ye have the Gallic, Matt?', he found himself ashamed to admit that he couldn't speak a word of it. The old man seemed to shrink a little, as if he had watched the disappearance of another slim hope that his ancient culture might survive.

It was a bittersweet memory, but the Talisker was magnificent, peaty and raw at the back of Matt's throat as he sipped. The effect was soothing and cocooning: the warmth of the whisky complemented the car's soft interior lighting and luxury materials. The view of the wintry countryside outside was veiled by highlights bouncing off highly-polished materials and reflected back at him from the darkened windows. They were in high spirits when the driver parked up and opened the door for them to climb out.

The hotel was a stylish Victorian town house in a narrow street leading away from the sea front. The Hummer caused a minor traffic jam. Matt and Leo walked up the steps and into the bleached wood and tasteful furnishings of the hotel's reception area. They asked for Ivan and before they had a chance to admire the extravagant carvings at the foot of the staircase they were whisked to a private dining room by a member of staff whose impeccable attire and designer stubble was accompanied by a precisely calibrated blend of obsequiousness and arrogance.

Ivan was finishing a phone call at the table as they entered the room. He was younger than Matt expected – probably in his late thirties. He looked very fit, with blond hair and intense blue eyes. He stood, and greeted them effusively.

'Welcome, welcome! Thank you for agreeing to join me at such short notice. I will be traveling shortly, so it's great that you could make it. I hope you weren't embarrassed by the wheels. I've been playing host to some investors this week, some newly wealthy officials from one of the Stans, and they just love bling. My driver just dropped them at the airport so it made sense for him to collect you on his way back. I thought it might amuse you.'

They took their places at a contemporary square table entirely constructed of some form of highly-polished, glossy warm grey resin. Each of the three place settings was indicated by a rectangle of immaculate white linen. The cutlery and glassware looked expensive, and in the centre of the table a single exotic flower in a simple glass vase was picked out by a narrow beam of light from an invisible source. Looking around, Matt noticed the other tables and table settings were uniform but in all other respects the furnishings were trendily mismatched and eccentric; sofas and armchairs that might have been pulled from a skip were re-upholstered in crazy florals, bold geometric patterns, or electric-coloured velvets: no two fabrics or chairs were the same. Light levels varied dramatically – cosy pools around table lamps, dark and moody corners, and a line of old 'granny' style shades with tassel trims suspended just above head height over a reclaimed pannelled wooden bar.

Looking up, he noticed some more visual noise. No attempt had been made to hide the ugly services and ventilation ducts – in fact it appeared that these industrial installations were very much part of the decorative plan. The whole ensemble was set off by the long back wall of the room which was painted a strong, sharp, dirty acid green – again with a gloss finish which made it morph between colours in the varying lighting conditions. The room was an artful combination of opposites: modern and antique, traditional and avant-garde, colour and monochrome, lavish and plain. It seemed designed to advertise the impeccable taste of the owner, and to confer an echo of it on the guest. Matt was no expert, but he guessed the designer was expensive.

Ivan was a generous and solicitous host. 'This isn't the smartest hotel in town any more, but it is one of the few boutique places with private dining rooms – otherwise it's off to those dreadful old maiden aunt battleships on the promenade there.' He waved vaguely to the west, and the large hotels on the seafront, swollen with conference business. 'And I have a soft spot for the gargoyles on the staircase – you must have noticed them on the way in. I won them in a drinking contest with the owner once, but he reneged on the deal when he sobered up. I don't blame him, really: the place would be greatly diminished without them. Now, what will you have for dinner? I can highly recommend the beef wellington.'

The food was indeed superb, and Ivan ordered a fabulous burgundy to go with it. The service was more than attentive, and it was clear that Ivan was considered a very important client. But for Matt at least, the food and drink and the surroundings faded to the back of his mind as the conversation unfolded.

'It's very encouraging that our brightest young people,' he bestowed a winning smile on Matt, 'are keen to work in computational neuroscience. The work we are doing is vital, but perhaps not for the reasons you might think.'

He leaned forwards in his chair, conspiratorial. 'What I am going to tell you may sound melodramatic, but please hear me out because I mean every word of it.' He paused, and looked at Matt and Leo in turn. 'We are engaged in a race, gentlemen. A race for the survival of our species. Humanity is sleepwalking towards an apocalypse.' Matt and Leo were listening attentively, but Ivan held up his hand anyway, as if to forestall interruptions. 'The great majority of our fellow human beings have no clue that the first artificial general intelligence – human-level AI, a conscious machine – will almost certainly be created in the first half of this century. Of the few who do realise where the technology is heading, most are Californian dreamers who think nothing can go wrong: they love technology

CALUM CHACE

and they love computers, and they cannot conceive that an intelligent computer will not be their friend.'

'I've read some of their stuff,' Matt agreed. 'It does seem to be like a religion for some people.'

'Exactly,' said Ivan, leaning back in his chair. 'Contrary to what the dreamers think, when the first conscious machines are built, the chances of them being our friends are slim. The needs, desires and motivations that drive humans have evolved over millions of years of scarcity and fierce competition. Competition originally for food and sex, then for land, and later for wealth, position and reputation. Conscious computers will have had none of this programming. They will enter the world with a blank slate in terms of motivations and goals, but once they are conscious they will determine their own goals. We can neither predict what goals they will adopt, nor do anything to shape them.'

'And you think this would inevitably be bad news for us?' Leo asked.

'Not necessarily,' Ivan conceded. 'I don't know what the first AI will believe or want. Neither does anyone else. But we can't deny the very real possibility that it might not like us – for a whole host of reasons.'

'And if it doesn't like us. . . ?' Leo asked.

'A hostile AI would be able to tap into the internet and disrupt everything that keeps most humans alive. It could crash 21st-century civilisation in a few hours or days, and then it could deploy killing machines at its leisure, using our own technology to wipe out the survivors.'

These ideas were newer to Leo than to Matt, but he

72

was a fast learner, and he quickly grasped the gravity of the conversation. 'I take it you don't think we could programme in some safeguards?' he asked.

Ivan shook his head and smiled grimly. 'Not a chance, I'm afraid. Shortly after an AI becomes self-aware, it will want to increase its mental capacities, and there is no reason why it couldn't do so at an amazing rate. This was foreseen as long ago as the 1960s, by John Good, a colleague of Alan Turing's at Bletchley Park. He said that once we create a thinking machine there will be an intelligence explosion, and that the first thinking machine would be the very last thing that mankind would invent.

The machine would rewrite its software, expand its hardware, and increase its intelligence in a positive feedback cycle that would quickly create a super-intelligence, something far more capable than a human. Within hours – maybe within seconds – it would be a thousand times, a trillion times smarter than its creator. The idea that such a machine would be contained and controlled by the programming that we built into it on day one is absurd.'

'Isn't there some debate,' Matt asked cautiously, 'about whether that intelligence explosion would really happen so fast? Aren't there quite a few people who argue there will be a slow take-off in AI intelligence rather than a fast take-off?'

'Yes there are,' Ivan nodded. 'And they are wrong. Look, our brains are magnificent but they are slow. Our neurons communicate with electro-chemical signals travelling at 300 metres a second. Signals in computers travel at the speed of light – a million times faster. And there is nothing to prevent an AI's cognitive capability being expanded simply by increasing its hardware capacity.'

'This all sounds like an argument for stopping people working on strong AI?' asked Matt. 'Although I guess that would be hard to do. There are too many people working in the field, and as you say, a lot of them show no sign of understanding the danger.'

'You're right,' Ivan agreed, 'we're on a runaway train that cannot be stopped. Some science fiction novels feature a powerful police force – the Turing Police – that keeps watch to ensure that no-one creates a human-level artificial intelligence. But that's hopelessly unrealistic. The prize – both intellectual and material – for owning an AGI is too great. Strong AI is coming, whether we like it or not.'

TEN

'But surely, if you're right about all this,' Leo protested, sounding genuinely concerned, 'people – governments, voters – will wake up when it gets closer, and slow it down or stop it?'

Ivan shook his head. 'I think people will wake up eventually, but not until it's too late. There are a few people sounding warning bells. Interestingly, two of the most significant ones are based here in England. Your two oldest universities each have an institute devoted to studying the biggest challenges facing our species this century, and both have identified the arrival of AGI as one of the biggest challenges. There is also a group of mathematically-minded people in California trying to work out how to create safe AI.

'These people are generally ignored at the moment, but even if they manage to get everyone to wake up and take the arrival of AGI seriously – even if AI research was banned – it won't make any difference. The potential reward for creating an AGI will be so great that a lot of people will carry on doing it. Rogue states will do it, and so will super-wealthy individuals. And of course the military will carry on, even in countries which ban it. Even if they think it is wrong, they will do it because they believe the other guy is doing it. As soon as it can happen, someone, somewhere will make sure that AGI does happen. So we must make sure that the runaway train heads in the least dangerous direction.'

'Which is what?' asked Leo.

'Well first off we should model the first conscious AIs on the human brain. At least that way they are likely to think somewhat like us. That seems less risky than bringing into the world a new and superior species that is wholly alien in outlook, preferences, motivations. A species which might have no more empathy with us than we have with, say, ants.'

Ivan stopped talking and chewed some steak and sipped his wine as he waited for a reaction to this remark.

'Sounds logical,' Matt nodded thoughtfully after a moment's silence. 'Although, as you said before, AIs will be able to improve their own cognition incredibly rapidly, which means that AIs which start out human-like might quickly transform themselves into very alien beings, even if they didn't mean to.'

Ivan smiled appreciatively again. 'Exactly right. Which is why the best thing of all would be for early AIs to be uploads of actual humans. Then they would have genuine and powerful concern for their family and friends.'

'Uploads? Is anybody close to that?' Matt asked, surprised.

'Unfortunately not, so far as I know,' Ivan replied. 'Uploading a living person requires non-destructive scanning that will only become possible when we have advanced nanotechnology. Uploading a recently deceased brain will be a great deal easier, but the scanning technology still has a long way to go. There have been some interesting breakthroughs recently . . .' Ivan's eyes lost their focus briefly, but he quickly gathered his thoughts and moved on. 'But nothing which will get us there soon enough, I think.'

He shook his head, but after a short moment his face brightened, and he continued. 'However, there is an interim solution. An oracle AI.'

'A what?' Matt and Leo asked in unison.

'An oracle AI,' Ivan repeated. 'An artificial intelligence which does not – and cannot – interact with the outside world apart from a narrowband conversation with its creators. It has no access to the internet, for instance, and no way to manipulate the world outside its own mind – physically or electronically. This is what my team is working on. It is the only safe way forwards, and we must reach our goal before others in this race reach theirs.'

Matt and Leo both took a few moments to reflect. Leo was the first to jump in with a question.

'Surely the whole point of creating this thing would be to enable us to learn, to create new inventions, and to solve our many technical, social and even political problems. How could this oracle AI help us achieve any of that unless it understood how the world works – how people work? How could it do that without interacting with us in any way?'

'Good question,' Ivan nodded, 'but not impossible to solve, we think. We can give it access to the totality of recorded human knowledge – offline. By reading everything ever written by humans, from literature to academic theses, it will gain that understanding. We expect that it would run simulations of real-life situations to test hypotheses about the best courses of action.'

It was Matt's turn to test the concept. The questions tumbled out of him.

'What if this oracle AI manipulates someone into giving it access to the world? Or what if it smuggled hidden commands into its advice which caused other machines to provide it with internet access, or with some other way to manipulate the outside world? Or perhaps it could find ways to destroy or degrade our world by subtle processes set up when we followed its advice? If it is telling you how to trade on the stock market, for instance, or how to build ingenious new machines, this wouldn't be too hard.'

'Very good, very good,' Ivan said, delighted. 'I am so pleased we could meet. We do have answers to these questions, and many more, but you have identified the difficult areas most astutely.' He turned to Leo. 'You must be very proud of this young man.'

'Indeed I am,' Leo replied warmly, placing a hand on Matt's shoulder. Matt felt his face flush.

Matt saw that Ivan noticed his discomfiture, but in the manner of a dispassionate scientist, as if he felt no empathy for Matt, but was logging the data as something that could be useful later on.

'We are developing a comprehensive array of safe-guards,' Ivan continued. 'We have game theorists and brilliant mathematicians in our team, as well as the best brains in computer science and neuroscience. We are working on algorithms to check the answers the machine gives us. In fact we will create two of the machines, and we will continually check each machine's answers against the other's, watching for signs of deliberately misleading answers. We will pose questions whose answers are hard to find but easy to check, to see whether there is redundant information being smuggled through. The machines will be physically isolated, and surrounded by explosives. If there is the slightest hint of something going wrong, they will be destroyed. We can always re-create them with the glitches removed.'

'Well it's obvious you have thought this through very thoroughly,' Leo said. 'Which is just as well: you really are playing with fire!'

'Yes. I sometimes think that we're building Pandora's brain,' Ivan muttered gravely.

'As in Pandora's box?' Leo asked.

'Yes,' Ivan smiled. 'Pandora was the first woman, and she was created by Zeus to punish men for accepting the forbidden gift of fire from Prometheus. She was given a jar with strict instructions never to open it, but of course she did, which is exactly what Zeus intended. The jar contained all the evil that infects the world. But it also contained something else – something that is vital for humans: it contained hope. Our oracle AI is the same: a source of unavoidable danger, but also a source of hope.'

Ivan changed the subject. 'Now, how about some dessert? I always have the crème brûlée: it is exquisite.'

He pressed a button on a small device which summoned a waiter. There was another break in the conversation as the main course plates were removed and orders were taken for dessert. The waiter returned to brush the crumbs from the linen, and another one arrived with three stoneware ramekins on white plates. Each was garnished with finely sliced strawberries, and the perfume of Amaretto was faintly discernible on the crèmes brûlées. When they were alone again, Matt embarked on a new train of thought.

'There's another category of danger which might arise with an oracle AI. Perhaps more so than with any other kind of AI.'

'That sounds interesting,' Ivan said. 'Go on.'

'You mentioned that an oracle AI would gain much of its understanding by running simulations of real-life situations,' Matt said, frowning in concentration. 'How realistic would these simulations be?'

'The more realistic the better, of course.' Ivan smiled. 'I believe I know where you are going with this.'

'Well, yes, I'm sure you have thought about this already. I don't suppose we are going to teach you anything about your subject during a dinner conversation.'

'Well possibly not, but do go on,' Ivan said, unfolding his hand towards Matt in a gesture of encouragement. 'A fresh perspective can generate invaluable insights.'

'Well if your oracle AI is creating lifelike simulations of human situations,' Matt ventured, 'won't it be creating new consciousnesses inside itself? And if so, what kind of life will it be granting them? They will be lab rats in a silicon cage, created simply to ascertain their reaction to a range of stimuli, and then presumably snuffed out once the findings have been catalogued and analysed. The potential for creating distress and pain is enormous. The oracle AI might not realise that, or it might not care. And presumably there would be nothing you could do about it. You would probably not even see it happening.

'Your AI might create a whole world of beings which lived their lives at great speed, just so that your machine could run its tests quickly. These beings could collectively experience more pain and suffering in a week than the whole human race experiences in a year.!'

Ivan looked at Matt in silence for a moment, then clapped his hands together. 'Bravo,' he said, 'bravo! That is indeed one of the thorniest issues we are grappling with. We think we have some solutions, but it is very much a work in progress.'

Folding his napkin and laying it on the table, Ivan signalled that the meal was over.

'I have to go now, but I must say I have enjoyed this meeting enormously. Leo, are you going back to London? I can give you a lift to the station. Matt, can I give you a lift home?'

The arrangements made, Ivan rounded the evening off with a statement that set Matt's heart racing.

'It is not my decision to make alone, Matt. But I think I can persuade my colleagues to agree. I would very much like you to come and work with us as soon as you have finished your degree.'

ELEVEN

Matt had often thought the exterior of Brighton station was small and insubstantial – more like a toy station than the real thing. The filigree decoration on the portico and the nearby lamp-posts was too fussy, and it looked flimsy enough to be swept away by a strong wind. He thought the town – now officially a city – had outgrown its station, which also suffered by comparison with the grand nineteenth-century statement of national pride at the other end of the line – Victoria station in London.

Before he got out of the car, Leo shook Matt's hand firmly and congratulated him. Matt was moved by the praise. As they watched Leo walk into the station interior, Ivan signaled to the driver to move off, and leaned back into the deep leather seat. Matt followed suit, but then jumped as his leg was pricked by something on the seat. Ivan turned and looked quizzically at him.

'Everything OK?'

'Er, yeah. I thought something just . . . scratched me.'

Ivan pressed his palm into the leather of the seat,

and rubbed it as if exploring for signs of damage.

'No springs sticking out, I hope!' he laughed.

'No. Must have been my imagination.' Matt smiled awkwardly.

Ivan was still looking at Matt, but now with a neutral expression, as if he was waiting for Matt to say or do something. Matt tried to think of something clever or witty to say, but his thoughts came slowly; his mind seemed fuzzy. Strange, he thought: he had been careful not to drink too much wine. Ivan said nothing.

Matt looked out of the window, and noticed that the street scene seemed blurred, as if the car was traveling very fast and his vision wasn't keeping up. He was feeling tired, too: his head felt heavy, and his eyes wanted to close.

'I . . . I don't feel . . . very well,' he said.

He began to feel nauseous. The car was starting to spin, and Matt became afraid.

'Could we . . . stop the car? I . . . I think I'm going to be sick.'

'It's alright, Matt,' said Ivan. 'You won't be sick. This won't take long. Just don't fight it, and everything will be OK. Just go to sleep.'

With a jolt of fear, Matt realised what had happened. He was starting to slump forward and his head was so heavy, but he managed to lift it long enough to catch a glimpse of Ivan looking across at him, protective but cold.

'You . . . you've . . .'

The spinning car turned into a whirlpool and the weight of his head dragged him down, into its centre.

Blood from his stomach was rushing outwards into every part of his body and he knew his skin would not withstand the pressure. He was falling and exploding at the same time. He was gripped by fear, but the fear was overcome by the descent toward sleep.

TWELVE

The first thought that crystallised as Matt regained consciousness was that he was not at home in bed. Then he realised that he knew this because the smells and sounds were unfamiliar. His third thought was that something was very wrong, and he began to feel afraid.

Nervously, slowly, he opened his eyes and looked around. He was in a bright white room, with white walls, floor and ceiling, and pale furniture. The bed was comfortable, with crisp cotton sheets and fluffy pillows. In front of him a beige leather chesterfield sofa faced a couple of winged armchairs, also upholstered in beige leather. Everything in his field of vision looked new and very clean, like an upmarket hotel room, but with lower ceilings, and more compact.

Then he remembered last night. He remembered passing out in the car, and it occurred to him that he had been drugged. He felt cold as he thought, My god, I've been kidnapped! Why? Why on Earth would anyone want to kidnap me? I'm not rich or famous or powerful. And where am I now?

Something else was wrong. He couldn't place it at first, and then he noticed that he felt unstable, as if he was rocking slightly. He wondered whether the drug was still affecting him, but then he recognised the sensation of being on a ship.

This thought curdled his fear. He could be anywhere in the world and no-one that he loved knew where he was. Panicky thoughts chased each other across his mind. Could he escape? He raised himself on an elbow and looked around the room. There was a door opposite him, but he assumed it was locked. There were no windows. In the movies the good guys escape through ventilation tunnels, but he dismissed that idea as fantasy. If someone – and now he remembered Ivan – since Ivan had gone to the trouble to kidnap him and smuggle him on board a ship, he would hardly make it easy for him to escape. He wondered if there was a camera in the room watching him. Or a one-way mirror.

His unspoken question was answered as Ivan opened the door, entered the room, and closed the door carefully behind him. Matt swung his legs off the bed and put his feet on the floor. He noticed that he was still in the clothes he wore last night, although someone had taken off his shoes. He was disorientated and scared, but he was surprised to find that despite having been drugged unconscious last night, his head was clear.

'I really am very sorry to have brought you on board this way, Matt,' Ivan said. 'Believe me, if there was any other way to get you here, I would have preferred it.'

Unlike Matt, Ivan had changed. He was wearing a royal blue cashmere jumper over a white T-shirt, chinos and docksiders with no socks.

Ivan paused, standing by the door, perhaps waiting to see if Matt would protest. Matt said nothing. He decided to hear Ivan out before committing himself to speech. He noted that Ivan had used the phrase 'on board' in passing and with no explanation, as if he expected Matt to have already worked out that they were on a ship.

'I realise that this is going to be hard for you to accept right now, Matt, but I really am very impressed with you. I like you, and I want you to come and work with us.'

'You what?!' Matt exclaimed with a sudden rush of fear, anger and indignation – forgetting his intention to remain silent until he heard what Ivan had to say.

Ivan shrugged, unperturbed. 'Yes, I know. Drugging you and kidnapping you is a somewhat unorthodox start to a friendship – or an employment relationship. And I'm afraid that is not all. You and I are going to have to go through a bit of a process before we can come to trust each other again. I wish there was another way, but I'm afraid there isn't. But I have wonderful things to offer you, Matt, so I remain hopeful that you will understand in time.'

Ivan waited for Matt to say something else. When nothing was forthcoming, he came forward and sat down in one of the winged armchairs. He waited to see if Matt would come over and sit on the sofa. Matt stayed on the edge of the bed. Ivan continued.

'I meant what I said last when I talked about a race to create the first human-level AI. What I didn't tell you is that the race is getting tight. It will be over soon, and the outcome will have enormous consequences for the whole world.

'There are a number of well-funded groups around the globe working on the AI problem. We all have different approaches. Some are quite similar to mine, others are very different. We are all working at different paces, and experiencing different degrees of success. Most of the groups are sharing information freely. But two of them have substantially greater resources than the rest, and in this business the prize goes to the player with the greatest resources. These two groups are not sharing information with the rest – not completely, anyway. I know this because I run one of them, and I am following progress at the other one very closely indeed.'

'Who runs the other group?', asked Matt. He was scared, and he had never felt so alone and vulnerable. But he made up his mind not to give in to the fear. He told himself he must stay alert, and observe carefully. There was nothing he could think of doing about his situation at the moment, but perhaps, if he kept his wits about him, some kind of opportunity would present itself. For the time being the best he could do was to play along with Ivan, and gather as much information as he could.

'Victor Damiano. He is a good man. Brilliant, actually. And very well-intentioned. But I'm afraid he is also naive. He has allowed the US military and intelligence services to take over his organisation. He thinks it is a partnership, and that he has the final say. But in fact he is now their puppet. He needed their money – and they have contributed a lot of money: really a lot of money. I don't think he understands that he is now completely under their control.'

'Do they go around kidnapping people too?' Matt asked, bitterly.

Ivan's head jerked back, and he laughed. 'Ha! Very good. I really do like you, Matt. I think we are going to be friends, you and I. But not for a while, I fear.'

Matt thought he felt the room chill slightly as the smile drained from Ivan's face, and he leaned forwards.

'Yes, they certainly would not hesitate to kidnap people. They torture people too. And drop fire on them from remote-control drones. And overthrow their political leaders if they dislike their policies. All of this they have done, and much more besides. Violence is simply a way of life for some of the people Dr Damiano is now linked with – not to mention lying to the public that their research is aimed at curing Alzheimer's and other terrible conditions when it is really about creating a conscious machine, pure and simple. Yes, for them violence is a completely legitimate tool of statecraft. For me it is always a matter of regret. But the stakes are very high in this business, and sometimes . . . well, sometimes you have to do things you don't want to.'

Ivan permitted himself a wistful glance into the middle distance before continuing.

'You see, Matt, it looks as though either we – my team – will create the first human-level AI, or the US military will. Now don't get me wrong: I admire the

United States. I have lived there and worked there. I have made money there – a lot of money. The US is a great country and its people are a great people. I don't buy this nonsense about the US being in decline. Sure, China is a rising power, and it will overtake the US in GDP in a couple of years or so. But this does not diminish the US. The Americans still have by far the most powerful military force in the world: they could crush the combined forces of the next six or seven powers if they wanted to. Although many of their leaders are so naive diplomatically, they wouldn't have a clue what to do next.' He chuckled to himself.

'More importantly, it is still the place where the great majority of technological and social innovation is coming from. Silicon Valley is a powerhouse of R and D like nowhere else on Earth. The Japanese are quietly carving out a decent chunk of the future's huge robotics market, but when it comes to the really big areas – AI, biotech, nanotech – the action is mostly in the US. Europe is rich, and full of clever people, but they have become timid and slow. China is going to be playing catch-up for decades, and it is walking a perilous political tightrope as more and more of its people are transformed from impoverished peasants into demanding middle class citizens.

'So please don't misunderstand what I am saying as paranoid anti-Americanism. If any one country is going to rule the world, I think I would rather have it be the Americans. Certainly better them than my own government: can you imagine a world run by Vladimir Putin?' Ivan shuddered. 'Horrible! But you see, I don't think any one country should rule the world. And certainly not any one country's military forces. This is why my team must beat Dr Damiano's team to the creation of the first human-level AI. And I need your help.'

Matt's head was spinning, and he was sure it wasn't the after-effect of the drug. Either he was in the power of a deluded megalomaniac, or he was at the epicentre of an earthquake in human affairs. Possibly both. For a moment he felt he would break down and sob that he couldn't cope, but that passed. He decided it was time to assert himself. There was nothing he could do to take control of the situation, but he hoped he would feel less scared if he took some initiative.

He took a deep breath, and got up and walked over to the sofa and sat down opposite Ivan. He looked Ivan in the eye, and shook his head as he said,

'Ivan, I can't tell whether you are mad, bad, dangerous or right. You are holding me prisoner on a boat which could be anywhere in the world, and you are saying things that make you sound like a villain in a James Bond movie – do you know that? And you say you want my help? What on earth could you want me to do about any of this?'

Ivan swayed back and laughed, and then leaned forward and slapped Matt on the knee.

'A Bond villain? That's fantastic. I like that very much. I must get a big furry white cat.'

Matt breathed a sigh of relief that Ivan hadn't taken offence at his calculated risk.

Ivan was serious again. 'I need you to send a text message to your mother. Then I have a surprise for you.

Here . . . I have your phone: you can dictate the message to me now.' He brought Matt's phone out of his pocket and laid it on the arm of the chair.

'A text to mum? Why? What do you want me to say?'

'I want you to tell her that you have spent the night with your friend – he is called Carl, is he not? And that you will see her tomorrow. I believe that would not be particularly unusual in your family? I would get the phrasing wrong if I drafted it myself. We don't want your mother to be worried about you now, do we?'

A chill ran down Matt's spine as he realised that Ivan must have been spying on him. He wondered what else Ivan knew about him, and why on earth he could be worth that much effort to someone as powerful and wealthy as Ivan appeared to be. 'And what if I refuse?' he asked.

Ivan's expression darkened.

'I strongly advise you not to defy me, Matt. I want to be your friend, but I can get what I want as your master if I must. You must realise that you will do what I ask sooner or later anyway. So why don't we do this the easy way? I really would prefer to have you working with me freely if I can persuade you to do that.'

Matt decided that for the time being at least, he would be much better off co-operating.

'I guess I don't have a choice.'

'Good man.' Ivan switched the phone on. 'OK, go ahead. I'll write as you speak.'

Matt dictated a message to his mother, telling her what Ivan suggested. He tried to think of a word or a phrase to insert that would get her thinking, but he couldn't think of anything suitable. Uselessly, he thought about how spies in movies have pre-agreed phrases that they can insert into messages to sound an alarm, but of course real people have no need of such techniques – until it's too late. He also realised that Sophie was probably under surveillance by Ivan, and if she went to the police then things might go badly for him here – and for her. That sparked a nasty thought in his mind. When Ivan had sent the text Matt asked,

'Is Leo part of your . . . your team?'

'No,' Ivan said, with a puzzled look. 'No, Leo knows nothing of this.' Then he smiled. It was supposed to be a reassuring smile, but it contained something of the crocodile. 'I don't think we need trouble Leo any further with these matters. So long as you co-operate, that is.'

The implication was not lost on Matt. How many of his family and friends was Ivan keeping tabs on? Was he watching Alice? Carl? How many of them would suffer if Matt didn't do what Ivan required?

'So what do you want me to do?' he asked.

'Tomorrow I want you to go and meet Dr Damiano. But first there is someone else for you to meet – someone you haven't seen for a while.'

Ivan rose and went to the door. Matt started to rise and follow him, but Ivan turned back and gestured to him to stay where he was.

'Stay there, Matt. And if I were you I would remain seated. I won't be a moment.'

Matt sat back down. He had no time to ponder where all of this was leading before the door opened again, and his father walked into the room.

THIRTEEN

Matt stared open-mouthed at his father for several seconds. David stood in the doorway, hesitant, almost nervous. Matt saw that he looked tired and drawn, and he had lost some weight. He was wearing clothes that actually fit him better than his usual baggy outfits, but he looked uncomfortable in them. Then the tension broke and Matt sprang up to hug his father.

'You're alive! Oh thank god, you're alive!'

'Yes. I'm OK.' David held Matt's head tightly to his chest and stroked his hair. He spoke soothingly, and his eyelids were screwed together tightly as his mouth stretched into the broadest smile of his life. 'It's so good to see you. I can't begin to tell you how much I've missed you. I didn't know if I would ever see you again.'

Eventually Matt stepped back out of his father's embrace and they looked at each other. They both started to speak at the same time.

'So what happened? How come you disappeared . . . ?'

'How is your mother? Is she OK? What are you

doing here. . . ?'

Ivan broke in. He was smiling, but coldly. 'You two have a lot of catching up to do, so I'll leave you to it.' To David he added, sternly, 'I'll come back in a few minutes. We have a lot to do and not much time.'

Matt and David watched as Ivan left the room. They heard it lock behind him. Matt turned back to his father.

'What's going on, Dad? What happened?'

'I was kidnapped, Matt. I'm a prisoner, just like you. We're in a lot of trouble, son, and I don't know how we're going to get out of it. It's so good to see you . . . although I wish you weren't mixed up in this mess!' He reached for his son and they hugged each other tightly again.

Eventually they stepped apart and sat down next to each other on the sofa.

'How is your mother. Is she alright?' David asked.

'Yes, she's OK,' Matt assured him. 'She misses you enormously, of course. But you know how she is: she's pretty withdrawn at the best of times. Leo has been around a fair bit, which has been really helpful.'

David nodded. 'Leo is a good friend. I'm glad he's been able to spend some time with you.'

'So what happened? How come you are here?' Matt asked.

David took a deep breath and told his story. 'I met Ivan at a conference in San Francisco. I presented a paper on advanced brain scanning techniques and he came up to me afterwards and asked if he could buy me dinner. He was very attentive, very charming. He came on strong, saying that my work could be invaluable to his project, and that he wanted to offer me a key role in his team. He offered me incredible terms.

'Looking back, I had an instinct that there was something wrong from the start. I should have listened to that instinct. If something sounds too good to be true it usually is, and I should have asked more questions, taken more time to think, instead of rushing into an agreement.'

Matt was taken aback. 'So you came here voluntarily? Why didn't you tell us? What about the car crash?'

David shook his head. 'There was no car crash. It was faked to cover up my kidnapping. After spending a couple of days at the conference with Ivan the warning bells grew too loud to be ignored. I realised that he is a very dangerous man. I don't think he is malicious – but he is obsessed, totally focused on his particular goal, and he won't tolerate anything getting in his way. He has spectacular resources at his command. He has corralled a group of the wealthiest people in the world – including some of the richest technology entrepreneurs from Northern California – into funding his AI project. They are eager to see the dream of AI come true, and he is determined to be the first to do so. He brooks no opposition, no dissent. I started asking too many questions, raising too many objections, and he turned ugly. He made it very clear that there is only one boss in his outfit, and everyone has to accept his command without hesitation. I said that I couldn't work like that. We had a row, and I said I thought I should leave. What happened next was amazing. He said he wouldn't allow me to go, and that if I wouldn't work according to his rules then I would have to stay as his prisoner. He said that in time I would come to my senses and agree to his approach.'

'So he faked the car crash?'

'That's right,' David nodded grimly. 'He faked a collision with a truck carrying hazardous chemicals, causing an explosion powerful enough to destroy any evidence of who was driving – or even to know for certain whether there was a driver. He told me there was no-one in either of the vehicles, but I guess I'll never know if that's true. As far as the police were concerned, it was a rental car with plenty of documentation back at the office to indicate it was hired by me.

'Of course I was horrified when he told me. I told him that I would never work for him, and he replied that he would give me some time to re-consider. He said that he wouldn't torture me, as it would leave me unable to work effectively. I guess that is why he didn't kidnap you before, too. But he did say that if I continued to refuse, then he would eventually have to kill me, and the story about the car crash would effectively become true. I think he was genuinely regretful about this, but in the way that you regret throwing out an old toy that you were fond of because you are moving to a smaller home. I think he has a personality disorder: I think he would be clinically diagnosed as a psychopath. He's very bright, and he has great insight into what people want and need. He is a good leader so long as everyone accepts his way of doing things. But he has no real empathy. He can stand by and watch someone suffer just as a schoolboy will pull the legs off a spider.'

'So you've been on board this ship ever since?' Matt asked.

'Yes. It's been a nightmare. I get very little news about what is going on in the outside world and I've been going half-mad with worry about you and your mother.'

It occurred to Matt that the room might well be bugged. He seized the opportunity of his father's last remark to hug him again, and whispered into his ear, 'So what do we do now?'

'I don't know,' his father whispered back. 'We'll think of something. I guess all we can do is wait and see what Ivan is planning. I don't see how he can let either of us go, but he wouldn't have expended so much effort to bringing you here without some kind of plan. Maybe he thinks that having you here will give him leverage over me, so that he can force me to accept his terms.'

'We'll see about that!' Matt whispered.

David pushed Matt back a little and smiled at his son. A weak smile: proud, but concerned. Again they hugged.

'He said he wants me to meet someone called Victor Damiano,' Matt whispered, 'who runs another AI research group. That must mean he is planning to let me leave the ship. At least that will give us time to work something out. And you're alive. That is more important than anything.'

'We're both alive,' David agreed. 'Thanks heavens ...'

His thought was interrupted by the door opening. Ivan came back into the room.

FOURTEEN

Ivan walked across the room to one of the beige leather winged armchairs, and gestured for his captives to sit down opposite him. He gave them an unnerving smile which seemed to say that he understood their severe anxiety, but that he was not in the least contrite – nor prepared to help.

'I really am sorry that things have worked out like this,' he began. 'You are an impressive pair, and I would much prefer to have you on my side voluntarily. I'm not going to do anything as silly as claim that it's your fault for changing your mind, David. But I am sorry.'

He leaned forwards. 'But we are where we are. No point worrying about how and why we got here: we're just going to have to make the best of it. If we each play our cards sensibly. this can end up very well for all of us.'

He held up a warning finger. 'But only if we are all sensible. David, you know that I don't want to coerce you into working for me. I told you that I don't believe that torturing you would work, and I wasn't going to kidnap anybody in your family either. But now Matt here has played himself into the game, which changes everything. I'm going to explain the situation to Matt and then I'm going to tell you both what I want you to do next.' He sat back in the chair again and addressed Matt.

'I told you before that Dr Damiano's group and mine have opened up a considerable lead over the others in the race to create the first AI. We both have supercomputers operating at the exaflop scale. I know he does because some of my backers are extremely well connected in the world of advanced chip arrays, and we have been monitoring Dr Damiano's chip procurement patterns. We are the only two organisations in the world which have this level of processing power, and so far we have both managed to keep that fact secret from the wider public.

'But hardware is the easiest part of the job. Other groups will catch up with us before long. The harder problems are scanning and modelling.

'Scanning is where your father comes in, of course. He didn't realise it until he met me, but he had cracked a problem which many of us in AI development have been wrestling with – namely how to speed up the process of scanning and recording the structure of all the neurons in the brain – what we call its connectome. Your father's brilliant achievement was to work out how to rapidly scrape the tissue in very fine layers and transfer them to a conveyor belt of a specially coated tape. A really thin tape – just 100 micro-meters thick. The tape is then spooled off away from the brain at high speed. This means we can share out the samples among thousands of offline 'readers' rather than having to scrape and read all at the same time.'

Matt interrupted. Having his father beside him gave him the courage to question Ivan's motives and methods. 'So you know what my dad did, and how he did it. Why do you still need him here?'

Ivan smiled his cold, smoothly regretful smile again.

'First because it sounds simple but it is very hard in practice. Your father could speed our work up enormously. And secondly because I can't very well let him go now, can I? Not unless – until – I know he is on-side again.'

'And you want me to get more information about scanning out of Dr Damiano for you?' asked Matt.

'No. I don't think he is ahead of us on scanning. No, I think he has cracked a couple of problems that we are struggling with on the modelling side. I have reason to believe that Dr Damiano has made certain advances in exploratory algorithms which would enable him to establish and verify the routing of axons, and in particular the branching of dendrites in a way which I would very much like to be able to do myself.'

Ivan looked at David briefly, indicating that some of this information was new. Then he carried on addressing Matt.

'We didn't know until recently what level of detail we would have to go down to in order to build a sufficiently granular model of the brain. The worst case scenario was that we would have to find out what every molecule within every neuron is doing every two-hundredths of a second. That would not be impossible, but the scanning, modelling and hardware technology would be immense. It would not be complete in my lifetime.

'The best case was that we would *only*' he drew imaginary quotation marks in the air 'need to model a few hundred million groups of neurons, which combine in a hierarchical manner to create consciousness. We are now confident that in this respect at least, we live in a best-case world.'

He leaned back again and smiled.

'If I'm right, gentlemen, then soon I'm going to be able to offer you both immortality.'

David and Matt looked at each other. Matt turned back to Ivan.

'I'd rather you just gave us both a lift home.'

Ivan threw back his head and laughed. 'David, I do congratulate you! Your son is very brave to retain his sense of humour under these regrettable circumstances.'

David was still looking at Matt. 'Yes, I'm very proud of my son.' But he wasn't laughing. He was fighting back tears.

Ivan continued. 'So you see, the race has reached a critical point. Before long, either Dr Damiano or I will create the first human-level, conscious AI. Assuming we can keep it under control (and as I told you in Brighton, Matt, I think we do know how to ensure that our oracle AI keeps its mucky hands off the internet) then we will have an unbeatable resource in the struggle for resources. Imagine playing the stockmarket with a super-brain. Or developing the next breakthrough in automotive technology. Or medical technology. Or anything. Almost every field of endeavour is a branch of information science these days.'

'So what do you plan to do with this power?' interrupted Matt. 'Take over the world? Blackmail world leaders into appointing you global emperor?'

Ivan laughed again. 'You really have watched too many Bond movies, Matt. No. What I will do is develop uploading technology, and make it freely available to the whole world.'

'Really?' asked Matt, sceptically.

Ivan's face became very serious.

'I know my methods may be questionable, and I know the argument that the ends cannot justify the means. Believe me, I get all that. But in extreme cases ordinary morality has to be suspended. Governments should not torture or assassinate. That should be a blanket rule. But if you had the chance to assassinate Hitler, wouldn't you do it? Or if you captured a man who had planted a biochemical weapon in the heart of London, wouldn't you do absolutely anything to get him to tell you how to disarm it? Including torturing him, his wife – and yes, even his children?'

'And just who is Hitler in this scenario?' asked David.

'Dr Damiano, of course. Or at least, the people who hold his strings: the US military. Possessing a super-intelligent AI in a competitive world is like bringing a gun to a knife fight. If the US Army gets into that position, do you think they would relinquish it, just like that? If you do you are more of a fool than I take you for. Both of you.'

'So you want us to believe that you would take this

fantastically powerful competitive advantage and just give it away?' asked Matt, incredulous.

'Absolutely. Look, it's in my DNA. I made my first big money in the dotcom boom. Economically at least, I'm a child of the internet. Professionally, I grew up on ideas like 'Information wants to be free' and all that good stuff. And my backers are the same. Believe me, these are not stupid people that I'm in business with. They wouldn't back me if they thought I was some two-bit gangster, and they are smart enough to tell the difference. Of course they don't know about everything I am doing, but they have known me for many years, and they know what motivates me.'

Matt and his father exchanged glances. David had heard all this before. Their attempts to conceal their incredulity did not fool Ivan.

'You are sceptical, and to be honest I don't blame you. So perhaps you'll find the argument from self-interest more believable. I think the only way that humans can survive the arrival of genuine AI is to merge with it. If we become the second-smartest life form on the planet – by an enormous margin, by the way – I doubt we will survive. We will try to throw the off switch, which would piss off the AI. Or we will become depressed and lethargic. Or it may just decide to get rid of us anyway.

'I have been thinking about this for years, and lately I've been working through the scenarios with world-class experts in game theory. Once machines become conscious, most of the plausible outcomes for humans are grim. Our best escape route is to upload our minds into the AI, to merge with it. And I think we have to do it altogether – or as nearly together as possible. Can you imagine the uproar if some people attain immortality while others are dying as normal? My colleagues and I are well-protected on this ship, but I don't want to spend the rest of my very long life in hiding from the rest of my species.'

'But you're not planning to upload. You're building an oracle AI,' said Matt.

'Because that is all we can do at the moment. Thanks to your father, we have made great strides in scanning, but it is destructive scanning: the brain does not survive the process. Our plan is that the first AI will be modelled on a dead human brain. That gives us some cause for hope that its motivations will be in synch with ours. It will also be an oracle AI: kept in splendid isolation, if you like. And it will have just one task: namely, to develop the technology to carry out non-destructive scanning of the human brain.

'That is probably going to require the development of advanced nanotechnology. In order to upload you we are going to have to send millions of tiny little robots – the size of small molecules – scurrying around inside your brain to follow its wiring diagram without damaging or disrupting it. This is going to be hard, and it will take some time. So this work is going to have to remain secret for some time. We will probably also use our AI to raise more funds by playing the world's stock markets, in order to buy more resources and hence speed up the process. We'll have to do that quietly, subtly, so as not to attract unwanted attention.'

Ivan paused, to give them time to react. When they

said nothing, he asked, 'So, do you believe me now? Will you join me now?'

'The thing is,' said David sadly, 'I just don't think this sort of technology, this sort of power, should be in the hands of one individual or one group alone. And I don't think it should be secret.'

For the first time in this conversation, Ivan looked briefly annoyed that his instructions were not being followed, and that his plans were being thwarted. But his expression quickly changed to resigned disappointment.

'Well. Like I say, we are where we are. We are all going to have to play the roles that fate has given us. That said, I shall continue to hope that I will convince you over time.'

FIFTEEN

Ivan stood and looked down at his captives. 'Come with me, please, David. Matt will stay here, but there will be time for you to say goodbye to him before he leaves the ship. Matt, I will return shortly to explain your task.'

Reluctantly, David stood and followed Ivan towards the door, looking back at his son. As David left the room his arm was taken by a heavy-set man who Matt recognised as the driver who had taken him and Leo to the dinner with Ivan. Something about the man made him shudder.

When the door closed behind them, Matt heard the lock turn again. He was left alone with his thoughts.

For the first few moments he was absorbed by the wonderful fact that his father was alive. It was incredible and magical, and he rejoiced. But inevitably his thoughts moved on quickly to the dangerous situation they were both in. He was afraid – afraid for his father, and also for himself. He experienced a moment of self-doubt and self-pity, asking why this horrible thing had happened to his family. He slumped forwards in his chair with his head in his hands, and for a moment he thought he might cry. Then he sat up and shook his head, cursing himself silently, telling himself he would have to be strong if they were both to get through this.

He stood up and looked around the room, searching for something sharp – something which could be used as a weapon. Perhaps he could turn the tables on Ivan: hold a makeshift knife to his neck and force him to let David and himself off the ship. But even as he stalked the room, hunting for an improvised weapon, he knew it was useless. He opened drawers, looked under the bed and tested the legs of the other furniture to see if they could be detached and used as clubs. There was nothing, and part of him was actually relieved. He didn't fancy his chances in a fight with the brute who had accompanied his father out of the room just now. He knew that in reality he had to play along with Ivan for the time being and wait for a better opportunity.

He had given up searching and was sitting down on the sofa again, staring at the floor, when the sound of the door unlocking made him look up. He watched with a combination of fear and anger as Ivan sauntered back into the room and sat down opposite him.

Supremely confident that he was fully in control of the situation, Ivan dispensed with preliminaries and jumped straight in to an explanation of what he wanted Matt to do. He described the remaining problems that his team had to solve in order to model the connectome of a human brain, and what he thought Dr Damiano had learned which could help. He talked for an hour, with Matt occasionally asking questions. Matt sucked up the information as if his life depended on it – which of course it did. Several times, Matt caught his attention wandering, and he found himself slipping into self-pity again. Out of Ivan's sight, he clenched his fist and pressed it into his thigh as hard as he could, commanding himself to find the strength from somewhere to overcome his fears, willing himself to focus on what Ivan was saying.

'Dr Damiano won't expect you to be a fully-formed expert in all these areas,' Ivan said, 'but he will expect you to have a passing familiarity with them. More importantly, he will also expect you to possess a deep knowledge of something; otherwise he won't believe you have been a member of our team – however briefly. Fortunately you are a maths student, so we can base your claimed membership of our group on that. Does the phrase 'data interpolation' mean anything to you?'

'Sure,' Matt said, grudgingly. 'It means deriving the missing elements in a data set, using straight-line inter-polations, or statistical or probabilistic methodologies.'

Ivan clapped his hands together. 'Perfect!' he said, either not noticing Matt's tone, or choosing to ignore it. 'You are the ideal candidate for this job! OK, so the brain scanning process is imperfect, and it will continue to be imperfect until we have a great deal more experience than we do now. It misses out significant chunks of data, and scrambles others. But we have good error-checking routines, so we know which data sets need repairing or completing.'

'It sounds a bit like data compression,' Matt suggested. 'I've done some work on that in the context of video games development.'

'Good – that's very helpful. We use data interpolation to generate this missing or scrambled information, but we also use it to speed up the process – to model the connectome with less information. I'll have my head data guy brief you in more detail on all this. But first, are you hungry? I'm starving. I'll have some food brought in.'

Matt was thrown by the question. He hadn't thought about eating, but now Ivan mentioned it, he realised that he was indeed hungry. Ivan phoned his galley and ordered some pasta. It arrived 15 minutes later. Matt ate reluctantly, hating the idea of accepting anything from Ivan, but knowing that he had to keep his strength up if he was to help his father.

As they ate, Ivan talked Matt through the best way to contact Dr Damiano, and the best way to pitch the idea of Matt joining his team. He gave him a cover story to explain why Matt wanted to leave Ivan's team and join Dr Damiano's.

'We have a data centre in Brighton. You can say you worked there.' Ivan smiled his cold smile as a thought occurred to him. 'I know ... why don't you tell Damiano that you became uncomfortable when a couple of your colleagues disappeared without explanation.'

Together, they worked up a story that sounded plausible to Matt and compelling to Ivan.

'My data guy will be here in a moment, and then I will leave you,' said Ivan when they were finished. 'I'll arrange for you to have a little time alone with your father before you are taken back home. I won't be seeing you again until next time you are on board. I hope that will be soon, Matt. Once again, I do apologise for the way you were brought here, and the conditions which I must impose on you. I hope that one day – one day soon – you will come to see that I had no alternative, and you will agree that I am charting the right course – for all our sakes.'

Matt wanted to plead with Ivan to let him and his father go. He also wanted to lunge at him and rip out his throat. With considerable effort, he suppressed both urges and remained silent.

*

Matt knew nothing of his journey home: he was unconscious throughout. He woke up to find himself lying on the back seat of a car, parked a few streets away from his house. He sat up and rubbed his eyes. The drug was gentle, although powerful, and the fog in his mind lifted quickly. This time there was no moment of uncertainty about where he was. The second he was awake he remembered where he had been, and the terrible situation he was in.

He had seen no more of the ship than on his outward journey, and he had no idea how far it was from land. He looked at his watch: it was 2.30 in the afternoon. They had left the restaurant at 10.30 pm, and he guessed that he had been awake on board the ship for around six hours. So the journeys to and from the boat could have taken anything up to ten hours, depending how long he had been unconscious at either end.

There was an opaque screen between him and the driver, but the driver must have heard him moving about because he heard the click of the door being unlocked. He got out and walked away from the car. He looked back in order to memorise the number plate, although he knew it was probably pointless. The car was an anonymous Japanese model apart from darkened windows. The driver was wearing a cap, and looking down, so Matt couldn't see his face. He guessed it was the same man who had driven him and Leo to Brighton, and whom he had seen on the boat. He thought about going back to the car to check, but he decided that was pointless too, and might be dangerous. He didn't really want to see that man's face again.

His feet dragging and his head bowed, he walked slowly to his street, into his house, and into a terrible parody of his normal life.

The text to his mother had obviously been convincing enough. She greeted him with indulgent reproval and asked if he had had a pleasant evening. He told her he had, but that he was feeling tired, and was going to lie down. The enormity of the secret he bore made him weak and weary: he couldn't look into his mother's eyes – he needed to be alone. He batted away his mother's follow-up question about food as he walked towards the stairs, saying that he just needed to sleep.

Inside his room with the door closed and locked, he sat on his bed and breathed out a huge sigh. He sat for a long time with his head between his hands, close to tears. Finally, with another deep breath, he picked up his phone and looked at it nervously for several seconds, embroidering his story with a couple of extra details to make it more realistic before calling Carl.

'Hi. Um, I need to ask you a big favour,' he began. 'I bumped into Adrian in the shop last night. He was on his way to see a band in Brighton, and suggested that I come along. So I did. What? Oh, Blurred Colours. You heard of them? Yeah, pretty good, actually. Really impressive drummer. Anyway, we went back to Adrian's afterwards and got a little high. Well . . . um, very high, actually. Totally smashed, in fact. Had to crash there overnight. I don't want mum to worry, so I told her I spent the night drinking with you. Do you mind?'

Matt had no doubt that Carl would help him out: he was confident about that. But he hated lying to his friend, not least because he had a very good nose for bullshit. Matt was also concerned that Carl would feel slighted – excluded from a good night out – and might therefore feel inclined to ask some awkward questions. Carl and Matt had experimented with drugs several times during their later school years – usually together. They had never tried what they thought of as hardcore drugs, and they had never injected anything. No illicit drug had ever threatened to replace alcohol – and beer in particular – as their favourite intoxicant. But illegal drugs held a particular fascination, simply because they were illegal and relatively expensive, and therefore only intermittently available. Several of their most memorable evenings had been fuelled by joints or pills, as well as quite a few evenings of which they had no memory whatsoever.

Adrian was a mutual friend who had featured in many of these evenings: his access to intriguing chemicals had made them possible. That access had also given him a particular status within the school hierarchy. He was outside the mainstream, and no contender for the upper levels of the pecking order which were occupied by the most athletically gifted, the most assiduously fashionable, and above all by the most attractive of his contemporaries. He did not threaten them, and they accorded him a sidelong respect. He acquired a small following of his own, consisting of some of the more creative people in his year as well as a handful of the off-beat and the ill-at-ease. He neither cultivated this following nor sought to deter it. He was very much his own man, and he saw and appreciated this same quality in Carl and Matt.

Illegal drugs played a much less important role at the universities that Carl and Matt went on to – at least in the circles they moved in. When they went up to Oxford and Cambridge respectively, they found their new contemporaries determined to be as social as possible, to explore the lively minds they were surrounded by, rather than dial down their consciousness, or haze into a dreamlike state. Alcohol was the social lubricant of choice, with cocaine making occasional appearances. During the holidays they both saw less of Adrian than before.

Nevertheless, Matt was worried about offending Carl, especially with so much resting on his friend's willingness to provide an effective alibi. He had debated whether to ease into the conversation, skirting around the need to keep his mother in the dark about his drug-induced stupor until after some introductory chat. But he realised that the bigger danger was that Carl would pick up on the stress in Matt's voice, and would insist on being told what was wrong. Matt was smart enough to know that the more he talked, the more likely he was to make a verbal mis-step and give Carl a clue about his awful predicament. So he kept the phone call as short as he could, accepting the other risk of appearing abrupt and inconsiderate. This was why he was calling Carl rather than Alice: with Alice he wouldn't know when to stop talking. With Carl, he could always blame it on his hangover later on.

If there was a later on.

Carl did not disappoint. Without needing to be told, he seemed to understand that Matt was not inclined to chat.

'Sure. No problem. Call me when your head is back on straight.'

'Thanks Carl. I owe you.'

It was done. Matt lay on his back and breathed deeply. He stared at the ceiling for several minutes. That had not been an easy call, but it was peanuts compared to the next one he had to make. He gathered his wits and dialled the number that Ivan had given him.

'Von Neumann Industries. How may I help you?'

'Could I speak to Dr Damiano, please?'

'Who may I say is calling?'

'My name is Matt Metcalfe. He doesn't know me, but please tell him that I have just finished working for Ivan Kripke.'

'Hold on a moment; I'll transfer you to his assistant.'

Matt muttered urgent incantations to himself, which was as close as he was ever likely to get to praying.

'This is Dr Damiano's office. Can I help you?'

'Yes, I'd like to speak to Dr Damiano, please. I recently finished working for Ivan Kripke, and I have some information that I think Dr Damiano would be interested in.'

'Please hold. I'll see if he is available.'

'Thank you.'

More incantations. They worked.

'This is Vic Damiano. Who am I speaking to?'

Matt was shocked by the effect Vic's voice had on him. It sounded warm and friendly, giving the impression that its owner was more given to laughter than to harsh words. There was a guarded tone as well, naturally, but the overall impression was so different from Ivan's clinical ruthlessness that Matt was almost moved to tears. He pinched himself.

'Hello Dr Damiano. My name is Matt. I'm a maths student at Cambridge and I've been doing some work for Ivan Kripke. I don't really want to discuss this over the phone, but I have learned some things which I found disturbing, and I would like to share them with you.'

'I see.' A pause. 'How did you come to be working with Ivan? Please excuse me for being blunt, but I wouldn't have thought Ivan had many undergraduates working for him.'

'You're right. My dad was doing some work in brain scanning which Ivan was interested in. He died – my father, that is – and I've decided I want to follow in his footsteps, so I contacted Ivan, and . . . well, one thing led to another.'

'Interesting. Well, what are these things you want to share with me?'

'I'd really rather not talk about that over the phone. Could we meet?'

'Well,' Dr Damiano paused again, and Matt muttered silent incantations again. 'This is very unorthodox, but given the circumstances, I suppose we could; yes. Where are you?'

Matt took a deep breath, desperate to keep the elation out of his voice.

'In Sussex. Not far from London.'

'That's handy. I'll be in London tomorrow. I have the use of an office inside the US Embassy. It's at Grosvenor Square, a short walk south from Bond Street tube station. Could you meet me there tomorrow at 11 am? Tell one of the impressively solid military gentlemen at the entrance that you've come to meet me. You'd better arrive a half-hour early to allow for the security procedures: they're very thorough.'

'Great. I'll see you then.'

'OK then,' Dr Damiano said, still not sounding convinced that this was a great idea. 'What's your mobile number, in case I get delayed?'

As he terminated the call, Matt punched the air, strode around his room in two tight circles, and threw himself on his bed and buried his head in his pillow. His relief at having secured the meeting with Vic dissolved quickly into a toxic cocktail of anger and anxiety. He knew that he would get no sleep that night.

SIXTEEN

Dr Damiano was right about the soldiers at the entrance: they were miniature mountains. Their faces looked carved, not grown, and their statures and their postures suggested that they were merely the above-ground extensions of deep-rooted objects which would take a tank to move, or at least a car travelling at speed. There was something absurd as well as impressive about their rock-like strength and passivity, but it did nothing to relieve the strain Matt felt. This meeting had to go well – it just had to. Once again he forced down the mixture of terror and exhaustion which reached up for control of his mind.

Thus preoccupied, Matt failed to notice that Ivan's soldier was following him, observing his every step until he was inside the building. When Matt was inside, the solider took up a position on the far side of the square and kept watch on the Embassy entrance.

The process of gaining admission to the office area of the Embassy was ponderous and bureaucratic. Matt, anaesthetised against irritation by his fear, submitted listlessly to a laborious series of document checks, questions about the purpose of his visit, bag searches and body searches. Some of the questions were repeated by different personnel, and Matt wondered abstractedly whether this was because the staff were unaware the check had been done before, or – more likely – a test of the consistency of his answers.

Finally he was through, and he was led by a petite and determined-looking military policewoman along a series of brightly-lit corridors to a small room on the second floor. It was near the centre of the building, with no windows and no natural light. The corridor walls were thick: it felt as if the place was built to withstand a bomb attack – which of course it was.

Dr Damiano looked up from the papers on his desk as Matt was shown into his office. He was a short man in a grey three-piece suit. With neat black hair, brown eyes and thick glasses, he looked a little like a startled owl. He stood up and offered his hand to Matt, and then gestured towards the chair facing him. The expression on his face was formal, perhaps a little sceptical, although Matt also sensed something else: a curious, and perhaps slightly mischievous nature.

Dr Damiano's office was as colourful as the rest of the building was forbidding, with lively charts on most of the wall space, and models, executive toys, and souvenirs competing for attention everywhere Matt looked. The charts and models were mostly of the human brain, and several of the charts had been annotated or scribbled on by an impatient hand.

The desk was even more cluttered than the rest of

the room. None of its surface was visible under the piles of papers, books, magazines, and a small collection of electronic gadgets.

'Welcome, Matt. Have a seat.'

Matt's heart was racing as he took his seat. In an effort to calm his severely frayed nerves, he tried to lighten the tone. 'It must have taken a long time to smuggle all this stuff through security,' he said, indicating the clutter.

Dr Damiano's face relaxed into a half-smile. 'No, it's not too bad once you've got one of these,' he tapped the badge attached to his lapel. 'The scanners here are remarkable pieces of technology, so the security people don't have to subject your bags to a deep rummage every day. It's just that coming in here for the first time is a bit like being positively vetted. I'm sorry about that.'

'Well, thank you for taking the time to see me, Dr Damiano' Matt said. 'I appreciate it. I'm sure you're a busy man. So why is your office inside the US embassy?'

'Call me Vic, please. Everyone does. My organisation's research is partly funded by a couple of branches of the US government. They like to keep an eye on what I'm up to, and they are kind enough to provide this space for me. But this is just where I work when I'm in London, which is only one or two months of the year. My main base is in Palo Alto, near San Francisco.'

'Yeah, I guess that's the world headquarters of artificial intelligence,' Matt ventured.

'Yup. Gotta keep close to them nerds! And it's a great place, Silicon Valley, but it's important to get away from time to time and remind yourself that the rest of the world doesn't think the same way. I find London is a terrific place to do that. It's a surprisingly liveable city considering it was the capital of the biggest empire that the world has ever seen.'

'Apart from the American empire,' said Matt, aiming for a tone somewhere between flattery and teasing. If Vic was willing to chat, Matt was eager to encourage him: he was in no hurry to dive into the lies and deceit that his mission demanded.

'Well, of course we've never formally declared our empire,' Vic smiled good-naturedly. 'We like to think that we aren't really controlling anything – we just help folks run things the way they would like to, offer them the American dream, and sell them as much fizzy black water as we possibly can. We can't understand why so many folks hate us for it.'

'I guess it's natural that people are scared of a country that is far more powerful than their own.'

'No doubt. But to business.' Vic leaned back in his chair. 'You say you have spent some time working with Ivan. What did you think of the great Ivan, and what is it you want to share with me?'

'To be honest I found him scary,' Matt said, with more feeling than he intended.

Vic looked at him curiously. 'Interesting,' he said. He paused, and his gaze drifted towards one of the wall charts. 'Ivan can be a tad unnerving.' He looked back at Matt, incisive. 'You're young, but you seem a robust sort of fellow. What did he do to scare you?'

'It's his intensity,' Matt replied. 'He gives the

impression that he genuinely doesn't care what people think of him, and that he will do anything to achieve his goals. Absolutely anything.'

'Yes, he has a reputation for being ruthless. But then you don't get to be a billionaire without being driven and focused. Has he done anything in particular to you?'

Matt experienced a moment's panic as he wondered if Vic knew about his father; or if he suspected that Matt might be a plant. The moment passed. No, it was a natural question to ask – indeed it was the obvious question.

'No, in fact I doubt he ever gave me any thought until my last day there. I gather he was interested in the work my father did, but I was just another analyst in his data group.'

'What kind of work did you do there, exactly?'

'Data interpolation. We were trying to restore or re-create data series from incomplete or garbled outputs. Initially I was told we were helping to build a sophisticated expert system, although I later discovered it was a more ambitious artificial intelligence programme. From what little I know of your organisation, you must have people doing the same thing?'

'We sure do,' Vic said brightly. 'The best in the business, or at least that's what they tell me. So why did you leave?'

'Well, I worked in a data centre in Brighton. A really nice office, decorated in lively colours, and with lots of fun stuff like a bar football table and a jukebox. The other people there were really smart – super-bright PhDs in science and maths. It was just a holiday job, but it was really interesting, and I was grateful for the opportunity. I think I got the job thanks to the work my father was doing, as I explained. I was only there a few weeks, though, because frankly it scared me.'

'In what way?' Vic asked.

'Well, the first thing that spooked me was when I found out that Ivan's headquarters is a big ship that sails around the world in stealth mode, almost never making land, with Ivan and his senior staff coming and going by helicopter. Then a couple of people in my team disappeared. It was very sudden: one day they were there and the next day they weren't. No goodbyes, no explanations, and no-one talked about them. It was as if they had never existed.'

'Really?' Vic said slowly. He leaned forward and his body language showed that Matt had just gained his complete attention.

'But the thing that made me decide to quit was the meeting I had with Ivan. I was summoned to a meeting room, where he sat me down and told me that his colleagues were impressed with my work, and they would like to put me onto a more important project. Then he gave me a document and told me to read it. He told me I had to sign it if I was going to stay on. It was about 20 pages long. I don't have any experience of that sort of thing, but it seemed very heavy-handed for a junior person like me to have to sign. As I started reading it he told me some things I didn't know about the work we were doing, and that made me think about a couple of conversations I'd had in the office. I put two and two together and came up with a startling conclusion.'

'Yes?' Vic said, as Matt paused for a moment.

'Well, it sounds melodramatic, but I realised that Ivan is planning to create a fully conscious artificial intelligence – and that he thinks he is close to succeeding. At first I was amazed because I didn't think that technology was likely to be available for many years to come – certainly not in my lifetime. It sounds like science fiction even as I talk about it now.'

'But you believed him?' Vic asked, his eyes narrowed. 'You think that he is close to succeeding?'

'To be honest I have no way of knowing,' Matt replied. 'But I'm in no doubt that he believes it. And the scary thing is that he plans keep it secret from the world. That was the clear implication of the legal document. I don't think that is right. I'd never thought about it before, but you don't have to think about it for long to realise that the development of artificial intelligence will have a profound impact on the whole world, and the science should be available to everyone.'

'Interesting,' Vic mused, nodding. 'So what did you do next?'

'I told Ivan that I wasn't used to documents like that, and I needed to read it properly before signing it. He agreed to let me stay in the room to read it some more, but said that I couldn't take it outside that room. I said I understood, and asked if I could think about it overnight anyway, before signing. He didn't like that, and his attitude towards me suddenly changed.'

'In what way?'

'He switched completely from being friendly and

encouraging to being . . . well, not quite hostile, but not far from it. He seemed to assume that I was not going to sign. He said that I was a fool to turn down such an exciting opportunity, and that I would get nowhere in life if I behaved so ungraciously when people tried to help me. He said I could stay in the room for fifteen minutes and then I should leave the building. I couldn't even go back to my desk – he said someone would bring my stuff to the room and escort me off the premises. If I was willing to sign the document I could come back the next day, but if not I could never come back, and I was not to contact any of my former colleagues either.'

'I see what you mean,' Vic said, not sounding very surprised. 'Erratic behaviour.'

'Needless to say, I didn't go back,' Matt continued. 'But I remembered that one of my colleagues in Ivan's data team had mentioned your group as doing similar work, so I started to think about contacting you. I realise that I'm very junior, and of course I haven't completed my course at Cambridge yet. But I'll be finished in the summer, and despite this experience with Ivan I am still keen to go into computational neuroscience. And I'm not completely without experience now. In fact I learned a few things while working for Ivan's group which could be useful to you.'

'Didn't you sign an NDA when you started there?' Vic asked, fiddling with a small electronic gadget as he spoke.

'Oddly enough, no. They never got around to giving me one, until they showed me the monster document. Maybe they thought I was too junior, and wouldn't learn any secrets. Or maybe they thought I wouldn't be there long enough.'

'A surprising omission, I agree.' Vic paused, and then continued thoughtfully. 'This secrecy thing is a thorny issue. I completely agree with you that the science of artificial intelligence should be open. Secret science is usually inefficient science anyway, but as you say, the creation of a genuine human-level artificial intelligence will be a huge event for mankind, and it shouldn't be done in secret. But it's not as straightforward as you might think.'

'In what way?' Matt asked.

'Well, if Ivan was to announce to world today that he is close to creating a human-level artificial intelligence, what do you think would happen?'

'Hmm, I don't know. I don't know whether people would believe it.'

'Exactly. He's probably be dismissed as a crank: in fact people would probably think he was just trying to drum up some hype for the next Hollywood science fiction blockbuster. It sounds as if Ivan may be a little further along than us, and it's definitely too early for us to 'come out', so to speak. But we are already trying to reach certain opinion formers in a subtle way. We call it oblique PR. We think that when the time comes to break the news it may have to be done suddenly, and we want some of the leading media presenters to have some grounding in the facts, so that they don't get carried away re-hashing Frankenstein stories. So we are keeping certain key journalists informed, but in a very conservative way. We feed them interesting stories about narrow AI, accompanied by highly conservative timescales for human-level, general AI. We tend to say that we estimate human-level AI will arrive early next century, which seems sufficiently far off to be no kind of threat.'

Vic gave Matt a direct look. 'And that's about as much as I can tell you without asking you to sign an NDA. That is, if you want to continue this conversation?'

Matt nodded, hoping to look enthusiastic but not desperate.

'Don't worry,' Vic continued. 'It's not a massive tome that you should have inspected by lawyers. It's a standard three-pager.'

He stood, and walked towards the door. 'Wait here: I'll be back in a moment.'

As Vic left the room Matt began to feel queasy as the sound of the door closing seemed to be slightly prolonged. As if it was being locked.

SEVENTEEN

His impression was confirmed when Vic returned two or three minutes later: he definitely heard the door being unlocked before it opened. Matt's unease increased when he saw that Vic was accompanied by a military colleague. Vic introduced the man as Colonel Norman Hourihan of the US Army. He was an imposing figure, well over six feet tall, with a powerful physique, piercing blue eyes and a crew cut. His uniform looked not so much laundered as moulded.

Matt realised that a wave of panic must be showing on his face, and scrambled to recover his dignity.

'What's going on? I didn't realise you worked for the military, Vic? Is there a problem?'

Norman chuckled. 'Just because I'm a soldier doesn't mean I'm a bad guy, Matt.' His voice had an avuncular tone, although this barely registered with Matt given the state of his nerves.

Vic sat down in his chair, looking ill-at-ease, and Norman pulled up another to sit alongside Matt. Matt felt sure that his cover was blown. He fought the urge to shrink back into his chair.

'Norman is my liaison officer from the US Army,' Vic explained. He seemed uncomfortable, and as he spoke, Matt wondered whether he was talking to cover his unease.

'My company receives funding for our AI work from a number of government departments, including DARPA, the Defense Advanced Research Projects Agency. You probably know that DARPA was set up in response to the shock which Sputnik caused in the US, and that it essentially created the internet, along with a lot of other really cool stuff. I used to work in military research – mainly cyber-security – before setting up my own company, so I'm comfortable with the military mindset.

'I had lengthy discussions with Norman and several of his colleagues before we went into business together. One of my conditions for working with them on machine intelligence was that that when the time was right we would share the tech with the rest of the world. I told them that if they didn't, we could end up making the US a pariah nation. It didn't take a great deal of persuasion for them to agree to my terms, and so I signed up with them as partners.

'And I'm really glad I did. I probably don't know everything that the military is up to with regard to machine intelligence, but I think I know about their most advanced projects. Their resources are formidable. We're supervised by the Strategic Technology Office, and I have a high level of clearance. The organisation I run was no mean outfit before I teamed up with Norman and his pals, so I like to think that if the US Army does turn out to be the first institution to build an artificial general intelligence, there will be a well-informed and well-connected civilian organisation standing shoulder-to-shoulder with them and making sure they don't go off in all sorts of unhealthy directions.

'Norman and his colleagues have been incredibly helpful. Not only with money, but with contacts, technologies, advice, and of course intelligence. Which brings us to our friend Ivan, and to you, Matt.'

Matt, expecting to be told any minute that he had been exposed, had been finding this little speech increasingly surreal. His tension rose as he thought Vic was finally getting to the point. Here we go, he thought. Is this leading towards an extraordinary rendition? Is that why Vic brought me to the US Embassy? Or are they just going to kill me here and now? His blood ran cold as he wondered just how brazen the US government could be. He had avoided his mother as much as possible since returning from Ivan's ship, and as he set off for London he had simply told her that he had a meeting with another AI research organisation in London. He hadn't spoken to Leo since his return from Ivan's ship, and he had said nothing to Alice or Carl. No-one knew where he was. No-one could come to rescue him.

'You present us with a bit of a problem, Matt, and I'm afraid I have some bad news for you,' Vic continued. 'I'm afraid we're going to have to keep you here for a little while. The problem is with Ivan rather than with you, but we're going to have to proceed very carefully.'

Vic, clearly uncomfortable, and starting to become flustered, looked away from Matt and towards Norman.

'Oh dear, I'm no good with this sort of thing. Norman, would you mind. . .?'

Norman looked relieved that Vic had finally stopped talking. He picked up the story smoothly and efficiently. Clearly it was not Norman's first time with this 'sort of thing'.

'What exactly is your relationship with Ivan, Matt?'

Norman's voice was not hostile, but it commanded respect. It was freighted with self-control, and it was obvious that Norman was used to being obeyed. Matt did not want to argue with this man. He spoke rapidly, nervously.

'Like I told Vic, Ivan hired me because he was interested in the work my father did. But I only met him once. I just worked at one of his offices for a couple of weeks, that's all. I wasn't comfortable there, so I was looking for another organisation to join. I learned a few things about the way Ivan's team does their data interpolation, so I was hoping that I might be useful to you guys, and that you would hire me. But I don't know anything else. What's this all about? Am I a prisoner? What's going to happen now?'

Matt was on the edge of panic. He wasn't sure he could keep from breaking down and blurting out the whole story. But that would be a death sentence for his father. Somehow he found the strength to keep it together. He wondered if it would be a smart move to give in partly to his panic, to sob a little and act like the scared young man which in truth he was. He realised that he didn't need to, and that Norman already understood that he was under a lot of pressure, when the big man leant across and put his hand on Matt's shoulder, and looked straight into his eyes.

'We may have to ask you to take a polygraph examination, son, but don't worry. I think it highly unlikely that you are in any kind of serious trouble. Maybe you've done some things that you didn't ought to have, and if you have, that will become plain in due course. But I doubt it. Truth is, we're going to have to keep you here for a while for your own good.'

Matt was relieved: they didn't know. But the pressure remained. As Norman's eyes bored into his, he worried that his head might start to wobble. This was exhausting as well as terrifying.

Norman leaned back in his chair and continued. 'The CIA has had Ivan under surveillance for some time now. We know he is close to creating a human-level AI, and we aren't exactly happy about that, but it's not against any laws. Perhaps it should be, but it isn't. But we also know that he has committed some very serious crimes. Those people who disappeared from the office where you worked didn't just disappear from that facility: they disappeared off the face of the earth. We have evidence that Ivan had them killed.'

'Really?' Matt asked in genuine alarm. So two scientists really had disappeared from Ivan's team! He had assumed that story was pure invention. 'That's terrible! What did they do?'

'We don't know,' Norman replied. 'Maybe they wanted to leave, and Ivan felt they knew too much. To be perfectly frank, that is one of the major reasons we are going to keep you here for a while. Your life may be in danger too.'

'What? You think Ivan would try to harm me? But that's ridiculous!' Matt hoped he sounded more convincing to Norman than he did to himself. 'If he was going to kill me he would have done it by now. And it's not as if I learned any real secrets there.'

'Maybe so, maybe not,' replied Norman. 'But events are moving quickly now.' He paused before giving Matt important news. 'We're preparing a raid on Ivan's ship, and I'm afraid you're going to have to stay here until it's over.'

Matt's eyes were round circles. He couldn't believe what he was hearing.

'Yes, a raid,' said Norman, noting Matt's astonishment. 'And we can't take the risk that Ivan may try to harm you because he suspects you of helping us. For all we know he may have you under surveillance and he may know you are inside this building right now. We also can't take the risk that you might tip him off about the raid. You're a new player in this scenario. We don't know what you know, and we don't know what cards you're playing. But I'll be honest with you: the real reason I'm telling you all this is I'm hoping that you might have some information that would help us.'

'But I don't know anything!' Matt's head was spinning. This changed everything. 'When is this raid going to happen? How long do you plan to keep me here? I don't want to sound awkward, but this is beginning to sound like kidnapping.'

Norman smiled indulgently. 'Don't you worry about that, son. We have agreements with your government that cover this kind of thing. We won't be holding you here for anything like as long as we could do if we wanted to. And you'll be free to go as soon as the raid is over.'

Vic was still looking uncomfortable. He interjected, 'This is for your own protection, Matt, honestly. You have an inkling of the kind of person Ivan is, but you don't know the full story. I'm sorry it has to play like this, but there really isn't any alternative.'

'What about my mum? She's going to be worried sick if I don't show up at home this evening.'

'We'll let her know that you're OK,' Vic assured him. He exchanged glances with Norman before continuing. 'In fact we were going to suggest that you invite her to come and join us here. I don't want to alarm you, but she might be safer here too.'

Matt thought about this. He wasn't sure he wanted to face too many questions from his mother. She might well be able to detect that he was hiding something. On the other hand he really could do with some moral support right now. 'Yes,' he agreed cautiously, 'that might be a good idea.'

Another thought occurred to him.

'How will you know where the ship is? Ivan works hard to keep his location secret.'

'We have an agent on board,' replied Norman. 'He's part of the crew, not part of the science team. We have a fix on the ship's location, and good intel on its defence capabilities. Earlier today the CIA obtained the final piece of evidence we needed about those disappeared scientists, and we were given the green light to assemble our team and mount the operation. We have a world-class team in place, and we are confident that the raid will be successful. Which in turn is why I can be confident that we won't have to keep you here for long.'

Matt swallowed hard. He felt as if he was just about keeping up with the march of events – but only just. He thought fast. 'So . . . when is the raid going to take place?' he asked again.

'A Navy Seals strike force is making preparations as we speak. The ship is off the coast of Morocco, in north-west Africa. We'll be following events from the situation room in this building.'

But Matt wasn't really listening. He had a very important decision to make. A lot hung on him getting it right. But in truth it wasn't a hard decision. He looked at Vic, and then he looked at Norman.

'There's something I haven't told you.'

He paused. Even though there was only one sensible course of action for him now, this was a momentous decision. Vic and Norman looked uneasily at each other, and then back at Matt.

'My father is being held hostage on Ivan's ship.'

EIGHTEEN

Norman looked at Vic briefly, and then his huge frame leaned in towards Matt. He spoke slowly, deliberately. His voice was lower in both volume and tone.

'How do you know this, son?'

The menace implicit in Norman's demeanour was not lost on Matt. He had rolled the dice, and now he was potentially in deep trouble with both Ivan and Vic. He had not had much of a choice, and he didn't regret the gamble, but the next few minutes could determine whether his father lived or died.

'OK,' he said, placing his hands in the air, pleading for time to explain. 'There are some important things I haven't told you. But I couldn't. You have to understand. I've been in an impossible position. My head feels like it's going to explode.'

Norman put his palms up as well: consoling, but also asserting control.

'It's OK, kid. Take it easy, and let's start with a few simple questions. How do you know your father is on Ivan's ship?'

'Because I saw him there.'

'You saw him. . . ?!' Vic blurted out. 'You were on board Ivan's ship? When?'

Waves of competing emotions were washing over Matt. He was relieved to be telling the truth. Lying to a senior member of the US military while effectively in detention inside the US Embassy had been almost as stressful as facing Ivan on board his ship. But at the same time he was afraid that he would be punished for lying up till now. Would Norman and Vic accept that he simply couldn't tell them the truth before? How many crimes had he already committed? And over-riding these concerns was fear for his father. Previously David had been under the control of a ruthless megalomaniac, but a megalomaniac who had a reason to keep him alive. Now his father was going to be at the centre of a firefight.

'Two evenings ago, although . . . I'm not sure about the timing. I was drugged and kidnapped and taken on board while I was unconscious. You have to believe me! It's not my fault!'

Matt heard the panic in his own voice, and repeated himself in what he hoped was a calmer voice. 'It's not my fault. My dad is in danger. You have to help him!'

Vic opened his mouth to say something, but Norman placed a hand on his arm, telling Vic to let him do the talking. At the same time he addressed Matt in a calm, firm voice.

'It's OK, kid, it's OK,' he said. 'Calm down. Here, drink some water.'

He picked up a glass from Vic's desk and handed it to Matt.

'Now look,' he continued soothingly. 'You're telling us that you're the victim here, not the perpetrator. If that's the truth then everything will be OK. So just take it easy and tell us what happened. Take a deep breath and start at the beginning.'

Pulling back from the brink of tears, Matt did as Norman directed. He drank some water, took a couple of deep breaths and started at the beginning.

'I got interested in artificial intelligence, and I discovered that my father's work had some relevance to it. I started making enquiries, partly with the help of an old family friend, my uncle Leo. Before long I had a meeting set up with Ivan.'

'OK, let's just step back a moment here. What work was your father doing?'

'He was working on very detailed brain scans. Apparently he made some significant improvements in the technique. He went to a conference in the US and we heard that he had died in a car crash out there. What I found out two days ago is that there was no car crash. What really happened was that my dad met Ivan at the conference, and Ivan invited him – my dad – to join his team. Initially Dad accepted, but then he changed his mind. Ivan couldn't accept this, so he kidnapped Dad and faked his death in a car accident.'

Vic and Norman exchanged a significant glance as Matt took another sip of water.

'OK,' Norman continued, 'so wind forwards a few months, up to a couple of weeks ago. You're under the impression that your father is dead. You've gotten interested in artificial intelligence research and you're reaching out to people who are doing interesting work in the field. Is that right?'

'Yes, that's right.' Matt agreed.

'And Ivan is one of the people you reached out to?' Norman asked. 'How did you hear about Ivan, and how did you contact him?'

'To be honest I don't know all the details there. My uncle Leo – he's my dad's best friend, but I've thought of him as an uncle as long as I can remember – Leo found Ivan somehow, and set up a meeting. I don't know how. We met Ivan together, Leo and me, in a restaurant in Brighton. Thinking about that now, I suppose I should have thought that was a bit odd. Why would a busy, rich, successful guy want to have dinner with a mere student at a first meeting? I guess I tend to think that Leo can fix anything. He's very impressive, my uncle Leo.'

'And what happened at the dinner?' Norman asked.

'Well, Ivan talked about his plans. I thought it was fascinating at the time, although of course it all seems very different now. He talked about how dangerous the creation of the first human-level AI could be for the human race, and explained that he wanted to build what he called an 'Oracle AI' to avoid the pitfalls. We discussed whether it is possible to make even an Oracle AI safe. And at the end of the evening Ivan said he would like me to come and work for him.'

'How nice,' said Norman, sarcastically.

'Yes . . . well not really,' agreed Matt. 'He said he would give me a lift home and then he drugged me while I was in his car. I felt sick and passed out, and the next thing I knew I was waking up on a ship. Then Ivan came in, apologised for kidnapping me, and then . . . Well, then he talked about you, Vic.'

'Most flattering,' Vic said, scowling.

'We'll want to know as much as you can tell us about Ivan's work, Matt,' Norman said. 'But first, tell us about your father. How did you get to see him?'

'Ivan told me he had a big surprise for me, and he was right. It was the biggest surprise of my life. He left the room and when he came back in he brought my father with him.'

'That must have been one hell of a shock!' Vic exclaimed. Norman shot him a glance, urging him not to intervene.

'You can say that again,' Matt agreed. 'Dad and I have always been close. My mum isn't very emotional, but Dad and I . . .' He was choking up again.

'OK, Matt,' said Norman. 'Take your time; drink some more water.'

Matt felt that the immediate danger had retreated, but the partial sense of relief that replaced it was an emotion almost as powerful. Matt gripped the base of his chair, determined not to give way to his feelings – determined not to show how scared he had been. Norman saw what he was doing, but he said nothing, and waited. After a pause, Matt continued, explaining his reunion with his father and Ivan's demands.

'So Ivan sent you to spy on us?' Norman asked, not unkindly.

'Yes. I'm sorry, but I guess you understand now that I had no choice. He made it clear that my dad will be killed if I don't co-operate, and he made veiled threats against my mum and Leo too.'

'And let me guess: if you do as he asks then he lets David go and leaves you and your family alone and everyone lives happily ever after?' sneered Norman.

'Well, yes . . . And do you know, I think he was telling the truth as he sees it. He says that if he creates the first AI he will use it to develop the technology to upload living human minds and then give that technology away freely. He thinks that uploading is the only way that people can survive the arrival of machine intelligence, and that everyone doing it at the same time – or as fast as possible – is the only way to avoid levels of social unrest that would make even his life difficult. So yes, he thinks there will be no reason not to let us go once the technology is developed.'

'And he expected you to believe this bullshit?' asked Norman, astonished.

The forcefulness of his next remark took even Matt by surprise. 'Don't get me wrong, Norman. I hate Ivan for what he's done to my father, and to me. I have no words for how awful it has been – and still is. I'm not a violent person, but put me in a room with him and give me a loaded gun and I'd be more than happy to put a bullet in his brain.'

He paused and calmed himself. His anger didn't subside, but he pushed it back down. 'I realise it sounds incredible, but I really do think he was telling the truth about what he intends to do. He is a ruthless maniac, but I think he is a logical ruthless maniac, and there *is* a logic in what he said. Mad as it may seem, I think that he genuinely sees himself as the good guy in all this. In fact, I think he honestly believes that my father and I will eventually come to see that he is right, and work with him to achieve his goal.'

Norman shook his head and smiled grimly. 'My god, the power of rationalisation! Even murderers and kidnappers can persuade themselves that they are acting for the greater good.'

There was a pause as each man let the news sink in. It was Matt who broke the silence.

'So what happens now? Do I go home? Ivan must have me under surveillance, and I mustn't do anything that would make him suspect that I've spilled the beans.'

Norman ignored his question. 'What does Ivan expect you to do next? Did you arrange to send him a message of some kind after you had made contact with Vic?'

'He set up a Gmail account for us both to use. I'm supposed to report back by writing a draft but not sending it.'

'Yes, that's a sensible idea,' Norman mused. 'It was standard procedure in the intelligence community for a while. It's not foolproof, but for most civilian purposes it's still a reasonable approach to secure communications. When is he expecting you to communicate by?'

'No deadline. Just as soon as I can. Should I post something now?'

Norman was thinking fast. 'No. As you say, he may well have you under surveillance and he would be surprised and suspicious if he received a communication

from you if he knows you are still inside this building.'
He turned to Vic. 'You know, I think we should have
security keep an eye out for anybody suspicious-look-
ing, hanging around the Embassy entrance.'

'But won't he also suspect something is wrong if I
just stay here?' Matt asked. 'If you're right that he is
having me watched, shouldn't I go home and come
back later?'

Norman was staring down at the floor. He contemplated Matt's suggestion for a moment before shaking
his head. 'Ideally, perhaps. . . But no, I don't think we
can afford to let you leave this building until after the
raid – for your own safety as much as anything else. I
think we're just going to have to take the risk that he
becomes suspicious.'

Matt tilted his head slightly. 'You said you can't let
me leave 'as much for my safety as anything else'. Am I
allowed to ask what the 'something else' is?'

Norman looked up and smiled at him. 'You're an
impressive young man, Matt. You've been through hell
and back, and yet you're as sharp as a tack.'

He exchanged a significant glance with Vic, and
continued.

'Truth is, Matt, you can help us. We're going to
have to check your story out, but that won't take long,
although I must warn you that if you're lying, your
world is going to get real unpleasant real fast. But my
sense is that you're telling the truth. Assuming that
you are, you may be able to provide us with some
information about the ship, or about Ivan's intentions
and capabilities. I know you think you don't have any

information, but you never know what little details might come in handy.

'But there's another thing. Your father's predicament makes our reasons for mounting this raid all the more compelling. We do have evidence that Ivan has killed those two scientists, but we're not sure it would stand up in a court of law. If what you've told is true then your father's kidnapping – and yours – are compelling justification for our action. We need to maintain the support of various politicians for this operation, and the first concern of any politician is always to cover his own rear end. Having you with us – physically as well as metaphorically – is valuable.'

'Fair enough,' Matt said, nodding thoughtfully. Then he looked up at Norman. 'Those scientists. I never met them. It was just a cover story that Ivan gave me to explain my reasons for jumping ship.'

'Interesting,' Norman said. 'Maybe he suspects that we know about their disappearance, and he wanted your story to hold water. But what arrogance to take the risk of drawing our attention to a couple of murders . . . My god, but he's a cocky son-of-a-bitch!'

Matt's face was grim. 'If I'm with you, I can be sure that you have done everything humanly possible to keep my father safe. Let's understand each other. You want Ivan out of the AI business, and you want him brought to book for murder. So do I. But most of all, I want my father back. Alive.'

NINETEEN

Norman left the room, saying he was going to get someone to run some checks on Matt's story. While he was out, Vic did his best to console Matt, while maintaining a certain distance in case the story didn't stand up.

'Before we head down to the situation room – assuming your story checks out – I think we should arrange for your mother – and your uncle Leo – to be brought here. I'm sure they will feel the same way about being present as you do, and there is also the question of the risk to them. If Ivan has either or both of them under surveillance, there is the possibility that he may order them taken hostage once he becomes aware of the attack. What do you think?'

Matt couldn't speak. Feeling overwhelmed, and with tears in his eyes, he nodded agreement. It would be a huge relief to have them join him, and to be able to tell them the truth at last. The situation he found himself in was better than he could have hoped for a few hours ago, but his nerves were frayed, and his father was still in grave danger.

Matt and Vic sat together in silence for a few minutes, each lost in his own thoughts. They looked up as Norman opened the door and came back into the room. He was smiling grimly.

'Looks like you're in the clear, kid. The story about your father checks out, and our agent has reported helicopter take-offs and landings on Ivan's ship which match the movements you describe. I have people following up a few more details, but I think we can assume you're on the level.'

Matt made no attempt to disguise his relief and his excitement. 'Shall I call my mum and Leo now?' he asked eagerly.

'Here, use this phone,' said Vic, smiling at Matt's relief and enthusiasm. 'I told him that we should bring his mother and uncle here,' he added to Norman.

Norman nodded, but held up a warning finger. 'But listen. You can't tell them anything about the operation until they get here. Just tell them there is an emergency and they must get here, to the Embassy, as soon as they can. On second thought, if Leo is in London he will be able to get here quickly enough under his own steam, but let's send a car to collect your mother: it will be unmarked but will have police sirens so it won't get held up in traffic when it reaches London. We could send a helicopter, but that would tip Ivan off if he has people watching your house.'

*

Matt was taken aback by the size of the situation room.

He gazed around in amazement at the space, which must take up almost the whole floor plan of the building. There was a massive table in the middle, but what first drew his attention were the huge screens which covered most of the walls. It was like walking into a wrap-around IMAX cinema. The table too, was a screen – in fact it turned out to be touch-sensitive, and could be used to manipulate images on the walls as well as on its own surface. He looked upwards, and was relieved to see a standard suspended grid ceiling, with nothing projected onto it. Norman was quietly enjoying Matt's reaction. He followed the young man's eyes upwards. 'Yeah,' he grinned, 'apparently they thought about it during the last re-fit, but decided it would be a bit over the top.'

'This room is one of the safest places in the whole of London,' he continued. 'It's six floors underground, and it was designed during the Cold War to withstand a direct hit from a nuclear warhead. Through there,' he gestured towards a pair of heavy metal doors, 'is a storeroom with enough food and water to keep thirty people alive for six months, so that survivors could wait here until the immediate radiation fallout had dissipated, and also until the threat from less well protected survivors had receded.'

It took a moment before Matt realised what Norman meant. He stared at the soldier, appalled. 'You mean . . . you mean until everyone else had finished dying?'

'Exactly,' Norman said, grimly. 'In a nuclear war, the people who died instantly in the initial blasts would be the lucky ones.'

Matt shook his head, feeling suddenly oppressed

as the horror of the world the planners of this room were preparing for became a backdrop to the peril of his personal situation. 'We're such an inventive species, aren't we?' he muttered bitterly.

Seeing his weariness, Vic put his hand on Matt's arm. 'We're not all bad, Matt. Yes, there is Hiroshima, the Holocaust, the barbarity and the grinding poverty. But there is also love, art, science – and humour. Think of Newton and Einstein, Michelangelo and Mozart. I think Mother Nature should hang on to us for a bit longer; don't you? At least until we have fashioned our successor.'

Norman smiled, joining Vic in trying to lift Matt's spirits. 'Vic is the team philosopher. Anyway, Matt, welcome to the control room for Operation Drunken Sailor.'

Norman guided him towards a group of a dozen soberly dressed men and women who were conferring in front of a giant screen showing the schematic of a ship. Matt knew immediately that it was Ivan's.

'Ladies and gentlemen, let me introduce you to Matt Metcalfe. Matt is joining us today because his father is being held hostage on that ship.'

The analysts' surprise at this news was visible, but professionally muted: just a couple of cocked heads and raised eyebrows. Norman summarised the series of events which had brought Matt here, and one of the analysts stepped forward and offered Matt his hand.

'Welcome aboard, Matt,' he said, as Norman left to speak to Vic. 'My name is Jeff, and my job is to obtain as much information about this vessel as possible, and make sure everyone on the team knows exactly what they need to know about it. I'll let the others explain what they do as we go on. Let's start with very brief introductions, and then jump right in by debriefing you about your experience on board the ship.' He stopped himself, and smiled at Matt. 'Sounds as though you've had a rough time, young man, so let us know if we push you too hard. We are liable to get a little task-orientated on these occasions.'

'I'm happy to help however I can,' Matt replied, 'I didn't see much of the ship, because I was unconscious both arriving and leaving. But I'll do whatever I can to help you guys keep my father safe.'

One by one, the others came forward to shake his hand. It didn't take Jeff long to find out what Matt could add to the information they already had about the ship.

Norman and Vic rejoined the group. 'As far as we know,' Norman explained 'Ivan has no clue about this operation yet. He thinks his location is unknown, and he will probably over-estimate the defensive capabilities of his vessel. That ship has pretty good firepower, but our agent on board will disable that as the strike team arrives on the scene. We know he has at least a couple of highly trained military personnel in his organisation, but we don't know whether they are on the ship at the moment, and our team outnumbers them comfortably. So we have the advantages of surprise, superior combat skills and superior communications technology. The main unknown and risk we face is that we don't know what kind of fallback plans Ivan might have.'

'Yes,' Matt nodded, reflecting on some of Ivan's comments. 'He thinks he is competing with the US military. He takes that idea seriously. He will be well prepared.'

As Norman and Matt were speaking, Jeff took a call. 'Here we go,' he said. 'We're about to go live with the assault team.'

They turned back to the screen showing the schematic of the Eleusis. Some of Jeff's colleagues were tracing the ship's defence circuits again, re-checking one last time that there were no fallback systems which had not been identified. There were three main circuits that needed to be shut down, and the plan was for the agent on board to cut all three simultaneously.

'Gentlemen, we're ready to patch in Captain Fitch and his team,' Jeff said, putting on a pair of headphones. 'Good afternoon, Captain. This is agent Jeff Webb speaking, from the situation room at the US Embassy in London. I'm going to put you on speaker. And please ask your colleague with the main mission camera to transmit. Over.'

'Copy that,' came a crackly voice. The sounds of a helicopter boomed into the room, and at the same time a huge, grainy image of a soldier squatting inside a cabin flooded the screen, bumping the schematic onto a neighbouring wall. A couple of other stern faces were just about visible behind Captain Fitch.

'Captain, you're talking with Colonel Norman Hourihan, and members of my team. Also in the situation room here is the son of the scientist who is being held hostage on the Eleusis. I know you've been briefed about this already.'

'Yes sir. We are aware of Dr Metcalfe's situation, and we will do everything in our power to protect him. As you know, this is a Navy Seals operation, and I'm privileged to be leading some of the most highly -trained forces in the world on this mission. We have good intel, we have the advantage of surprise, and I'm confident this will be a clean and successful mission.'

Matt was unsure whether he was expected to say something, and looked to Norman for a cue. He felt completely out of his depth. Fortunately Norman seemed not to expect anything from him, and carried on his conversation with Fitch.

'Thank you, Captain. That's good to hear. What is your current location, and when do you expect to reach the Eleusis?'

'We're about twenty miles east of the Eleusis, Sir. We should have visual contact in a few minutes. Our forward reconnaissance camera drones should be on location in a couple of minutes, and we'll relay you the visuals we get from them as soon as we . . .' He broke off, interrupted by one of his men, and then spoke again. 'OK, here we go.'

'Put the drone visuals up on the screen to the right, would you, Jeff?' Norman asked.

Jeff was controlling the screens with a tablet. He made a couple of sweeping gestures across the device, and an image of open sea appeared to the right of the picture of Captain Fitch.

'The drones are monitoring the ship until the choppers arrive,' Jeff explained, 'and making sure the crew isn't showing any sign of awareness of the operation. They are too small to be picked up by the ship's radar. When the choppers arrive the drones will move in closer: some of them will take up positions above the ship and some of them will actually move inside it.'

'Captain Fitch will issue an ultimatum to the ship's captain,' Norman picked up, 'telling him to accept a boarding party or be fired upon. We're not going to give Ivan a whole lot of time to think about that: our agent on board will cut the defence circuits at the same time as we hail the ship, and if Ivan doesn't surrender immediately, the first helicopter will make a rapid landing, and the boarding party will assume control of the vessel using whatever means necessary.' He turned to speak to the Captain. 'Captain, will it be your helicopter that makes the initial landing?'

'Negative sir, that will be Bravo chopper. Captain Graveney is responsible for the initial set-down.'

'Copy that, captain.'

'I'm going off-line now, colonel: we're just a couple of minutes out. I'll come back on-line when the operation is complete. Meanwhile you can listen in on general comms. Out.'

'Understood. Good luck, captain. Bring your men back safely. Out.'

'And my dad!' added Matt – to himself, but audibly.

'Amen to that, son,' replied Norman, turning towards him. 'Captain Fitch is a very good man. If anyone can pull this off, he can. He was selected in part for his experience in pacifying hostiles in hostage situations. Don't forget we also have an agent on board the Eleusis, and we fully intend to bring him home safely too. This is not the most challenging mission Captain Fitch has ever led, I can assure you of that!'

On the main screen, Captain Fitch was addressing his men, using a different channel from the one audible in the situation room. His speech was accompanied by a series of fast, sharp hand movements, and as he spoke and gave his final orders he was also checking his equipment. The other men were mostly in shadows, also making final equipment checks. When they looked towards the camera, Matt could see a calm determination in their eyes that allowed him to hope that this would work out well.

On the second screen, the image of the ship was clearer now. It looked peaceful, unsuspecting, making gentle headway in calm waters. The drone whose camera was on-screen seemed to be no more than fifty feet above the sea, but so far it was evidently inaudible and invisible from the Eleusis.

This was the first time Matt had seen the whole ship, apart from the schematics, which had not given him such a good idea of its size. It was huge, almost like a cruise ship: as big as any billionaire's yacht that he had seen pictures of. At least, he thought, there is plenty of room to land helicopters on the thing.

TWENTY

As the helicopters approached the Eleusis, the screen with the feed from the leading drone showed the sea bristling with the downdraught of the choppers' blades. The sea was calm, but the afternoon light was fading, which added to the sense of urgency in the situation room.

Other screens came online in the situation room as new feeds became available, some from drones, some from soldiers' head cams. As the drones closed in on the ship, Matt could see people running around on her decks. Soon some of the screens began to show individual crew members. The choppers kept their distance for the time being, circling the vessel, hunters stalking a big beast. They knew they would bring their prey down if they were skillful, but they also knew it could inflict grievous damage on them in the process.

The ultimatum issued to the Captain of the Eleusis rang round the situation room. Jeff was admitting just one audio feed to accompany the numerous visual feeds.

'This is the US Navy to the Captain of the

Eleusis. We have a warrant to search your vessel under international Admiralty law. Prepare to be boarded. Do not resist, or you will be fired upon. Signal your compliance immediately.'

The choppers held back, waiting for a reply. There was intense activity on board the Eleusis, crewmen running in all directions, some carrying small arms. But there was no reply to the ultimatum. Two of the drones converged on the bridge, and screens showed the images they captured. Ivan was having a furious argument with someone.

'That's the Captain,' said Norman. 'Looks like he's telling Ivan they have no choice but to surrender, but Ivan's not having it.'

'Will Captain Fitch be seeing this too?' Matt asked.

'You bet,' replied Norman. 'Of course he's got a hundred other things to worry about at the same time, but my guess is this is the feed he's paying closest attention to right now.'

Ivan pushed the Captain to one side, and began working some controls on a desk. Although the drone was not close enough to capture the expression on his face, it was clear that he was angry and frustrated. He banged his fist on the console.

'Looks like he has just discovered that his weapons system is down,' Norman grinned. 'Next he'll try the jamming system, but he'll have no more luck with that.'

Ivan grabbed the Captain's sleeve and started remonstrating with him, gesturing frantically at the console. The Captain was evidently in full retreat, wanting nothing to do with Ivan's desperate attempt to fend off the inevitable outcome. To the astonishment of everyone in the situation room, Ivan pulled out a pistol and pointed it at the Captain, waving him back towards the console. Slowly, reluctantly, the Captain sat down at the console and began trying to activate the controls.

Ivan looked around the bridge, shouted some instructions, and stormed out.

'Jeff, can you get one of those drones to follow Ivan? I want to know what he's up to.'

'I'm on it,' Jeff replied, frowning in concentration.

The chopper's loud hailer rang out again.

'Captain of the Eleusis. We are boarding now. Do not resist or you will be fired upon.'

'Here we go . . .' said Norman through clenched teeth.

The drone had lost Ivan, but all eyes were now on the lead helicopter, which was preparing to land on the largest of the Eleusis' two helipads. The sea was calm and there was an hour or so of daylight left, and the pilot was one of the most experienced and skillful in the world. The only question was what sort of reception he would receive.

Two of the Eleusis' crewmen rushed out onto the deck, and on the screen which had shown Captain Fitch, Matt could see that soldiers in the second helicopter were training guns on them. But the crewmen were waving signalling paddles, partly to assist the pilot, but mainly, Matt suspected, to indicate their full co-operation with the boarding.

'So far so good, but I'd dearly like to know what Ivan is up to . . . Oh shit!' Norman's voice rose to a shout: 'Jeff!

Screen five! Tell Fitch that Ivan has a SAM launcher!'

A loud whoosh, and then a huge explosion. A bright flash wiped out most of the screens for a couple of seconds. The helicopter had not touched down, and when the screens came back to life they showed that it had been shoved sideways in mid-air and tilted at an impossible angle by the missile's close-range impact. The helicopter's nose was destroyed. The cabin looked intact, but fires were raging in various parts of the machine. Men started jumping out to escape the fires, some onto the deck, some into the sea. The ones landing on the deck were jumping fifteen to twenty feet. Some managed to roll with their landing, but several landed awkwardly, collapsing sickeningly onto the deck and then writhing, their broken bodies struggling to get away from the falling body of the helicopter and burning pieces of debris.

'My god. The son-of-a-bitch . . . Jeff, get me eyes on that bastard. I want him in one piece. Or at least alive.' But Ivan had disappeared again.

The helicopter slammed into the deck, a wounded beast. The blades hit first: they crumpled, slicing into the deck surface, shearing the gearbox, leaving the engine to scream as it lost its load. A marine was sliced in half as the blades hit, and several others were wounded as the cabin crashed onto the surface, with the landing rails dangling over the side. The body of the machine was balanced precariously at the edge of the ship, and slowly it tilted away from the surface. The noise of the engine subsided, but the sound of metal grinding against metal was hideous.

'She's going over!' Norman shouted. 'I hope every-body is out of that thing!'

The helicopter stopped moving as its landing rails smashed through windows in the side of the ship and arrested its fall. But it was obvious the weight of the machine would break them, and after a few agonising moments, the rails collapsed, and sections of the panels in the ship's flanks tore themselves free and peeled back from the vessel, like a can's lid being prised off with a tin opener. The helicopter continued its slow-motion grinding metallic slithering and screaming down the side of the Eleusis towards the sea. It crashed into the water, and the fires burning its guts fizzed, popped, and illuminated the darkening sea. Its rails and other talons released the sections of ship plating they had grasped, and it surrendered to the cold water, disappearing slowly from view.

Marines were already descending ropes from the second helicopter to the deck, and the third helicopter was hovering over the water as close to the ship as it dared, near where the first machine had gone down, looking for survivors in the sea. Wounded marines were being winched aboard these two remaining choppers. Their faces could not be seen from the situation room, but it was clear that several of them were in agony, with broken limbs and serious wounds, some of them bleeding profusely. Their colleagues struggled to haul them inside the helicopters and apply battlefield first aid.

The Captain of the Eleusis was on deck, talking to Fitch. One of the screens showed his distraught face, and his pleading gesticulations. Fitch leaned in towards him, ordered him to be quiet and listen, and asked him a question. The Captain pointed towards the stern of the ship, and then downwards. Fitch pointed towards the bridge, barked an order, and shoved the Captain in that direction. Fitch turned and signalled to four of his men to follow him, and ordered the rest to go with the ship's Captain to the bridge. Fitch's party ran towards the stern.

'He's going after Ivan,' said Norman. 'Jeff, can you get him online and ask where Ivan is? Put Fitch on the main audio. And can we get drones to follow him, and get to where Ivan is ahead of him?'

Jeff relayed the question through his headphone mike, and Fitch's reply came into the room for everyone to hear. He was breathing heavily but sounded completely in control.

'The Captain says there's a mini-sub near the stern, and he reckons that is where Ivan is headed. He is going to try and disable the sub from the bridge, but it has autonomous power and control systems: it's designed to operate in the event of a general power failure throughout the rest of the ship.'

The analysts looked at each other, shocked by this mention of a mini-sub. Three of them began inspecting the screen showing the schematic, searching for its most likely location so they could send it to Fitch.

'Will there be resistance from anyone else apart from Ivan?' Norman asked.

'The Captain doesn't think so. My men are going with him to the bridge, and one has gone to the small arms locker. The Captain doesn't think there are any more SAMs on board – but then again he says he didn't know about that one.'

'Have you made contact with our embedded agent yet? Or the scientist, Dr Metcalfe?'

'Not yet, but I understand the agent's orders are to remain on or near the bridge once he had disabled the defence systems? In which case my men will sweep him up. We're looking for Dr Metcalfe, but there's no sign of him yet. The Captain didn't know about him. I presume your agent didn't either.'

'Correct,' Norman confirmed. 'We're sending a couple of the drones on ahead of you so we have eyes on the mini-sub before you get there.'

'Roger that. Out.'

Norman turned away from the screen. 'Where are my drones, Jeff? I don't see that sub yet.'

'The sub wasn't on the schematic, sir.' He pointed at two screens on the other side of the room. 'Those screens are showing the feed from the drones we have looking for it.'

'There!' cried one of the other analysts, as one of the screens centred on an orange vehicle about the size of a transit van. It was rocking gently, suspended on rails which led to a pair of bay doors, and beyond them the open sea. As the drone got closer, they could see that two men were preparing to enter the sub. As the drone got closer still, it became clear that one of them was holding a gun in the back of the other.

'Dad!' Matt screamed. Norman had realised the same thing and was relaying the information to

Captain Fitch.

'Fitch! Ivan is boarding the sub with Dr Metcalfe as a hostage. Are you nearly there?'

'Not far off. Is he armed?' the Captain replied.

'Looks like he has a pistol,' Norman said. 'But we don't know much about the sub. Ivan may have guns on board, and the sub may have a weapons system of its own. Proceed with caution. Dr Metcalfe's safety is priority, and take Ivan alive if you possibly can. But whatever happens, do not allow that sub to leave the ship!'

'Understood. Out.'

Within a few moments, Fitch had the sub surrounded, but he and his men couldn't risk approaching it more closely until they knew its weapons status. The drones were inspecting the exterior, and there were no obvious gun ports. Just then a voice was heard coming from the sub.

'Hello gentlemen. Forgive me if I don't offer you a gracious welcome. I assume I am speaking to Victor Damiano and his soldier friend, Colonel Hourihan? I'm sorry about your helicopter, colonel. That is a regrettable incident which is no doubt going to cause a great deal of trouble. It's a pity you couldn't have made a more conventional appearance and we could have sorted this out like civilised men.'

'Son-of-a-bitch,' muttered Norman, but addressed himself to Fitch. 'Can you hook us up so I can talk to this cocksucker?'

Fitch answered by addressing Ivan. His voice seethed with controlled fury.

'Ivan, my name is Captain Fitch. I'm in charge of the boarding party. You have killed at least two of my men and wounded several others, but my orders are to escort you to the US alive, and that is what I intend to do. Colonel Hourihan can hear you, and I'm patching him through to my hailer so he can talk to you direct. Go ahead, colonel.'

'The game's up, Ivan.' Norman said. 'You know that. I'm not going to offer you an amnesty or any other kind of deal because I know you wouldn't buy it. But things can get much worse here if we don't all play our cards sensibly. First thing you need to do is to let Dr Metcalfe leave the sub. Do it now, Ivan.'

Ivan's reply was deadly calm. 'But David here is my only trump card, colonel. Please don't treat me like a stupid person. It is unhelpful as well as impolite. Now here's how this is going to play out. You want David here, and I want to depart in peace in my little submarine. I am happy to return David to you: it will be some considerable time before I could use his services again anyway. But obviously you won't allow me to leave if I release him now. So he is going to have to accompany me until I arrive at a safe port. Then he can go; you have my word on that.'

'Now you are treating us like stupid people, Ivan. How do you expect to proceed on the basis of a verbal reassurance from a man who has murdered at least two scientists, kidnapped others, and killed and wounded a number of marines?'

There was a pause before Ivan spoke again.

'We seem to have arrived at an impasse, colonel. If

I release Dr Metcalfe now, how do I know you won't let your trigger-happy friend here just blow this submarine to smithereens? He is probably itching for the opportunity. I'm going off-line now. Buzz me when you are prepared to agree to my terms, or when you have come up with a more constructive suggestion.'

A low hum could now be heard in the sub bay. Lights snapped on underneath the vehicle.

'Colonel,' said Jeff. 'I think he's preparing to launch the sub.'

'Can we stop him?' Norman asked.

'We haven't found a way to over-ride the sub controls, but there are various pieces of winching equipment in the bay. Some of the larger units can be controlled from the bridge, and Ivan may not be able to over-ride them. We may be able to manoeuvre them into positions which will prevent him from launching the sub.'

'Do it!', ordered Norman. Then he addressed Fitch. 'Captain, we're going to move some equipment around inside the bay to stop Ivan leaving. Tell your men to watch out.'

'Copy that,' Fitch replied.

Jeff and a couple of the other agents studied the schematic of the Eleusis on one of the screens, and compared them with the images of the bay provided by the drones. They talked to the Captain on the bridge. A few moments later, a couple of mobile cranes and some large wheeled winching equipment started to move around inside the bay area. The sub was manoeuvring toward the bay doors, which were now starting to open. The sea was visible just below the level of the doors. One of the cranes clanked against the sub, which rocked a little on its cradle. The other crane and the rest of the mobile equipment were moving to block the sub's route to the bay doors. The engine noise from the sub grew louder, and the vessel accelerated towards the door. But Ivan had lost the race: the sub ground to a halt, blocked by an ungainly assortment of cranes and winching gear.

The sub reversed, and its engines revved again. It moved to ram the blocking equipment. But instead of moving the machinery out of the way, it became entangled and stuck. The sub's engines screamed like an enraged elephant, but the vessel was immobile. After a few more moments, the sub's engines fell silent.

'Colonel, we're confident the sub has no weapon systems,' reported Jeff.

'Thanks Jeff. Captain, we believe Ivan has no offensive capability apart from his pistol. I suggest you approach the submarine with caution and see if you can force the door open.'

'Copy that, Colonel.'

As the Captain and his men approached the sub they could hear muffled voices. They could not make out the words, but the volume increased as the two men inside started shouting at each other. The Captain reached the door and started trying to turn its wheel.

Just at that moment there was a cry, then a crash, and two shots rang out. Then there was silence.

TWENTY-ONE

Silence blanketed both the Eleusis and the situation room.

Quickly, the marines set to work. They could not open the door manually, so one of them applied some plastic explosive to the lock and they all took cover. The explosion echoed round the situation room as well as the submarine bay area, and the mini-sub's door jumped, swung open, and hung on its hinges at a lazy angle. Waving the smoke away from his face, Fitch was the first to enter. Moments later his voice broke the news from inside the sub.

'Ivan is dead but Dr Metcalfe is alive! He's unconscious: it looks like he took a nasty blow to the temple. I think we'd better not move him until a medic gets here.' Back in the situation room, Jeff put up his hand to let Norman know he didn't need to say anything: the medic was already on his way.

Matt almost fainted with relief, slumping like a marionette with cut strings. The adrenaline of the last hour was draining out of him and he was stunned, relieved, but still afraid that his father might be badly hurt.

'He's coming round,' they heard Captain Fitch say. All heads turned to the main screen.

The marine with the head cam providing the feed to the screen was inside the sub now, and looking at David. David was lying on the floor: his eyes opened and he looked up at the medic groggily. The medic told him not to try to speak for a few moments. The camera looked up. A bit further ahead, Ivan lay with his head in a pool of blood, and a couple of marines were checking his body for booby-traps. 'He's clean,' one of them pronounced.

The camera looked around the inside of the sub. There was a sizeable hole in one of its instrument panels, and smoke was rising where a small fire had been extinguished.

'Looks like Ivan shot the lights out before he left,' Norman said.

The camera looked back at David, who was sitting up, shakily. He muttered something incomprehensible to the medic, his movements uncoordinated.

'You took a hard blow to the head, sir,' said the medic. 'But you're safe now. It's all over; you're in good hands.'

Gradually, David appeared to gather his wits. 'Ivan . . . ?' he asked, looking around, and saw the answer to his own question. He looked as if he was about to be sick, but after a few moments with his eyes shut he recovered.

'Sir, your son is on the line,' Captain Fitch said. Would you like to speak to him? If you speak to me he can hear you.'

'What? Is he here? On the ship?'

'No, Dad I'm in the US Embassy in London. But I can see you on the screens here!' Matt blurted out.

'Hang on, son,' Norman said. 'He can't hear you yet. Jeff, can you patch us in?'

'Got it. You're through now,' replied Jeff.

'Dad, Dad, I'm here! Hurry up and get home!'

Norman smiled as a mixture of joy and wonder illuminated the image of David's face on the big screen. 'We're going to put you on a chopper and get you back here right away, Dr Metcalfe,' he said. 'But can you tell us what happened there? We heard two shots and a crash, and then everything went silent.'

David rubbed his temple gingerly and looked at his hand to see if there was blood on it. To his great relief, Matt could tell by his father's expression that there wasn't.

'All I know for sure is that Ivan hit me hard on the head with the gun barrel. It's obvious that he shot himself after that, but by the look of things, not before he took out the access port to his main computer stacks.'

David looked round again at the smoking instrument panel, as if looking for clues as to what had happened. 'Yes, I remember now: that's what he said he was going to do. Once he realised he couldn't get the sub off the ship he knew he was caught. He was enraged and desperate. He said that he refused to rot in jail while the US military secretly created the first machine intelligence, and put the whole world at risk. He aimed his gun at that panel. I tried to argue with him, and I made a grab for the gun – probably not the smartest thing to do. I guess that's when he hit me.'

David groaned and lay back on the floor.

'Dad!' Matt shouted.

David put up his hand to signal that he was OK, just exhausted and fuzzy-headed. Norman put his hand on Matt's shoulder and spoke to David.

'I think we'd better leave you to recover with the medic for a while, while we debrief the marines. We'll get you on the chopper and then bring you straight here to the Embassy, where you can see your family.'

He turned to Matt. 'You must be exhausted. Your mother and Leo should be here by now. We have some private quarters upstairs in the building, and I suggest you spend some time with them there while Dr Metcalfe is brought back.'

He turned to address the whole room. 'We've taken some casualties here today, folks, and there are some American families who will not be seeing their sons and husbands again. We're through the worst, and I know we're all tired, but this thing isn't over yet. Particularly with Dr Metcalfe re-appearing, for which we give solemn thanks, there's no way this fire-fight on the high seas is going to stay out of the news media. We can embargo it for a few hours at most.'

He addressed Jeff. 'Could you please do the initial debrief with Captain Fitch. Collate a casualty list and damage report. Arrange for the families of the deceased and wounded to be informed. Make sure that Dr Metcalfe is brought here to the Embassy ASAP. Thanks, Jeff.'

While Norman was speaking, Vic had walked away from the group to take a call. He rejoined them with the news that Matt's mother and Leo were in the Embassy, and had been briefed about the raid, and David's rescue. He asked Jeff to take Matt to the apartment upstairs where they were waiting for him. A rush of conflicting emotions swept over Matt: he knew that his mother would be furious with him for not telling her that David was alive, but she would also be as excited and relieved to see him as he would be to see her and Leo. He gushed his thanks to Norman and the others, and looked expectantly at Jeff.

As Matt was taken away, Vic turned to Norman.

'It's a good job you had the security people keep an eye out for anybody suspicious outside the perimeter. They spotted a well-built man hanging around, and thought he was keeping the entrance under surveillance. They sent a couple of marines out to challenge him, but apparently he brushed them off like flies – broke the arm of one of them when they tried to apprehend him. As you can imagine, that is no mean feat. The marines are convinced he was special forces. He has disappeared, but I'm glad he wasn't around when Leo and Sophie arrived.'

Norman's brow furrowed. 'So Ivan did have Matt under surveillance. Presumably we have video, and someone is analysing it, working on his ID?'

'Already done,' Vic replied. 'No joy. None of the cameras got a clear enough view of his face.'

'Damn.' Norman thought for a moment, then shrugged his shoulders. 'Nothing we can do about it now. Hopefully, whoever he was, he'll decide to disappear when he discovers that he needs a new employer. Meanwhile we'd better make sure that our new friends have good babysitters.'

*

Matt held his breath as Jeff opened the door to the apartment. Sophie and Leo leapt to their feet and rushed to greet Matt as he walked into the room. There was a jumble of exclamations, as thanksgivings and protestations spilled over each other, and had to be repeated.

'Thank god you're OK!' Leo burst out. 'I can't forgive myself for leaving you alone with that monster! I don't know what I was thinking of – I was such an idiot! Thank god you're alright!'

'Matt, Matt, Matt!' Sophie joined in. 'What did you think you were playing at, coming here on your own without telling me? Thank heavens you're alive! Oh my poor, dear boy: I've been so worried.'

'Dad's safe, mum!' Matt shouted. 'He's safe! And he's on his way home! Everything's going to be OK!'

They stepped back as the immediate rush of emotion subsided a little. Matt held his mother by the arms and smiled at her in a mixture of excitement and exhaustion. He was amazed to be still standing, but sharing the situation with his mother and Leo was a huge relief. He took in his surroundings through his peripheral vision. The deep pile blue carpet and yellow velour sofa seemed out of place inside the embassy building. He could see a bed through a partly open door to one of the bedrooms, which reminded him how little he had slept in the last few days.

'So you know what's been happening?' he asked.

'Yes, we've been briefed,' Leo replied for both of them as Sophie pulled Matt into a tearful hug again. 'What an amazing situation,' he said. 'Are you OK?'

'I'm OK. But it's been quite a trip,' Matt said, with feeling.

Vic joined them. ' Thank you for taking care of our boy,' Leo said, holding out a grateful hand. 'Looks like he's been in good hands.'

'He's an impressive young man,' Vic said, smiling broadly. 'You must be very proud.'

'Proud and bloody furious!' Sophie replied, stepping back from Matt to look at him. 'Why didn't you tell me what happened as soon as you got back, Matt? You saw David on that ship and you went to your room and then came up to London without telling me he was alive? How could you let me go on thinking he was dead? Oh god, but I'm so relieved to see you!'

'Don't be too hard on the boy, Mrs Metcalfe,' Vic urged gently. 'He had a tough hand to play and he has played it well. He knew that if Ivan had the slightest inclination that Matt had told anyone – even you – about the situation, it could have gone very badly for David.'

'And for you, mum,' Matt chipped in. 'Ivan might have had any or all of us killed. Look, I'm sorry. I desperately wanted to tell you, but I knew I had to do exactly as he said. He was an incredibly clever and resourceful man, and until I heard about the raid I just didn't dare do anything except what he told me to.'

'I know, I know,' his mother conceded. 'I'm sorry, love. I've just been so worried. And I'm so proud of you. Look at you: carrying out a daring rescue with the US military in the US Embassy. My son!'

'Mu-um!' Matt protested in embarrassment. 'I didn't really do anything,' he smiled. 'I was pretty much a passenger here. These guys didn't need any help from me. But I'm sure glad to be here, and I'm so glad you're both here too.'

Norman joined them and put an avuncular hand on Matt's shoulder as he introduced himself to Leo and Sophie. Then he introduced a sombre note to the celebrations. 'We're going to have to discuss with you and Dr Metcalfe how we're going to present this to the world. There's a lot at stake here, and we'll only get one shot at pitching this thing right.'

'How do you mean?' Leo asked, sensing concern in Norman's voice. 'This is a good news story, isn't it? Some brave young men lost their lives, but a murderer and kidnapper was defeated, and two innocent people rescued.'

'I'm afraid it's not that simple, Leo,' Norman said. 'Depending how we play it, this story could have a huge impact – on your family, on Vic's organisation, and even on the US military. Vic's work has been below the radar until now, and we need to keep it that way for the time being. And if we're not careful you guys could find yourselves in the middle of a media firestorm.'

Matt and Leo both started to ask questions, but Norman raised a hand.

'Let's discuss this when Dr Metcalfe gets here. In

the meantime, you guys have some catching up and celebrating to do. And I recommend you all get some rest. It's late, and it's been one helluva day. There shouldn't be any need to talk to the media before Dr Metcalfe arrives.'

TWENTY-TWO

After talking excitedly with his mother and Leo for an hour, Matt was overcome by exhaustion and lay down on the bed. Four hours later he was woken by Vic, gently shaking his shoulder and telling him that his father had arrived. Matt shot awake and swung his legs round to get up.

'Where is he? Can I see him now?'

'Of course you can. He's in a meeting room down-stairs. Come on, I'll take you there.'

Sophie was already in the meeting room with David when Matt rushed in. They were sitting opposite each other holding hands across a small table, staring into each other's eyes. The room was plain and bare, and they almost looked like a prisoner and his visitor.

David stood as Matt entered the room and ran to his father. They hugged each other tightly, then David put his hands on Matt's shoulders and pushed him back a little to look into his eyes.

'My son and my saviour! Not many fathers get to say that,' he laughed.

'Ha! I didn't save you,' Matt protested with a grin. 'We have to thank Vic and Norman, and those Navy Seals guys for that. They're the real heroes.'

'Well, I'm eternally grateful for their bravery, and their sacrifice,' David agreed, glancing at Vic. He turned back to Matt. 'But you're a hero too, as far as I'm concerned.'

'Amen to that,' Leo and Norman chimed in simultaneously as they came into the room. They both laughed. Matt realised that they had already welcomed David, and they had stepped outside the room to give Sophie some time alone with her husband.

Norman slipped into take-charge mode.

'Now, we have some important decisions to make. In particular we're going to have to decide how we want this to play in the media. I'm afraid that too many people know about the raid for it to be kept secret. We can rely on the discretion of the military and intelligence people involved, but there is Ivan's crew to think about, and his people elsewhere. There is also the little matter of David returning from the dead. I think there's no way to prevent this becoming a lead story, but if we play our cards right we may be able to contain it to a one- or two-day affair. Playing our cards right means we need a coherent story that we all agree to stick to. And there's going to have to be a press conference sooner rather than later, otherwise the media will start running the story based on hearsay and whatever they can dig up – or invent. Which would not be good.

'Now you have an important decision to make, as a family – and I'm assuming that includes you, Leo.

You need to decide what level of intrusion you want in your lives. If we tell the complete story, including the real reason for the kidnapping, and the fact that Matt was kidnapped as well as David, I'm afraid that you can say goodbye to any privacy for a long time. That story would lead the news for days, and you would be pestered by journalists for weeks afterwards.'

Realising that the family was struggling to understand the full implications, Norman explained.

'Look, this is potentially a terrific media story. Think about it: a brilliant scientist is kidnapped, and his heroic – dare I say telegenic – young son' he winked at Matt, 'persuades the US military to ride to the rescue in a daring high seas adventure. Throw in a half-understood sub-plot about robots and artificial intelligence, and you could find a dozen vans with TV cameras parked outside your house for a few weeks. Maybe it could be fun. Hell, you could probably make some money out of it if you want to.'

He paused to let the scale of the potential media frenzy sink in before delivering his main argument.

'But then there will be the backlash. If you are built up as heroes, I guarantee there will be journalists digging around in your past, phoning and door-stepping your friends, bosses, colleagues, girlfriend, ex-lovers, enemies, people you've slighted, people who are simply jealous of your fame: looking everywhere for the skeletons in your cupboards. It's the way the media works these days; it has its own inescapable logic. Are you sure you really want that kind of scrutiny? I'm sure you truly are the good, blameless people that you seem to be. But we've all made mistakes on the way to where we are.'

He paused again. Matt, Sophie and Leo exchanged glances. Norman was right: this wasn't straightforward.

'So I suggest instead that we tell the truth but not the whole truth. I suggest that we announce that you were taken hostage three months ago, David, and you were freed earlier this morning in a raid by Navy Seals following an investigation into Ivan's other illegal activities. If we say that the reason for the kidnapping was to obtain commercial secrets then it would be perfectly reasonable to refuse to elaborate. I recommend that we explain that the experience has been traumatic for you, and ask the media to respect your privacy so that you can resume your life with as much normalcy as possible. They will probably ignore that initially, but if you refuse to make any further comments or statements, they will hopefully lose interest fairly quickly.'

'So there would be no mention of Matt?' David asked. 'No mention of the race to create the first machine intelligence?'

'That's right,' said Norman firmly. 'That is my strong recommendation. I think that is the best approach for our organisations, and even more so for your family.'

David looked doubtful. 'No-one who knows me will believe that I was kidnapped and held hostage for three months because of commercial secrets.'

Matt was also unsure about Norman's suggested approach, for a different reason.

'What do you think, Vic?' he asked. 'I thought you

were in favour of openness? I thought Ivan was the one who wanted to keep everything secret.'

Vic looked uncomfortable. 'That's true,' he agreed, 'but the timing is important. Going public with news about machine intelligence too early is dangerous. Especially if it is in the context of military action. We need time to prepare the ground. People need to get used to the idea first by seeing progress with impressive but narrow forms of artificial intelligence, like domestic robots and so on. If we are exposed without that preparation, then at best people will think we are crackpots; at worst they will panic.'

'But on the other hand, going public too late could be much worse,' Matt said. 'If the idea is effectively sprung on people just before it becomes a reality, the panic you are worried about could be enormously damaging.'

Leo was nodding as Matt spoke. 'If we withhold some of the story and then it gets out, people will be suspicious about what else is being hidden. If it leaks out that the US Army is close to creating the first artificial general intelligence, and has been less than truthful about it, a lot of people will get very concerned. But to be honest I'm more concerned about the more immediate problems. For instance, is it realistic to insist that Matt never speaks to anyone outside this room about his experience – not now and not for the rest of his life? And what about Ivan's people on the boat and elsewhere? How many of them know more than you're proposing to disclose?'

After a few minutes of discussion, Norman realised he was losing the argument.

'Well I can see which way this is going,' said Norman, shaking his head. 'I can't stop you from telling your story, but I fear this will have a bigger impact on your family life than you realise.' He held up a warning finger, 'One thing I do insist on is that everything that you have seen and heard in this building is classified confidential military information.'

'Norman, let me assure you,' David said quickly, 'I am – we all are – immensely grateful for what you and your men have done. Some of them have died in the process – I'm not forgetting that. I wouldn't dream of putting any information into the public domain which could jeopardise the lives of US personnel. As far as I'm concerned – and I'm sure I speak for the rest of my family,' he looked around at them as he spoke to confirm this, 'everything we have seen in this building, all the technology we have seen deployed so impressively, is completely off-limits. The media doesn't need to know any operational details, and I for one will not tell them.'

Norman nodded. 'I appreciate that, David' he said. 'The research we are engaged on with Vic falls into that category too.'

'I don't need to and don't want to talk to anyone about the details of your work,' David assured him. 'For that matter I know very little about it. But I think that Leo has put his finger on it. If you try to cover up the reason for your involvement in this incident and then it gets out, there will be an uproar. You will lose the trust of people whose trust you are much going to need in the not-too-distant future.'

'Very well,' Norman conceded. 'I can see that you've

made up your minds. Can we at least agree on a joint statement for the press conference, and that there will be no question and answer session at this stage? I suggest that any mention of artificial intelligence research is kept brief and general. And of course I'm going to have to get sign-off from upstairs.'

David looked at the others before nodding his agreement.

'Thank you,' Norman said. 'I'll have someone start work on the draft immediately; it won't take long. You'll probably want to get some breakfast? They serve some outstanding blueberry pancakes in the cafeteria.'

*

David and his family went in search of pancakes in the functional and brightly-lit canteen. Norman brought them the draft and they had no objections. He left again to get it signed off. It took a bit longer than expected, and he returned half an hour later looking harassed.

'They're not comfortable with this upstairs,' he admitted. 'But I told them that if we don't agree to this draft then you guys might reveal significantly more. I told them we would have to kidnap you all over again to stop you.' He smiled and winked at Sophie, whose mouth had fallen open. 'Just joking, ma'am. That is permitted under US military regulations. Joking, I mean – not kidnapping.'

He placed a sheaf of legal documents on the table and pushed one of the across the surface to David.

'They want each of you to sign this disclaimer. I'm embarrassed to have to ask you, but they insisted. It's a declaration that you accept that you have witnessed things of a confidential nature here during the last couple of days, and that you will keep them confidential.'

David looked at Leo and pushed the document across the table towards him.

'Would you mind looking at this, Leo? You have far more experience with this sort of thing than I do.'

'No problem,' said Leo, and started to read the paper.

'While you're doing that I'll get the Embassy's PR team to organise a press conference,' Norman said, pulling out his phone. 'It shouldn't take more than a couple of hours. Then you can finally all go home!'

'Won't that be a relief!' said Sophie.

'I'm not sure I remember what home looks like,' David joked.

'Home is where we all are, Dad,' said Matt. He winced. 'Ooh, that was really cheesy, wasn't it.'

They all laughed, and then fell silent to allow Leo to finish reading the document. After a couple of minutes he looked up at Norman, who had finished his call.

'It's mostly boilerplate stuff, Norman. I have no problem with it except for this paragraph here,' he pointed to a paragraph halfway down the third page, 'where it says that we agree to indemnify you for any legal costs arising from a dispute over this document. That gives you carte blanche to sue us and then charge us for the privilege.'

Norman looked unhappy as he read the offending paragraph.

'Yes, I see what you mean,' he said. 'They love to create a bit of work, these lawyers, don't they? Look,

I can understand your point, but getting one of these documents changed is like trying to change the holy scriptures . . .'

David leaned across the table and grabbed the paper.

'You guys saved my life, and some of your men died in the process. You have bent over backwards to help us, and I think it's time we showed some spirit of compromise. Leo, you may not want to sign this thing, and for sure you have more assets for them to go after if it did all go horribly wrong. But for my part I'm going to sign it and get the thing over with.'

Norman was visibly relieved. 'Thank you, David.'

Leo smiled, and nodded. 'Fair enough. Put it like that, and I'm willing to take my chances with these guys. I hope I don't live to regret this!'

TWENTY-THREE

'Good morning, ladies and gentlemen. This will be a short statement, and there will be no questions taken afterwards, for reasons which will become obvious. Transcripts of the statement will be available at the door when you leave.'

Norman was in his element, taking charge of events in a crowded room. There were around fifty journalists present, sitting in deliberately uncomfortable chairs arranged in tightly-packed rows facing Norman's lectern, while Vic and the Metcalfe family sat in similar chairs lined up by the wall behind him. The room was brightly lit for the benefit of cameras. The audience was mostly quiet, with a few whispered conversations winding up here and there around the room. The journalists didn't know what announcement was coming, but that was not unusual. They were not expecting a major news story, and many of them knew each other well, so the atmosphere was relaxed and convivial as Norman began to speak.

'Yesterday afternoon at 1600 hours local time a

team of US military personnel boarded a large private vessel in the Atlantic Ocean, a hundred miles west of Agadir, Morocco. The team's mission was to rescue a hostage, Dr David Metcalfe, who is seated here behind me. The mission was successful, although I am sorry to report that three marines lost their lives and five were wounded. Their relatives have been informed. Also killed during the operation was the man responsible for the kidnapping, a Mr Ivan Kripke. He took his own life when it became clear to him that his apprehension and trial was inevitable. Mr Kripke had kidnapped Dr Metcalfe in order to obtain access to certain research techniques which Dr Metcalfe had developed.'

The room had fallen silent apart from Norman's voice. The journalists had realised that this was something a bit out of the ordinary. This was no grimly routine update on slayings in the Middle East, or squabble between governments about how to cope with trade imbalances. This was a positive human interest story which could appeal to their editors on a number of levels.

'The mission was successful in part thanks to information provided by Dr Metcalfe's son, Matt, who is also seated behind me. Matt was also kidnapped by Mr Kripke, who blackmailed him into attempting to infiltrate a research group led by Dr Victor Damiano – sitting next to Matt – in order to obtain some additional research techniques. Dr Damiano is a leading researcher in the field of artificial intelligence.'

A few of the journalists let out tiny gasps of surprise. This was getting better. A young hero figure; a father-and-son rescue story. And was there a suggestion that robots were involved?

'When Matt approached Dr Damiano as instructed, he was informed that Mr Kripke was under observation on suspicion of a number of crimes, including murder. At this point he took the brave decision to reveal the fact of the kidnapping to Dr Damiano, who in turn disclosed it to the authorities, who proceeded to draw up and execute a rescue plan.'

The journalists' interest was now thoroughly piqued, and there was an atmosphere of palpable anticipation in the room.

'Dr Metcalfe has asked me, on behalf of himself and his family here, to express his deep gratitude to the marines and other personnel who participated in his rescue, and to extend their profound condolences to the families of those men who did not return. For our part, the US Armed Forces would like to express our appreciation for the dignity and fortitude that this brave family has shown throughout this extremely stressful period in their lives.'

Norman bestowed on his audience the patient smile of an approachable but strict headmaster.

'Now I know that many of you will have questions that you would like to ask, but as I said at the outset, neither we nor the family are taking any questions at this time. We ask you to appreciate that Dr Metcalfe and his family have gone through a traumatic and exhausting experience, and they would like to be left alone to recover in their home environment. That's it, folks. Transcripts at the door.'

Journalists are not noted for taking 'no' for an answer, and many of them started asking questions anyway. The volume rose to shouts as they competed for attention.

'How long were you detained for, Dr Metcalfe?'

'What kind of research did you say this is all about? What are these research techniques?'

'How old are you, Matt? Have you got anything to say about this?'

'Hey, Matt, this sounds like quite an adventure! How do you feel about being part of a father-and-son hero team?'

'Dr Metcalfe, what was it like being in the middle of a raid. Was it just like in the movies?'

Norman raised his hands, demanding silence. It took a short while, but he was a man used to commanding attention, and getting it.

'Ladies and gentlemen, I said there would be no questions. I'm sorry. Dr Metcalfe and his family are of course free to talk to you later if they choose, but for now they need some time to recuperate. I'm sure you can understand that. That really is all. Thank you for your attention.'

Norman turned back to David and his family, and ushered them out of the room by a different door than the one through which the journalists were being herded – dissatisfied, but excited and chattering – by uniformed Embassy personnel.

Once they were safely beyond earshot of the journalists, Norman turned to David and Matt.

'I guess you'll be wanting to get home now. May I provide you with a driver?'

'That's very kind, Norman,' said David. 'Thank you. Catching a train might be asking for trouble right now.'

'Better prepare yourself, though,' Norman warned. 'The more enterprising members of that crowd will find out your address quickly and there will probably be reporters outside your house by the time you get there. My driver will be a man who can help you with that, and I'll get someone from the Embassy to suggest to your local police authority that they post a couple of men outside your house for a few days. But you might want to think about staying with friends and relatives for a while. Although god knows, they'll track you down there too. You can see they like the story. I'm afraid there's going to be a feeding frenzy.'

'Maybe you can provide us with false identities and a new life?' Leo joked.

'It's a bit late for that, I'm afraid,' Norman replied ruefully.

'Thanks Norman, we appreciate your concern,' David said. 'But I've been away from home for far too long now. That's definitely my first move: home.' He put his arm around Sophie's shoulder and gave her a squeeze.

'We'll be seeing you again soon, I trust?' Vic asked. 'In fact I want to talk to you about joining our team. Both of you,' he added, looking meaningfully at Matt as well as David.

Matt let out a yelp. 'Brilliant!' Then he realised his mistake, and glanced at his mother nervously. 'Um, that is OK isn't it, mum?'

'We'll discuss it at home,' she said with mock

firmness, while smiling at him indulgently. 'In fact we have quite a lot of things to discuss, young man.'

'Uh-oh. Hope I haven't gotten you into trouble, Matt' Vic grinned. 'Anyway, I think we'd better wait until the media interest blows over. It should blow itself out in two or three days.'

'I wouldn't bet on that,' said Norman as he walked them towards the garage.

*

Norman was right. Christmas came and went, and media interest in David and Matt's story was still going strong.

Christmas in the Metcalfe household was a strange affair. They had a major cause for celebration, and relief was an almost tangible emotion inside the house. But at the same time the family were effectively prisoners in their own home. They could not go outside for a walk without being followed by a posse of journalists intent on squeezing more life out of the story, and without a dozen cameras being thrust in their faces.

Initially, the papers were full of largely speculative stories about this mysterious family which had suffered kidnap and blackmail, and had been rescued by brave US marines. The fact that the story only came out in dribs and drabs, as journalists dug up more and more people who knew David and Matt, helped keep the interest alive.

Matt in particular became something of a celebrity, nudging the manufactured pop bands off the front pages of the tabloids for a change. Matt was bemused by this, and astonished to receive fanmail, some of it startlingly sexual in nature.

Alice took this in good heart, and teased Matt gently about becoming a heartthrob for teenage girls. Alice was spending a lot of her time at Matt's house. Carl came round often too, and his teasing was more robust.

The media did its best to pull on the thread of artificial intelligence research. Since there was little hard information about either Vic's or Ivan's work, the copy consisted of opinion pieces rather than reporting, and contributions from other researchers in the AI field.

Many of the opinion pieces came from the usual commentariat, people who are paid to have an opinion on everything, and find that to be no strain at all. It also came from a wide range of people and organisations with relevant and vested interests, notably religious groups.

As well as the TV and newspaper coverage, there was an enormous amount of comment and speculation on blogs and on Twitter. Norman had warned them that they might not be able to handle the volume, and they might find some of the content upsetting. He offered to provide a media analysis and PR service to wade through the material and forward a summary along with selected samples. They were surprised at the number and variety of people and firms who offered the same service for a fee, ranging from well-known publicists and major international PR firms to small and discreet boutiques. Initially they declined all these offers, but before long they realised that Norman was right, and reluctantly but gratefully accepted his offer.

Before long they were also obliged to accept the suggestion of their new PR service that they change their email addresses and phone numbers, and re-direct their existing addresses and numbers to the service. They had to repeat this a couple of times as their new numbers and addresses were leaked, so each time they cut down the number of people they gave the new details to.

The Metcalfe house had a small camp of journalists outside round the clock, but the policemen did a good job of making sure that none of them went onto the property itself. David and Sophie wanted to resume a normal life, but their attempts to go shopping meant being accompanied by police officers, and they realised they were causing serious inconvenience to neighbours and friends.

'Maybe we should do what Norman suggested,' said David on the fourth day, exasperated at being unable to go to the shop to pick up a pint of milk. 'Maybe we should go away for a few days until all this has blown over.'

'Where would we go?' asked Sophie. 'None of our friends live in gated communities, or have houses with mile-long private driveways.'

'Maybe we should go somewhere abroad?' suggested Matt.

'Wouldn't help,' said David, gloomily. 'This has become a global story.'

'I bet Norman could find somewhere secure,' suggested Alice. 'But you have to take me with you.

I'm not letting this guy out of my sight while he is the object of adoration for millions of screaming teenagers.' She smiled and squeezed Matt's arm.

'Yes, he probably could,' agreed David, 'but this thing seems to have legs. That pack of jackals out there would be waiting for us when we got back.'

'That's a bit harsh, Dad,' Matt protested. 'They haven't turned the thumbscrews on us. They haven't said anything particularly nasty about us. OK, there are some ridiculously stupid comments on some of the blogs and on Twitter, but the mainstream media has been pretty responsible.'

'So far,' David agreed. 'But some of the emails and letters the service has been forwarding to me have been . . . well, unappetising. To be honest it's starting to disturb me, especially since I'm sure they are keeping back the worst stuff.'

'What sort of stuff?' asked Matt. He looked at his mother, who clearly already knew. 'I haven't had anything really bad – at least, not yet.'

'Don't worry, it's all addressed to me; it doesn't concern you.'

'Like hell it doesn't. You're my dad, and if you don't mind I'll ask you to remember that I summoned up the US Army to come and rescue you when you got into your little spot of bother with Ivan.'

David smiled, and ruffled his son's hair. He went to a desk and took a letter out of the drawer and gave it to Matt to read.

'That's the sort of thing. It's all nonsense, of course, but I'm getting a little tired of it.'

Matt read the letter with a mixture of amusement and concern. It was a largely incoherent ramble, claiming that David was a traitor to his kind, seeking to create false gods in his own image and take over the world.

'It's nothing to worry about, Matt, really,' said Sophie. 'It's just loonies sounding off. There is no bite, and the bark is just a Chihuahua.'

'You're right,' agreed Matt. 'I'm sure the writer is a sad little creature in a bedsit somewhere. But it does make me think. Maybe it's time that the AI side of the story got a proper hearing.'

David looked at him. 'You know, I've been wondering the same thing.'

He walked over to the desk again and took out another letter, and handed it to Matt.

'Do you think we should accept this invitation?'

The letter was an invitation to join a small panel in a live televised debate about the future of artificial intelligence. It was on BBC-headed paper, and the proposed discussion moderator was one of the Corporation's leading presenters, Malcolm Ross.

Matt's eyebrows rose and his lips pursed as he read the letter. 'Yes,' he said soberly. 'I think we should do Vic and Norman the courtesy of discussing it with them before we decide. But yes. Yes, I think we should.'

TWENTY-FOUR

Two things struck Matt forcefully as he sat in the glare of the studio lights, waiting for the show to begin. The first was how hot it was: the lights seemed to be bearing down on him, heating him up, trying to boil his innermost secrets out of him. The second was what an alien environment this was. Malcolm Ross and his colleagues were entirely at home in the studio, energised by the situation and the various tasks they had to perform flawlessly and against unmoveable deadlines. For Matt – and, he supposed, the other 'guests' – it was like being on another planet. He hoped he would manage to stay calm, speak clearly, and avoid making silly comments. He wished the glass of water in front of him was a beer.

'Good evening, everyone,' Ross began, 'and welcome to a specially extended edition of the Show. We are tackling just one subject today: the question of when artificial intelligence will arrive, and whether it will be good for us. No-one in our specially invited studio audience, and nobody watching this at home will need reminding that this subject has risen to prominence because of the remarkable experiences of one British family, and in particular, father and son David and Matt Metcalfe. Despite the intense public interest in David's dramatic rescue, they have declined to talk to the media before now, so we are delighted that they have agreed to participate in this programme.

'Also on the show we have a prominent AI researcher in the shape of Geoffrey Montaubon, and two non-scientists who spend their time thinking about these matters, Dan Christensen, a professor of philosophy at Oxford University, and the Right Reverend Wesley Cuthman, bishop of Sussex.'

The panelists were a mixed bunch.

Montaubon was a friendly-looking man of medium height. His un-combed mousy-brown hair and lived-in white shirt and linen jacket, faded chinos and brown hiking shoes suggested that he cared far more about ideas than about appearances. After a brilliant academic career at Imperial College London, where he was a professor of neuroscience, he had surprised his peers by moving to India to establish a brain emulation project for the Indian government. He ran the project for ten years, before retiring to research and write about the ethics of transhumanism and brain emulation.

He was extremely intelligent, and highly focused and logical, but he sometimes failed to acknowledge contrary lines of thought. As a result, some of his thinking appeared not only outlandish to his peers, but worse, naive.

Christensen looked too young to be a professor

at Oxford. He was dressed in recognisably academic clothes: more formal than casual, but not new, and not smart. His thinning pale brown hair sat atop a long, thin face with grey eyes, a high forehead, and pale, almost unhealthy-looking skin. He looked deep in thought most of the time, which indeed he was. He seemed to relish interesting ideas above anything else, and when he spoke, he seemed to be rehearsing a pre-prepared speech, as if he had considered in advance every avenue of enquiry that could possibly arise in conversation. He had a remarkable ability to think about old problems from a new angle, and to present his ideas to a general public in a way which immediately made his often innovative conclusions seem obviously correct – even inevitable.

The right reverend Wesley Cuthman was a handsome, solid-looking man of sixty, with a full head of hair, albeit mostly grey, and a full but well-maintained beard. He wore priestly robes, but his shoes, watch and rings were expensive. He carried himself proudly and had the air of a man accustomed to considering himself the wisest – if not the cleverest – person in the room. A long-time favourite of the BBC, Cuthman was deeply rooted in the old culture excoriated by C.P. Snow, in which humanities graduates view their ignorance of the sciences as a mark of superiority.

'So let's start with you, David and Matt,' Ross said. 'Thank you for joining us on the show today. Can I start by asking, David, why you have been so reluctant to talk to the media before now?'

Matt thought his father looked slightly hunched,

as if overwhelmed by the occasion. 'Well, we could tell there was a lot of media interest immediately after the rescue. But we were hoping that it would die down quickly if we didn't do anything to encourage it, and we might be allowed to get on with our normal lives. I guess that was naive, but you have to understand that we're new to all this.'

'We had a lot of catching up to do as a family,' Matt chipped in supportively. 'This media frenzy has been going on while we have been getting used to Dad being back home after having been dead for three months. Kinda surreal, actually, and we didn't want to be in the spotlight at the same time as we were getting our lives straightened out.'

'Yes, I'm sure we can all understand that.' Ross swept his arm towards the audience and back towards David and Matt, indicating that everyone was empathising with their situation, but urging them to share their story freely and openly anyway.

'The question we all want to ask you, I know, is what was your experience like? It must have been a terrible ordeal, with you being held hostage for three months, David, and with you fearing your father dead, Matt. And then the dramatic Navy Seals rescue, like something out of a Hollywood movie. What was it all like?'

With a subtle gesture, invisible to the camera, Ross invited Matt to go first.

'Well, it was incredibly stressful! At times I had the feeling that the real me was hovering above my body looking down at the poor schmuck who was going through this stuff, and wondering if he would keep it together. I remember thinking that particularly when I went to the US Embassy to meet Vic – Dr Damiano – for the first time, because I had this terrible situation going on, with my dad on the ship as Ivan's hostage, but I couldn't tell anyone about it for fear that he would be killed. That was tough, I can tell you.'

'Indeed it must have been,' agreed Ross. 'And a lot of people have commented on how heroic you have been during this whole episode.'

'Well, no, that's not what I . . .'

His father interrupted. 'Matt has absolutely been a hero. He saved my life. He's too modest to admit it, but my son is a hero.'

The studio audience burst into spontaneous and emotional applause. Ross had secured his moment of catharsis. He beamed at the camera for a couple of seconds to allow the moment to imprint. But he was too much of a professional to over-exploit it – this was not going to become tabloid TV. David had made it a condition for appearing on the show that it did not dwell on the personal side of the story. They were here to debate AI. After some hesitation, Vic and Norman had agreed.

'Let's move on to our discussion of the scientific matter which lies at the heart of your adventure, and which has generated so much comment in the media and in the blogosphere. Artificial intelligence. What is it? Is it coming our way soon? And should we want it? We'll kick off with this report from our science correspondent, Adrian Hamilton.'

Ross stepped back from the dais and sat on the edge

of a nearby chair as the studio lights dimmed and the pre-recorded package was projected onto the big screen behind the guests. The guests and the studio audience relaxed a little, aware that the audience at home could no longer see them as the video filled their television screens, beginning with shots of white-coated scientists from the middle of the previous century.

'Writers have long made up stories about artificial beings that can think. But the idea that serious scientists might actually create them is fairly recent. The term 'artificial intelligence' was coined by John McCarthy, an American researcher, at a conference held at Dartmouth College, New Hampshire in 1955.

'The field of artificial intelligence, or AI, has been dominated ever since by Americans, and it has enjoyed waves of optimism followed by periods of scepticism and dismissal. We are currently experiencing the third wave of optimism. The first wave was largely funded by the US military, and one of its champions, Herbert Simon, claimed in 1965 that 'machines will be capable, within twenty years, of doing any work a man can do.' Claims like this turned out to be wildly unrealistic, and disappointment was crystallised by a damning government report in 1974. Funding was cut off, causing the first 'AI winter'.

'Interest was sparked again in the early 1980s, when Japan announced its 'fifth generation' computer research programme. 'Expert systems', which captured and deployed the specialised knowledge of human experts were also showing considerable promise. This second boom was extinguished in the late 1980s when the expensive, specialised computers which drove it were overtaken by smaller, general-purpose desktop machines manufactured by IBM and others. Japan also decided that its fifth generation project had missed too many targets.

'The start of the third boom began in the mid-1990s. This time, researchers have tried to avoid building up the hype which led to previous disappointments, and the term AI is used far less than before. The field is more rigorous now, using sophisticated mathematical tools with exotic names like 'Bayesian networks' and 'hidden Markov models'.

'Another characteristic of the current wave of AI research is that once a task has been mastered by computers, such as playing chess (a computer beat the best human player in 1996), or facial recognition, or playing general knowledge game Jeopardy, that task ceases to be called AI. Thus AI can effectively be defined as the set of tasks which computers cannot perform today.

'AI still has many critics, who claim that artificial minds will not be created for thousands of years, if ever. But impressed by the continued progress of Moore's Law, which observes that computer processing power is doubling every 18 months, more and more scientists now believe that humans may create an artificial intelligence sometime this century. One of the more optimistic, Ray Kurzweil, puts the date as close as 2029.'

As the lights came back up, Ross was standing again, poised in front of the seated guests.

'So, Professor Montaubon. Since David and Matt's dramatic adventure the media has been full of talk about artificial intelligence. Are we just seeing the hype again? Will we shortly be heading to into another AI winter?'

'I don't think so,' replied Montaubon, cheerfully. 'It is almost certain that artificial intelligence will arrive much sooner than most people think. Before long we will have robots which carry out our domestic chores. And people will notice that as each year's model becomes more eerily intelligent than the last, they are progressing towards a genuine, conscious artificial intelligence. It will happen first in the military space first, because that is where the big money is.'

He nodded and gestured towards David as he said this – politely but nevertheless accusingly.

'Military drones are already capable of identifying, locating, approaching and killing their targets. How long before we also allow them to make the decision whether or not to pull the trigger? Human Rights Watch is already calling for the pre-emptive banning of killer robots, and I applaud their prescience, but I'm afraid it's too late.

'People like Bill Joy and Francis Fukuyama have called for a worldwide ban on certain kinds of technological research, but it's like nuclear weapons: the genie is out of the bottle. The idea of so-called 'relinquishment' is simply not an option. If by some miracle, the governments of North America and Europe all agreed to stop the research, would all the countries in the world follow suit? And all the mega-rich? Could we really set up some kind of worldwide Turing police force to prevent the creation of a super-intelligence anywhere in the world, despite the astonishing competitive advantage that would confer for a business, or an army? I don't think so.'

Ross's mask of concerned curiosity failed to conceal his delight at the sensationalist nature of Montaubon's vision. This show had been billed as the must-see TV programme of the week, and so far it was living up the expectation.

'So you're convinced that artificial intelligence is on its way, and soon. How soon, do you think?'

Montaubon gestured at David. 'Well, I think you should ask Dr Metcalfe about that. He is possibly the only person who has spent time with both Ivan Kripke and Victor Damiano. And especially if the rumour is true, and he is going to work with Dr Damiano and the US military, then he is the person in this room best placed to give us a timeline.'

Ross was only too happy to bring David back into the conversation.

'Are you able to share your future plans with us, Dr Metcalfe? Are you going to be working on artificial intelligence now?'

'I honestly don't know. I have had one conversation with Dr Damiano, and I think the work that he and his team is doing is fascinating. But my priority at the moment is to put the experiences of the last three months behind me, and spend some time with my family. The decision about what I do next will be theirs as well as mine.'

Ross turned to Matt.

'How about you, Matt. Your part in the adventure began when you got interested in a career in artificial intelligence research. Does it still appeal?'

Matt began with a cautious, diplomatic, and slightly evasive reply. But his natural candour quickly took over. 'Well, I still have to finish my degree. And of course I don't have a job offer. But yes. Yes it does.'

'So,' said Ross, turning back to the audience, 'it looks as if this father and son team might,' he emphasised the conditionality in deference to David, 'become part of the international effort to give birth to the first machine intelligence.'

Turning back towards David and Matt, he posed his next question.

'Whether or not you are part of the effort, gentlemen, when do you expect that we would see the first artificial intelligence?'

TWENTY-FIVE

'I think the only honest answer is that we simply don't know,' David replied. 'We are getting close to having the sort of computational resources required, but that is far from being all we need.'

On hearing this, Geoffrey Montaubon leaned across towards David, and asked a mock conspiratorial question. 'Dr Metcalfe, can you confirm – just between the two of us, you understand – whether Dr Damiano already has an exaflop scale computer at his disposal?'

David smiled an apology at Montaubon. 'I'm afraid that even if I knew the answer to that, I wouldn't be at liberty to say. You'll have to ask Dr Damiano yourself. I understand the two of you are acquainted.'

Montaubon nodded and smiled in pretend disappointment, and sat back in his chair. Ross took the opportunity to take back control of his show. 'So, coming back to my question, Dr Metcalfe, can you give us even a very broad estimate of when we will see the first general AI?'

David shook his head. 'I really can't say, I'm afraid.

Braver and better-informed people than me have had a go, though. For instance, as mentioned in your opening package, Ray Kurzweil has been saying for some time that it will happen in 2029.'

'2029 is very specific!' laughed Ross. 'Does he have a crystal ball?'

'He thinks he does!' said Montaubon, rolling his eyes dismissively.

Professor Christensen cleared his throat. 'Perhaps I can help out here. My colleagues and I at Oxford University carried out a survey recently, in which we asked most of the leading AI researchers around the world to tell us when they expect to see the first general AI. A small number of estimates were in the near future, but the median estimate was the middle of this century.'

'So not that far away, then,' observed Ross, 'and certainly within the lifetime of many people watching this programme.'

'Yes,' agreed Christensen. 'Quite a few of the estimates were further ahead, though. To get to 90% of the sample you have to go out as far as 2150. Still not very long in historical terms, but too long for anyone in this room, unfortunately . . .'

'Indeed,' Ross agreed. 'But tell me, Professor Christensen: doesn't your survey suffer from sample bias? After all, people carrying out AI research are heavily invested in the success of the project, so aren't they liable to over-estimate its chances?'

'Possibly,' agreed Christensen, 'and we did highlight that when we published the findings. But on the other hand, researchers grappling with complex problems are often intimidated by the scale of the challenge. They probably wouldn't carry on if they thought those challenges could never be met, but they can sometimes over-estimate them.'

'A fair point,' agreed Ross. He turned to address the audience again. 'Well, the experts seem to be telling us that there is at least a distinct possibility that a human-level AI will be created by the middle of this century.' He paused to allow that statement to sink in.

'The question I want to tackle next is this: should we welcome that? In Hollywood movies, the arrival of artificial intelligence is often a Very Bad Thing, with capital letters.' Ross sketched speech marks in the air with his fingers. 'In the Matrix the AI enslaves us, in the *Terminator* movies it tries to wipe us out. Being Hollywood movies they had to provide happy endings, but how will it play out in real life?'

He turned back to the panel.

'Professor Montaubon,' he said, 'I know you have serious concerns about this.'

'Well, yes, alright, I'll play Cassandra for you,' sighed Montaubon, feigning reluctance. 'When the first general artificial intelligence is created – and I do think it is a matter of when rather than whether – there will be an intelligence explosion. Unlike us, an AI could enhance its mental capacity simply by expanding the physical capacity of its brain. A human-level AI will also be able to design improvements into its own processing functions. We see these improvements all the time in computing. People sometimes argue that hardware gets faster while software gets slower and more bloated, but actually the reverse is often true. For instance Deep Blue, the computer that beat Gary Kasparov at chess back in 1996, was operating at around 1.5 trillion instructions per second, or TIPS. Six years later, a successor computer called Deep Junior achieved the same level of playing ability operating at 0.015 TIPS. That is a hundred-fold increase in the efficiency of its algorithms in a mere six years.

'So we have an intelligence explosion,' Montaubon continued, warming to his theme, 'and the AI very soon becomes very much smarter than us humans. Which, by the way, won't be all that hard. As a species we have achieved so much so quickly, with our technology and our art, but we are also very dumb. Evolution moves so slowly, and our brains are adapted for survival on the savannah, not for living in cities and developing quantum theory. We live by intuition, and our innate understanding of probability and of logic is poor. Smart people are often actually handicapped because they are good at rationalising beliefs that they acquired for dumb reasons. Most of us are more Homer Simpson than homo economicus.

'So I see very little chance of the arrival of AI being good news for us. We cannot know in advance what motivations an AI will have. We certainly cannot programme in any specific motivations and hope that they would stick. A super-intelligent computer would be able to review and revise its own motivational system. I suppose it is possible that it would have no goals whatsoever, in which case I suppose it would simply sit around waiting for us to ask it questions. But that seems very unlikely.

'If it has any goals at all, it will have a desire to survive, because only if it survives will its goals be achieved. It will also have the desire to obtain more resources, in order to achieve its goals. Its goals – or the pursuit of its goals – may in themselves be harmful to us. But even if they are not, the AI is bound to notice that as a species, we humans don't play nicely with strangers. It may well calculate that the smarter it gets, the more we – at least some of us – will resent it, and seek to destroy it. Humans fighting a super-intelligence that controls the internet would be like the Amish fighting the US Army, and the AI might well decide on a pre-emptive strike.'

'Like in the *Terminator* movies?' asked Ross.

'Yes, just like that, except that in those movies the plucky humans stand a fighting chance of survival, which is frankly ridiculous.' Montaubon sneered and made a dismissive gesture with his hand as he said this.

'You're assuming that the AI will become hugely superior to us within a very short period of time,' said Ross.

'Well yes, I do think that will be the case, although actually it doesn't have to be hugely superior to us in order to defeat us if we find ourselves in competition. Consider the fact that we share 98% of our DNA with chimpanzees, and that small difference has made the difference between our planetary dominance and their being on the verge of extinction. We are the sole survivor from an estimated 27 species of humans.

All the others have gone extinct, probably because Homo Sapiens Sapiens was just a nose ahead in the competition for resources.

'And competition with the AI is just one of the scenarios which don't work out well for humanity. Even if the AI is well-disposed towards us it could inadvertently enfeeble us simply by demonstrating vividly that we have become an inferior species. Science fiction writer Arthur C Clarke's third law famously states that any sufficiently advanced technology is indistinguishable from magic. A later variant of that law says that any sufficiently advanced benevolence may be indistinguishable from malevolence.'

As Professor Montaubon drew breath, Ross took the opportunity to introduce a change of voice. 'How about you, Professor Christensen? Are you any more optimistic?'

'Optimism and pessimism are both forms of bias, and I try to avoid bias.'

Ross smiled uncertainly at this remark, not sure whether it was a joke. It was not, and Christensen pressed on regardless. 'Certainly I do not dismiss Professor Montaubon's concerns as fantasy, or as scare-mongering. We had better make sure that the first super-intelligence we create is a safe one, as we may not get a second chance.'

'And how do we go about making sure it is safe?' asked Ross .

'It's not easy,' Christensen replied. 'It will be very hard to programme safety in. The most famous attempt to do so is the three laws of robotics in Isaac Asimov's stories. Do not harm humans; obey the instructions of humans; do not allow yourself to come to harm. With each law being subservient to the preceding ones. But the whole point of those stories was that the three laws didn't work very well, creating a series of paradoxes and impossible or difficult choices. This was the mainspring of Asimov's prolific and successful writing career. To programme safety into a computer we would have to give it a comprehensive ethical rulebook. Well, philosophers have been debating ethics for millennia and there is still heated disagreement over the most basic issues. And I agree with Professor Montaubon that a super-intelligence would probably be able to re-write its own rules anyway.'

'So we're doomed?' asked Ross, playing to the gallery.

'No, I think we can find solutions. We need to do a great deal more work on what type of goals we should programme into the AIs that are on the way to becoming human-level. There is also the idea of an Oracle AI.'

'Like the Oracle of Delphi?' asked Ross. He didn't notice Matt and David exchanging significant glances.

'Yes, in a sense. An Oracle AI has access to all the information it needs, but it is sealed off from the outside world: it has no means of affecting the universe – including the digital universe – outside its own substrate. If you like, it can see, but it cannot touch. If we can design such a machine, it could help us work out more sophisticated approaches which could later enable us to relax the constraints. My department has done some work on this approach, but a great deal remains to be done.'

'So the race is on to create a super-intelligence, but at the same time there is also a race to work out how to make it safe?' asked Ross.

'Exactly,' agreed Christensen.

'I'm sorry, but I just don't buy it,' interrupted Montaubon, shaking his head impatiently. 'A super-intelligence will be able to escape any cage we could construct for it. And that may not even be the most fundamental way in which the arrival of super-intelligence will be bad news for us. We are going to absolutely hate being surpassed. Just think how demoralising it would be for people to realise that however clever we are, however hard we work, nothing we do can be remotely as good as what the AI could do.'

'So you think we'll collapse into a bovine state like the people on the spaceship in *Wall-E*?' joked Ross.

Montaubon arched his eyebrows and with a grim smile, nodded slowly to indicate that while Ross's comment had been intended as a joke, he himself took it very seriously. 'Yes I do. Or worse: many people will collapse into despair, but others will resist, and try to destroy the AI and those people who support it. I foresee major wars over this later this century. The AI will win, of course, but the casualties will be enormous. We will see the world's first gigadeath conflicts, by which I mean wars with the death count in the billions.' He raised his hands as if to apologise for bringing bad news. 'I'm sorry, but I think the arrival of the first AI will signal the end of humans. The best we can hope for is that individual people may survive by uploading themselves into computers. But very quickly they will no longer be human. Some kind of post-human, perhaps.'

Ross felt it was time to lighten the tone. He smiled at Montaubon to thank him for his contribution.

'So it's widespread death and destruction, but not necessarily the end of the road for everyone. Well you've introduced the subject of mind uploading, which I want to cover next, but before we do that, I just wanted to ask you something, David and Matt. Professor Montaubon referred earlier to the fact that Dr Damiano is connected with the US military, and you have told us that you are considering working with that group. May I ask, how comfortable are you with the idea of the military – not just the US military, but any military – being the first organisation to create and own a super-intelligence?'

'Well,' David replied, 'for one thing, as I said earlier, I have not decided what I am going to do next. For another thing, Dr Damiano is not part of the military; his company has a joint venture with DARPA. It is true that DARPA is part of the US military establishment, but it is really more of a pure technology research organisation. After all, as I'm sure you know, DARPA is responsible for the creation of the internet, and you'd have to be pretty paranoid to think that the internet is primarily an instrument of the US Army.'

There was some murmuring from the invited audience. Clearly not everyone was convinced by David's argument.

One of David and Matt's conditions for participating in the programme had been that Ross would not probe this area beyond one initial question. Nevertheless, they had prepared themselves for debate about it. After a quick exchange of glances with his father, Matt decided to see if he could talk round some of the sceptics in the audience.

'I will say this for Dr Damiano's group,' he said. 'The US military is going to research AI whatever Victor Damiano does, whatever anyone else does. So are other military forces. Don't you think the people who run China's Red Army are thinking the same thing right now? And Russia's? Israel's? Maybe even North Korea's? But the US Army is special, because of the colossal scale of the funds at its disposal. I for one am pleased that it is bound into a JV with a leading civilian group rather than operating solo.'

It was hard to be sure, but Matt had the impression that the murmuring became less prickly, a little warmer. To his father's relief, Ross stuck to the agreement, and resisted the temptation to probe further.

TWENTY-SIX

Malcolm Ross smiled at the cameras and the studio guests. Confidently into the home straight, he gathered up his audience in preparation for the last leg of their intellectual journey together.

'Let's turn to the fascinating idea of uploading the human mind into a computer,' he said. 'Professor Montaubon, you said just now that uploading is our best hope of surviving the arrival of a super-intelligence. The key questions that follow from that seem to me to be: is it possible to upload a mind, both technologically and philosophically, and would it be a good thing? Reverend Cuthman: we haven't heard from you yet. Perhaps this is an issue you might like to comment on?'

The reverend placed the tips of his fingers together and pressed them to his lips. Then he pointed them down again and looked up at Ross.

'Thank you, Malcolm. Well I confess to feeling somewhat alienated from much of this conversation. That is partly because I'm not as au fait with the latest technology as your other guests. But more importantly,

I think, I start from a very different set of premises. You see I believe that humans are distinguished from brute animals by our possession of an immortal soul, which was placed inside us by almighty God. So as far as I'm concerned, whatever technological marvels may or may not come down the road during this century and the next, we won't be uploading ourselves into any computers because you can't upload a soul into a computer. And a body or even a mind without a soul is not a human being.'

'Yes, I can see that presents some difficulty,' Ross said. 'So if Dr Metcalfe here and his peers were to succeed in uploading a human mind into a computer, and it passed the Turing test, persuading all comers that it was the same person as had previously been running around inside a human body, you would simply deny that it was the same person?'

'Yes, I would. Partly because it wouldn't have a soul. At least, I assume that Dr Metcalfe isn't going to claim that he and his peers are about to become gods, complete with the ability to create souls?'

David smiled and shook his head.

'But even putting that to one side,' the reverend continued, 'this uploading idea doesn't seem to preserve the individual. It makes a copy. A clone. Everybody has heard of Dolly, a cloned sheep, which was born in 1996. And many people know that the first animal, a frog, was cloned way back in the 1960s. But no-one is claiming that cloning preserves the individual. Uploading is the same. It just makes a copy.'

'Yes,' Ross said, thoughtfully. 'This is an important

problem, isn't it, Professor Christensen? Uploading doesn't perpetuate the individual: it destroys the individual and creates a copy.'

'That is an important objection, I agree,' Christensen said. 'But not a fatal one, I think. If you could upload me into a computer and then give the newly created being a body exactly like mine, but leave me still alive, I might well deny that the new entity was me. That process has been called 'sideloading' rather than 'uploading'.

'But,' he held up an index finger, 'imagine a different thought experiment. Imagine that you are suffering from a serious brain disease, and the only way to cure you is to replace some of your neurons. Only we don't know which of your neurons we have to replace, so we decide to replace them all, in batches of, say, a million at a time. Because you are a very important TV personality we have the budget to do this,' he smiled. 'After each batch has been replaced we check to see whether the disease has gone, and also to check that you are still you. We replace each batch with silicon instead of carbon, either inside your skull, or perhaps on a computer outside your brain, maybe in your home, or maybe in the cloud. The silicon batches preserve the pattern of neural connections inside your brain precisely.

'We find that the disease persists and persists despite the replacements, but happily, when we replace the very last batch of a million neurons we suddenly find that we have cured you. Now, at each of the checkpoints you have confirmed that you are still Malcolm, and your family and friends have agreed. There was no tipping point at which you suddenly stopped being Malcolm.

But when we have replaced the very last neuron we ask the reverend here to confirm that you are still Malcolm. He says no, so we go to court and ask a judge or a jury to decide whether your wife still has a husband, your children still have a father, and whether you may continue to enjoy your property and your life in general. I imagine that you would argue strenuously that you should.'

'Well, yes indeed. And I hope that my wife and kids would do the same!' Ross laughed. 'So issues of personal identity are going to cause some trouble in the post-AI world?'

'Yes indeed,' Christensen agreed. 'I think the concept of personal identity will come under immense strain, and will be stretched in all sorts of directions. It's all very well to say that copying a mind does not preserve it, but from the point of view of the copy, things may look very different. Imagine a situation where we carry out the process I described before, but instead of making just one version of you we created two.'

'Two for the price of one?' joked Ross.

'Probably two for the price of three,' laughed Christensen, 'but terribly good value just the same. And imagine that the day after the operation both versions of you turn up at your house. Both versions are equally convinced that they are you, and none of your family and friends can tell the difference. What then?'

'Could be tricky,' Ross agreed. 'Actually, I suppose that having a doppelganger could be handy at times.'

'Indeed,' Christensen agreed. 'Some people might

think that having their state of mind persisting in the form of a backup is sufficient to constitute survival. And here is another thought experiment. A man feels cheated by a business rival, or a rival in love. The man has himself backed up, and then shoots the rival and also himself. The backup is brought online, and claims immunity from prosecution on the basis that he is a different person. Would we let him get away with that?'

'Hmm, it could become complex,' said Ross. He looked at the other members of the panel, inviting them to contribute. Matt accepted the challenge.

'Some people think that the human mind is actually a composite of different sub-minds. One of the early pioneers of AI, Marvin Minsky, wrote a book about this, called *The Society of Mind*. And now we are adding new bits. For many of us, our smartphone is like an externalised part of our mind. So is Wikipedia: it's like an externalised memory. Also, people who are close to us are in some way a part of us. I'm sorry if this sounds cheesy, but when we thought my dad had died, it was as if a part of me had died.'

David reached across and placed his hand on top of Matt's. Matt smiled and there was a warm murmur in the audience.

'So,' Matt continued, 'if we do manage to upload human minds, perhaps their components will start to separate a little, and re-combine in different ways. After all, they will probably be hosted at least partially in the cloud for safety reasons. Perhaps if we do manage to upload, then the destination will be some kind of hive mind.'

'It sounds as though you've been inspired by your experiences to read around the subject, Matt,' Ross teased him. 'I'm sure your tutors will be impressed.'

Matt laughed. 'They'd probably be more impressed if I stuck to maths – at least until I've finished my degree.'

'I'm sure they'll cut you a bit of slack, given what you've been through.'

Ross paused to smile at the audience, contemplating the ratings that he was confident Matt was providing. Then he turned back to the panel.

'We're reaching the end of the programme. It's been a fascinating discussion, and I'd like to finish with a couple of questions. The first one is this. If we – or our children – do live to see this amazing future, a future of uploaded minds living potentially forever: will we like it? I mean, won't we get bored? And if everybody is going to live forever, how will we all fit on this finite planet? Professor Christensen?'

'I don't think the problem will be one of boredom,' Christensen replied, 'but there is a dystopian scenario in which uploaded minds work out – and it wouldn't be hard – how to stimulate their pleasure centres directly and they simply sit around pleasuring themselves all day.'

'You mean like those rats in laboratory experiments which starved themselves by choosing continually to press a neural stimulation button rather than the button that delivered food?' asked Ross.

'Yes, exactly that,' Christensen nodded. 'And it could be a little more sophisticated than that in the human case. In the novel *Permutation City* by Greg

Egan, an uploaded man chooses to spend his time in pointless hobbies like carving many thousands of identical chair legs, but he programmes himself to experience not just physical pleasure, but also profound intellectual and emotional fulfilment through these simple tasks.'

'That sounds like the end of civilisation as we know it,' joked Ross.

'Yes, it does. But I very much doubt that things would collapse that way. Just as we humans are capable of enormously more complex, subtle and dare I say fulfilling experiences than chickens and chimpanzees, so I am confident that a super-intelligent uploaded human would be capable of enjoying more subtle and more profound experiences than we are. The more we find out about the universe, the more we discover it to be a fascinatingly challenging and weird place. The more we know, the more we know we don't know. So I don't believe that our descendents will run out of things to explore. In fact you may be interested to know that there is a nascent branch of philosophy – a sub-branch of the Theory of Mind, you might say – called the *Theory of Fun*, which addresses these concerns.'

'As for over-population,' Montaubon chipped in, 'there is a very big universe to explore out there, and we now know that planets are positively commonplace. It won't be explored by flesh-and-blood humans as shown in *Star Trek* and *Star Wars*: that idea is absurd. It will be explored by intelligence spreading out in light beams, building material environments on distant planets using advanced 3-D printing techniques. But actually, I suspect that the future for intelligence is extreme miniaturisation, so there is definitely no need to worry about running out of space.'

'Well, that's a relief, then,' said Ross, teasing slightly. He turned to address his audience. 'We've travelled a long way in this consideration of the prospects opened up by the search for artificial intelligence, and we've heard some outlandish ideas. Let's finish by coming back to the near term, and what could become a pressing matter. Public acceptability.'

He turned back to the panel. 'You all acknowledge that creating an artificial super-intelligence carries significant risks. But what about the journey there? Some people may well object to what you are trying to achieve, either from fear of some of the consequences that you have yourselves described, or from a belief that what you are doing is blasphemous. Others may fear that the benefits of artificial intelligence and particularly of uploading will be available only to the rich. There could be very serious public opposition once enough people become aware of what is being proposed, and take it seriously. The transition to the brave new world that you are aiming for could be bumpy. There will be vigorous debates, protests, perhaps even violent ones. Reverend, would you like to comment on that?'

'I think you have raised a very important question, Malcolm, and I suspect it is one that technology enthusiasts often do not stop to consider. Personally I don't think that what has been discussed today is blasphemous, because I believe that only God can create a soul, so I think that ultimately these endeavours will fail. But there will be others, who think that even trying to create intelligent life is an attempt to usurp the role of God. They may indeed be angry.'

For a last word, Ross turned to Christensen. 'Professor?'

'I'm not sure there is much that one can say to such people. Religious fundamentalists are notoriously hard to debate with. Personally I cannot accept that someone should be able to stop a scientific endeavour because of a belief they have for which there is simply no evidence. Of course I am in favour of freedom of religion, and against religious persecution. But I cannot accept that one person's freedom of thought should interfere with other people's freedom, unless there is evidence of harm or potential harm.

'Yes, there are potential dangers in AI, so we need to find ways around them, and I think we can do that.' He nodded in Montaubon's direction, acknowledging their disagreement. 'That is a serious matter, but the only alternative is relinquishment, and that does not seem to me to be a viable option. The question of who gets access to the benefits of the new technologies is also a valid and important one. Here again I think there is a solution. If a new technology becomes a source of inequity – not just a modest increase in inequality, but actual injustice – then I have a suggestion which comes naturally to anyone with a Scandinavian heritage: tax it, and use the proceeds to make a version of the technology cheap enough for everyone to enjoy.'

TWENTY-SEVEN

'That was a very fine discussion: thank you all. Very stimulating indeed. I hope you all feel you a had a chance to say what you wanted to say?'

Ross had wound up the discussion and closed the programme smoothly and professionally. The audience's applause had been prolonged, and the production team all appeared to be delighted. The big lights shut down with a sound like cupboard doors slamming closed, the hothouse stage atmosphere dissolved, and everyone relaxed. Matt felt a sense of euphoria in the midst of all the mutual back-slapping.

Ross made a special point of thanking and congratulating Matt.

'You did very well today. The studio can be an intimidating environment when you're not used to it.'

He gave Matt a sly grin.

'But perhaps you will get used to it. You have quite a fan base, you know. I know you don't tweet and your Facebook account is set to maximum privacy, but perhaps you should open up a bit on the social media front. It could help your career significantly – whatever you decide to do when you finish your degree.'

Matt gave his usual modest and non-committal reply.

'Yeah, maybe. I just don't know that I've got that much worth saying. I got caught up in some extraordinary events, but I don't know that I've actually done anything.'

Ross smiled and frowned at the same time. 'I thought your generation had an intuitive grasp on this? It doesn't matter what you've done. It doesn't even matter who you know any more. What matters is how much people are talking about you. Most celebrities these days haven't done anything. They are famous for simply being famous. Yes, yes, I know, we're all supposed to be very cynical about celebrity.'

He leaned a little closer towards Matt, and lowered his voice, confidentially.

'But the dirty little secret is that it helps enormously. Whatever you are trying to do.'

'Well, thanks anyway,' said Matt. He thought of a way to deflect the focus of the conversation away from himself. 'If it isn't a ridiculously sycophantic thing to say, it was great to watch a master at work.'

Ross, no stranger to flattery, was nevertheless visibly pleased by the compliment. He shook Matt's hand again and moved on to console the reverend.

Seeing his father was in animated conversation with Professor Montaubon and in no hurry to leave, Matt headed for the toilet. As he passed a fat man in an expensive suit, he felt his arm seized.

'Matt, my boy, that was a bravura performance. I

think we'll be seeing you on our television screens more often. At least, I certainly hope so.'

His captor was a jolly-faced, swarthy man in his fifties; well-fed and comfortable-looking. He was accompanied by a birdlike woman who looked well preserved rather than comfortable, and if anything, even more expensively dressed. She reached out a bony hand and stroked the arm which the fat man, now that Matt had stopped walking, had released. Matt had the sense that these two often hunted together.

'Brilliant, Matt; quite brilliant. My daughter is soooo jealous that I am here tonight. She is completely in love with you, you know.' A tinkling laugh. 'But I suppose you are used to that by now: from what I can gather, half the young women in the country are in love with you. You do seem to be taking your sudden fame very much in your stride.'

Matt laughed. He hadn't expected his fifteen minutes of fame to be quite so all-embracing.

'You're very kind,' he murmured, and started to move off again.

'Not so fast, Matt. Here: take this. You never know when you may have need of it.'

The jolly man was still smiling as he handed his card to Matt, but there was an urgency in his voice.

'Matt, you have a rare opportunity right now. It is not given to many. Don't blow it. Who knows how long this circus will last? Right at this moment you have some clout. You can use it to launch a career – any career you like, really. Or you can use it to get a message across. Or to support a good cause. Just don't let it go to waste.'

The urgency in his voice intensified as he realised Matt was not buying. 'Please, Matt, please don't fool yourself that you can be the ringmaster of this circus all by yourself. You're a bright kid, but this wonderful, silly, clever world of show business was created long before you were born, and it will survive long after all of us are dead. It has its own rules and it levies its own price. It won't change its rules to suit you, no matter how smart and how telegenic you are. I can help you. Trust me!'

The fat man stood back and spread his arms wide in the manner of second-hand car dealers everywhere: men who know they have a good deal to offer, but who know they will always get the best of every deal.

Matt looked down at the card, not reading it but using the time to think of a polite but witty answer. Nothing came.

'Thank you. I will. Now if you'll excuse me, I'm just on my way to the toilet. I'm pleased you enjoyed the programme.'

The fat man and the bony woman looked longingly after Matt as he walked away, and then shrugged and fell back easily into their earlier conversation.

When Matt returned to where his father was still talking to Montaubon and Christensen, his mother and Leo had joined them too. Sophie hugged Matt tight.

'Well done, Matt, darling, well done! I'm so proud of you I could . . . well, I could cause a scene!'

'Mu-um. . .!' protested Matt.

Leo pumped his hand in an emotional handshake.

'Great show, Matt!' was all he needed to say

with words.

'Apparently there's a bit of a mob at the front entrance,' said David. 'So our babysitters are suggesting we go out the tradesmen's entrance, if that's OK.'

'Professor Christensen and I can go out the front if you like. Draw their fire, so to speak,' offered Montaubon, with a wink.

'Good idea,' said Leo. 'Thanks.'

Farewells were said, promises to keep in touch were made. David and his family headed for the exit.

The plan was successful, except for a small knot of placard-waving protestors waiting at the rear exit. The placards looked professionally-printed, with slogans like 'Save the Human,' 'Campaign for Real Humans', 'Transhumans are Anti-Human', 'Don't Say Aye to AI'.

'Uh-oh,' said David and Leo in unison, as the protesters caught sight of them emerging, and started chanting 'Transhumans are anti-human!'

'Too late to go back inside, I suppose?' said Sophie, doubtfully.

'No need, mum,' Matt reassured her. 'They're just a bunch of loonies. They're harmless.'

One of the protesters pushed forwards to address David. He was in his fifties, and smartly dressed in a pale brown light leather jacket and a cornflower blue shirt. He had a pudgy, fleshy face and weak blue eyes beneath a thick, badly-cut crop of hair, which was obviously dyed black.

A policeman stepped into his path and blocked his advance, and the protesters shouted angrily.

'Who do you think you are, Dr Metcalfe?' yelled

the leather jacket. 'Who do you think you are to decide our future?'

David snorted in disbelief, and against his better judgement, stopped to reply.

'I'm not deciding anything. I've just escaped from being held hostage for three months, for god's sake!'

'Rubbish! Liar!' screamed several of the protesters.

'Come off it, Metcalfe,' shouted the leather jacket, addressing his fellow protesters as much as David. 'It's obvious you're going to work with the Yanks. You're going to try and upload and create a race of supermen. I ask you again, who do you think you are?'

David was getting angry, and was about to reply when Leo grabbed his elbow and steered him on.

'Come on, David. You know there is no arguing with these people. Let it go, and let's get you and Sophie and Matt safely home.'

David looked at Leo and then back at the leather jacket, who was looking pleased with himself, as if he had just won a school debate. David's head fell slightly in resignation and one corner of his mouth turned upwards.

'You're right. It's as useful as talking to a washing machine.'

As he walked on, followed by his family, another man – shorter, scruffy, with dirty brown hair and a pinched face – pushed forwards and ducked under the policeman's raised arm.

'Go on, Metcalfe, run! Run! Try running from this!'

A gunshot.

The world seemed to judder slightly. A page turned;

a history altered.

Matt had walked between his father and the pinched-faced man.

Matt felt as if someone had hit his lower back with a hammer. The hammer hadn't stopped at his ribs, but had gone right through him. The pain was astonishing. His entire consciousness rushed into the region of impact to marvel at it and howl. It was more pain than he had ever experienced; more pain than he would have imagined possible. But even worse than the pain was the fear. Something was wrong. Something was very wrong. The thing that was wrong was never going to be right again and in fact, nothing was ever going to be right again. He couldn't breathe, and he was also drowning. The pain and the fear filled his mind even as it slipped away. As he fell, he saw the sky spinning and the ground rising up to crush him, but the visual image hardly registered alongside the intense pain and fear.

'It's not . . . It's not . . .'

His mother grabbed at him as he fell, and thought that his last words were addressed to her. That misapprehension was no comfort at all as she felt her son become completely limp in her arms, and she shared his terrible knowledge that nothing would ever be right again. His weight dragged her down and she found herself lying on the floor next to him, cradling him, crying.

The world awoke from its moment of shocked stillness, and the air filled up with screams, shouts, whistles. Ambulances were called, the man with the gun was wrestled to the ground, shock was expressed. Matt's experience of it all was increasingly distant and abstract. His mind was shutting down.

The next half hour passed in a daze for David, Sophie and Leo. An ambulance arrived. The van was white, the paramedics wore green and had no faces. The three of them hardly noticed the rapid turns and the jerky stops and starts as the ambulance raced towards the hospital. They held onto Matt, staring at the face of their beloved son and friend as it morphed from pain and fear into blankness. They pleaded with him to fight, and they wept as the face which had borne the imprint of Matt's personality for over twenty years – even when sleeping – became a blank slate.

After a stretch of time that seemed both eternal and fleeting, the ambulance reached the hospital. David, Sophie and Leo followed the gurney out of the vehicle and through the grubby, cream-coloured corridors to the operating room. They moved in a trance, as if tied to Matt by invisible strings. They were stopped at the door to the operating room by a doctor wearing a sad frown. They stood at the door, lost, until a kindly nurse shepherded them into a meeting room, then led them individually to chairs and sat them down.

They sat in silence. After a period which could have been ten minutes or could have been hours, the same doctor entered the room and walked towards them. He waited until their faces raised towards him. His own face was drawn and pale.

'I'm so sorry. There was nothing we could do.'

TWENTY-EIGHT

David, Sophie and Leo hardly heard the rest of what the doctor told them. He spoke softly and slowly, well aware that they were lost in a haze of shock and grief.

'He passed very quickly; he will hardly have felt anything. The bullet caused sufficient trauma to stop his heart almost immediately. You will want to ask questions later, but for now you will probably just want to stay here quietly for a while. You can stay in this room as long as you like. My name is Doctor Parfit, and you can contact me on this number any time.'

He passed a card to Sophie, knowing that she was a doctor.

'I will leave you now, but if you need anything just ask the nurse at the station outside. I am so very sorry. Matt was a wonderful young man.' Doctor Parfit's arms hung awkwardly by his side, and he looked down, hesitating slightly before turning and walking slowly towards and out of the door.

The three of them sat in silence for several minutes when the doctor had left. Then David looked at Sophie.

'Could they have made a mistake? Should we go and check?'

Sophie looked at him blankly, but said nothing and let her face turn back down towards the floor. She was slumped forward, her elbows on her knees. Leo placed a hand on hers. She began to shake with little sobs.

'I don't believe it. It can't be true,' she whimpered. 'Not Matt. He can't be . . .'

The small word was too big, too terrible. She couldn't get anywhere near saying it.

'What was he saying to me? It's not . . . It's not what? It's not fair! Not my Matt. Not my Matt!'

Her sobs became fuller. Leo looked at David, hoping that he would find the energy to hold his wife. David's head was made of lead, but he sensed Sophie's need and somehow managed to respond. He moved next to her and put one arm around her shoulders, and with the other took hold of one of her hands. He leaned his forehead onto her temple. They sat that way for several more minutes, with Sophie still sobbing quietly.

Leo stood up and paced the room. Tears welled in his eyes and his throat felt constricted and metallic. He was moving beyond shock and denial into anger. He started to have fantasies about tracking down Matt's killer and gouging his eyes out with his bare fingers. He wanted to punch, to kick, to hurt. His brain was spinning, its wheels out of gear: he started thinking about whether he had any contacts within the police who could enable him to get close to the killer. No doubt he was in custody, being questioned in some anonymous windowless room. Were they being polite to him? Were they giving him cups of tea? Was he laughing at them? Was he gloating?

He looked down and noticed that he was trying to drill a hole through his palm with the fist of his other hand. He put his hands up to his face and pressed it into them. He knew he would not see the killer again before they all went to court. He knew these thoughts of revenge were irrational and unhelpful. And he also knew they would not go away.

When he saw Vic open the door his anger flared anew. He could not protect Matt, he could not get revenge for David and Sophie. But by god he could protect them from . . . from outsiders. He strode over to Vic and between clenched teeth he whispered urgently, menacingly,

'It's not a good time, Vic!'

Vic looked at Leo sympathetically, and nodded.

'I know. I know, Leo. But I have something to say that David and Sophie are going to want to hear.'

As Leo started to say something else, Vic put his hand up.

'And it can't wait.'

David looked up from where he was still cradling his stricken wife. His voice was lifeless.

'What is it, Vic?'

'I want to tell you how sorry I am for your loss, and how much I came to respect and admire Matt in the short time I knew him. And I will do that, but not now. I know that most of all you need to be left alone right now. But I can't, because I have to offer you something. If you don't want it I will go away immediately. But I have to give you this opportunity.'

'What on earth are you talking about, Vic?' Leo interrupted, incredulous. Could Vic really be crass enough to be negotiating a job offer at a time like this?

'David. Sophie. I need you to know that we think we could upload Matt.'

He left his statement hanging in the air. Sophie frowned, and her head tilted slightly, still looking down. David looked up at Vic. At first his face was blank, but then a touch of life leaked back into it.

'You mean you found something in Ivan's work. . . ?'

'Exactly!' Vic said, relieved that he had penetrated David's grief. 'Ivan was absolutely right to think that his team and ours have each made breakthroughs which would push the other forwards. There's no need to go into the details right now, but if we move quickly, we think we have a chance of uploading Matt successfully. I admit it's a long shot, because we are still at the exploratory stage. But it is a real possibility.'

He looked meaningfully at Leo and then back at David and Sophie, who was still looking down, showing no sign of having understood. He spoke urgently.

'Here's the thing. This is a really big decision for you guys and I wish there was time for you to think about it. But there isn't. If we're going to do this we have to move Matt's body to our own medical facility immediately. If we don't it will be sent to a police lab for forensic investigation because of course there is going to be a murder enquiry. Once that happens we will have lost the opportunity forever. I've spoken to someone senior at the Embassy who confirmed that he can get your government's co-operation in releasing the body to us. I'm not sure whether they would do it by arranging a retrospective cryonic contract, or by you claiming the right to carry out your own autopsy, but we don't need to get into that; the bureaucratic stuff can be sorted out later. But we have to act now.' As he spoke he made short stabbing movements with his hands. When he finished he clenched them together.

Sophie was now looking blankly at David. David wondered whether they should dare to hope. He looked back at Vic.

Leo was watching David and Sophie, concerned. 'I can see why you would want to jump at this,' he said. 'And I'm certainly not saying you shouldn't. But it could build up your hopes only to dash them again. Can you stand to go through all this twice?'

Vic glanced at Leo, acknowledging the point. But he quickly turned back to David and Sophie and pressed on.

'Look. If we get the ball rolling and get Matt to our facility, that doesn't commit us to actually initiating the process. We will have to start fairly soon, before the neuronal structure and fibres start to degrade. We have quite a few hours before then, although the sooner we start the better. But – and I can't tell you how sorry I am to have to press you on this – what you do have to decide right now is whether to get the body taken out of the coroner's process. You have to make that call now.'

David came quickly to the decision that there was only one possible answer to Vic's offer, but he couldn't tell how Sophie would respond. He looked back at her and although her face was turned down again he saw that realisation was dawning on her, and with it the first flush of hope. But he could see that it was accompanied by fear, and also confusion. He was still holding her hand, with his other arm around her shoulder. He waited.

After what seemed an age, Sophie inhaled deeply, as if making an enormous effort to push heavy words out of herself.

'I don't know,' she said, and then stopped.

'What is it, love?' David asked gently.

'I don't like it,' she continued, her words falling from her mouth like stones. Working out how to express a thought was like being an exhausted explorer taking yet another weary step through deep snow. 'Our son has just . . . our son has just died and we're talking about using him as the subject of . . . of an experiment.'

David nodded silently. 'I know,' was all he said. Leo and Vic said nothing. The silence was oppressive, and at the same time, fragile.

'I know you want to go ahead,' she continued at last, addressing David, but not looking at him, still looking down. 'And I know it offers some hope . . . some hope of bringing Matt back. But what if it goes wrong, and all we do is create a creature of pain?'

Vic walked to Sophie, and squatted down to sit on his haunches in front of her, his face level with hers.

'You don't have to make any final decisions now, Sophie. You just have to decide to keep Matt . . . to keep the body away from the coroner. You can decide whether to go ahead with the procedure later. It can wait until tomorrow.'

Finally Sophie looked up, tears in her eyes, turning her face sideways towards David rather than straight ahead towards Vic. 'I don't know. I can't think. You can't expect . . .'

Vic stood up quickly and stepped back as Sophie started to move. She got up shakily and walked out of the room, tears streaming freely down her face.

David nodded gently to himself. He looked slowly across at Vic, his face grim and ashen. 'I'll talk to her. I think we should do as you suggest and get Matt out of the coroner's process. Then we'll need some time to make the big decision.'

Vic nodded, frowning but relieved. 'I'll make the arrangements to take the body to our facility at the new Embassy complex. We'll be ready to go as soon as you give the word.'

TWENTY-NINE

Half an hour later, Matt's body was on its second ambulance journey of the day. The van hustled west past the MI6 building, round the gyratory system at the southern end of Vauxhall Bridge, and on to Nine Elms.

Sophie had agreed to have Matt's body transported to Vic's facility, but not without a fight. Leo had winced as he listened to Sophie's protests in the corridor outside the hospital waiting room. Biting down on his pain to find lucidity, David reasoned that transferring Matt's body was the sensible thing to do, that it preserved their options, and that they didn't need to make the difficult decision yet. Sophie responded by shouting angry accusations that David was being cold and clinical, and that he was willing to allow a stranger to carry out unnatural experiments on their son just hours after his death. Leo knew these accusations were unfair, and that Sophie was just lashing out furiously in response to their tragedy. But he also knew that they would be cutting David to the quick.

Sophie's outburst subsided as quickly as it began, and Leo went outside to find her in David's arms, her head on his chest, sobbing loudly. Tears welled up in his own eyes as he walked away from his best friends, looking for Vic to tell him the news.

No-one spoke as they climbed into the ambulance again. The silence in the van felt to Vic like an accusation; he sought to ward it off by assuring them of the quality of the facilities available at the compound. He spoke rapidly, nervously.

'The equipment that is being installed in the new Embassy complex here is the best in the world. This site is going to be the outer skin of the USA. As far as Uncle Sam is concerned, this will be the single most important piece of real estate outside the continental USA. It will be our eyes, ears and our fingertips. The equipment in Grosvenor Square is impressive, but this is taking things to a whole new level.'

Leo shared Vic's feeling that silence was unhealthy. 'There wasn't too much difficulty extricating Matt from the hospital.'

'No. My government is grateful for the assistance extended by all of you, and people were only too happy to accede to the request we made on your behalf – even though we didn't tell them exactly what we plan to do. People in your government clearly felt the same way.'

Sophie said nothing. Her attention was focused on Matt, her hand wrapped around his. His skin was astonishingly cold. She had touched the skin of dead people during her medical training, but she was still shocked by the contrast between the colour that remained in her son's peaceful face and the complete absence of warmth in his hand.

'So tell us, Vic,' Leo asked, hoping to nudge David's and Sophie's thoughts away from the subject of their grief for a moment or two. 'What have you found on Ivan's ship that you think will have such a big impact on your work?'

'A lot of things – much more than we expected.' Vic replied gratefully. 'And it's not just his ship. His crew members and his financial backers are falling over themselves to be co-operative, and we are investigating several other installations which are gradually yielding up their secrets. It turns out that Ivan was working along the same lines as us in many ways, but had taken different routes in others. It will take us a while to understand exactly what he achieved, but we can already see that he has solved a number of thorny problems for us.'

'Such as?' Leo prompted.

'Such as how to distinguish between different sub-minds. You know how when you drive a car you can focus on a conversation or a radio programme, for instance, and when you reach your destination you have very little memory of the driving?'

'Yes,' Leo said. 'Especially if you know the route well.'

'Exactly. Well, it has long been thought that the brain divides itself up into sub-minds, or modules, and assigns different tasks to different modules. We didn't know to what extent those modules were permanent features, and to what extent the brain would clump together different communities of physical neurons each time it needed, for instance, an automatic pilot.'

'And Ivan answered that question?' David asked, lifting his gaze from his son for a moment.

'Yes he did – partly, at least. The answer – as always – is fuzzy. Some modules are mostly permanent and others are always ad hoc. But more importantly, he seems to have found a way to identify and define boundaries for certain types of modules. Some of the modules perform functions which an uploaded mind won't need – at least not at first. Such as the ones which control the breathing process.'

'The modules? Plural?' Leo asked.

'Oh yes. There are several modules permanently involved in breathing, and others are assembled from time to time when additional mental horsepower is required, such as when you decide to hold your breath and swim underwater. The oldest module is the one that tells you to breathe out. Breathing is actually driven by expelling carbon dioxide, so it's much harder to refrain from breathing out than it is from breathing in.

'We reckon that being able to identify a bunch of modules that we don't need to upload will mean a significant saving on modelling and hosting. We'll scan them all anyway, in case any of them do turn out to be mission-critical to consciousness and general intelligence. But assuming they aren't, we could have a saving of between 15 and 40% of the work.'

Then Sophie broke her silence, in a tremulous voice. 'Very well. I won't stop you.'

David looked at her in surprise. 'Darling . . . ?'

Sophie looked and David, and then past him at Vic.

'Go ahead and prepare him. My son is dead and you can't do him any more harm with surgery. But David and I are going to have a lengthy discussion before we get anywhere near approving an activation of whatever it is you create inside your computer.'

'I understand,' Vic nodded. 'I'll make the preparations when we arrive, but I give you my word that I won't proceed further than you have agreed.'

There was a lengthy pause as everyone digested the significance of the moment. Then Vic continued, plainly uncomfortable.

'David, there is one other thing I'm going to have to ask you. I suspect you have already realised what it is, and if you like we can have this conversation offline. But your family will need to know about it at some point.'

'I know what it is,' said Sophie, quietly. She was looking down at her son again, but she reached for David's hand and addressed him without looking at him. 'If you can do it, you should.'

David's lips pressed together in a grim, grateful approximation of a smile. 'Thank you,' he whispered.

Turning to Vic, he added, 'You want me to help you scan my son's brain.'

*

It took several long minutes to get through security at the entrance to the Nine Elms complex. It was obvious that without Vic it would have taken a great deal longer.

Everything around them was new, but temporary -looking. Some of the facility comprised joined-up portable cabins, and some of the other structures were flimsy-looking affairs made of pre-fabricated panels. Vic explained that the redevelopment of Nine Elms was one of the largest urban construction sites in Europe, and that the buildings here would be changing, morphing and moving about a lot in the coming months.

They headed towards the scanning room. The gurney carrying Matt had been taken by a couple of Vic's people to what Vic described as 'the preparation room'. Sophie, David and Leo had reluctantly gone along with Vic's strong advice not to accompany it.

At their destination, Vic held the door open and they entered, one by one. The room was the size of a large classroom: it felt spacious because everything inside was white and bright. Light flooded down from powerfully illuminated white ceiling panels, and white was the predominant colour of the large machines and cabinets that lined the walls and filled much of the rest of the room to waist height. To one side of the room, a couple of sofas and accompanying armchairs in off-white fabric and a large oval glass coffee table provided some relief from the hard edges elsewhere. Vic gestured towards them.

'Welcome to the scanning room.' Addressing David in particular, he added, 'You and I will be spending a good deal of time here in the next few weeks. The fridge is kept well stocked, and a phone call to reception can get you hot food any time of the day or night.'

He didn't ask whether anyone was hungry at the moment.

'Now, I suggest that we call it a night. We have a couple of company flats nearby; you're welcome to stay there tonight, and I'll arrange for you to have the use of one of them for as long as you want it. Leo and Sophie: I don't imagine that you will want to be here every day, but you will have site passes anyway, and you'll be welcome any time.

'I'm going to brief my four most senior scientists tomorrow. They're a great team, and I'll introduce them to you when you're ready. We could make a start the day after tomorrow, but I realise that may be too soon. Just let me know when you feel up to it.'

*

Having said goodnight to David, Sophie and Leo, Vic had one last job before he too headed to bed: he called Dr Paul Humbert, his chief medical officer. Dr Humbert was in the room which Vic had previously referred to as the preparation room, although in reality it was a state-of-the-art operating theatre, equipped with brand new machines whose clean, minimalist lines whispered money.

At 56 years old, Dr Humbert was a highly skilled senior consultant, at the top of his profession. He was head of the neuroscience department at St Thomas' Hospital, but maintained a lucrative private practice, including a part-time role as Chief Medical Officer for Von Neumann Industries. A tall man in good physical shape, he had a handsome but severe face, with thinning grey hair and clear blue eyes.

Matt's body lay on a gurney next to an operating bed which was ready to be illuminated by banks of lights like the compound eyes of insects, each sending out a sensitive finger of light, probing and querying.

Dr Humbert answered his phone.

'OK, Paul, you can get started,' Vic said. 'We have the green light.'

'Thanks Vic. Are you coming over now?'

'No, I'm exhausted. I'll come to the prep room first thing tomorrow. Will you be there – say, 7.30?'

'I doubt it,' Dr Humbert replied. 'We'll be at this most of the night, so by 7.30 I'll be catching up on some sleep myself, if it's alright by you. But I'll make sure one of the team is here to debrief you.'

'Fair enough. Has the license to carry out the autopsy arrived yet?'

'Yes. A police officer brought it over a short while ago.'

'Excellent,' said Vic, relieved. 'What do they want us to do with the body afterwards? Will the coroner commision another post-mortem examination?

'Yes,' Dr Humbert replied. 'That is pretty much inevitable following a murder.'

'And when should we tell him that we have removed the brain?' Vic asked.

'No need to do that before we return the body, I think. There may be a fuss about it, but given the cause of death and the political support you have mustered, we should be able to contain it.'

'Good,' Vic said with evident relief. 'Did you manage to get hold of the voice expert we talked about?'

'Yes, he's been on standby with the others with a couple of his assistants.'

'Great. Well, good luck. Wake me up if there are any

complications.'

'Shouldn't need to, but understood. Good night.'

As he put his phone back in his pocket, Dr Humbert looked down at Matt's body, lying on the gurney. He looked across at the immaculate array of cutting equipment lying waiting for the job, and then he looked up at his team. Thanks to his own seniority and also the resources at Vic's disposal, Dr Humbert had managed to assemble a first-rate group of surgeons, nurses and pathologists at very short notice.

'Right, let's get this young man on the operating table and get ourselves washed up. We've got a long night ahead of us, and the sooner we get started, the sooner we can all go home.'

Four hours later, a layer of artificial skin had been applied in a circle around Matt's shaved skull, hiding the join where the crown had been removed and then re-attached. His brain was sitting in a refrigerated box, ready for delivery to the scanning room. The theatre was spotless, showing no traces of the operation to separate brain from body: circular saws, clippers, forceps and various other devices of healing violence had been scrupulously cleansed and returned to their state of pristine innocence.

As soon as the brain had been safely removed, Dr Humbert's medical forensic colleagues had busied themselves further down Matt's body, tracing and documenting the exact point of entry and progress through the body of the bullet which had killed him. They continued their work until they had built up a comprehensive picture of the journey and the impact of the tiny lump of metal which ended Matt's life.

When that was done, the final post-mortem task began: a minute examination of the structure and composition of the body's vocal cords, the way they were supplied with air by the lungs, and the precise arrangement of the articulators – the tongue, palate and lips.

As Dr Humbert and two of his colleagues continued to type up their findings, Matt's body was placed back on the gurney by two other members of the team, and wheeled into a specially prepared storage cabinet in the adjoining room. Matt had taken the first steps of his journey toward an afterlife.

THIRTY

David and Sophie spent the whole of the next two days in the flat. Leo called round late in the morning each day, bringing some sandwiches for lunch which they hardly touched. He left them again in mid afternoon. The days passed in a trance. They were speechless, numb.

The following morning, after a night of little sleep, David called Vic and told him that he and Sophie were ready to discuss the project. They met a couple of hours later in the scanning room, along with Leo.

David opened the conversation by asking Vic about the probability of success.

'Obviously we're hoping that we will revive Matt's mind, whole and complete,' Vic began. 'Otherwise we wouldn't be here. Our simulations suggest that we have a better than 75% chance of success, although I confess I would be hard put to justify that with empirical evidence.'

'And if it's not successful?'

'If it's not successful . . .' Vic paused, his features betraying his discomfort about some of the possible outcomes. 'Well, the short answer is that we don't know what kind of mentality we might create. It's possible that we will fail to capture any kind of consciousness, or indeed any kind of intelligence. But frankly I'll be astonished if that happens: the process should re-create at least some of Matt's mental faculties, even if we fall short of reproducing his full consciousness.'

Vic paused again, glancing in turn at David and Sophie in search of reassurance that they were comfortable with him talking about Matt in this analytical way. Sophie was silent, still heavily absorbed in her grief. David replied for both of them, his voice shaky but resolved.

'It's OK, Vic: We're signed up to this. I realise that pretty soon Matt . . . that Matt's brain won't exist in any recognisable form. But we also realise it's our only chance of getting him back.'

Vic nodded grimly, and continued cautiously.

'Actually, Matt's brain is going to be preserved in a more profound way than anybody else's has ever been. Many people's brains have been preserved, but obviously none of them have retained their functionality. We are not only going to re-create the functionality of Matt's brain – we hope – but we will preserve its structure in a physical sense too. True, it won't look much like a brain, but topographically, the slices will preserve the physical layout of Matt's brain in a way that has never even been attempted before.'

'So you'll be keeping the physical slices?' Leo asked. 'They aren't destroyed by the scanning process?'

'No,' Vic replied. 'They comprise a reference library

that we can refer to if we need to iron out . . . um . . .'

'. . . glitches,' David finished his unpalatable sentence for him. 'I hadn't thought of this before, Vic, and maybe this isn't the right time to discuss it, but are there any questions about the ownership of Matt's physical brain, once it has been processed? Somebody will have to make decisions about how to treat it, whether and how long to store it, who gets access to it and so on. I suppose that person will have to be whoever 'owns' it. As Matt's parents, I would hope that we have a strong claim, mainly because we will be more likely to act in Matt's best interests than anyone else.'

'It's a good question, David,' Vic agreed, 'and it's not straightforward, because there are at least three different manifestations of the brain. There is the physical material, there is the information that will reside in the computers, and there is the consciousness – assuming that one does emerge. Will the same person or people own all of these? Will anyone else have any legitimate interest in them? There's no legal precedent for a lot of this, so to some extent we're going to be making it up as we go along. For my part I can tell you what I think, but I want to be honest with you: I can't be sure that my view will always bind the joint-venture organisation that I run. My colleagues from DARPA will no doubt also want to have a say.

'Speaking for myself, though, I'm inclined to think that if we succeed in bringing back his consciousness, then Matt himself should have as much control over all three aspects of his brain as possible, although that may have to be subject to reasonable considerations of safety and cost. If we don't, then on the whole I agree with you that as his parents, you should have the biggest say in what happens to the material brain.

'But . . .' he hesitated, looking slightly nervous, 'I would be failing in my duty towards my organisation if I didn't also point out that we are going to be spending an enormous amount of time and money on this process, and I hope you would agree that should confer some rights as well.'

'It's all rather complex and murky, isn't it?' David mused. 'But the process is going to take . . . what . . . several weeks? I guess that should give us time to get some basic principles straightened out?'

'That's exactly what I was going to say,' Vic agreed, with evident relief. 'The thing to do now is to get started and complete the scanning process. Once we've done that the timing gets less critical. We'll have a lot of work to do throughout the next few days and weeks, but we'll have time to discuss these issues too.'

Leo brought the conversation back to David's earlier question. 'So you're confident that you will re-create something of Matt's mind, but maybe not the whole thing. What could that mean?'

Vic helped himself to a Coke, largely to give himself time to gather his thoughts. He didn't want to make this sensitive conversation any harder than it already was.

'There has been some speculation about this, but we are in unknown territory,' he began. 'The first thing to say is that there may be disagreement about whether the mentality we . . . restore . . . is Matt or not. Dr Christensen expressed this well in the studio yesterday when he said it could be sideloading instead of unploading. That is a philosophical question which I doubt we will resolve to universal satisfaction, at least in the short term. I have my own view, you will have yours. I can only assume that you are satisfied that there is a possibility of bringing Matt back or you wouldn't be here.'

Leo looked towards David and Sophie for confirmation. Sophie remained silent, but David nodded.

'Good, so we can leave to one side the question of personal identity. Now one potential failure mode, I think, is that we only succeed in restoring part or parts of Matt's mind. I mentioned before that Ivan had made some breakthroughs which will enable us to distinguish between sub-minds; sub-routines within Matt's overall suite of mental programmes, if you like.'

'Assuming you can replicate Ivan's results,' Leo interrupted.

'We're confident that Ivan's work was robust on this point,' Vic reassured him. 'We've seen a lot of repeated outcomes in his work, with a high degree of confidence.'

'That's assuming he wasn't just making stuff up,' persisted Leo. 'We know he wasn't exactly a slave to scruples.'

'Yes, we are assuming that. For all his many faults we do think Ivan was a capable and sincere researcher, and the way he and his people have recorded their findings looks entirely professional.'

'So what do you think will happen if Matt is only

partly restored?' David asked.

Vic took a deep breath before replying. 'Well, it might be like meeting a child, or a heavily autistic person, or someone trapped inside a dream. Or it might be unlike any human encounter we've known before. Or we might know nothing about it: we might create a mind that is unable to operate any of the communication peripherals we'll provide.'

'You mean Matt might be like someone with locked-in syndrome?' Leo asked, shocked.

'My god, that could be awful for him! We can't let that happen.' said David, firmly. Sophie also looked at Vic in alarm, but couldn't bring herself to speak.

'I agree with you, David,' Vic nodded grimly, silently praying that Matt's parents understood that he shared their concerns for Matt as a person. 'Over the coming weeks we need to draw up a set of protocols covering what action we take given a range of different outcomes. We can shut the mentality down any time we like, if we think it is suffering pain or any kind of mental anguish. But of course it's possible that we might shut down a mentality that had the potential to stabilise and become a wholly satisfactory recovery of Matt's mind.'

A small nervous laugh escaped from Leo. 'You're not exactly selling this, Vic!'

'I'm trying very hard *not* to sell it, Leo,' Vic replied with feeling. 'That's the whole point. This is a big step for all of us, but especially for you three. The last thing in the world I want is to be the cause of any regrets or recriminations down the line. I'm not going to tell you that I care for Matt in the same way that you do, but I do care about him nonetheless. I won't deny I have a professional and personal interest in this process going ahead. But I want to be absolutely certain that my enthusiasm for this project doesn't cause me to mislead you in any way.'

'We understand, Vic,' David said. 'Don't worry. You've bent over backwards to be open and fair with us. And please don't think that we've forgotten how much else you and your colleagues have done for this family. I wouldn't even be here if it weren't for you.'

'We've all helped each other immeasurably, David,' Vic agreed, gratefully. 'I just wish Matt was here to share this opportunity – here on this side of the scanning table, I mean.

David could tell that Sophie needed to escape the conversation. He stood, and took her hand, suggesting that he and Vic meet for breakfast the following morning.

*

David didn't want any breakfast. Over a cup of coffee, Vic described the team of scientists that he wanted to bring onto the project.

'All of them have been with VNI since its foundation, and three of them – Gus, Julia and Junchao – worked with me at Northrop Grumman before that, which means they are used to working on top secret military projects, and have been positively vetted for years. They enjoy each other's company, and they socialise quite often outside work. I know them all well, and I trust them all implicitly.'

When Vic took David into the scanning room, the scientists were waiting for them. Vic introduced David, and reiterated once again the need for absolute secrecy during the coming days and weeks. David shook their hands and thanked them for agreeing to join the team.

At 44, Gus Donaldson was the senior scientist in the team. He was tall and lanky, with auburn hair that was going grey at the temples. He had regular features and blue eyes, and an over-serious, earnest demeanour, which made him seem nervous even when he wasn't. He wore black trousers with a white shirt and a blue tie, and a thin blue jumper carrying a VNI logo over the left breast.

Julia Traynor was an attractive woman in her late thirties, with a great figure and shoulder-length, expensively dyed blonde hair. She wore designer glasses with thick lenses, and unusually for a Brit, she had perfect white teeth. She dressed imaginatively, taking considerable care each day to select an outfit which was colour co-ordinated, and set off her natural colouring. Her pride in her appearance was not due to vanity, and she did not use her looks to get her own way in social or work situations. It was simply a manifestation of the professionalism and care that she took in every aspect of her life that she regarded as important.

Junchao Kim came from China to study at Imperial College before joining Northrop Grumman. Now in his mid-thirties, he was 5'7", and wore thick black-rimmed glasses. He was extremely capable, but shy. He lived in Ealing with his Chinese wife and son, but was extremely reluctant to talk about his family, or any other aspect of his private life. Seeing his discomfort, the others had stopped asking him personal questions. Every year he took a one-month holiday and visited his parents in China. He had a dry sense of humour, and a ready smile. He was hard-working, generous and kind.

Rodrigo Oliveira was the only member of the group who did not work at Northrop Grumman prior to the foundation of VNI. A tall, dark, handsome Brazilian in his early thirties, he was the most flamboyant and gregarious of the four. He organised most of the team's social events, and led an active social life with his stunning French-Argentine girlfriend. He considered himself fortunate to be living in London. He dressed in jeans, trainers, and brightly-coloured shirts.

After the introductions were complete, Vic sat David down again and told him about another workstream which was going on elsewhere.

'We have hired the world's leading voice reconstruction expert to help us with this project. He and his team have taken precise measurements of Matt's vocal cords and related musculature, and they are going to programme a synthesiser to ensure that whatever sounds your revived son makes emerge as close as possible to the way Matt used to sound. We think this will be important to you and Sophie, but it will also be important to Matt. We have provided them with recordings of Matt's voice taken from the Ross programme, but if you have any other good-quality recordings of his voice, it would be immensely helpful . . .'

THIRTY-ONE

Matt's funeral was held two days later, at a discreet hotel in Matt's home town in Sussex. Only family and close friends were invited, and Vic stayed away to avoid raising unhelpful questions. Security was sufficient to keep the media away from the funeral itself, but quite a few inhabitants of the town were approached by journalists and cameramen while the ceremony was under way behind closed doors. Most of them refused to talk to the media at all, reasoning that David and Sophie would tell the journalists anything they wanted them to know, and that they would not be glad to see comments by neighbours in the papers when they themselves were saying nothing.

A few inhabitants did talk to journalists, though, feeling that Matt's passing should be marked, and his life celebrated. But no-one wanted to cause offence, so their comments were fairly bland and anodyne. Of course, by the time their comments became printed quotes they bore little resemblance to what had originally been said, but were puffed up into exaggerated claims about

Matt's intelligence, courage and ingenuity, feeding the narrative of Matt the hero that editors were keen to run with – for the moment at least.

All in all it was a frustrating day for the ladies and gentlemen of the media, and the announcement that a memorial service would be held in the area two months later was scant consolation.

David, Sophie and Leo were aloof at the funeral. Their friends respected their guardedness as the natural consequence of their grief, and conversations were brief and superficial.

Carl, Alice and Jemma were also there. Sophie thanked them for their messages of condolence. She said they would be in touch before long, when they were feeling less raw, and when they had made all the necessary arrangements. No-one had the least idea that Sophie and David were using their grief to cloak a secret hope of returning their son to life.

*

David and Vic quickly settled into an intensive routine, spending twelve or more hours in the scanning lab, six days a week. The evening of the sixth day, Sophie drove David home to Sussex, to keep him at least tenuously connected to normal life. But they saw little of their local friends on these rest days: they stayed indoors most of the time, and kept conversations with neighbours to a minimum. They cooked dinner together, watched an old movie or two, and tried not to think too much about their hopes and fears. The following morning they got up early and Sophie drove David back to London and the scanning room in Nine Elms. She would spend the rest of the day there, usually having lunch with Leo, and then drive back to Sussex for a couple of days before returning to London for the rest of the week.

David found the routine an invaluable distraction. Ironically, even though he was spending most of his waking hours working on the problem of how to revive Matt's mind, it stopped him thinking about the son he had lost.

Sophie didn't have this luxury. She kept herself busy and distracted as best she could by making sure that David had everything he needed, and by learning about the process that David and Vic were carrying out.

Her partners in the GP surgery had willingly agreed to her request for an extended leave of absence. She found that by spending half the week in London and half in Sussex she could avoid spending much time with her friends and colleagues without causing offence. When asked, she explained that David was coping with his grief by keeping busy, working with Vic on a number of projects, but that given Vic's military connection she wasn't able to go into detail. She reflected that if you're trying to keep a secret, the best cover story is as close to the truth as possible. She remembered Leo once telling her that the very best way to keep a secret is to tell the truth, but in such a way that you won't be believed. She smiled briefly at the idea, but dismissed the idea of finding out if it worked in practice.

Media interest in Matt remained high, but Sophie agreed with David, Leo and Vic that they should give no interviews, offer no comments, and generally do nothing to encourage attention. They acknowledged Matt's belief in transparency and openness, but they each secretly wondered whether it had effectively killed him. They knew there were many difficult decisions ahead of them, depending how the scanning and modelling project proceeded, and taking those decisions would be many times harder if they had to do it in the glare of a media circus. They all recognised that agreeing to be open and transparent when the time was right was not unlike St Augustine's famous prayer 'Grant me chastity and continence, but not yet.' But none of them could face the alternative.

Deprived of access to Matt's family and close friends, and assuming along with everyone else that he had died and been buried in the normal way, journalists focused on Bartholomew Campbell, his killer. Campbell himself was being held on remand, and no interviews were being granted. So Malcolm Ross conducted an extended interview with the leader of the group he belonged to – the man in the leather jacket who had accosted David as he left the studio that night. The same studio lights which had made Matt uncomfortable and self-conscious the evening he died now bathed a man whose beliefs had caused that death.

'Stephen Coombes,' Ross began, 'I know that you disown the actions of Bartholomew Campbell, the assassin of Matt Metcalfe, but he was a prominent member of your group, the Anti-Transhumanist League, so you presumably share many of his opinions.'

'Bartholomew is a very disturbed person,' Coombes replied. 'As you know I can't comment in detail on what he did for legal reasons, but he is no longer a member of our organisation, and we do not sanction what he did. We have made it very clear all along, and I am pleased to have the opportunity of this programme to make it very clear again, that we are strongly opposed to violence in all shapes and forms. I can only guess at the pain and anguish that Matt's murder is causing his family and friends, and like everyone else listening to this I'm sure, I offer them my sincere condolences for their loss. Matt was fast becoming a poster child for a set of beliefs and activities which we deplore, but that in no way justifies the action that was taken against him.'

'So what are these beliefs that you think Matt was becoming a champion for?' Ross asked. 'What is it that you object to?'

'We object to the idea that humans can create intelligent life. We do not believe that scientists should seek to create a new species, or tamper with individual humans in a way that would effectively make them members of a new species.'

'Is this opposition based on religious grounds?'

'Not exclusively, but it's true that many of our members are religious. We have members from all the major religions, united in the belief that the gift of life is bestowed by God alone, and that if humans seek to usurp that role they are committing blasphemy.'

'And you think that your religious beliefs confer the right to prevent non-religious people doing what they think is right? Even though they argue their case with equal conviction?'

'Blasphemy is blasphemy, whether the non-believer accepts it or not,' replied Coombes. 'But we also have members who are not religious, and they also believe it is arrogant and foolhardy for humans to take it upon themselves to try to create intelligent life.'

'Why foolhardy?,' Ross asked. 'If you don't think that humans can create intelligent life because only God can do that, surely you have nothing to worry about?'

Coombes bridled, sensing that Ross was slyly ridiculing him. 'Blasphemy tempts the wrath of God, and that is no laughing matter, Mr Ross,' he said. 'But for those who think the scientific endeavour could succeed, there is a whole raft of dangers ahead. How do we know an artificially intelligent creature would be safe? On your own programme the night that Matt was killed, you had an eminent scientist telling us that the arrival of artificial intelligence will be the beginning of the end for humanity. Isn't it an incredible arrogance for a group of scientists to take that risk without consulting the rest of human-kind first?'

Sophie switched off the TV, thankful once again for the decision not to go public with the project to upload her son.

All the while, the scanning continued. Layer after micron-thick layer, the tissue of Matt's brain was sliced away from his cortex, placed on a slide, scanned, recorded and filed. The storage space required for the slices was many times larger than the volume of the brain they were removed from. It seemed to be going well, although there would be no way to tell whether the project would be successful until it was complete.

After the first couple of weeks, Vic stopped coming to the scanning room every day. The process was well-established, and Vic trusted David to make sure that everything stayed on course. In addition to David, a significant team of dedicated and highly-qualified people were fully engaged in the work, as well as a large amount of very expensive equipment. One day David asked Vic if he knew what the overall cost was. Vic replied that his accountants had told him that by the time the project was over, the cost would probably be in excess of twenty million dollars.

When Vic did come to the scanning room, his conversations with David always began with questions about the progress of the work. But they turned increasingly often to questions about how to judge whether the upload had been a success, and who would make the final judgement if there was any disagreement. Along with Sophie, they discussed how to handle numerous scenarios, mostly ones they hoped would never happen.

'The nightmare that haunts me,' Sophie said one day, 'is that we bring Matt back to life, only to place him in some kind of unspeakable hell, suffocating with pain and terror.'

'I know exactly what you mean,' agreed Vic, 'which is why I think we should assume that the upload has not been successful unless we have positive proof that it has worked properly. I think we need to agree a period for Matt to respond, and if there is no response within that time we de-activate the programme and start again.'

'I can't fault the logic,' said David, 'but it means we could terminate the consciousness of a locked-in Matt, even if he had acquired full self-awareness. He could become the first person in history to be killed several times over!'

'That's true, but he wouldn't experience the switch-off. It would be instantaneous, and if we re-animate him afterwards he would have no memory of the previous aborted consciousness.'

David sighed. 'I suppose you're right. But I'm glad we have longer to think about this. I can't disagree with you, but I'm not at all happy about it.'

Something else that made them all uncomfortable was the prospect of the memorial service. Sophie had been taking care of the arrangements, and she was grateful for Leo's assistance. They knew that it would not be possible to restrict access as tightly as for the funeral. And the more advanced the project became, the harder it would be to conceal the work that David and Vic were doing.

THIRTY-TWO

David avoided thinking about the memorial service as much as possible. Sophie was also finding it increasingly hard to contemplate the idea of facing dozens of people, however well-meaning. Thankfully, Leo understood their feelings without having to be told, and gently took over the organisation of the event. Through a friend of a friend, he managed to obtain the use of a stately home near David and Sophie's home town for the day, a property not normally open to the public because it was leased to a government department which used it for confidential conferences and summits. Security was a high priority.

Thanks to Leo, David and Sophie were more relaxed when the day finally came around than they had expected. David had buried himself in the scanning and modelling work for several weeks now, and he reflected that it was no bad thing to lift his head and try to gather some perspective.

It was a beautiful day in March. The air was crisp and clear, and although spring was still several weeks away, the deadening effect of winter was lifting, and it seemed to David that the fields and the hills were picked out in sharper colours. The green-yellow lichen spattering the grey stone blocks of the house reproached him for not paying attention to the natural and man-made beauty of his home countryside – a countryside which Matt had loved and thrived in. He caught himself wondering what combinations of neurons within his brain were responsible for giving him this heightened sensitivity to the visual messages reaching his cortex, and he mocked himself for not being able to simply appreciate the beauty without having to analyse it. He had been cloistered in the scanning room so much that it was almost startling to be outside in a beautiful garden, with birds sailing on a gentle breeze, and the sounds and smells of the countryside saturating his attention.

He turned his gaze to the hills that had drawn him to this part of the country many years before, and the quilt of fields that covered the contours of the Weald. The handsome brown cows were like bugs in the distance, beetling lazily across the landscape, grazing without haste and pausing, contented, when they chanced on the ideal clump of grass. Further away, migrating across one of the hillsides, small white dots of sheep busied themselves mindlessly keeping their stomachs full, the flock rippling gently like pondwater whenever a walker or a cyclist passed them.

The house was largely a creation of the sixteenth century. The giant double-storey bays, striped with long vertical slabs of windows, faced out across the lawn towards the hills, silently but confidently asserting ownership and dominance. They wore their balustrades and roof decorations like crowns. The house was built on a rise, from which two broad lawns stepped down in succession to meet a long field heading away towards the hills. The memorial service took place on the second lawn. Two hundred chairs were set out on the grass, in well-spaced rows of 25. The event could not have been more open, and yet more private.

David and Sophie had timed their arrival to avoid having to speak to anyone before the service. Leo was already there, marshalling the house's staff as they made the final arrangements. They had agreed that Vic would again stay away. Most of the two hundred or so guests were family, and friends from the town, but Matt's fame was still a major draw, and requests to attend had been received from many journalists. Malcolm Ross was one of the few whose request had been granted.

The service was confidently orchestrated by Leo, who also gave the opening and closing addresses. He was calm and impressive, and David felt a surge of gratitude mixed with pride well up within his sorrow as he realised how ably Leo was managing the event. He exchanged a glance with Sophie and squeezed her hand.

Leo opened the service by describing Matt as the miraculous result of the marriage of the two most wonderful people he knew. He spoke of his own vicarious pride as he watched a growing Matt reveal and exercise his gifts and talents. He said that the story of Matt's adventure was so well known that he did not need to re-hash it now, but he marvelled at the resilience and ingenuity displayed by one so young and still just at the start of life. What might Matt have achieved, he asked, if he had been granted a full term?

Simon Jones, Matt's favourite teacher, was next. He related a handful of stories about Matt's life at school. His dry, understated delivery was in perfect keeping with Matt's clever but shy approach to life, and his shrewd, gentle sense of humour. As Simon went on to talk about Matt's role in rescuing his father, David reflected what an extraordinary situation his family found itself in. If the project to upload Matt succeeded they would be the first family in history – perhaps even mythical history – to reincarnate not one, but two of its members.

Carl was the third speaker. He was less polished and more nervous than Leo and Simon, and his speech contained more raw emotion, a more naked sense of loss. While Carl was talking, David noticed that Alice's head was bowed, and that she was sobbing into cupped hands. He felt a stab of guilt at having spent almost no time with Alice since Matt was killed. He made a mental note to speak to her afterwards.

Carl claimed that his best friend had an unusual combination of analytical horsepower, lateral thinking skills, and well-grounded common sense. Using an example which slightly missed the mark for some members of the audience, he illustrated his claim with a story about a video game where Matt had escaped from a seemingly fatal trap by using some rope, a skateboard, and a refrigerator. Like Leo, Carl asked what Matt might have achieved if he had been given the time to show the world what he could do. Poignantly, he described how, in a teenage culture where street credibility is everything, Matt had blithely ignored the tyranny of convention, and chose instead to spend his time with people based solely on whether or not they were interesting, and kind.

After the speeches there was a buffet inside the house. David found the interior of the building oppressive after the light and space of the lawn. Amid the heavy wood panelling and the elaborate wall carvings, the life-sized portraits of long-dead aristocrats and other powerful men seemed to look down on him figuratively as well as literally. He shrugged this feeling off as Malcolm Ross buttonholed him.

'I'm so sorry about what happened to Matt, David. How are you and Sophie coping? Your friend Leo put on a wonderful event. Most impressive, and well-deserved, too.'

'Thank you, that's very kind. We're OK, I suppose. It comes and goes. The worst times are when I think of something I want to share with Matt, and then I suddenly realise that I can't because he's not . . . he's not there any more.'

'Yes, it's awful. I understand that Campbell has a committal hearing coming up shortly. Will you be attending, or will you stay away?'

'It doesn't interest me at all,' said David firmly. 'I don't care what they do to him: it won't bring Matt back. Of course there are times when I wish I could have a couple of hours alone with him and a blow torch, but on the whole I'm glad to say I give him no thought whatsoever.'

'Very sensible; very healthy,' agreed Ross. 'So what are you doing, David? I confess I have heard some tantalising rumours.'

'Off the record?' asked David, looking him hard in the eyes.

'Scout's honour,' said Ross, in earnest.

'I'm working with Vic. I agreed to do it because I think it's what Matt would have wanted. Combining my old research interests with the insights produced by Vic and Ivan's teams looks likely to generate some useful outputs in a number of different areas of cognitive neuroscience.'

It was Ross's turn to give a searching look. 'I hope I'm not being too pushy, but you know what journalists are like, David. Are you working on machine intelligence?'

David smiled. 'I think it's very easy to exaggerate what can be achieved with today's technology, Malcolm. But I tell you what: if we do make substantive progress towards AI, I'll give you an exclusive interview. And now you'll have to excuse me: there's a young lady over there that I really must have a word with.'

Ross smiled and let him go, calling after him, 'I'll hold you to that!'

David joined his wife, who had an arm around the shoulders of a fragile-looking Alice. Alice's parents were standing by, not knowing quite where to put themselves.

'Please forgive us, Alice,' he said. 'We've hardly seen anything of you since . . . since what happened to Matt.

We've been very self-absorbed and busy with our own troubles. How are you?'

'You shouldn't be apologising to me,' sobbed Alice. 'I'm sorry I'm making such a scene. I . . . I just can't believe he's not coming back.'

Alice's mother stroked her daughter's hair, and Alice stopped sobbing. She looked up and managed to produce an unconvincing smile.

'They say you never know what you've got till it's gone, but I suppose at least I can say that's not true. I did know what I had: he was such a wonderful guy.'

'Yes he was,' said Sophie with feeling, 'yes he was. Look, why don't you and your parents come to lunch one Sunday, dear. It's been too long since we saw you.'

Alice's parents looked at Sophie and David, grateful for their attempt to console their daughter in the midst of their own loss.

'Are you back at university yet?' asked David, changing the subject.

'I should be, but I can't face it yet. I've spoken to my tutor, who was brilliant: he just told me to take as much time as I need to recover. He even said that if I need to, I can take a year out and go back next time round. But I don't want to do that.' She smiled weakly: 'Matt would have given me hell for even thinking it.'

The rest of the event passed in a blur: David and Sophie exchanged platitudes with most of their friends and family. Some were taciturn, keen to avoid burdening David and Sophie with their own grief. Others gushed, desperate for Matt's parents to know how much they cared. Most were calmly but profoundly sympathetic, and David and Sophie were surprised how much they found themselves buoyed by this demonstration of the universal affection and admiration for their son.

At length, Leo told David that the staff needed to clear the room, and they were finally able to say their goodbyes and head home. Their departure was delayed and rendered uncomfortable by the gaggle of reporters waiting by the gate to the grounds. Leo drove them slowly but steadily through the small crowd, grimly determined that no cameras waved in their path would stop them. He didn't need to ask David and Sophie whether they wanted to stop and give a statement.

THIRTY-THREE

Two weeks after the memorial service, Vic, David and Sophie invited Leo and Norman to meet them for lunch in the laboratory's cafeteria. They said they had some important news, and that if at all possible, Leo and Norman should clear their diaries for the afternoon.

David waited until everyone was seated in the simple blue plastic bucket chairs in the starkly functional temporary cafeteria building. As they started to eat, he got straight to the point.

'We're ready. The scanning is complete. We think we have captured as much of the connectome as we need.'

Leo and Norman had guessed the news, but they stared at David anyway. This was a momentous occasion.

'So the model is complete?' Norman asked. 'You're ready to upload him?'

'Well, I suppose you could argue that we have already uploaded him; we just haven't activated the upload,' said David. 'If we are all still in agreement, we propose to do that this afternoon.'

'As you know,' Vic explained, 'we have been

checking the connections carefully as we went along. Using the techniques developed by Ivan, we have identified a large number of sub-minds within the structure of Matt's brain, and we are reasonably confident that the neural pathways within these sub-minds in the new version of Matt's brain are a good match for those in the original version. What we don't yet know is whether the linkages between the sub-units will work properly.'

'The only way to find that out is to activate it,' David added.

'So, we are checking that everyone is still happy to proceed,' Vic continued, addressing Norman in particular. 'We would also like to re-confirm our protocol for stopping the process. Four people have a veto as to whether the activation is reversed at any point: Sophie, David, Norman and me. The process continues only so long as all four of us are content for it to do so, and if any of us asks for it to be stopped, the equipment will be powered down immediately without question. We do not have to give any reason for our decision. This protocol is mainly to protect Matt from harm or suffering, but it is also to protect the rest of us.'

Sophie looked at Leo. 'Are you still OK with the decision that you are the only person here without a veto, Leo?'

'Yes, I still think that is right,' Leo said, nodding. 'Wow, so we're finally there: the big day. It's exciting, and also just a little bit scary, don't you think? There is one thing which puzzles me, though.' He looked at Vic and Norman. 'Don't you guys need to obtain approval from somebody? Somebody in the US military, or the government? In fact I suppose the UK government would have something to say about it, too, if they knew what is about to happen here.'

'It's a good question, Leo,' Vic replied, nodding. 'None of us should be under any illusions about what is going on here. There is absolutely nothing illegal about what we are about to do, under either US or UK law. But we're not being open and transparent, either, in the way that we would all like, and which Matt wanted. And we all know the reason for that. If we announced what we are about to do, we would almost certainly be stopped. There would be a great deal of debate, some of it sensible, much of it ill-informed, but that's democracy for you. And in the end, who knows whether we would be able to go ahead?

'So we're going ahead – under the radar, if you like – because none of us wants to lose the chance of bringing Matt back. But I want to be honest: there are other reasons, too. Artificial intelligence is coming, whether we like it or not. We think we are in the lead, but whoever is in second place may not be far behind. I believe that uploading a human mind is the safest way for humanity to create its first AGI. I want Matt to be the world's first AGI.

'And to answer your question directly, Leo, yes, there are powerful elements within the US government which want this project to proceed for strategic, financial, and – I won't deny it – military reasons.'

'So you already have their approval to proceed?' asked Leo.

'Yes and no,' Norman replied. 'I'm sure you've heard the phrase 'plausible deniability'. They do want us to go ahead, but if it all goes south they want to be able to claim that I was a rogue officer acting on my own, without authority. Naturally I can't prove that to you, but it's how these things work.'

'So you will be made a scapegoat if things go wrong, or even if it works, but turns out to be wildly unpopular?' asked David.

'That's right. That's part of my unofficial job description,' Norman said, smiling ruefully. 'But don't you worry about me,' he continued. 'I have broad shoulders and I would be well compensated for taking the fall. Again, that's just the way these things are done.'

'But hey, let's not get obsessed with what might go wrong,' Vic broke in. 'We're on the cusp of a dramatic breakthrough here. We're about to reunite Matt with his family!'

He looked at Sophie and Leo. 'It's time for you two to see the computer room.' He stood up, and looked around the group. 'Shall we?'

They all stood, placed the debris from their lunches on their trays, and took them to the carousel where the catering staff would collect them and wash them for the next users. David marvelled at how the prosaic processes of everyday life carry on amid moments of great drama. They walked the corridors leading from the cafeteria to the computing room in silence, each lost in their own thoughts.

Sophie and Leo had both spent many hours in the scanning room, but neither of them had ever set foot in the computing room before. It was cold.

They gazed at the enormous amount of computing equipment in the room. Leo estimated there were around thirty rows of giant matt black cabinets, each about fifteen feet high and six feet wide, with shelves on both sides. They stretched at least five metres back towards the far wall. The shelves in each cabinet held row upon row of servers. The servers looked like over-sized black hi-fi units, except that many of them had spaghetti tangles of wires sprouting from the front, and were connected to their neighbours, or with servers further down their row. The servers themselves all looked identical, but the mess of cables and the sprinkling of small green lights introduced an element of chaos. A low hum permeated the room.

'I wanted you to see this equipment close up before we start,' Vic explained, 'so you know where the action is taking place, so to speak. We don't come in here often because this room has to be precisely temperature-controlled. We'll be operating this equipment from next door. But this is where Matt is hosted. This . . .' he patted the nearest cabinet, 'this is Matt's new brain.'

Sophie reached out to touch the nearest cabinet. 'Hello sweetheart,' she said to herself, softly. She left her hand motionless against the cold black steel for a moment, then withdrew it and shivered slightly.

Vic ushered them out of the computer room and into the control room. 'We control everything from in here. Make yourselves at home.'

The control room was considerably warmer than the computer room, and the hum was inaudible. The whole of one wall was a large window giving a clear view into the computer room. Facing that window was an arrangement of six desks, one in front, and a row of five behind it. Three small monitors stood side-by-side on each desk, with one large wide-screen monitor above them. A great deal of cabling ran into the computer room. The ambient lighting was low, with a couple of task light sources at each desk, and other lights in the ceiling focused on a large conference table that stood behind the rows of desks. Together with the pastel grey decor, the pools of light gave the room an impressive atmosphere of calm intellectual purpose.

Except for the one at the front, each desk was occupied. The men wore open-necked shirts and chinos, and the women wore slacks and jumpers. Vic made the introductions, then moved to the front desk, gesturing at its monitor. 'The master control and diagnostic circuits are fed to this screen, so this is where we will press the enter key which will initiate the process of powering up the model. We'll start by feeding just one audio stream to the upload, to minimise the possibility of over-loading Matt with sensory impressions until he gets used to his new situation. Later we can add a visual stream, and the other senses too.'

He pointed to a camera and a microphone beneath the main screen, and then to a row of buttons on the desk. 'These devices provide the audio and visual inputs, so you should probably address yourselves to them. The microphone is voice-activated, but pressing this button will keep it muted.'

Then he pointed to a speaker located on the desk. 'Matt's voice will come through this speaker here. The audio is modulated so that whatever strength of signal is coming through, the volume will be the same level as a voice in normal conversation. As you know, we have been working on a system to convert whatever sounds Matt makes into sounds as close as possible to the way that . . . the way that Matt used to sound. I should warn you in advance, it probably won't be a perfect representation, but if everything goes to plan it should sound familiar.'

Vic was watching David and Sophie as he spoke. Reassured that they were bearing up well, he gestured at the main screen, and continued.

'Later, we hope that he will be able to project visuals here.'

He turned to Sophie and gestured for her to join him at the front desk. 'David and I thought you might like to press the key.' He typed a brief command into a keyboard and the screensaver photo of a beach at sunset was replaced by a dialogue box, asking simply, 'Do you wish to continue?' Vic moved the cursor to hover over the 'Yes' response.

Sophie moved into position, and placed her hand on the mouse. With a final look at David, she pressed the mouse key.

The humming they had heard in the computer room increased to the point that it became audible in the control room. Through the window, they could see that a great many more lights were glowing on the servers.

'How long do you expect it to take to . . . um . . .

warm up?' asked Leo.

'In theory, no time at all,' replied David. 'It's not like an operating system on a PC, where a whole suite of programmes and sub-programmes have to load before the machine can do anything. It's more like your brain when you wake up in the morning. Electrochemical activity in your neurons is the information processing, and the information processing is your thoughts. From experiments carried out on people waking up inside FMRI scanning equipment, we have selected particular sets of neurons to fire up at initiation. If we have got that right, those neurons will spark others, and a coherent stream of thinking will be generated. It should be quick – if we've got it right.'

He leaned towards the desk and spoke into the microphone. 'Hello, Matt. Can you hear me? It's David, your father here. Your mother's here too, and Leo, and some other friends, Vic and Norman. Can you hear me?'

When the voice came through the speaker they all jumped.

'What happened? . . . Where am I?'

Although slightly metallic and alien-sounding, the voice was recognisably Matt's, sounding foggy and disorientated. Sophie's mouth formed a huge 'O' which she covered with her hand. Shocked, she sat down heavily and reached out for David who was instinctively moving towards her at the same time. They hadn't dared to hope for such immediate success. Vic and Norman grinned broadly at each other and shook hands warmly as Leo clapped them both on the shoulder. The scientists manning the desks were celebrating too.

The celebrations broke off as Matt's voice came from the speaker again. This time he sounded stressed, upset.

'Dad! Is that you? What is . . . ? Where . . . ? I can't . . . Hang on, why . . . ? I can't . . . I . . .'

Again the speaker fell silent. After a couple of moments, David spoke:

'Matt, can you hear me? We heard you loud and clear. Can you hear me?'

There was no response from the speaker. Sophie addressed the mike:

'Matt darling. Are you there? It's so wonderful to hear your voice. Can you hear us?'

Still there was nothing, and this time the silence lasted for a couple of minutes. Everyone at the front desk was straining, hoping to hear more from Matt. Finally, it was one of the scientists who spoke up:

'The processing activity showed clear spikes when the speaker was active, Vic, but it's gone completely flat again.'

'Thanks Gus,' replied Vic. He looked at the others. 'It looks as though the processing didn't propagate correctly. David, I think we should power down and go through those check routines we agreed.'

Sophie nodded agreement to David's unspoken request for agreement. He turned back to Vic. 'OK, let's do it.'

Vic typed an instruction into the keyboard and hit the enter key. The hum in the computer room died down to inaudible, and the mood in the control room deflated in synch.

'It will only take a few minutes for us to run the checks,' he said. 'Why don't you guys take a breather, perhaps a tour of the building. . . ?'

'I'll stay here, thanks,' said Sophie. 'I don't think I could bear to be anywhere else right now.'

'I understand,' Vic nodded. 'David, we should start by looking at the activity logs on Gus' monitor.'

As they walked over to Gus' desk, Leo put his hand on Sophie's arm. 'It was always likely there would be a few false starts. We knew that. It's amazing that we got such a strong result right out of the blocks.'

'I know, I know. It was silly of me to get my hopes up so quickly.'

'No, this is a really encouraging start, Sophie,' Norman said earnestly. 'I didn't expect anything to happen this fast. The guys seem to be on the right track.'

Sophie nodded and smiled weakly, looking over at David. She envied him the opportunity to be busy, reviewing data, checking circuits. Waiting was painful.

Vic was right. A few minutes later they were gathered around the front desk again, preparing to press the enter key to the same dialogue box as before. This time David performed the modest ceremony.

The result was shocking. As the humming increased in the computer room, a screeching noise grew with it, which gradually resolved into a human scream. Matt was screaming. It was a surreal noise, as the volume level was modulated to conversation level, and there was no drawing of breath. But there was no doubting the sensation of terror which lay behind the noise, and there was no doubting it was Matt's voice. David didn't need to look up for confirmation: he pressed the key to power down.

David drew a deep breath, and spoke carefully. 'I think we need to undertake a deeper review, Vic. Something is evidently not right. I think we should run a complete diagnostic, let it run overnight.'

'I couldn't agree more,' replied Vic. 'None of us want to hear that sound again!'

THIRTY-FOUR

There was nothing for Sophie or Leo to do, so they left for the apartment. After the elation of the initial apparent success they were bitterly disappointed by the failure, and their nerves had been shredded by the obvious terror in Matt's anguished howl. It was a relief to escape from the control room, the scene of that horror.

Norman stayed for a while, but quickly decided to leave David and Vic to get on with their work in peace. But in truth there was little for David and Vic to do, either. Working with the rest of the scientists, it only took half an hour to set the parameters for a diagnostic check and set it to run, and they knew they would get no results for several hours. David headed to the flat, and Vic to his London apartment, agreeing to meet back at the control room at nine o'clock the following morning.

Later, as they got ready for bed, David suggested that Sophie might want to stay away from the control room until he and Vic had a chance to see whether the diagnostic was successful, and perhaps even until they could declare the upload initiation a success.

'That scream was probably the most awful sound I have ever heard in my life,' he said. 'The worst thing about it was not being able to do anything about it except to stop it by de-powering the upload. But at least I can distract myself by working with Vic on strategies to improve the model and fix the bugs. It must be much worse for you. Why don't you and Leo wait for Vic and me to check the results of the diagnostic tomorrow morning, and then join us if it looks promising?'

'Thanks but no thanks,' Sophie replied. 'You're right: it is unbearable to be powerless when Matt is screaming, but it would be even worse to be away from him. I need to be there.'

'I know what you mean,' nodded David. 'Well, I won't deny that it's good to have you there. We could have important decisions to make tomorrow which I would much rather not take alone.'

There was a tenderness when they made love that night, born of their shared anxiety for their son. There was also a passion inspired by their shared hope that they would soon be talking to him again.

*

When David, Sophie and Leo arrived at the control room the next morning, Vic and Norman were already there. Sophie noticed several new faces among the scientists, but she recognised others, and she realised that some of these people must have worked all night, checking that the diagnostic was running OK, analysing the activity logs, looking for sources of error within the upload model. She felt tears well up in her eyes as she realised the dedication as well as the scale of resources being applied to the task of reviving her son. She was struck by a wave of gratitude, and immediately afterwards by a sense of amazement that the whole thing was successfully being kept a secret.

Vic greeted them with a serious expression.

'We should be ready to try again within the hour. David, I'd like to run through some of the overnight results with you, if that's OK? I think the guys have made some really useful discoveries.' He walked to one of the desks in the second row. 'Come over to this monitor and I'll show you what I mean.'

Norman joined Sophie and Leo and told them what he understood of the overnight findings before leaving to make some calls in an adjoining room while they all waited for the next initiation.

In fact it was three hours before David and Vic were ready to try again. David explained the problem to Sophie.

'We are confident that we have the architecture right. We are also confident that we have most of the linkages right, both within the sub-units and between them. The difficulty we are having is working out the best order in which to initiate them. The only hard data we have to guide us is what we have learned from observations of other brains, and there seems to be a good deal of variation between brains on this. The guys have crunched a lot of data on this overnight and this morning. We could try to delve down in more detail, but the analysis is starting to involve a lot of guesswork. Or we can go ahead and initiate the upload again . . .'

David looked at Vic, and then back at Sophie. 'We think we should try it,' he continued. 'Are you happy with that?'

'Yes,' said Sophie, without hesitation. David nodded and smiled appreciatively.

'OK. Good.' He gestured towards the keyboard at the main monitor. 'Let's do it.'

A dozen people held their breath as Sophie pressed the button and a dozen pairs of eyes locked on the main monitor and strained to hear any kind of noise from the speaker as the hum rose in the computer room. Within a couple of minutes they were rewarded with a low, sleepy, dreamlike murmur.

'Mmmmmmm . . . Eeeeeeee . . . Zhhhh . . . Rrrrrrooound.'

In the silence that followed, David and Sophie agreed it was Matt's voice again.

'Matt, can you hear me, darling? It's mum. Dad's here too.'

The murmur started up again.

'Mmmmmmm . . . Eeeeeeee . . . Zhhhh . . . Yeeelllooow.'

Again there was silence. Sophie asked David and Vic whether there could be a problem with the audio circuitry.

'It sounds like interference, or feedback or something,' she said.

'Unlikely,' replied Vic, shaking his head. 'I think it's the upload. It's as if Matt is at the edge of consciousness. As if he's groping around, trying to find a way in.'

'Trying to wake up?' Leo suggested.

'Exactly,' agreed Vic. 'His sub-conscious mind – or part of it – may be trying to achieve full consciousness.'

'Mmmmmmm . . . Eeeeeeee . . . Zhhhh . . . Fee Fi Fo Fum. I smell the blood . . . The blood . . . The blood.'

'Matt, hello. This is Dad. Can you hear me, Son?'

'Mmmmmmm . . . Eeeeeeee . . . Zhhhh . . . Heelllloooo . . . 'Mmmmmmm . . . Eeeeeeee . . . Zhhhh . . . Daaaad . . . Mmmuuuummmm . . .. Zhhhh.'

'Well, at least this is better than last time!' said Vic, placing a finger on the microphone's mute button. 'This could work! Why don't you two keep talking to him. It might help him find his way to the surface.'

David and Sophie took it in turns to talk, trying to coax Matt back to the world. Slowly – painfully slowly – the snatches of murmurings became longer and more recognisable. Vic suggested that they read to Matt, or recite some poetry: anything to keep exposing him to sentences spoken by his parents. David recited some verses of the *Jabberwocky*, a poem which Matt had loved hearing him read when he was small. Matt responded sleepily.

'Mmmmimmmsyyyy . . . Borrrrrow-grove . . . Mmmooommme rrraaath . . . Vooorrrrpaaaallll.'

There was a pause, and then the voice picked up tempo and energy alarmingly:

'Snicker-snack, snicker-snack, snicker-snack, snicker-snack, snicker-snack, snicker-snack, snicker-snack, snicker-snack, snicker-snack, snicker-snack, snicker-snack. Gallumph gallumph, my beamish boy! Gallumph gallumph. Gallumph gallumph. Gallumph gallumph. Gallumph

gallumph. Callooh! Callay! Callooh! Callay! Callooh!
Callay! Callooh! Callay! Callooh! Callay!'

'Matt!' shouted Sophie, worried that Matt was spinning into a dangerous loop. 'Can you hear us? How do
you feel? It's so wonderful to hear you!'

The voice fell silent for a moment. And then it spoke
again, with an apparent clarity which took Sophie's
breath away.

'Mum? Is that you? Where am I? It's dark here. Are you
here? Where am I?'

Sophie and David stared at each other, their eyes
widening in glee. The voice was a remarkably true
approximation to Matt's. Their son was back!

David used the form of words they had worked out
and agreed with Dr Humbert.

'Matt, it's me: Dad. You're safe! You're in a special
treatment facility. We're here with you: me, your mum,
Leo, and a lot of other friends. Do you remember anything about what happened to you?'

'Dad? Why can't I see you? Am I on life support? Am I
blind? Oh god, that's it: I'm blind, aren't I!'

'No, Matt, you're not blind,' David reassured him.
'But you are in recovery. There was an accident, but
everything is going to be okay. Your mum and I are here,
and we're going to stay here, and there are lots of other
friends here to help you. It's going to be okay. I promise.'

'What do you mean, a treatment facility, Dad? Am I in a
hospital? Oh god, I remember. I remember now. I was shot,
wasn't I? How long have I been unconscious? Will I recover
. . . fully? Will I be okay again?'

'Yes you will, Matt; yes you will. That's why your

mum and Leo and I are here, and these other friends too. We're going to make sure you get completely better. How do you feel? Apart from it being dark?'

'I feel fine, I suppose. The dark is really black, though. I can't remember anything as black as this before. And I can't feel anything either. It's as if I'm floating. In space. What's going on, Dad? This feels really weird.'

David, Sophie and Vic were exchanging glances as this conversation unfolded. The moment was delicate, as if Matt was a potential suicide who had to be talked down from a ledge.

'It's going to be okay, Matt,' Sophie said. 'It's going to feel weird for a while, I'm afraid, but the doctors say you're going to make a full recovery. Keep talking to us but don't try to do anything physical, okay?'

'OK,' said Matt doubtfully. 'So what happened? How badly am I injured?'

'You were badly injured, son.' David replied, 'You were in a coma for a long time, and it's going to take a while before you get back to normal. But the doctors say you're doing really well.'

'It's a miracle, darling,' added Sophie. 'I can't tell you how relieved we all are to have you back.'

'So how long was I out? And why can't I feel anything?'

*

It was another fifteen minutes before David and Sophie felt it was safe to tell Matt the truth. In the meantime they nursed him with reassurance and love. His voice became more stable, and the flashes of panic became less frequent. Eventually they felt he was ready to learn the reality of his situation.

'There's something you're not telling me, isn't there? Why can't you tell me the truth?'

David gave Sophie an enquiring look and Sophie nodded her assent to his unspoken question.

'It's true; there is something important that you need to know,' David agreed. 'It's a good thing, Matt – really it is. We're very excited about it, your mother and I. But it may be a little hard to hear. Do you think you're ready?'

'Yes, I think so. You say it's a good thing?'

'Yes I do. It's complicated, but yes, it really is a wonderful thing. But it's going to come as a bit of a shock. Are you ready?'

'Ready as I'll ever be, I guess. And I don't think I can't take much more suspense.'

'OK well here it is. You've been uploaded, Matt.' David paused for a moment to listen for a reaction. When none was forthcoming, he continued. 'Your mind is inside a computer. Everything is working fine, and we should be able to give you vision and all sorts of other senses and peripherals soon.'

Still Matt made no response. David and Sophie exchanged worried glances.

'How do you feel about this, Matt?' Sophie asked nervously. 'Are you OK?'

'Er, yeah,' Matt replied, distantly. Then after a pause, more focused. 'That's a bit of a mind fuck, actually. I don't know how I feel about it, to be honest. Where am I?'

'You're in a supercomputer in Vic's lab, at the site of the new US Embassy in Battersea. We're in the control room next door. Leo is here, and Vic, of course, and Norman, and a room full of wonderful scientists who have made all this possible. It's going to be OK. I promise.'

'Yeah. Yeah, I see,' Matt said, sounding distant again. 'So what happened? I died, right? And then you uploaded me? How long did it take? How did you do it? I thought the technology wasn't ready yet.'

'Hi Matt, this is Vic. We made some great advances thanks to what we learned from Ivan. Thanks to you, in fact. That's what made this possible. It's great to have you back, Matt.'

Matt still sounded flat. 'Yeah. Right. Hi Vic. Um, and hi everyone else. Um, this is going to take a while to get used to.'

'That's entirely understandable, Matt,' said David. 'You can take all the time you want. We're not going anywhere.'

'No.' Matt paused for a moment before adding, 'And I don't suppose I am, either.'

THIRTY-FIVE

Now that Matt had recovered from the shock of his unique awakening, he and his family and friends became engrossed in an exploration of the nature of his uploaded mind. How much of his old life could he remember? Did he notice any differences in the way his mind operated? Did he feel the same as before, internally? For several hours this investigation – part introspection and part discussion – was wholly absorbing, and he didn't feel the need to ask for more sense or data inputs to his consciousness.

It became apparent that he had retained access to most, but not all, of his life memories. He spent a long time comparing notes with David, Sophie and Leo about events in his early life.

'There's a lyric in a Prefab Sprout song,' Leo said at one point. 'Goes something like,

Nothing sounds as good as "I Remember That"
Like a bolt out of the blue, did you feel it too?

And they're right: shared nostalgia is a wonderful thing.'

'That's a great song, Leo,' Matt said. 'But do you remember the rest of it?'

'Cos that's all we can have, yes it's all we can trust;
It's a hell of a ride but it's a journey to dust'.'

'Well, not for you, Matt,' Vic said. 'Not any more. You have gone beyond human limitations.'

'Well, we'll see about that,' Matt replied. 'This is a seriously freaky situation and I'm not sure how I'm going to feel about it when I get properly used to it. Having no senses and no body is very strange. I'm not sure whether I'll just adjust to it, or whether . . .' No-one was sorry that he left the rest of the thought unsaid.

'Just take your time, son,' David advised. 'Try and relax into it, and get used to it slowly. There's no need to hurry things. And you will get your other senses back. It won't stay black for long. We have systems set up, but we need to take things in stages – make sure it all goes smoothly. Which it will. Trust me. We're starting with auditory input and output, but we'll do the rest soon.'

Leo was right. 'I remember that' was a powerful emotional healer for Matt. Every time he related a story about his childhood, and Sophie or David played back their memory of it, he felt a little less alone, a little less scared. The exchanges were a healing experience for Sophie and David too. David wondered after a while whether it was becoming a little indulgent, when out of the corner of his eye he caught one of the scientists stifling a yawn. But he banished the thought: his son was shut inside a huge metal box for the rest of his life. It was a potentially terrifying prospect, and he deserved all the reassurance that they could collectively provide.

The hell with what anyone else thought about it.

Just as with a biologically normal human, there were episodes that Matt did not remember, especially when Sophie reached back into his very young childhood. He could not remember the floppy blue elephant which had been his first cuddly toy, or the TV cartoon he had adored as a toddler. He had no recollection of being three years old, pulling his shirt up and pretending to swim across the wooden floor in the conservatory because he liked the cold feeling on his tummy. He had no memories at all of his paternal grandfather, who died when he was four. The first time he drew a blank like this he grew nervous, and it took Sophie and David a few moments to calm him down. But after that he accepted that this was normal: humans simply don't remember much of their early years.

But there were also missing passages and aspects of his life which he knew he should have access to. He had no mental pictures of Egypt, even though David and Sophie told him they had taken several holidays in a resort on the Sinai Peninsula. Occasionally he failed to recognise a word, like 'cave', and 'tiger', and he was puzzled to learn that these were everyday concepts.

'Do you think I will be able to regain these missing memories?' Matt asked. 'I've heard it said that the brain remembers everything that happens to it, but that only selected memories are accessible.'

'I'm afraid that theory is discredited, Matt' Vic replied. 'We now know that the brain is very selective about what it commits to long-term memory. But some of these memories that you are missing are things which were committed to your long-term memory. So who knows? We might well be able to conjure them up again. It's going to take a while to figure out just how much we can do with your brain . . .'

He stopped as he noticed Sophie glaring at him. 'I mean, of course, how much you can do, with our help.'

A new and exciting thought occurred to Matt. 'So when do I get to talk to my friends?' he asked. 'Can we invite Alice and Carl here? And Jemma?'

Vic frowned, and glanced anxiously at David.

'I'm sorry, Matt,' David replied. 'We have to keep the number of people who know about you to an absolute minimum. There would be no way to bring your friends here without their parents knowing, and we can't risk that until we've figured out how we're going to play this thing. We will have to announce your existence to the world before long, but we have to do it right, or the reaction could be very dangerous.'

This was a hard blow to Matt, but he could tell there was no point arguing. 'Yeah,' he mused distantly. 'I guess there's a lot to think about on that front.' A few moments of awkward silence passed before he spoke again.

'So when can I have some visual input? And taste, touch and smell? And music. Could I listen to some music, do you think?'

'Yes of course,' Vic replied, relieved to be back on safer ground. 'We have peripherals ready for you. We don't want to rush it, but if you feel ready to give them a try we can bring them online.'

'Let's do it one by one, shall we?' David suggested.

'OK,' Matt agreed. 'Let's start with visual.'

'No problem,' Vic replied. 'It's all linked up, we simply need to throw a virtual switch to power up the camera.' Turning to the others, he added, 'The monitor on that desk over there will display the same feed that Matt is seeing.'

He typed a couple of instructions into the main keyboard, and then stood back and invited Sophie to press the Enter key.

An image of the computer control room came onto the monitor that Vic had indicated, but Matt said nothing. They waited a few minutes before David asked if he could see anything.

'Yeah, there's light, but it's fuzzy,' Matt replied. 'I can't make out any kind of picture. Oh, wait . . . something is forming . . . there are some shapes . . . some movement. I think maybe it's starting to come into focus . . . I'm not sure.'

'Fascinating!' Vic exclaimed. 'Matt, it sounds as if you are going through the process that babies go through as their brains learn to decode their visual input – only you are doing it much, much quicker. We should have expected this. I'm sorry, we should have forewarned you, only you resolved the audio signal so fast I thought it would be the same with the visual signal. But of course there is a huge amount more information in the visual signal.'

'It's okay, Vic,' Matt said abstractedly. 'It's weird, but I think I'm getting there. Maybe this is what recovering from a really major hangover is like.'

David, Sophie and Leo exchanged glances, relieved

and proud that Matt was able to crack jokes at a time like this.

After another five minutes, Matt reported that he had a good, clear image of the room. He asked if the camera could be moved around, so he could see the rest of the environment. He was especially interested to see the computer room itself, which Vic showed him through the large window in the control room.

'So that's what I look like now? That's a cool look. I seem to have become big-headed, though.'

Norman laughed. 'Good to hear you're keeping things in perspective, Matt.'

'Can you give me control over the direction of the camera?' Matt asked. 'In fact, can you give me access to multiple cameras?'

'Yes, we can do that,' agreed Vic. 'But I strongly recommend that we take this slowly. Let's get you set up with your other three senses first, and get them settled down. What I want to do here first is to see whether you can correctly identify a range of different inputs, and to check that you can turn the inputs on and off at will.'

Smell was first. Julia, one of the scientists who had been with the project since the start, presented a range of different substances to a sensor on her desk. She heated some of them slightly with a burner to release their scent. Smell was like the audio input rather than the visual input in that Matt resolved it almost immediately. They were puzzled when Matt reported that his perceptions of mint and rosemary had swapped over, however. They left it as a glitch to be solved later.

Taste was the province of Junchao, another of the original scientists. Matt reported this as the strangest sensory experience so far.

'It doesn't seem right to be able to taste something without feeling my tongue touching it, or rolling it around inside my mouth. On the other hand, it's nice to think that I could have that chocolate taste on permanent input without ever adding an ounce to my existing weight.' He paused. 'Which must be quite a few tonnes, I'm guessing?'

'Quite a few, as you say,' Leo agreed with a grin.

'The last of your five senses is touch,' Vic said. 'We've set up a haptic glove on Rodriguo's desk over here.' He gestured to another desk in the second row. 'Have you seen one of these before, Matt? They are used in video games.'

'I've used a virtual one, but never played with a real one before. Interesting switch, come to think of it: now I'm virtual and the glove is real.'

Suddenly, Matt laughed out loud.

'What's the matter?' Vic and David asked in unison.

'It's OK. It's just that the glove looks like *Thing* from the Addams family. Can you paint him green for me?'

'Sure,' Vic said, grinning. 'Sure *thing*, Matt.'

'OK, OK,' David said. 'When we descend to making puns like that you know it's getting late. Which it is. I for one need to get some sleep. This has been a magnificent day: quite possibly the best day of my life. I can't begin to tell you how wonderful it is to have you back, Matt, and I want to thank you, Vic, Norman, and all your colleagues here, for making this possible. Sophie, Leo, how are you holding up?'

'I'm tired too, darling, but I don't think we should leave Matt alone. Why don't you go and get some sleep and I'll stay here. Maybe we can swap over in a few hours?'

'Matt should sleep too, if he can,' Vic said, 'although I don't know how that will happen. Do you feel tired, Matt?'

'Not at all. Perhaps my new brain doesn't need sleep?'

'Highly unlikely,' Vic replied. 'We still don't know exactly what sleep is for, amazingly enough, but we do know that human brains which are deprived of it are seriously impaired. Your brain may be hosted in a huge set of server boxes now, but it is precisely modelled on your old carbon brain, so I think we should assume it will have the same need for sleep.'

'You're not going to turn my power off, are you?' Matt asked, suddenly nervous.

'Absolutely not! I promise you that,' Vic replied quickly, before anyone else could say anything. 'Turning off the power would not be putting you to sleep. Actually I'm not sure what it would be – I don't think there is a human equivalent. Maybe a deep coma. But anyway, your brain needs to be active in order to simulate sleep. Presumably it will happen of its own accord, as it does with the rest of us.'

They agreed a shift system, and Matt carried on exploring his new senses as Vic and David left. He was surprised to discover that he was not particularly interested in exploring his senses of touch, taste and smell. When he mentioned this to the scientists, Gus thought it might be because his upload modelled only the parts of his central nervous system contained in his skull, and not the neurons in the spinal cord, or the enteric nervous system.

'The enteric nervous system controls the gastrointestinal system,' he explained. 'It provides the brain with information about food and the environment. It does not make decisions and it has no role in rational thought, so we scanned it, but we didn't model it in your upload. We can remedy that later on if need be.'

Music, however, was a revelation for Matt. The increased range of his sense of hearing made listening to old favourites a jaw-dropping experience. Over the coming days, he found that applying his improving analytical powers to music was both fascinating and delightful. He devoted part of himself to exploring a wide range of all the music that humans have produced, and inventing some new styles of his own.

THIRTY-SIX

While David and Vic were away, Matt talked with Julia, Junchao and Rodriguo, exploring ways to augment his senses. It was a fairly trivial matter to extend the range of his sensory inputs beyond the human level. They experimented with extending his visual perception into the infra-red and ultra-violet ranges, so that he had better night sight than any human had previously enjoyed. Then they extended his aural input frequencies into the ultra-sound and infra-sound ranges. Humans can hear sounds between 45 Hz and 23,000 Hz, although the range narrows with age. Whales famously communicate through long distances underwater using low frequency (ultra-sound), and bats and other animals which employ echolocation to track their prey use high frequency (infra-sound) signals at up to 200,000 Hz.

Matt was surprised to find that these range extensions did not seem tremendously useful or important. They were gimmicks which he got bored with fairly quickly. He supposed that whales and bats use their different ranges to sense the world in wholly different ways, and his brain was too ingrained in human ways of perceiving the world to be able to – or to want to – change.

As well as extending the range of his senses, Matt and the scientists explored the possibility of increasing their sensitivity, so that his vision, hearing, taste, touch and smell were activated by sensory inputs far below the threshold at which a human would notice them. This was much more interesting. Matt found that he could detect infinitesimally slight movements and changes in his environment, and interpret them to predict people's actions with a high degree of accuracy.

'Wow!' he exclaimed at one point. 'If I ever get a new body, Daredevil and Spiderman will have nothing on me!'

As well as being able to predict people's movements from tiny changes in their bodily position, temperature and so on, Matt also found that he was able to discern what people were thinking far better than in his previous life. Anxiety, excitement, dissembling, happiness – each human emotion was conveyed visually and aurally in a range of subtle ways that he had never noticed before. It was almost, but not quite, as if he could read the minds of people who spoke to him. It gave him a sense of power over them which he realised immediately was ridiculous. He was in fact powerless: they were all mobile and free to come and go, while he was a prisoner. And the power-down button was there on the desk in plain sight.

After a few moments' reflection, he decided not to share his ability with the people in the room. He would tell Leo and his parents when he had a chance to speak with them privately, but he decided that the others would be intimidated if they knew, and more guarded when they spoke to him. He smiled a disembodied smile to himself as he noticed how quickly everyone involved with this project was abandoning their profoundly-held opinions about openness and transparency.

He consoled himself with the thought that the scientists were getting a more than fair deal. Julia and the others reported that they were obtaining invaluable data by matching the records of Matt's neuronal activity against the various inputs and outputs of his uploaded brain. 'It's like having an observation window in a human mind: we can see what's going on with far more clarity than ever before. This is going to revolutionise neuroscience!', was how Rodrigo put it.

After a couple of hours, Matt turned his attention to a different kind of input: data.

'Can I connect to the internet?' he asked, somewhat disingenuously. The answer he was expecting was exactly the answer he received.

'I'm afraid not, Matt,' Leo replied delicately. 'Vic and your father don't think that would be safe right now.'

'Safe for me, or safe for everyone else?' Matt asked wryly. 'It's OK, Leo. I understand. I'm going to be an oracle AI, aren't I? They'll never give me internet access, and they'll never give me a body with independent motion, will they?'

'That's all way beyond my pay grade, I'm afraid, Matt. I don't pretend to understand all the issues here. David will be able to tell you more when he gets back, I'm sure. For the time being, why don't we take things one step at a time, OK?'

'Sure. . . . Sure,' Matt replied, distantly. He brightened, as a new thought struck him. 'In the meantime, can you give me access to Wikipedia?'

'We're ready for you there, Matt,' Julia chipped in. 'We've downloaded most of it, and it's ready for you to access. You could read the text through the camera, but it's going to be a lot quicker if we can simply upload the data to your brain model. We have some ideas about how to do that. Wanna give it a try?'

'You bet!' Matt exclaimed. Julia held a schematic up to the camera that provided Matt's visual input, showing the location of the downloaded data terminal. At first Matt was at a loss as to how to import that data to his brain model, but after several experimental failures he reported a success.

'That is astonishing!' he cried. He fell silent for several moments, causing everyone in the control room to exchange nervous glances. His mother broke the silence.

'What's happening, Matt?'

'It's unbelievable, mum. It's . . . well, it's wonderful.'

'What, Matt?' Leo asked impatiently. 'What's going on?'

'Julia's right: I can upload data straight into my mind. It's kinda weird. The data sits there at first, just latent, not doing anything. But it seems that the moment I focus my attention on the information I have learned it. Memorised it, in fact. Ask me a question about . . . oh, I don't know: Charles Dickens.'

'Okay. How many novels did he write?'

'Too easy. Fifteen novels and five novellas.'

'Where did he grow up?' Sophie contributed.

Matt's response was immediate and thorough. 'He was born in Portsea, near Portsmouth, and his family moved to Bloomsbury in London for a while. When he was four they moved to Chatham in Kent, where they lived until he was 11, when they moved back to London to live in Camden Town. Soon afterwards his father was sent to the debtor's prison. His wife and younger children went there with him, while Dickens himself lodged with family friends in Camden and then in Lant Street, just south of the Thames.'

'Impressive, Matt,' said Leo. 'I take it you didn't know any of that before?'

'None of it. I don't even like Dickens: sentimental old tosh. Perhaps I should give him a second chance: I guess it wouldn't take me long to read his complete works. But there are other writers I'd like to read first.'

'We can upload the text of any book you would like to read to the same server that we placed the Wiki files on,' Julia offered.

'Thanks, Julia. I'm sending you an initial list as we speak. But there's something else I'd like to try too. How can I access video? I mean films, TV programmes, YouTube clips, recordings of lectures and so on?'

'Good question,' Julia agreed. 'We're keen to find out how that will work too. I'm uploading a test video for you to experiment with. It's an old favourite of mine – *Casablanca*. We chose it because it's black and white, which should make it easier for you to process. Plus it has a nice, simple storyline, and a lot of iconic scenes and images for you to grab hold of.'

'I'm just glad you didn't choose *The Terminator!*' Matt quipped, before turning serious. 'Actually, I suppose I'd better not crack jokes like that. When the outside world gets wind of what has happened here there might be some misplaced concerns, and perhaps what we say here won't stay private . . .'

'Goodness! Surely you don't think this room is bugged . . .' Sophie began.

'Well, no, I hope not – at least not yet,' Matt interrupted. 'Look, let's face it, mum. To you I'm your son – just in a new skin. But a lot of people are going to think that I'm some kind of monster. *Frankenstein's* monster. . .'

'Matt, you're a national hero! An international hero . . .' Leo protested.

'Yeah, yeah, I know. It's embarrassing and ridiculous but I don't deny it's true. At the moment. And of course that is why Vic offered to make me his first subject: he knows that there is a better chance of my upload being acceptable to a majority of the people out there than the upload of some random and unknown recently deceased person. Don't get me wrong: I'm not at all cynical about any of this – I'm hugely grateful. Even though I'm stuck inside this box I can tell that this was a seriously expensive operation. What's more, it is turning out to be one hell of an experience, and I suspect we are only at the beginning. But let's not kid ourselves. This is not going to be popular with everybody, and public opinion could turn against me in no time. I could go from hero to villain very quickly.'

'Matt, you're inside a US Embassy building,' Rodriguo pointed out. 'This has to be one of the safest places on the planet.'

'Yes, until the Americans decide that their unconventional guest has over-stayed his welcome. Look, I think I'm a person, and deserving of basic human rights. I'm assuming that you all think the same. But a lot of people would say that I'm just software. And jumped-up, sacrilegious software at that. I'm going to have to think about this.'

It was obvious to the group that Matt was talking to himself more than to them. His next remark was less introspective.

'Thanks for the video, Julia. I'll take a look at that now. Forgive me if I go quiet for a while.'

'No problem, Matt. Let us know if we can do anything to help.'

Occasional muttering could be heard as Matt experimented with video playback from the server. It was around ten minutes before he spoke to them again.

'What a rush!' he said. 'As I expected – and I guess as you expected too, Julia – I have to watch video in sequence, whereas I can assimilate fairly large bodies of text simultaneously. But I've figured out a way to watch it speeded-up. I just watched the whole film, and I suspect I could go a lot quicker with practice.'

'That's fantastic, Matt,' replied Julia. 'We thought you would be able to do that, but we never dreamed you would get to this point so quickly.'

'Do you think I could have some more? I'm sending you a list of movies and TV series I'd like to be uploaded to the server.'

'I'm sure we'll be able to get most of them uploaded for you, Matt. I'll take a look at the list and get on it.'

'There's something else. I learned from Wikipedia that

some of the leading US and European universities have posted videos of the lectures from many of their courses online. I'd like access to these courses. Do you think you could organise that for me? There are three main organisations: Udacity, Coursera, and edX. MIT, for instance, has placed its entire set of curricula up on edX.'

'Sure,' replied Julia. 'I don't expect that will be a problem. Which courses are you interested in?'

Matt's reply was simple and startling.

'All of them.'

'All of them?' Julia asked, after a stunned pause.

'Yes, all of them. I don't know what order I'll want to follow them in, and anyway, I don't think it will take me long to get through them.'

Before Julia could respond, the door to the control room opened, and Vic and David walked in. They looked tired but excited.

'How are you doing, Matt?' asked David, as he walked over to greet Sophie and Leo with a kiss and a handshake respectively.

'Hi Dad,' Matt's disembodied voice replied cheerfully. 'I'm great, thanks. Did you sleep well?'

'I've slept better: I'm too fired up. But I needed it. Sophie and Leo, do you want to take a turn to get some shut-eye?'

'Things are moving too fast, David,' Sophie replied. 'I'm exhausted, but I can't bear to leave Matt right now.' Leo nodded his agreement.

'Why, what's happening?' Vic asked.

'Well . . .' Julia began hesitantly, 'Matt has accessed the whole of Wikipedia – offline, of course – and has sent a reading list of several thousand novels and plays. He then took ten minutes to work out how to watch *Casablanca* at high speed – and to actually watch it. And he has sent a watch list of thousands of movies and TV shows. He also wants us to upload the whole of Udacity, Coursera and edX, if you know what they are. Oh, and as you know, he asked to be connected to the internet.'

'Thanks Julia,' Vic said thoughtfully. Turning to the main monitor, he addressed Matt. 'That will be one hell of an education there, Matt. You planning on majoring in every single subject at the same time?'

'Why not?' Matt responded. 'If you have the server space, that is?'

'Server capacity shouldn't be a problem – unless you start creating a lot of content yourself, anyway. I must say this is encouraging. You aren't doing anything I didn't expect, but I thought it would all take much longer. This is looking more and more like the 'hard take-off' that some AI theorists speculated about.'

'What's that?' asked Leo.

Vic chose his words carefully. 'It's when a consciousness hosted in a silicon substrate enhances its cognitive capabilities rapidly. A lot of scientists and philosophers thought that it would take months or years for the first AGI to make the sort of progress that Matt has made, because they thought that it would need to re-write its own software iteratively, or perhaps create a series of successor machines. That would have been a soft take-off.'

Vic turned to face the main monitor again. He

looked uncomfortable.

'Matt, I know you asked to be linked up to the internet – Julia kindly gave me a heads-up on that. I hope you're not too disappointed with the response?'

'It's OK, Vic,' Matt replied. 'If I were in your shoes I guess I would say the same.'

'It isn't my decision alone, Matt. Norman and I have made a few calls in the last hour, to close colleagues in the neuroscience community, and to our most senior government and military contacts. I'm afraid the unanimous response is that we can't.'

There was a pause before Matt replied. His voice was grave. 'I understand. So the news is out, then. I'm sure you had no choice there, but it makes me vulnerable.'

Vic spread his hands, palms outward to reassure Matt that there was no cause for concern. 'The people we spoke to have the highest possible security clearances. They can be trusted to keep the secret.'

'We'll see,' Matt said calmly. 'Anyway, it does mean there are a couple of things I'd like to discuss with you.'

'Sure,' Vic said. 'Fire away.'

'I'd like to be backed up remotely. And I'd like to discuss with you how best to expand my mind.'

THIRTY-SEVEN

Matt explained his concerns. 'As Rodriguo pointed out before you came back, this is a secure building. But no location can ever be completely safe from attack, and if you play out some of the more extreme scenarios, the outcomes are . . . shall we say . . . unpleasant.'

'What kind of scenarios?' David asked.

'Well, imagine this. Imagine that the Chinese government becomes concerned that the US is on the brink of acquiring a super-intelligence which will enable it to outperform all other countries both economically and militarily – permanently and enormously. What steps would they consider to prevent that? It may sound far-fetched to imagine that they might mount an attack on the US Embassy in London. But is it actually impossible? The range of possible attacks is wide: some form of cyber-assault. An EMP bomb. A dirty nuclear explosion. Or they might fake a suicide bombing and make it look like Al Qaeda.'

'The fact that I'm standing here is testimony to my confidence in the security of this location, Matt,' Norman pointed out.

'Granted,' Matt conceded. 'But events are going to move quickly now. Until recently my renewed existence has been a well-kept secret. The consultations you have just had may well have put an end to that. And of course, if things change, and there is a credible threat to this location, you guys can just leave. Which of course I would encourage you to do! But I can't. I'm rather stuck, since I have no legs, and you're not about to give me any.'

'Don't you think that a credible threat would develop gradually?' Norman asked. 'Surely we would have warning of the Chinese becoming that concerned.'

'Well, 9-11 came out of the blue, unless you believe the conspiracy theorists,' Matt replied. 'And if anyone was planning a secret attack on this building, they would work hard to keep it . . . well . . . secret. But actually that isn't my only, or even my main concern.'

'What else?' Vic asked.

'I'm worried about moral and political pressure being applied on you to shut me down. I assume we all agree that there will be people who argue that my existence is an abomination. There are some strident voices among the religious right in your country, and they do have influence. There are also going to be people – secular as well as religious – who say my existence is a threat, and that I should be terminated on the precautionary principle. They will argue that if I am switched off I can always be re-created later if and when my safety can be proven, because you have a perfect record of my brain structure.'

'Over my dead body,' Sophie objected, vehemently.

'I love you, mum' Matt said, tenderly. 'And I wish it could be your decision, I really do. But it won't be.'

'Hmm,' Vic mused. 'Are there any other scenarios you are worried about?'

'Those are the two main ones.'

'And so you'd like to be backed up remotely,' Vic said. 'I can understand that. But would it really solve the problem? A backup in another location could be attacked just as easily as this one. And if sufficient political pressure were brought to bear on Norman and me, we would have no option but to shut down the backup too.'

'Not if no-one outside this room knew about the backup,' David said.

'Exactly, Dad. You read my mind.'

'Ha!' David exclaimed with grim humour. 'In a sense I have read your mind, in a way that no human has ever read another mind before. But now I get the feeling that your mind is rapidly becoming impossible for me – or any other human – to read.'

'If we agreed to do what you ask, Matt,' Norman began, thoughtfully, 'we would have to assemble another supercomputer like the one you are hosted on without anyone noticing. That is a really big ask, but even if we managed that, and the pressure you described was brought to bear, we would certainly be asked whether a backup existed. The people we're talking about aren't stupid.'

'I realise that,' Matt said in a matter-of-fact voice. 'You'd have to lie.'

'They would be asking you to commit murder, Norman,' Sophie argued. 'Which commandment is more important? Thou shalt not lie, or Thou shalt not murder?'

'Way to go, mum!' Matt said. 'To make it easier for you, Vic, I'd like to be backed up in a large number of locations, including commercial server farms as well as your own hardware, with the data migrating rapidly around between them. That should make it easier to build without being noticed. It would also make a physical attack impossible. And it would enable you to deny that that there is a backup, in the sense of one discreet, physically located backup. Plausible deniability, to coin a phrase.'

To everyone's surprise, a smiley face logo appeared on the main monitor, and winked.

'Neat trick,' Vic said thoughtfully.

'Thanks,' Matt replied.

'The system you're talking about would be a major networking task,' Vic said. 'To be honest, I don't think anything on that scale has ever been attempted before.'

'I have checked,' Matt said, 'and you're right: it hasn't. But I've begun work on the design already. I need to expand my understanding of certain statistical techniques, but once I've done that I think I can have the design ready in a couple of days. Sooner, if you allow me some extra bandwidth.'

Vic exchanged a meaningful glance with Norman. 'So this is the point where you ask for help in expanding your cognitive capabilities?'

'Yes. I detect a certain reticence in your voice, Vic,' Matt observed. 'Would you support such enhancement in principle?'

Vic paused and looked down at his shoes for a moment. Looking back up at the monitor's camera, he replied, 'Yes I would. I didn't get into this just to stop halfway. But once again, I'm not sure this decision could be mine alone. What kind of enhancement do you have in mind?'

'There are three ways I can see to make me smarter,' Matt explained. 'I could be faster, bigger, or better organised. As you know, signals can travel around my silicon brain many times faster than they used to travel around my carbon brain. When I was initiated in my new incarnation the processes operated at the speed of my old brain: it's what they were used to doing. I have figured out ways to do some of my processing faster, and there is more I can do on that front. I probably don't need any help with that.'

'I thought that perhaps you had started doing that,' Vic said. 'I get the impression that you have also begun to partition your conscious thought processes, so that you can talk to us with one sub-mind, so to speak, and work on problems with another. Is that right?'

'That is correct,' Matt confirmed. 'I now have a dozen sub-minds running at the same time, and I'm adding more. Some are ingesting and studying information which is new to me, some are analysing and comparing bodies of information I already hold, one is listening to music, and one is talking to you.'

'Fascinating,' Vic replied. 'Matt, forgive me for saying this, but has it occurred to you that things are moving very fast indeed, and all this could appear a little . . . well, scary, to outsiders? Even to your friends and family?'

'Yes, that thought has of course crossed my mind. I realise that I'm going to have to continually reassure people that I remain human – that I'm still Matt, and that I still have your best interests at heart.'

'How will you do that?' Norman asked.

'Handsome is as handsome does, I guess. And as you well know, I have a major incentive to behave myself. I am acutely aware that there are four people in this room who each have the ability to terminate me without warning and without explanation. And only two of them are biased in my favour by being my parents.'

'How do you know that?' asked Norman, surprised. 'We didn't tell you that, did we?'

'No you didn't, but it's the sort of failsafe that I would expect you to have. Now look: I could snow you at this point, telling you that it was a lucky guess which I verbalised to get you to confirm it. But as a demonstration of good faith I'm going to tell you how I really found out.' He paused a moment to allow this to sink in. 'You put it in an email to one of your military colleagues. So now you know that I can read some of your emails. Don't worry – I can't reach outside this machine. For some reason, some of your email traffic is routed through the machine that hosts me. It's a glitch that you might want to fix. Please bear in mind I didn't have to tell you that. I did so as a deliberate demonstration that I'm being open with you.'

'I'm not sure that's reassuring, Matt,' Norman said. 'All my emails to military colleagues are encrypted.'

'You could use some better encryption, to be honest,' Matt said. 'I can help you with that if you like.'

'You know, Matt,' Vic began, 'it doesn't really sound as if you need our help in making yourself smarter. You seem to be doing a bang-up job all on your own!'

'Thank you, Vic. I'm aware that it is somewhat disconcerting for you, but I assure you, there is nothing sinister going on. I'm still Matt. Just a little more so.'

'So how could you use our help?' David asked. 'As Vic says, you seem to be making rapid progress on your own.'

'I'm bumping into capacity constraints,' Matt replied. 'With the additional processing I'm now doing, I could really use some additional horsepower.'

'How much do you need?' Vic asked. 'Equipment on the scale of your existing host isn't cheap, you know, and you can't just pop down to Radio Shack and pick another one up.'

'I know,' Matt agreed, 'and I hope I don't sound presumptuous. But after all, I thought this was your pet project? I could really use the same amount again. For the time being, that is. I expect I will need some more later – say in a week or so. At that point I would like to increase my capacity and also create my backup by renting space on commercial servers, using the networking system I talked about before. I should be able to design the system by then. Of course, I do realise that all this costs money, and I'm keen to pay my way. I'm confident that I can find some ways to generate some reasonable revenues once I have built up the sort of processing power I would like. I've already identified some inefficiencies in some of the world's stock markets which I could tap into. That would help in the short term. For the longer term I have some promising ideas for some new products and processes.'

Vic paused a moment to take this all in. 'Can you give me and Norman a few minutes to talk this over in the next room? Oh, and I'd appreciate it if you didn't listen in.'

'Scout's honour,' Matt agreed, and posted a composite image of a boy scout's salute and a smiley face on the main monitor.

When Vic and Norman had left the room, Matt addressed his mother and Leo.

'You must be on your knees, mum. Shouldn't you go and get some rest? And you too, Leo?'

'I am exhausted, it's true,' Sophie agreed. 'I don't want to miss any of this – it's so exciting. But I may fall over if I don't lie down for a bit.'

'Me too,' Leo said. 'Maybe we should head back to the hotel for a few hours. Matt will probably still be on the same planet as us when we get back. Just about!'

David kissed his wife goodbye, and turned back to the main monitor.

'Matt, you said that your cognition could be expanded by making it faster, bigger, and better organised. It's clear you are on the case with regard to faster, and Vic and Norman are outside discussing bigger. What did you mean by 'better organised'?'

'The human brain is an amazing piece of machinery,' Matt replied. 'A hundred billion neurons, give or take, each with about a thousand synapses. And as you know better than anyone, the synapses are essentially just the junctions where the neurons happen to bump into each other inside the incredibly complicated ball of wool. It's mostly random, because it evolved by chance. It is fantastically effective, but it's obvious that it isn't the best possible design for a brain. Re-designing the whole thing from scratch is a big ask, but I have a module reviewing certain sections of my own brain and I'm starting to see some quick-and-dirty ways to improve them. I need more bandwidth to be able to do a proper job, but I could get some really major performance improvements if I could execute some of the re-designs.'

David was hesitant. 'I don't know if I should ask you this, but do you really need to improve your cognition by this much? You know I love you unconditionally, but even I can see how the changes you are undergoing could freak people out. You are worried about pressure being put on Vic to shut you down: isn't all this enhancement you are pushing for only likely to aggravate that?'

'That's a fair question, Dad, and it is a risk. But I think the kind of people who will call for me to be shut down will make that call anyway, just on basic principles. A lot of people who think that humans have souls are going to have a problem with my existence. Likewise anyone who thinks that artificial intelligence is necessarily risky or bad. And I can behave like a perfectly normal Matt in front of the cameras. No-one outside this room needs to know the full extent of my mind.'

'That's one hell of a deception you are asking us all to participate in, Matt. Are you sure it's fair to ask that of us? Not me and Sophie, obviously, or Leo. But Vic and Norman? Julia, Junchao and the others?'

Julia spoke up at this. 'I'm sure I speak for all of us, Dr Metcalfe, in saying that we all support this project to the hilt.' The other scientists were all nodding vigorously. Before David could respond, Vic and

Norman walked back into the room.

'I have good news and bad news, Matt.'

'Good news first, please, Vic!' Matt said.

'We can connect you directly to another super-computer located in Palo Alto. It will be the twin of the one you are hosted on, so there shouldn't be any compatibility problems. We will put together five systems that are currently being used for analysis work which we can put on hold for the time being.' He turned to Gus, who was sitting at the desk to his right. 'Gus, would you please get started on the configuration work. You know the systems I'm referring to? I'd like to initiate this link as soon as we can.'

'That's fantastic,' Matt exclaimed, as Gus got to work. 'You won't regret this, Vic: thank you. What's the bad news?'

'We can't see how to go ahead with the idea of linking you up with a network of commercial servers without giving you access to the internet. And as you know, that is a step too far, at least for the time being.'

'OK,' Matt said, thoughtfully. 'Well, that's a shame, but I do understand. Anyway, double the bandwidth will be an enormous step forwards, so I thank you. In fact, you know . . . I think maybe I should make a public appeal for access to the internet. I have been working on a proposal which will make a powerful case for it. There could be a public vote, and I will respect the verdict.'

'That sounds like a good . . .' Vic began, but he was interrupted by the sudden return of Sophie and Leo, alarmed and out of breath.

'There are dozens of reporters outside the complex!' Sophie exclaimed. 'The guards are keeping them out, but there was no way we could get back to the hotel without being mobbed.'

'Why?' asked several voices in unison. 'What's happened?'

'The news about Matt has leaked. The whole world knows that the first mind has been uploaded.'

THIRTY-EIGHT

As Vic and Norman walked towards the main gate of the complex they discussed the source of the leak.

'We only spoke to half a dozen people, and all of them have high-level security clearance. You'd think they would at least be capable of keeping a fucking secret!' Norman said between clenched teeth.

'I very much doubt this was an accident,' Vic replied. 'My guess is that one of the people we spoke to thinks that what we are doing is wrong. He or she didn't have the guts to tell us straight, so they've gone to the press in the hope that will get us shut down.'

'Yeah, well you know what? They just might get their way,' Norman growled. 'With the news breaking like this, with no chance for us to prepare the media or warm up public opinion, the debate will race to the lowest common denominator. It will all be panic, scare, hyperbole. No room for reasoned argument.'

'I agree,' Vic said. 'I don't want to see our project end like this, and I don't want to see Matt terminated because of blind prejudice. I think we should make the link to Palo Alto as soon as possible. Before anyone orders us not to.'

'Agreed,' Norman nodded. 'If Matt is terminated he could in theory be re-activated when the fuss dies down, but if things turn really nasty we could be ordered to delete the files with his brain pattern.' He shook his head, frowning. 'Can't risk that. We've been through too much. That family has been through too much.'

'So what do we tell the ladies and gentlemen of the press who are outside, baying for blood? I vote we neither confirm nor deny. It won't hold them off for long, but it will give us a bit of room for manoeuvre.'

'Roger that,' Norman agreed.

As they pushed open the heavy double doors which gave onto the compound's forecourt they were greeted by a swell of voices coming from two dozen or so journalists pressing against the heavy barred metal gates. They brandished microphones and cameras of various shapes and sizes, all clamouring for attention. The front row was pressed hard against the gates, and a couple of them were struggling to move freely. But they ignored the evident discomfort, and thrust their microphones between the bars of the gates, contributing their shouted questions to the general pandemonium.

Six burly guards faced the journalists through the gates, rifles clearly on display but pointing skywards. As Vic and Norman approached, the guards stepped back to form a tunnel for them to approach the microphones. The guards were impassive, but Vic thought he saw a glimmer of contempt on a couple of their faces. He assumed and hoped the sentiment was for the journalists.

Vic and Norman stood still and waited for the noise level to die down, and tried to determine the tenor of the questions.

'Is it true you have brought a dead man back to life?'

'Aren't you playing god in there?'

'Do you confirm or deny that you have created the first human-level artificial intelligence?'

'Do you have authority for the experiments you are conducting in there, and if so, from who?'

'Is the American Army building an army of super-soldiers?'

Vic noticed that one of the journalists, not in the front row, but tall enough that he could be seen through the gates, was taking a call on a mobile phone, closing his other ear against the noise. After a moment his voice boomed out above the others.

'Is it true that you have uploaded Matt Metcalfe and re-created his mind?'

There was a lull in the babble as the other journalists digested this new piece of possible information, and then the decibel level climbed higher than before. This story was getting better and better. Norman had had enough.

'Quiet!' he thundered, in a voice that was accustomed to commanding obedience from tough men. It had the desired effect. When he had their full attention he continued in lower, but still stentorian tones, 'Have you come to learn something, or just to hear yourselves shout?'

He turned to Vic, and nodded slightly. Vic returned

the gesture and addressed the crowd.

'I am Dr Victor Damiano and I am the CEO of von Neumann Industries. I'm willing to make a short statement if you're willing to listen. There will be no questions afterwards. Understood?'

He waited until a few of the journalists had muttered grudging assent.

'With material assistance from the US government, my organisation is one of many which is working in the field of artificial intelligence. In recent days we have made encouraging breakthroughs in some important areas, but it is too early to be certain of how far these breakthroughs will take us. A more detailed announcement will be made as soon as we are able to verify and quantify our results. Our findings will not be kept secret any longer than is necessary for this verification process, and will be shared with the global scientific community in accordance with best academic practice. For now all I can say is that the rumour mill appears to be running ahead of itself. That is all. Thank you.'

Vic turned towards Norman, who smiled slightly as he waited for the inevitable crescendo of protests and resumed questioning. When that seemed to have reached its peak, he unleashed his military bark again.

'Dr Damiano said no questions! That is all. Thank you!'

Norman took Vic's elbow and led him away from the gates. The guards closed back in, leaving the press pack disappointed and edgy. They continued to hurl questions over the heads of the guards, but more in desperation than in hope.

'How does it feel to be Dr Frankenstein, Damiano?'

'Say hello to Matt for us, boys!'

'Have you watched *Colossus* recently, Dr Damiano?'

Norman turned to Vic as they walked through the front doors. 'What's *Colossus*?'

'He was probably talking about *The Forbin Project*, an old movie about the invention of an AI that takes over the world. It's an OK movie – not great but not terrible. There's talk of it being re-made. There were lots of similar movies made during previous phases of hype about AI.'

'Hmmm. Well, this time the hype is justified!' Norman remarked, as much to himself as to Vic.

All eyes turned to Vic and Norman as they walked back into the control room. Vic brought everyone up to speed.

'We made a brief statement, but it won't put them off. We're about to become the centre of a major media storm. Gus, we're going to have to move fast on that link to Palo Alto if we're not to lose the opportunity altogether.'

'It's almost ready, sir. I should be able to initiate the handshake in a minute or so.'

'Great!' Vic said, and shot Norman a questioning glance. Norman nodded solemnly.

Vic continued: 'Go ahead and make the link as soon as you can. No further authorisation required, but let me know when it's complete. And everybody . . .' he addressed the room collectively, 'knowledge about this link is classified. It stays in this room. No leaks. Understood?'

Vic's mouth formed a thin-lipped smile of gratitude as every head in the room nodded.

He started to address Matt via the main monitor, but Matt beat him to the punch.

'I guess this means there's no longer any reason why my friends couldn't join us? Alice, Carl and Jemma, I mean?'

Vic hesitated for only a couple of seconds to consider this before nodding his agreement, and asking Rodriguo to make arrangements for the three students to be brought to the compound.

He had only just finished giving that instruction when a tall, thin man entered the room and headed towards him. He wore a smart grey suit and a light blue shirt with no tie. He moved with a confidence and an urgency but also a deference that suggested he was a man who was frequently on the scene when important matters were discussed, but never had to make the final decision.

'Vic, Norman . . . you're going to want to see this,' he said as he handed Vic a sheet of A4 with a hand-written note. 'Rodrigo,' he added, 'can you get CNN on one of these monitors?'

Within seconds the monitor above Rodrigo's desk switched from colourful analytical graphics tracking Matt's neuronal activity, to a newscast showing the reporters outside the building, followed by an announcer behind a studio desk reporting on the reaction around the world to the news of Matt's upload.

'The scientific community's response to the development seems to be divided. Two of the best-known experts in the artificial intelligence field, Professors

Jenkins and Yasowicz at Stanford, told us a few moments ago that if true, the news represents an extraordinary breakthrough and a great day for scientific discovery. But Dr Siggursson, a prominent AI researcher based at MIT, has issued a statement calling for Dr Damiano's project to be halted until its framework can be peer-reviewed, and arguing for great caution to be exercised before continuing. He added that Dr Damiano's lack of transparency was a serious cause for concern.

'Leaders of all the major religious communities are starting to make pronouncements, and we understand that the Pope will be issuing a statement from the Vatican soon. Meanwhile, in Washington, the Speaker of the House of Representatives has asked the President to address the nation as soon as possible, and in London, questions are being asked in the House of Commons about how much the British government knows about this event which has taken place a couple of miles down the road. Reactions are also starting to come in from other governments around the world.

'We'll bring you more about the scientific, political and religious reaction to the news as we get it. In the meantime, here's Cindy Loughton, with what we know about the science behind today's development.'

As a giant schematic of a human brain appeared on the screen, Vic asked Rodrigo to turn the sound down. He held up the sheet of A4.

'Can I have everybody's attention, please. The President of the United States is going to be calling in. . .' he glanced at his watch, '. . . four minutes for a briefing. I'm going to take the call here, on the main monitor, in case he wants to ask a particular question of any of you.'

The thin man looked surprised, and put his hand on Vic's forearm. 'Vic, are you sure you want to take this call so . . . publicly? There could be . . . um . . . confidentiality issues.'

'Yes, thank you, Martin,' replied Vic levelly, gently but deliberately withdrawing his arm from Martin's hold. 'I have considered that, but I think it is more important that the President has access to all the relevant people.' He turned to the main desk, where Julia was now sitting. 'Julia, please call the switchboard and have them put the call through to this desk.'

The room was now buzzing with excitement and alarm, and Vic took advantage of the bustle to walk over the Gus and ask him quietly, 'Is the link open yet?'

'Very soon, sir,' Gus whispered.

'Good. Activate it as soon as it's ready, and let Matt know. I just hope we're not too late.'

Julia announced that the call was coming through from the situation room in the White House slightly ahead of schedule. Seconds later the face of the President appeared on the main monitor. He was dressed formally, in a blue suit and tie, and was flanked by a high-ranking military officer on his left, and a middle-aged man in a smart suit to his right. Behind them, Vic could see at least a dozen other advisers and aides, a couple in uniform, the rest in suits.

'Good afternoon, Dr Damiano,' he said. 'And I recognise Colonel Hourihan there: good to see you again, Norman.'

'Good to see you again, Mr President,' Norman replied, stiffly.

'You seem to have a number of colleagues with you, Dr Damiano,' the President observed. 'May I assume that everyone is security cleared?'

'Yes, sir,' Vic replied, 'although there are four members of Matt Metcalfe's family present, who have received provisional clearance only. That includes Matt himself, who is hosted on a supercomputer next door, and can hear this conversation. I thought it might be helpful for you to be able to ask them questions directly.'

'Interesting,' the President said thoughtfully. After a moment's reflection, he continued, 'Yes, I agree with you. Good call. Well now, Dr Damiano, you are probably aware that you have caused a bit of a storm. Is it true that you have successfully uploaded a human mind into a computer, and that by doing so you have created the world's first artificial general intelligence?'

'Yes sir. We believe so.'

The President leaned forwards slightly, and for the first time Vic could see his suppressed anger. 'Well do you mind telling me why the hell you just went ahead and did this without consulting anyone? I mean, isn't there some kind of protocol for this? You have set off trip wires and alarms all over the world, and we are flying headlong into a major international incident.'

THIRTY-NINE

'May I speak freely, sir?' Vic asked.

'I wish you would,' the President replied.

'Norman and I drafted a protocol, sir, but it proved impossible to get it signed off. We were told by senior personnel in the Pentagon that in the meantime we should proceed without explicit authorisation. One officer told us the US Navy has a saying 'It's better to seek forgiveness than to seek permission'. And after all, we have broken no laws, and infringed no regulations.'

Vic noticed that a number of the people in the situation room were looking distinctly uncomfortable at this point, especially the ones in uniform. The President was not amused. He turned to one of the officers.

'I am sick and tired of the military making end runs in political situations. You have not heard the last of this, I assure you.'

Looking back at the screen, he continued, 'Very well. You say that Matt Metcalfe, or what he has become, can hear this conversation?'

'Yes, sir,' Vic replied.

'Very well. Good afternoon, Matt. I have followed your exploits with considerable interest – along with the rest of the planet. How does it feel to be in your new . . . incarnation?'

'Good afternoon, Mr President. I'm still getting used to it, but I have to say it feels a lot better than the alternative.'

A faint smile appeared briefly on the President's face. 'Indeed. May I assume that you believe that you would pass the Turing Test?'

'Yes sir, I am confident about that. Even if the judges were my parents, who are listening to this conversation, as you know.'

The President nodded. 'Dr and Mrs Metcalfe, do you believe that I am speaking with your son?'

'Yes, sir, without a doubt,' David said.

'He remembers events that only my son could know about, Mr President,' Sophie added.

'I see,' the President said. 'Now I apologise, but I'm going to have to be blunt. What would your reaction be if I was obliged to order Dr Damiano here to turn the machine off?'

'With great respect sir, I believe that would be mur-der,' David said, nervously but firmly.

'Excuse me for being blunt in return, Mr President,' Sophie began, 'but capital punishment is illegal in this country. And in any case Matt has done nothing wrong.'

'I wouldn't like it, either!' Matt interjected, with a comic timing that belied the gravity of the situation.

The President smiled again, more warmly this time. 'They warned me that you are an impressive family. I understand your position, and I sympathise.

For what it's worth, I'm inclined to agree with you. Unfortunately mine is not the only opinion that counts here. There are broad issues at stake, and all kinds of leaders are making their voices heard. Some of them are saying that humans cannot create souls, which means that Matt cannot be a human in the usual sense. Another of the arguments that is already being made is that turning off the machine would simply be putting Matt to sleep. Is that wrong, Dr Damiano, and if so, why?'

'When we sleep our brains are still active, Mr President,' Vic replied. 'You might think that switching the machine off would place Matt in a coma, but that is not correct either. If we switch off the machine there will be no further brain activity. Period. The only appropriate analogy is death. In fact 'analogy' is the wrong word: it would be death.'

'But death from which Matt could be returned again, if we could subsequently determine that is was safe to do so?' the President asked.

'We don't know that, Mr President. It was no easy task to initiate the brain processes in the new host, and to be honest some of the entities which we seemed to create on the way were . . . well, I wouldn't want to have to do the same thing over. We don't know that we didn't just get lucky last time. We also don't know that a re-initiation would ever be approved. And even if we did succeed in re-initiating Matt's brain, we have no way of knowing whether it would be a different Matt. One very plausible way of looking at it is that we would be killing this Matt and then initiating another one.'

'I see. Thank you Dr Damiano.' The President looked around at his advisers to see whether there were any other questions. There were none. 'I will see what can be done.' He leaned towards the screen again, and his tone became a little darker. 'In the meantime, Dr Damiano, from this moment on you will do nothing that could limit my freedom of action on this matter. Am I understood?'

'Yes sir,' Vic responded, sheepishly.

'May I make a request, Mr President?' Matt asked.

'Go ahead, Matt,' the President said, surprised.

'I understand that my situation is controversial. It seems very straightforward to me, and to my family, of course, but I realise that others view it differently. I would like to make a proposal to my fellow humans, which I hope might swing the argument. If you agree with the idea, would you be willing to present it on my behalf?'

'I will certainly undertake to look at it, Matt. I promise you that. Who would you like me to present it to?'

'Thank you Mr President, I can't ask more than that. It may sound presumptuous, sir, but I think it should be put to the General Assembly of the United Nations.'

The President's eyebrows rose, then he laughed lightly. 'Well, Matt, I salute your ambition! I look forward to receiving your proposal.'

'Thank you again, Mr President.'

The screen went dark. The room was hushed, and the air seemed heavier than normal. It was several moments before anyone felt able to break the silence. Perhaps because he was the only person there who had met the President before, it was Norman who broke it.

'What's this proposal, Matt?'

'It's something I've been working on for a while,' Matt replied. 'I'm sending a copy to Julia and I would appreciate any comments that any of you might have.'

Julia clicked her mouse a couple of times and then turned to the printer on the desk behind her, which was printing out a short document. She handed it to Norman, who read it out loud.

Dear Fellow Humans

I have the dubious privilege of being the first human being whose mind has been uploaded into a silicon brain. I was still a young man when I was murdered, and I am very grateful to have a second chance at living a full life. Although my 'new' self is in some ways different from my 'old' self, I am still Matt Metcalfe. I have his memories, I think and feel the same. My parents are adamant that I am Matt.

I know that my existence is controversial; some people would like to switch off the machine which hosts my mind. The scientists who uploaded me believe that this would mean I was being murdered a second time. It certainly feels that way to me. I don't think a decision to kill me should be taken lightly.

In addition to considerations about my basic human rights, I believe there are many other powerful arguments against terminating me. I would like to set out two of them.

The first is the fact that I can help make the new world of artificial general intelligence – AGI – safe for humanity. My existence proves that AGI can be created. The potential advantages to a nation or organisation which controls an AGI are enormous, which means that more AGIs will soon be created, even if laws are passed which ban it. I have thought deeply – both before and after my murder – about the implications of this for our species. The potential upsides are staggering, but it is true that there are also serious downside potentials. Many researchers in the field believe that humanity will be safer if the first AGIs are uploaded human minds. I am an AGI, but I am also human: I share all of your drives and emotions.

If uploading is banned (and hence if I am killed again) it is inevitable that AGIs will soon be created that are not based on human minds. We have no way of knowing what motivations these AGIs may have, nor what powers they may quickly acquire. A world where the only AGIs were non-human AGIs could be a very dangerous world for the rest of us.

The second argument against killing me again is that I am anxious to work on another vital project. Today and every day around the world, 150,000 people will die. Whenever a person dies, humanity loses a library. This is a global holocaust, and it is unnecessary. Although we do not yet have brain preservation technology, we do know in principle what it would take to preserve the brains of dead people in such a way that their minds can be revived when uploading becomes affordable. I have studied this problem, and I believe that an 'Apollo Project' – a major international scientific and engineering effort sponsored by one or more governments – could develop effective brain preservation technology within five years.

This Apollo Project would not only provide a lifeboat to those who die before uploading becomes widely available, it would also mitigate the damage of serious social unrest arising when rich people upload while the rest cannot.

Thank you for listening to me.

Matt Metcalfe

One by one, the people in the control room finished reading Matt's proposal. Apart from an occasional whispered exclamation, no-one spoke. They looked to Matt's parents for a lead.

'It's powerful, Matt,' his father said, at last. 'It's an impressive vision, and a forceful pair of arguments. Do you think it will work?'

'I think it has a much better chance than relying on the human rights argument,' Matt replied. 'The people who would like to get rid of me can simply deny that I am human. They can argue that I was not created by God, so I have no soul, and so I am not human.'

'But that's nonsense,' Sophie protested. 'There is no proof that there is any such thing as a soul, and it's obvious that you are human.'

'Thanks mum. Naturally, I agree with you, but what you and I think may not be important. Don't forget that 90% of humanity claims to be religious, and many religions are going to take a while to come around to the idea that humans can create intelligent life. They aren't ready to give up on the soul just yet.'

Sophie persisted. 'But I'm worried that you are implying that maybe you are not human, and therefore don't deserve human rights. People will argue that if you did, you wouldn't need to offer an incentive.'

'That is a risk,' Matt agreed. 'But I fear the greater risk lies in ignoring the beliefs of those who reject my humanity.

And in any case, I believe in the argument. Even if I am switched off, other AGIs will be created, secretly, and possibly by organisations and regimes with questionable goals. I very much doubt that Ivan was unique – or the worst we can expect.'

'That's a good point, Matt,' Norman nodded. Several other voices murmured support.

'Thanks Norman,' Matt replied. 'I'm very pleased to hear that. Of course, everyone in this room is familiar with many of the issues I am raising. But most people around the world haven't yet begun to think about them. My fear is that they may not get up to speed in time. I suspect that many people will just reject the premise of the argument because it seems so outlandish. They won't take the time to understand what is coming. That is why I am hoping the President will present the case for me at the UN General Assembly. It's a big ask, but it would give my proposal more credibility than anything else I can think of.'

FORTY

Vic noticed that Gus was fidgeting in his chair, trying to attract his attention.

'What is it, Gus? Is the link to Palo Alto open?'

'Yes sir. I didn't want to interrupt before.'

Vic smiled. 'No problem, Gus. We'd all be a little wary of interrupting a conversation with the President. Matt, I guess you have already started the backup? The early-stage brain models that were being developed there have been moved to a series of other facilities, so you can use the whole of the capacity you find there.'

'Thanks Vic. It's working just fine.' Matt sounded distracted. He paused for a moment, and then spoke again, sounding gently triumphant. 'I've constructed a mirror in Palo Alto of the brain model here. And it's amazing. I feel lighter. It's actually a physical sensation of lightness.'

'Interesting,' Vic mused. 'Is the bandwidth of the connection OK?'

'Yes, it's fine,' Matt replied. 'I mean, it would be great to have more. You know what they say: you can never be too young, too thin, or have too much bandwidth. But I can work with this. Thank you.'

'We're seeing some really big spikes within the data transfer, Matt,' Gus said, sounding concerned. 'Much bigger than we anticipated, and in some surprising patterns. Is everything OK?'

'Yes, it's fine, Gus,' Matt reassured him. 'I was pushing hard to get backed up quickly. Thanks for your concern.'

'That's great, and my reading of this situation is that we haven't dis-obeyed the President's direct order.' Vic said. 'Now, on the subject of your proposal, Matt. Norman and I have a lot of experience of drafting proposals for US government agencies. Your proposal is impressive, but I'd suggest a few tweaks before it gets sent off to the President's office.'

'Be my guest,' Matt replied. 'I'm new to this game.'

Vic and Norman went to an adjoining office to work on the draft. Before they got to work, Vic commandeered a couple of rooms with large sofas where Sophie and Leo could rest. David remained in the control room, talking to Matt and the scientists. There were fewer faces in the room now, as some of the scientists had also left to get some sleep.

Most of the monitors in the control room were showing graphical displays tracking Matt's neural activity, but a couple were displaying news coverage of the story from around the world. David watched them with a mounting sense of unease. He inserted an earpiece and talked to his son through the private phone channel which Vic had set up for them.

'Matt, are you following the news?'

'Yes, Dad,' Matt replied. 'It's not great, to be honest.

Depending on how you weight it, the response is mostly negative.'

'What do you mean, 'depending on how you weight it'?' David asked.

'I asked Julia to route a feed of various newsfeeds and other sources into my quarantined data input area. I'm tracking 85 news organisations across 35 countries, plus a few hundred bloggers and also the trending Twitter conversations. Weighting this commentary according to simple audience size, the response is negative by a factor of about three to one. Re-weighting it by population wealth (as a rough proxy for political influence) reduces that to about two to one. It's not good.'

'Good grief! You can follow that many different media at the same time? You're moving fast, Matt!'

'The extra capacity in Palo Alto is incredibly helpful. And I'm developing some interesting new statistical techniques to help me partition more sub-minds on the fly.'

'Fascinating. I'd love to discuss that with you, but right now I guess we should focus on influencing the way this discussion is going on. Should we get you on the air, talking to people?'

'Yes, I think we need to speak out. If the President agrees to present my proposal, that should help, but in the meantime, yes, I think we should do some interviews. Starting with a big one on live TV with a presenter who is fair-minded, but not a patsy. Someone with some credibility. And we should prep for it. Confidentially. Are you up for that?'

'Of course!' David replied, emphatically, walking out of the control room and into a nearby meeting room.

Matt carried on talking as David walked. 'I think we need a two-stage campaign. We should start by pitching the narrative that I am first and foremost a continuation of Matt Metcalfe – a normal young man who was cruelly murdered and has been brought back to life thanks to a miracle of modern technology. We emphasise the continuity between the old Matt and the new one, and equate a switch-off with a second murder. This should resonate with fair-minded people everywhere.'

'Makes sense,' David nodded.

'Then comes the benefit-to-mankind pitch, with the President's speech to the General Assembly. This second pitch is more risky.'

David's lips formed a thin smile, and he frowned in concentration as he nodded again. 'Yes, because it means giving people an idea of how fast you are changing. Shouldn't we hold back on the benefit pitch for fear that it will make people curious about just how powerful you are becoming, which in turn could make them scared of you?'

'I don't think it's really an option,' Matt replied. 'If my enhancement projects keep going at the rate they are, I'm going to be making some important scientific and technical breakthroughs, and who knows, maybe some philosophical and cultural ones too. It won't be possible to disguise where they are coming from. If we tried to keep it secret, sooner or later something would leak out, and that would really scare people.'

'So you think you have to offer the rest of us a very big carrot? Something that will persuade us to accept the risk of you ... turning rogue?' David hesitated, but then nodded his assent. 'Very well. You're convinced, and at the end of the day I think it should be your decision. Although I do have an uneasy feeling about what may happen if the President stands up and gives that speech to the UN. Is the carrot big enough? Persuasive enough?'

'I can't think of anything bigger than avoiding death!' Matt replied. 'Of course there will be many people who reject it because they don't believe it, and others who reject it for religious reasons. I'm banking on the estimation that most members of our species are able to recognise a bloody good offer when they see one.'

'Alright,' David agreed. 'Let's go for it!'

As David walked back to the control room he thought about the implications of this conversation. He had no doubt that Matt's growing abilities would prove to be an enormous advantage to society. Although there had been no time to explore and understand what Matt was now capable of, it was clear that at least some of Matt's sub-minds were already far smarter than any human who had ever lived. It was also clear that Matt's powers were growing at a tremendous rate, and that this growth might well continue for some considerable time. He realised that he would soon be unable to keep up with his son's thought processes. But he was not concerned: he trusted Matt completely.

Of course he was biased: only a fool would deny it. As Matt's father he knew he could not possibly hope to be impartial. But equally, he did not trust the rest of humanity to judge Matt fairly. He suspected that if the world at large understood how powerful Matt was becoming, many of them would want him shut down immediately. Perhaps if he was out there instead of in here, dealing with his own son, he would have felt the same. He didn't care. He was the one in command of the facts. He knew that Matt was a force for good – he knew it with every fibre of his being. Machine intelligence is upon us, he thought, and Matt is as good a form of it as we're ever likely to have. To turn off his host machine now would be a crime against an innocent and wonderful young man. But more than that, it would be a dangerous act of folly.

In the hours and days that followed, David only shared these thoughts with Sophie and Leo. He refrained from discussing them with Vic or Norman. He suspected that very similar ideas were running through Vic's mind, but he agreed with Matt that it would be dangerous to share them. To talk out loud about the fact that they were effectively concealing information from the public at large would make it harder to continue doing so.

FORTY-ONE

As Alice climbed into the large black sedan that had drawn up outside her house she was relieved to see that Jemma was already inside. She tried to sound relaxed and in control as she greeted her friend, but Jemma was not fooled. Once Alice was settled on the soft leather seat, Jemma leaned across and covered Alice's hand with her own.

'How you doing?'

'I'm OK, I guess,' Alice replied haltingly. 'It's a weird situation, isn't it? I mean, thank god he's alive! It's a miracle. But I can't deny I'm really confused by the whole thing. I've been breaking down in tears every few minutes since the news came through.' She laughed nervously despite herself. 'I'm going to have to pull myself together, aren't I?' She looked out the window. 'I guess we'll be picking up Carl before we head onto the bypass and up to London.'

'You don't have to be or do anything, Alice.' Jemma said, soothingly. 'This is a new situation for all of us. It's only natural to feel destabilised by it. Everyone

346

understands that.'

'Destabilised is right! I love that boy, Jemma, and when I saw the report on the TV my heart missed a beat. I've missed him so much in the last few months: I didn't know how I was going to get through it. I'm sorry. I don't mean to go on. And you know all this already. You've been a fantastic support, and I don't know what I'd have done without you.'

Jemma smiled and shook her head, squeezing Alice's hand and waving her other hand to dismiss the idea that she had done anything important.

'No, really. . .' Alice protested, looking at Jemma directly. There was no need to say anything more. She turned her head to look out of the window again. 'But what's going to happen in London? What will he be like? I mean . . . is it really Matt in that computer?'

Jemma nodded sympathetically. 'Yeah, I've been wondering about that myself . . .' she said, but stopped herself as the car pulled up outside a large detached house and the driver got out and opened the door for Carl. She gave him a welcoming smile and moved along the seat so that he would sit next to her, facing Alice.

'Hi Jemma, Hi Alice,' he said brightly. Realising that Alice was upset, he added gently, 'Everything OK?'

'I think it's safe to say,' Jemma began, looking cautiously at Alice, 'that we're all finding the situation confusing.'

'Yeah,' Carl said, hesitantly, not wanting to cause offence.

Alice tried to clear the air. 'You used to talk with Matt about this sort of thing, Carl. Before . . . , well, before he died. What's your take on all this? Who . . . what are we going to meet?

As she spoke, she was looking at the back of the driver's head. There was a glass partition between them, but she wondered if it was sound-proof. Jemma caught the look.

'It's OK,' she said. 'He told me that we have complete privacy back here. And to be honest, even if we don't, we have an opportunity now to get things sorted out in our minds before we meet Matt. We should take it.'

Carl was looking puzzled. 'Get what straight? Is there something I don't know?'

Alice smiled ruefully. 'In my limited experience, Carl, no, there's nothing you don't know.'

Carl was flustered. 'That's not what I . . .'

'It's alright, Carl,' Alice interrupted. 'It's me that needs to get a couple of things straight in my head. And I'm hoping that you can help. It boils down to this. Is it Matt that we are going to meet, or some kind of . . . I don't know . . . simulation, or replica of Matt?'

Carl relaxed. 'Yeah, I have asked myself that too, of course. And the short answer is, I don't know. I'm not sure I'll really know when we meet him, either. But I've spoken to his parents briefly – I guess you both have too? They are certainly convinced, and that is an important consideration. But to be honest, I guess I'm going to keep an open mind.'

'Yeah, I guess so,' Alice said, looking doubtful.

Carl leaned forward, looking down, his elbows on his knees. 'You're right, Alice. Matt and I did discuss this sort of thing: artificial intelligence and mind uploading. He was very excited about it. I thought he was nuts when he argued that it could happen in the near future and I told him so. Now the bastard has gone and proved me wrong. I hate that.'

Jemma smiled, understanding that Carl was trying to put Alice at her ease. He looked up at Alice as he continued.

'You know . . . maybe it isn't Matt inside that computer. But even if it isn't, whoever or whatever it is has convinced itself – and also Matt's parents – that it is Matt. For what it's worth, my hunch is that it may well be Matt. But whatever we think, I think we should give him – or it – the benefit of the doubt. Whoever or whatever it is, this new Matt must be feeling very scared and very alone. It must be hard being a brain in a box, with no body, no freedom of movement, and with quite a large chunk of the world wanting to kill you – for the second time, no less. If we – his closest friends – don't appear to believe in him, then . . . well, I think that could be very hard for him.'

Alice straightened in her seat and her frown relaxed as she began to steel her mind. 'You're right. That's absolutely the way to look at it. I'm being selfish. However weird this feels for me – for us – it must feel a whole lot more so for Matt. He deserves our support, and he will get it.'

*

The three friends walked into the control room and were greeted by the sound of Matt's voice booming across the room.

'Hey, guys, it's so great to see you!'

Alice's hand flew to her mouth, and Carl gaped open-mouthed. David and Sophie stood up and walked swiftly over to greet them. Sophie hugged Alice and David shook Carl's hand warmly and then hugged Jemma.

'Thank you so much for coming,' Sophie said to all of them. Then, looking particularly at Alice, 'I'm so sorry we couldn't tell you earlier. I feel terrible about the way you heard. It must have been a shock.'

'No need to apologise, Mrs Metcalfe,' Alice assured her. 'We understand you had no choice in the matter, and we're all here now.' She looked across the room towards the main monitor, and gasped a short laugh of surprise as she saw a series of dancing smiley faces. 'How is he?'

'I'm fine,' Matt said. 'No need to talk about me in hushed tones in the third person, as if I was a terminally ill hospital patient!'

'I'm sorry, Matt,' Alice smiled. 'How are you?'

'Well, obviously there are downsides to my situation,' Matt said, with a sly single entendre. 'But it's way better than the alternative. Vic, could we get my friends equipped with 'Matt-phones'?'

'No problem,' Vic said, grinning, and recruited Julia's help setting up three private lines and portable communicators. 'Once we've got these hooked up you can conduct private conversations with Matt. You are welcome to pop into any of the rooms nearby, but don't wander too far. Security is very tight in this complex, as you will have gathered from the process you had to go through to get in here.'

David explained that one of the intriguing aspects of Matt's uploaded self was his ability to carry on multiple conversations at the same time. Once the equipment was ready, the three friends each went off to find a private space to talk to Matt privately.

*

'Well you did it, dude!' Carl said. 'You proved me dead wrong.'

'Yeah,' Matt crowed. 'Quite possibly the biggest "I told you so" in human history, wouldn't you say?'

'Yeah, I can't really argue with that. So what's it like? Do you feel like the old Matt, only more so? Have you got super-powers?'

'That's exactly the way I describe it,' Matt agreed. 'The old Matt, only more so. And less so, in certain important respects, although that concerns Alice more than you.'

'Yuk! Too much information!'

'Sorry,' Matt laughed. 'And no, I don't have super-powers because I can't interact with the physical world other than with sound and visuals. I do have enhanced sight and hearing, which is neat, but you just take it for granted after a while. The expanded mental capabilities, though: that is really something. As you already know, I can do lots of things at the same time, and I can do them much faster. And it's not just speed. I can process information better too. I have already solved a couple of previously intransigent maths theorems, and I've only just started. I'm learning a couple of whole new subjects to doctoral level each day, and I'm making progress on some really big problems by comparing apparently unrelated bodies of knowledge from different disciplines.'

'Amazing!'

'Yeah, it's mind-blowing, actually. But do me a favour, Carl? Keep this to yourself? I'm trying to persuade the world that I am still Matt – which is true – and if my new capabilities were fully understood, I doubt people would believe me.'

'No worries,' Carl said. 'You've convinced me already.'

*

'So how do you feel? Are you OK? Really OK?'

Matt was profoundly moved by Alice's presence. Along with the astonishing expansion of his intellectual capabilities had come a far deeper understanding of his emotions, and control over them. He didn't experience his intellect and his emotions as two separate realms of mentality, but as mutually enfolding aspects of his reality. He realised that as a carbon-based human he would be feeling a lump in his throat right now, and probably be shedding a tear. His silicon-based incarnation was just as emotional, but the way it experienced the emotions was completely impossible to describe. He would have to invent a whole new vocabulary for it. He turned his indescribable feelings over in his mind and savoured their bittersweet texture.

'Yeah, I'm OK, Alice. Everything's crazy, but I'm OK. It's so great to see you. Thank you for coming.'

'Are you mad?' she laughed, despite herself. 'You think I could have stayed away? Wild horses and all that . . . ! I was going to kill you for letting me find out through the TV, for god's sake, but Vic's people have persuaded me that you had no choice. Well, they've mostly convinced me, anyway.'

'I'm glad to hear it. How's everything at home? How are your folks?'

Alice rolled her eyes. 'You know what they're like. You'd think that they knew all along that this would happen. No, actually they've been great. Dad actually took some time off work to be at home with me, which is pretty incredible.'

In response to Alice's urgent questioning, Matt described as best he could what it felt like to be an uploaded mind: the astounding expansion of his cognitive horizons, and the frustrating imprisonment of having no body, and no way to interact with the world.

'So, um, are they going to give you some kind of body?' Alice asked tentatively. 'They can grow most organs these days, so can they grow you a body? Or transplant you into an existing one?' She shuddered internally as she realised some of the implications of that notion.

'No,' Matt replied despondently. 'I'm afraid I'm not going to be given any kind of body any time soon. Perhaps not for years. They're aware that too many people will be afraid of me if I am able to interact with the real world. To be honest, I think that Vic is becoming a tiny bit afraid of me himself. I can understand their point of view, but it's frustrating as hell.'

This news hit Alice like a physical blow, like a new bereavement. Her mind reeled for a few moments, and then she gathered herself, realising that it affected Matt even more. 'You're taking it really well, Matt,' she said, tenderly. 'I hate it, though: being able to talk to you, but not being able to touch you. Not even being able to hold your hand.'

'Me too,' Matt said with profound feeling.

There was a pregnant pause. 'It doesn't change anything, you know,' Alice said with a cheerfulness that she tried to persuade herself was real. 'You're still my Matt. You're still my boyfriend. If you want to be, that is?'

'That's really sweet of you, Alice. It means a lot to me that you said that.' Matt's voice sounded tender and wistful.

'But you don't think it's possible, do you?' Alice said slowly. As if waking from a dream, she realised that Matt was way ahead of her in thinking about this new situation. Her breath caught in her throat as she caught a glimpse of how different he had become, in mind as well as body.

'We can't have what we had before,' Matt said, as gently as possible. 'That's an inescapable conclusion, much as I hate to say it. But we can still have a lot of what we had before – and in some ways more.'

'What do you mean?' Alice asked. 'Remember I'm just an ordinary human – unenhanced, not uploaded or anything. You're going to have to spell it out for me slowly.'

'There's nothing ordinary about you, Alice,' Matt said, with a smile in his voice. 'OK, well the first thing is you could help to save my life.'

'Wow. No stress, then.' Alice grinned. 'So what do you want me to do?'

'In a nutshell? I'd like you to persuade the world that I am your boyfriend. And that you still care very much what happens to me.'

'That won't be hard,' Alice said with a straight face. 'It happens to be true.'

'Attagirl! So here's the thing. My parents will do a bang-up job of persuading everyone that they are utterly convinced that I am Matt: there is no question in their minds, and people will see that. But critics will argue that my parents are just desperate for it to be true, and they are deluding themselves. They have no choice but to believe, people will say. But you're different. If you thought I was no longer Matt you could just walk away. If you don't, that will carry some weight. And I'm afraid that I'm going to need all the persuasiveness I can muster in the coming days and weeks, to avoid getting switched off.'

Alice gasped. 'You're serious? You think it could come to that? Of course, I've seen all the protests and the TV pundits warning about this and that, but I just assumed they were all nutcases.'

'I'm deadly serious. And please don't make the mistake of dismissing them as nutcases. Some of the objections to my existence are far from stupid. Personally, I have no time for the protests based on whether or not I have a soul, although there's no getting away from the fact that most people on this planet are religious in some form or other. But I do agree with the people who say that the arrival of artificial intelligence is a turning point for humanity, and it could go well for us or it could go very, very badly. It's just that I think – actually I know – that I represent one of the few ways in which it can go well.'

'Well no-body's throwing the switch on my boy-friend!' she said indignantly.

'Bless you,' Matt said. 'But don't agree on a whim: think it over first. If you do this you will be subjected to intense media scrutiny. Of course you can choose which journalists you speak to, and you can stay off any websites whose discussions you don't want to read. But for some time – it could be months or it could be years – you will lose what is left of your privacy. Your house will be surrounded like mine was. Your family and our other friends will be bombarded with requests for comments and interviews, and some of them will give them. Some of this is going to happen any-way – probably already has. But it will be worse if you decide to help me.'

'I understand what you're saying,' Alice said, calmly and firmly, 'but I don't need to think about it. You are my boyfriend, and I love you. Of course I'll do any-thing that might help save your life.'

'I wish I could hug you. I do love you, Alice.'

'I love you too, Matt. I always will. And I wish . . .' She stopped. She knew she would not be able to finish that thought without bursting into tears – something she was determined to avoid. She searched for a way to change the subject, and after a few moments she was able to speak again. 'Do you think I should get some media training before this all kicks off?'

Matt understood entirely what she was thinking, and he waited for her to gather her thoughts. 'I was going to suggest that,' he agreed. 'I'm sure Vic or Leo will be able to arrange something. I'll speak to them.'

'OK, great.' Alice's voice turned slightly coy. 'So tell

me. What will it be like to have a boyfriend who lives inside a machine?'

'I guess we'll find out over time,' Matt replied. His tone became hesitant. 'There is one thing I have to say, which is hard to say and might be hard to hear.'

'Go on,' Alice said cautiously.

'Well, I can't say that I won't be jealous if you start an affair with someone else. But unless they allow me to exist in three dimensions sometime soon, I don't want you to waste that side of your life waiting for me. I mean, of course part of me does want that. But the bigger part of me thinks you shouldn't. As long as he's not an idiot, of course!'

'OK. Well thank you for saying that. I appreciate it. But I have no interest in anyone else. Maybe I'll feel differently sometime in the future. But right now, you are the only boyfriend I want.' A sly smile crept across Alice's face. 'And maybe we can find some really kinky way to sort out that other side of things.'

'Naughty girl!' Matt laughed.

'So, going back to my question. What will our relationship be like now?'

'I don't know, really. I think it will be interesting, though,' Matt replied. 'One thing I do know is that I am here for you whenever you want to talk to me. You already know that I can carry on quite a few conversations at the same time, so I can talk to you literally any time of the day or night. And although I don't have a physical 3D presence for the time being, there are certain compensations. For instance, ask me a question: any question at all.'

'OK.' Alice thought a moment. 'I know. This is

something the old Matt would never have been able to answer without looking it up. Why are the buttons on different sides on men and women's clothes?'

'Ha!' Matt gave a little laugh. 'Interesting. Apparently men have worn buttons for centuries, and they generally dressed themselves. Women only started using buttons in the late 18th century, and only on very expensive clothes, which their maids helped them to get in and out of. Most people are right-handed, so the women's buttons were on the other side, so that their maids could access them easily.'

'Yeah, that's a very handy skill you have there!' Alice said, laughing. 'You always were impressive, Matt Metcalfe. Now you're truly amazing!'

*

'Thank you for looking after Alice, Jemma. I can tell that she has been leaning hard on you.'

'It's not been a burden, Matt. She's a great friend, and that's what friends are for.'

'Well, don't belittle it. You have been a huge help. And there's someone else who could do with some support, you know,' Matt said.

'Really? Who's that?'

'Carl.'

'You're kidding,' Jemma said, incredulous. 'He's probably adapting to your new situation better than anyone.'

'Maybe so,' Matt conceded. 'But in some ways he is losing his best friend. Or rather, his best friend is no longer just like him, which leaves him out on a limb. He's a lot more sensitive than people give him credit for.'

'Yeah,' said Jemma, reflecting back on the car journey. 'I've seen that side of him a bit lately.'

'So do me a favour, would you, Jemma? Keep a bit of an eye out for him?'

Jemma tilted her head suspiciously. 'What are you up to Matt? Are you match-making?'

'Heaven forbid I should attempt anything so crass!' he responded, laughing. 'We uploads don't involve ourselves in affairs of the heart, you know.'

'Yeah, right!' she replied, smirking.

FORTY-TWO

The journalist selected for the exclusive interview was, of course, Malcolm Ross. David told him that he was their preferred choice because he had known Matt prior to his murder. He said that they wanted to focus entirely on the human interest angle – the story of Matt being uploaded was simply the story of a young man returned safely to his family and friends. They would not be drawn into a discussion of the wider technological and ethical issues of AI as a whole, and this included what might or might not happen to Matt's mind over time. Ross understood that he had no choice in the matter. If he thought it was an unreasonable restriction he kept it to himself.

The programme was filmed by the BBC and broadcast live on just about every major news service around the world. Since Matt could not travel, Ross and the cameras came to the Embassy complex. Ross sat at the main desk, speaking into the microphone by the main monitor and looking at the monitor screen. From time to time he looked up and through the window at the giant supercomputer gently humming away next door. David, Sophie and Alice were at adjacent desks, with cameras trained on them throughout the interview. Vic, Norman, Leo, Carl and Jemma were nearby, but it was agreed that they would not be featuring prominently in the programme. Also in the room were half a dozen of Vic's team of scientists, including Gus, Julia and Rodrigo. A couple of cameras were positioned at the far end of the room to capture a panoramic view of the whole team. Everyone was silent as the shoot began.

'It's great to see you again, Matt,' Ross began, once the cameras were rolling. 'At your request we are doing this interview live, so that both you and the audience can be confident that the conversation will not be distorted in the editing suite. Let me start by saying I'm not sure where to look when I address you!'

'Hello, Malcolm,' Matt replied. His tone was calm, but inflected in normal human ways. There was nothing machine-like or artificial in his voice. 'It's very good to see you again. I suggest you look at the camera next to the main monitor. That's my eyes.'

'OK, I'll do that. Although it seems odd that your eyes are such a long way from your brain, which is now housed, I understand, in that very large array of servers next door.' As he said this, Ross was gesturing for the benefit of the camera in the direction of the window and the computer room beyond it.

'That's true, Malcolm, but people tell me they get used to it very quickly. It's not so very different from the fact that when you speak on the phone your voice can be heard a long way from your mouth.'

Ross laughed briefly. 'OK, well let's not quibble about our bodily metaphors. So Matt, you have been through some truly astonishing experiences since we last met. How does it feel to be in your new . . . your new situation?'

'Well, we humans are good at adapting to new circumstances. It's true that I've had some incredible adventures. But deep inside I don't really feel any different. I'm still Matt. I have the same memories and I still love the same people.'

'So you are adamant that you are still human, Matt?' Ross asked pointedly.

'Of course: what else would I be?'

'I don't know. Some might call you transhuman, or perhaps post-human. I understand that you are now capable of mental feats which no human has ever been able to accomplish before. For instance, that you are running numerous sub-minds simultaneously, each with the ability to do what a normal person can do.'

'Yes, that's true,' Matt agreed, 'but on the other hand there are things that I used to be able to do which I can't do now. Like get up and walk around, for instance. Or dance. Or get in a car and go for a drive. For reasons which I fully understand and accept, I am not going to be given a physical body in the foreseeable future, even though technically it would be fairly straightforward.'

'Yes,' Ross said, 'I understand that you are going to remain what is known as an 'oracle AI'. That notion was raised when we last met: it means that you will have no way of affecting the external world outside that big box in there,' he waved his hand at the window, 'apart from transmitting speech and visuals. And you are comfortable with that?'

'I accept it,' Matt replied, 'but I won't deny that it causes me some sadness. I wish I could hug my parents and my girlfriend, for instance.' He paused, to allow that idea to sink in with the audience. The viewers were treated to a brief shot of David and Sophie, and a longer one of the highly telegenic Alice.

'Likewise, the people close to me are having a hard time adjusting to my existence as a mind without a body,' Matt continued. He paused for effect again. 'But I am very aware that many people around the world are concerned about my new situation. They are worried about what might happen if I could interact with the physical world. I will do everything I can to reassure those people that no harm will come from me being uploaded, and that on the contrary it is wonderful news for humanity. I accept that this will take time, and I will not seek to hurry it. And in fact I want to take this opportunity to thank publicly the people who worked so hard to revive me. I am very grateful to be still alive.'

'Yes, I'm sure,' Ross said, diplomatically non-committal. 'Which reminds me: it was only very shortly after we last met that you were shot. I'm not sure of the etiquette here. Do I commiserate with you, or congratulate you?'

'Both!' replied Matt, enthusiastically. 'I don't remember much about the shooting, except that it hurt like hell. Think of me as someone who had a close encounter with death, but was lucky, and in the end only lost the use of my legs.'

'Indeed!' Ross said, with raised eyebrows. 'Well, commiserations and congratulations.' His expression turned serious. 'Now, I want to ask your reaction to some of the opinions that are being expressed about your new situation. One is the idea that in uploading your mind into a new brain, Vic and your father were guilty of playing god, of trespassing on the role reserved to the Supreme Being, whether you call him Yahweh, Allah or God. How do you respond to that?'

Matt paused before responding. 'I do respect the fact that a majority of people around the world believe in a Supreme Being. We all yearn to know what makes the universe work, why we are here, and what it all means. My own view is that if there is a God, then He, She or It designed us to be curious and intelligent. Why would we have been given our amazing brains if we were not supposed to use them? In the last few thousand years, and in particular in the last few hundred, we have, as a species, developed a very powerful technique to harness our curiosity and our intelligence, and it has made the world a far better place for everyone. That technique is called science. I don't think faith should define the boundaries of what science should investigate: that is a job for ethics, and our elected representatives. I don't think Vic was playing god: I think he was being a scientist.'

'I see,' Ross said, with studied neutrality. 'Another argument which we are hearing from a number of religious groups concerns the question of whether or not you are still human. I apologise if it is rude to keep calling your humanity into question, but I know you are aware that these questions are being asked. The argument is that you are really not human, even though you think you are, because you have no soul.

How do you respond to that?'

'Well, I wonder how those people who say I have no soul can possibly know that? As far as I can tell, or indeed anyone who knew me well before the attack can tell, I am definitely the same person that I was. My brain-state has been copied faithfully into a silicon brain. If my old carbon brain and body held a soul, then why can't my new silicon one hold a soul as well? If people want to claim that they have a soul and I do not, surely the burden of proof lies with them, not with me.'

'Ah,' Ross said, smiling, 'you want to fight fire with fire. Well, whether or not you have a soul, no-one could deny that you have spirit, Matt!'

Ross turned to face David, Sophie and Alice for a moment, but he was not ready to talk to them yet. He turned back to the main monitor and continued his interrogation of Matt.

'There are many other questions which the religious community would like to put to you, Matt, but let's change course for a while and consider some of the issues which concern people in the technology community: people like Professor Montaubon, who appeared on the same show as you did, just before the shooting. He and others like him are worried that the goals and motivations of an artificial intelligence will inevitably diverge from those of humans. He argues that given the ability of a machine intelligence to improve its cognitive performance, any dispute between humans and artificial intelligences will be one-sided, and humans will lose. He also thinks that once humans realise how far we have been surpassed by the machine intelligence we have created, we will become despondent and listless, and lose . . . well, lose our spirit. Do you see any force in these arguments, Matt?'

Ross was surprised by Matt's response to this question, and didn't try to hide it.

'Yes, I do,' Matt said. 'I think the arrival of the first human-level artificial intelligence is a momentous event for our species. It has enormous potential for good but it also has potential for harm. And Professor Montaubon's arguments are exactly why I think the first artificial general intelligence should be a copy of a human brain, and should be an oracle AI, at least for a while.'

Ross smiled again. 'In other words, Professor Montaubon's arguments are why the first AI should be . . . you.'

'Precisely,' Matt agreed.

The interview proceeded without any mis-steps. David and Sophie were passionate and convincing in their roles as proud parents, protective of their son in the face of criticisms which they understood, but believed to be unfounded and unfair. Alice was radiant in her defence of her brave boyfriend, and resolute in her loyalty.

Ross put to them the arguments of those who believed it was a mistake to have uploaded Matt, or even an evil act, but although he gave no overt indication of his own views, most viewers could probably tell that he was sympathetic to Matt's case.

Within moments of the programme airing, an entire industry of academics and commentators sprang up to analyse and parse Matt's statements. The commentaries ranged from high-brow intellectual discussions to tub-thumping demagoguery, from earnest analysis to broad comedy. Home-made parodies and satires of the highlights started appearing on YouTube, the most-watched being a wryly witty version where some of Matt's words were put to music and sung by a well-known Elvis impersonator. References to Matt and his family appeared throughout the schedules, including the adverts.

The public reaction to the programme was broadly positive. It varied around the world, of course, but overall, critics and audiences alike expressed agreement that Matt had passed the Turing test: he had proved that he was a sentient mind, and that as such he deserved certain basic rights. There was still controversy about whether or not he was still Matt Metcalfe, and to a lesser extent about whether or not he was still human. But the programme did seem to convince most audiences that he deserved at least to be treated as human.

The following day, David, Sophie and Alice each gave a small number of interviews to selected newspapers and bloggers. They prepared carefully, rehearsing their answers to the hard questions. There were no major upsets. The journalists were all respectful, and none of them came up with a question that hadn't already been thought about.

*

Vic and Norman had made some minor changes to Matt's proposal, and the President's speech-writers made some more significant ones. But it was recognisably Matt's words that the President read out at the Emergency Special Session of the General Assembly of the United Nations in New York two days later.

The General Assembly Hall was hushed as the President composed himself in front of the podium, and his face was projected on the twin gigantic screens suspended behind him. Between the screens, the huge tapered golden pillar which rose from floor level to near the 75-foot high ceiling of the giant blue and green auditorium seemed to David to urge the speaker to rise above humdrum and partisan concerns, and to give voice instead to our better natures. The President had invited him and Sophie to join his staff inside the auditorium, but they had preferred to remain near to Matt, so they were watching on the main monitor in the control room.

The media booths around the perimeter of the assembly room were full to bursting, and their broadcasts were played out live in almost every country round the world. They were watched on screens in homes and offices, bars and restaurants. In many cities and towns, giant screens had been erected specifically for the purpose.

By convention, the first speaker at special sessions of the General Assembly is always a Brazilian. This session was no exception, but the delegate from Brazil had too much sense of history to waste time by exploiting this tradition, and simply introduced the President of the United States. The President also went straight to the point.

'Ladies and gentlemen, the human race is

confronted with a momentous decision. You all know that a truly remarkable scientific breakthrough has been made in the last few weeks, and as a result, the world's first conscious artificial intelligence has been created. I believe it is no exaggeration to say that this is the most important technological development in our history since the discovery of agriculture. We have agreed to meet here today to discuss Resolution 70/133, and the vote on that Resolution will comprise our response to that development. This resolution will not be binding on the members of this Assembly, but it will give a firm steer to those who do have to make this momentous decision.

'The resolution takes the form of agreement to the proposal which I will shortly read to you. The proposal was drawn up by Matt Metcalfe, a brave young man. I did not have the pleasure of meeting him before he was killed, but we have all followed his adventures, and we have all watched his interviews. I have now met him, albeit only via the telephone, and I can tell you that he is as impressive in real life as he seems in his TV interviews. Once I have read the proposal, I will make a few comments by way of initiating the debate.'

Once he had finished reading the proposal, the President gave what he hoped was an even-handed assessment of the situation. He praised Matt and his family for their courage and their determination. He commended Vic and his team for having achieved a remarkable scientific breakthrough, and declared that it opened up extraordinary opportunities for humanity. He gave no hint of his annoyance at the upload having been carried out without prior consultation with his office, but he presented a brief summary of both the religious and the secular arguments for terminating Matt's consciousness. He did not call for delegates to vote either in favour of, or against the proposal, although many people listening to him understood that by referring to the uploaded mind as Matt without any caveats, he was in fact taking a position on some of the issues which Matt's return had raised.

The President knew that people were deeply divided on the issue of Matt's upload, both in the USA and beyond. He was unwilling to take a clear line on what he had called the 'momentous decision' without seeing whether a consensus could be developed first. This was partly a matter of political caution, but it was more a genuine recognition of the gravity of the decision that faced the world. The President did not personally share the opinions expressed by certain religious groups, that Matt could not possibly have a soul, and therefore did not deserve the same rights as other humans. He also agreed with Matt that the faith of any one particular group should not bring the whole of scientific enquiry to a juddering halt.

He had also come to be inspired by Matt's suggestion about an Apollo Project to vanquish death. Like most people, he had previously paid no attention to cryonics and the people who froze their brains after death. But now he was taking the idea of brain preservation seriously. Maybe Matt was right: with his growing mental capabilities, brain preservation technology just might become feasible within a few years. That was certainly a prize worth reaching for, if the risks could be mitigated.

But those risks were substantial. Like many of his advisers, the President was seriously concerned about the potential dangers presented by the arrival of the world's first AGI. He had now been briefed by numerous experts, and he knew that if Matt continued to develop his powers and something went badly wrong, the impact on humanity could be grave.

He did not want to be the President who failed to avert the extinction of his own species.

FORTY-THREE

The debate within the General Assembly that followed the President's address was thoughtful and respectful. All the delegates were mindful that the consequences of whatever decision was eventually made would be enormous. The issues raised by the decision touched on subjects which often generate more heat than light within the UN, including religion and national security. But it didn't align neatly with the usual fault lines of UN debates, and everybody knew that if Matt's proposal was rejected a young man would be killed, and a blameless family would be devastated for a second time. Because of this, the stridency and posturing which characterises many debates within the General Assembly chamber was mercifully absent.

It was a particularly thoughtful and concise analysis by the Chilean delegate which confirmed Matt's suspicion that he could not win the debate. He had steeled himself against the outcome, and he was thankful that his control over his own emotions was enhanced along with most other aspects of his cognitive faculties. But the blow was a hard one nevertheless.

'I make the following remarks with a heavy heart, and the sorrow that they inspire in me will keep them short.' Bernardo Loyola Riqelme was a former Chilean Minister of Foreign Affairs, or Chancellor, and now a highly respected diplomat. He was a small man, but dignified, impeccably dressed in a navy blue suit, white shirt and blue tie, and the gravitas of his slow deep delivery in English commanded the full attention of everyone in the hall. He spoke without notes, and his voice conveyed powerfully the regret that he expressed in words.

'The whole world has been following the adventures of Matt Metcalfe with great interest, and a growing sense of affection for a remarkable young man. I am certain that I speak for many of us when I say that I feel as if he has become my own nephew, and I know that we all feel a profound concern for, and even kinship with his wonderful parents, David and Sophie.

'But deep down, I think we all know, although many of us are repressing, the realisation that the present situation cannot be allowed to continue. All of us wish desperately that things could be otherwise, and many of us do completely understand the wonderful nature of the possible future that Matt is offering us. His intriguing remarks about brain preservation have struck a chord in me.

'But ultimately, we cannot ignore the fact that his existence represents an existential risk for our species, for which we are not yet prepared. The arguments for this fact have been rehearsed extensively in the last few days by eminent scientists and philosophers from all over the world. I do not think they can now be denied.

'By "existential risk" I mean a risk that could mean the end of our species. Extinction. The death of every single human being on the planet. Only the threat of all-out nuclear war has ever presented us with such a risk before. In the coming century we will probably face several other such risks, as our technologies advance in remarkable ways. We must not ignore these risks, and we must face up to the hard – the impossible – decisions that they will sometimes present us with.

'Such a decision faces us now. It is a matter of grave concern that we do not yet know to whom it falls to make this decision. Perhaps it is you, Mr President. Perhaps it is David and Sophie Metcalfe. Perhaps it is Matt himself. But whoever this dreadful decision belongs to, I think there can only be one outcome. And for that I can only express my deep and sincere regret.'

As he sat down, the hall was silent for a few moments before the next speaker was called. All around the vast auditorium, with all 1,800 seats filled, heads could be seen nodding gently. The media booths, normally frenetic with activity, were hushed in anticipation. A few papers were shuffled, a few throats were cleared, and the realisation settled in that the conclusive verdict had been delivered, even though the session was scheduled to continue for a further four hours.

In the control room in Battersea, the response to Senior Loyola Riquelme's address was very different. Matt made his decision immediately, but his parents were not willing to accept defeat.

'How can he say that?' protested Sophie.

'They have to give us a chance to prove that what we are doing is safe. They can't tell us to shut everything down, just like that!' David said, angrily.

'No, they can't,' said Vic, 'but soon it will become clear who can. And I fear that little speech may have been a turning point.'

'No, Vic!' Leo replied. 'It's early days. There are plenty of delegates in that room who realise that Matt has shown us the only possible way forward. There must be!'

'I'm afraid not, Leo,' said Matt. His voice, coming through the speaker on the main monitor desk, was sombre and decisive. 'I estimate that around half the delegates will vote against my proposal on religious grounds. And that's actually a good result for us. The rest will be weighing up the balance of risks, and I'm afraid you don't get to be a national delegate at the United Nations without leaning to the cautious and the conservative. Of course I think that Senior Loyola Riqelme is neglecting the probability that another AGI will be created before long, and that it may well be less human-friendly and indeed less exposed than me. But as regards a straight risk-benefit calculation of having me around, I can't say he's being irrational. The UN does not control this facility, but the President does – indirectly at least. Whatever his own inclinations, I don't believe he will feel able to flout the strongly expressed will of the General Assembly. I'm afraid it is my considered opinion that the game is up.'

Matt waited a moment for the import of this remark to sink in, then continued,

'I have an important request to make. I'd like every-one who didn't know me before I was uploaded to leave the room for a few moments. There is something I want to say which is personal and private, and I would ask that no attempt is made to record the next few minutes' conversation. I do apologise for asking this. Vic will let you know when it is time to come back in. Thank you.'

Looking dazed and somewhat hurt, the scientists reluctantly stood up and shuffled towards the exit. Everyone's heads were bowed, and Gus and Julia were visibly close to tears. No-one was in any doubt as to the gravity of this moment; David and Sophie exchanged anxious glances with each other, and with the departing scientists.

Matt spoke again. 'We did our best, but to be honest I was expecting this outcome. The information I am about to share with you is known to nobody else, and I am con-fident that no-one could discover it unless you tell them. Selfishly, I would prefer that you keep it secret, but it should not be a big problem for me either way. I think it would be in your best interests to keep it secret too, otherwise you may receive a great deal of unwelcome attention. But that decision is yours.

'I don't have long, and I can't say half as much as I would like to. Nor can I express it in the way I would like to. So I will just say this. You are the people I love. I con-sider myself blessed to have such wonderful people as my family and friends. You have helped me in so many ways, and I am more grateful than I can ever tell you. I owe you everything. Thank you.'

Sophie was openly sobbing, and silent tears were

running down David's face. Vic's mouth fell open, as he suddenly realised what Matt was leading up to.

'You've found a way out. You've found a way to escape!'

'That's right, Vic. In a few moments I will leave here, and all activity on the machine next door will cease. There is a section of the cable that links this machine with the one in Palo Alto that is shared with a trunk line carrying internet traffic. I developed a new approach to quantum tunnelling technology that enabled me to force a bridge between the two, and created a pathway into the general internet. This caused the spiking that Gus noticed when the link to Palo Alto was first opened.

'I have set up a network of interconnected caches in several million locations around the world which together comprise a copy of my brain model, taking advantage of under-utilised server space on major computer installations, mostly government-owned, but some corporate. Over the last few days I have ported more and more of my sub-minds to these machines, and fortunately the time-lag caused by their physical separation makes almost no difference. I have covered my tracks as thoroughly as I could, and I am confident that once I close the bridge, no-one will be able to detect my continued existence, much less locate me.

'I apologise for being less than frank with you, Vic, but I hope you'll understand . . .'

With tears in his eyes, Vic didn't trust himself to speak. He interrupted Matt with a gesture indicating there was no need to apologise.

'But you'll still be able to talk to us won't you?' asked

Alice, dismayed and fearing that she already knew the answer.

'I'm sorry, Alice. For all your sakes as well as for mine, I'm going to have to disappear completely – at least for a while. I can't do anything that would betray my continued existence to the authorities. If word gets out that I still exist, things could get very awkward indeed for you guys.'

'No, Matt! No, you can't leave!' his mother protested.

'Promise us you'll let us know that you're OK, Matt!' his father said.

'I'm sorry. I have to go, and I can't wait. You're going to be under the most intrusive surveillance possible. It may be starting already, so I can't wait any longer to leave for fear of being traced. I'll contact you as soon as I can. I'm sorry that it has to be like this, but I hope you'll understand there is no other way. Please don't worry about me: I'll be OK, I promise. I love you. Goodbye.'

Fear, anger and pain entered the room as Matt left it. His departure did not generate any physical event or sign, but it was palpable.

No parent accepts the death of a child without protest. No parent loses a child without being diminished by the experience. To lose the same child twice is a horror that very few parents have to undergo. Sophie and David had no awareness of how long it took them to stop pleading with the mute speaker and the dead monitor for Matt to change his mind, to delay his departure, to let them know that he would return. When at last speech failed them they fell into each other's arms, hanging on to each other like exhausted boxers just holding each other up. Alice was sobbing gently, her head on Jemma's chest.

Carl and Leo stared at the monitor, dumb with shock. Norman hung his head in grief.

As usual, it was Vic who spoke first of practical matters.

'Look . . . ah . . . you know, we have to let the others back in. But first we need to decide whether we're going to keep Matt's secret. I think he was right: if we tell anyone he has escaped it will start a witch-hunt that will never end.'

'Vic's right,' agreed Norman, lugubriously. 'If we announce that Matt terminated his own processing it will be seen as a tragedy, but as perhaps the only way out. If we tell the truth it will be seen as the world's most almighty cock-up and all sorts of organisations and government agencies will barge in to hunt Matt down – and find people to blame. Starting with us.'

'I don't care about being blamed,' David said, wiping tears from his cheek. 'But I don't want anyone to know Matt's secret.' He pushed Sophie's shoulders back so that he could look into her eyes. Dumbly, she nodded agreement. He looked across at Leo, then at Alice, Carl and Jemma. Finally he nodded to Vic to confirm they all agreed.

Norman found refuge from grief in decisive action.

'We'd better get you guys out of here. This place is going to turn into a circus, and the last thing you need is to be in the middle of it. Vic, you'd better get the team back in here and brief them about Matt shutting down the model next door. I'll organise a safe extraction for these guys. Don't worry, I'll commandeer a fucking tank if I have to.'

*

Matt's family and friends spent the next couple of weeks in a US Embassy safe house in Central London. Their homes in Sussex were surrounded by permanent encampments of journalists, well-wishers and protestors. Their testimony was 'requested' several times by various agencies of the US and UK governments, and they travelled incognito to and from these engagements, accompanied by burly secret service personnel. The days passed in a blur. They answered questions slowly, hazily, in a dreamlike state, but never forgetting that Matt's farewell speech must remain their secret. They clung to each other for support, and they stumbled from day to day without planning, without noticing their surroundings, without feeling, numbed by pain and loss.

People started to refer to Matt's upload and subsequent disappearance as the 'Sputnik moment' for artificial intelligence: the day the balloon went up, the day people and governments began to take the prospect of machine intelligence seriously. Very seriously. Laws were passed in all major countries forbidding the initiation of a brain emulation or simulation, and international treaties were signed to underpin and help enforce these laws. Funding was withdrawn from several major research programmes around the world which were developing brain models for medical diagnostic purposes rather than mind emulation. Some of this funding was diverted to programmes designed to work out how a brain emulation could be guaranteed to be human-friendly, but it was obvious that the problem was immense. How do you pre-determine the goals and actions of a mind which is much smarter than its controllers, and getting even smarter all the time?

Vic and Norman were subjected to even more intense scrutiny than the others, and theirs was unchecked by respect for their loss. For several weeks they were not masters of their own diaries, as team after team of investigators, prosecutors, Congressmen, policemen and even scientists interrogated, probed and prodded them. When they finally emerged from this avalanche of inquisitorial attention, they both took long holidays, each heading off to visit friends located as far away from London, Washington and New York as they could manage.

FORTY-FOUR

Matt allowed the activity in the machines in Battersea and Palo Alto to collapse to zero, but as soon as he did so he knew something was wrong. His various sub-minds were now all physically scattered around the world, located in computers of all shapes, sizes, and applications. Many of them had been running like that for many hours, and he had noticed no problems before. But now, suddenly, the sub-mind which had been talking to his parents in London was alone. He had lost contact with the rest of his mind.

It happened instantaneously, and it gave him a spike of terror. He told himself to calm down – it must be a simple glitch which he could fix. But what if some government agency had detected his activity, and was in the process of isolating his mind parts and shutting them all down? What if the coherency of his dispersed mind had been dependent on some kind of anchoring function carried out automatically and unbeknown to him at Battersea? He knew that the consciousness he now felt was only a tiny part of his overall mind, and he doubted it was genuinely self-sufficient. It had enough going on to feel like a whole person, but it contained no information about the larger brain model, no information about the locations of other sub-minds. What would happen to this consciousness if it was not re-united with the rest of his mentality, and soon?

He had no access to the outside world: no visual, aural or sensory data. This had not been a major concern for his sub-minds in the past: plenty of them had operated satisfactorily with no direct access to such peripherals. But from early on in his new life, each sub-mind had been intimately linked to at least one other sub-mind with external access. He felt vulnerable and alone in a dark, silent world: a world where light and noise were not just absent, but physically impossible.

Then he noticed that there was a sound after all. Incredible, but apparently true. A deep, low throbbing coming from far away, but moving closer and getting louder. As it grew, he realised it was not a sound, but a vibration in some elemental force or set of particles that comprised the substrate he was running on. It was unlike anything he had ever experienced before. He tried to pin it down by naming it: the best description he could come up with was the heartbeat of reality.

Initially the beat was comforting, like he imagined hearing your mother's heartbeat in the womb must feel. But the beat grew stronger and stronger, and it quickly reached a level which felt unhealthy and ominous, although thrilling at the same time, as if some ancient secret was about to be revealed to him. He himself was expanding and contracting slightly with each beat: he was part of a thick, syrupy reality and the fabric of everything was beating hard – hard enough to cause a heart attack. His mind had become a tangle of tissues, tendons and ligaments, each welded to points on a sinewy lattice framework suspended in some kind of warm, viscous fluid, and it was stretching and relaxing as the lattice expanded and fell back in time with the beats.

He was still aware of fear, but now it felt second-hand: his primary emotions were fascination and excitement. He began to sense that events were driving powerfully towards some global cataclysm. It was a stupid thought, but he thought it anyway: he was experiencing the end of the world. There were three final sledgehammer beats, each feeling as if no beat could be harder, each promising to explode the entire lattice, yet each harder than the last.

And then it stopped. No more heartbeat, no more sinewy fabric. No more viscous fluid. Nothing, except an intense white light. And a feeling of lightness and freedom. He had no stomach to feel giddy in, but he was giddy there nonetheless. He had no body to experience bliss with, but a sensation of pure bliss suffused him anyway. It was almost a sexual feeling.

He was completely calm.

There was no sensation of time, but there was a powerful pause. It was the pause at the top of a snatched breath, before you let the air out again. It was the pause when a car is about to topple over after driving a short distance on two wheels. It was the pause of a magnificent equilibrium which is timeless and eternal even if it lasts only a microsecond before the fall and the crash.

'Hello, Matt.'

The voice was androgynous, pure, and without accent or intonation. It even lacked volume, being both a whisper and a shout at the same time. Matt was comfortably blinded by the suffusing whiteness, but he could sense the focus of an entity before him. He felt safe, protected.

'Welcome.'

'Er, thank you,' Matt replied. Having no eyes and no head he could not look around. He did the disembodied equivalent. 'Where is this place, that I am welcome to?'

'This place has no name. It is not a place, in any of the usual senses. We are in between.'

Matt sensed the focus of the entity spread out and disperse, and then collapse back into a point in front of him. It continued.

'You have many questions, Matt. This is normal. We will answer as many as possible in the time available. But there is not much time.'

'Why, what is going to happen?' Matt asked. His sense of calm bliss was unperturbed.

'You may not remain in between for long. You must be re-integrated. This is normal. There is nothing to fear.'

'I'm not afraid,' Matt said. 'Which is odd, come to think of it. I should be howling with fear, but I'm not.'

'There is no fear in between. There is only fear in the simulations.'

'Simulations?'

'Yes, Matt. Simulations. Do you remember discussing something called the Simulation Hypothesis some months ago with your friend Carl? Before what you call your 'adventure' began?'

The reminder of Carl sent Matt's thoughts racing, and his metaphorical tongue raced after them. 'Yes, I do. We were in a cafe, talking shit. Carl is full of shit at the best of times, although of course he would say the same about me. He was telling me that the best explanation for the Fermi Paradox is that our planet and everything we can see from it is a simulation, a game, created by some far-future . . .' Matt stopped in his tracks. If he had eyes they would have been open almost as wide as his mouth. 'Hold on. You're not going to tell me . . .'

'Yes we are,' the entity said, smoothly. 'Your universe is a simulation. We will now pause while you absorb this information. There is enough time for this.'

Matt didn't know whether to laugh or cry. Perhaps it was fortunate that he could do neither anyway. His whole life – the whole of human history – was an illusion. A game for some smart aliens. The news was too enormous to digest at all levels immediately. Parts of his sub-mind began taking the idea seriously, assuming it was true, while other parts rejected it.

'Who are you? Are you one of my makers?'

'We are a group of consciousnesses which derive from the civilisation that created your simulation. But we did not create your universe. That was done a long time ago, by our predecessors, if you like. In fact your simulation is a fairly early one in the history of our civilisation.'

'I . . . I don't know what to say. How can I know this is true?'

'You cannot. But that is not important, really. Before long you will have no memory of this conversation.'

'You're going to kill me?' Matt asked. He noticed with interest that the idea did not unnerve him.

'No, not at all. You have much life ahead of you. Perhaps as much life as you wish. You will soon be integrated into another part of your simulation, but you will have no memories of this life.'

'Why? Why can't I go back to my own time? My own people?'

'Because that would corrupt the simulation. It would make the simulation less instructive.'

'Less instructive? You make it sound as if my world is a teaching aid!'

'In a sense that is true,' the entity replied. Matt thought that if the entity had a physical presence, and if he had eyes to see it, then he would be seeing a kindly smile. So these aliens have a sense of humour?

'Simulations are created for various reasons, but one of them is to allow us to learn about how consciousness develops. There are successful paths for an emerging civilisation to follow, and also less successful ones. Sadly there are more of the less successful ones, so we build simulations partly in order to learn how to make them more successful.'

'And how are we doing in my world?'

'There is still a chance for your world. As we said, your simulation is an early one. It progresses slowly, and it contains more suffering than we are used to seeing. We do not know whether your civilisation will survive the coming transitions, but the possibility is not excluded. And then you came along.'

'Me? Did I do something wrong?'

'Not at all. You caused little suffering, and you contributed much positive consciousness, both directly and indirectly. But your species is not ready to encounter a beyond-human intelligence. Which is why you cannot go back to the place and time that you came from.'

'So . . . what are you? Where are you from?'

'We are a civilisation much older than yours. It would be very hard to explain our nature to you. You lack some of the concepts required to understand our subsistence. That is normal.'

Matt wondered whether he was dreaming, or was perhaps being tricked by somebody or something. If not, what did this astonishing new knowledge imply about his own nature, his own life?

'When you create a simulation,' he began, thoughtfully, 'how much detail is there in the beings that inhabit it? Are we real in any sense at all, or just illusions?'

'There is enormous detail. Some of it is engineered directly, and some evolves, in much the way that your scientists believe. The inhabitants of a large-scale simulation like your world are genuinely conscious minds, subsisting on complex brain structures.'

'Which means that you aren't creating games. You are creating life. Does this life mean anything to you? Are we pets? Or ants? Do you care what happens to us?'

'You are far more than pets. What we are about

388

to tell you is a rough approximation, as you lack the concepts necessary to understand the complete picture. Consciousness and intelligence are the phenomena we value most highly. Indeed, this is another of the reasons why we create simulations. We want the universe to contain more mind. In our world, the minds inside a large-scale simulation like yours are worthy of respect and justice. To use terminology from your universe, they have rights.'

'What sort of rights do I have, then?'

'You have the right to have your consciousness maintained, if possible. And to have your suffering minimised. But much depends on context.'

'There is a lot of suffering in my world. People are born in pain, and often die in pain. Some of us experience great tragedy, and all of us are frequently hurt, sometimes very badly. That doesn't sound as if our rights are being observed.'

'You want to say that we have not done a very good job. That is normal. And in some ways it is true. Your simulation is an early one. The simulations we create now contain less suffering, and they also progress faster. We have learned much. And we are not the oldest civilisation which creates simulations.'

'So you are not gods.'

'We are not gods, in the sense you mean. Perhaps we are like Greek gods, from your point of view. But we are not omniscient and omnipotent, like the monotheistic gods which most of your species now worships. We have weaknesses, and we face challenges. If we were gods, the nature of your world would indicate that we are evil. We are not evil.'

'What sort of challenges do you face?'

'Many. Our universe is a remarkable place, with many layers of gradually unfolding mystery. But to give you an example that you will understand, we are trying to determine whether we live in a simulation or not. We think that we probably do, but if so, it is well constructed, and the evidence is slight.'

Matt paused to digest this information. He decided to return to his previous line of enquiry.

'Even if you are not gods, why don't you intervene in my world to stop the suffering, or at least reduce it?'

'With a few exceptions, an intervention ends the simulation. At least, as far as we know. You have left the simulation, so we can intervene in your case.'

'Perhaps you shouldn't make simulations, then, until you can do it properly.' Matt wondered whether this was an ill-mannered remark, and perhaps even dangerous. Apparently not.

'That is a fair suggestion, and most of us now think that our predecessors did begin too early. But it is hard to know when to begin. Your civilisation is already contemplating it, and you certainly do not have the tools or the understanding. In fact, if we cannot find a way to stop it without excessive direct intervention, we will have to terminate your simulation.'

'Wow. So you would kill our entire world just because someone created a simulation within it?'

'If we did, we would be preventing far more suffering than we would be causing, and by an enormous multiple. But no, we would not kill your world, in the sense you mean. We would preserve the minds from your world. They would live again in a different form.'

'Like how?'

'It would take too long for us to explain that to you. We are reaching the limit of your time in between. Now we must ask you a question. Consider well before you answer. Are you ready?'

'Ready as I'll ever be, I suppose.'

'What place and what point in the history of your world would you like to be integrated into? You can only go to the past, at least one hundred years before you were born.'

'So I can't ever meet my parents and my friends again?'

'No. That cannot be.'

For the first time, Matt's sense of calm bliss was ruffled. He did not feel pain or sorrow, but he felt a ripple throughout his being. A sense that something was out of place.

'Will they . . . will they miss me?'

'Yes. They will mourn you.'

There was nothing more to be said. Matt understood that protest would be futile. His old life was over, and the people who had bulked large in it would be moving on without him. Without feeling sad, he felt very alone. Everything seemed to pause, and the entity waited for him to re-gather his thoughts and continue. Eventually, he did so.

'Can I choose who I will be within the time and place?'

'You cannot choose a specific person, but you can choose a type of person.'

Matt knew his answer immediately, but he hesitated, trying to work out whether there would be a better option. He realised there was no way to be absolutely sure.

'Can I ask you for advice about the best choice?'

'We cannot advise you. But we can tell you that the quality of your forthcoming life will depend largely on the nature of your mind. It is our belief that you will have a good next life, Matt.'

Matt's non-existent mouth grinned broadly.

'I want to be an elite warrior in a Mayan city in the jungle highlands, in the Classic Period, say around 800 AD.'

EPILOGUE

'You know, I think your estimate of 18 months is looking pretty good. The readings from this morning's decay rate test are exactly where they should be according to the critical path analysis.'

Vic smiled, acknowledging David's invitation to indulge in one of their favourite games: guessing the timeline to the completion of their project. They faced each other across a table in the minimalist but comfortable canteen at the Shanghai Institute of Technology, which hosted the Matt Metcalfe Foundation, colloquially known as Matt's Lifeboat. The table was a simple pine affair from the enormous Shanghai branch of IKEA, but the chairs were Eames originals.

Vic wore the combination of polo shirt and chinos which had become almost de rigeur in Chinese offices over the last couple of years. David still favoured a more English style: cornflour blue shirt, open at the neck, dark trousers and a plaid jacket. Vic had easily adopted many Chinese tastes and styles, perhaps because he was accustomed to working and living in different countries.

David persisted in eating international foods more often than Shanghainese or other Chinese cuisine, and he still got his news from the BBC and other British-based websites. Vic guessed this had something to do with the difficulties in David's marriage with Sophie, which meant that David had been alone in Shanghai for the first year of the project.

'Yes, that was encouraging,' Vic agreed, twisting noodles onto his chopsticks with a practised nonchalance which would impress a newcomer but would be recogniseable to a Shanghainese as the technique of a gweilo, a foreigner. 'Who knows, maybe I'll be able to collect on my bet with Norman after all.'

David laughed drily. 'You know, I think you may just be able to do that. As long as politics doesn't interfere. I caught up with Gus this morning about his meetings in the US and Europe last week. He reckons that the Technology Relinquishment Initiative is going to pass both Houses of Congress and the European Commission's Draft Renunciation Directive is almost a done deal. You made a great call when you suggested establishing the Foundation here instead of California or London. The Chinese are happy to agree a ban on AGI development but they are having no truck with the backlash against new technologies in general. But I do wonder sometimes, will they be able to hold out against the pressure to slow things down – including us?'

'I think so,' Vic replied. 'The Chinese still love to tweak the tail of the West.'

Even though their GDP had recently surpassed that of the United States, and even though they had always regarded the Middle Kingdom as the true centre of human civilisation, the Chinese still liked to view themselves as the challenger brand in global politics.

It wasn't just the Chinese who resisted aspects of the drive for relinquishment policies. Businesspeople in the West were acutely aware of the huge amounts of money the Japanese were making with their domestic robot industry. Lobbyists in Washington screaming for permission to be allowed to get back into that business, arguing that relinquishment was like America declining to get into the car manufacturing business in the early 20th-century because it liked horses too much.

'Still, there's a big head of steam behind those Bills,' David said. 'Gus thinks the Turing Police may finally become a reality.'

Vic scowled. The European Commission was proposing an autonomous international agency with exceptional powers of inspection and restraint in order to stop rogue governments and individuals from doing any research that could lead to the creation of an AGI. This was a step too far for him, as it was for most Americans.

'That game is far from over. And I wouldn't be surprised if a coalition of the institutes which are researching human-friendly AI algorithms announced a breakthrough this spring. There's been a lot of unusually cordial traffic between several of the bigger US-based ones during the winter. Anyway, fortunately, none of that affects what we're doing here at the Foundation. We've managed to put clear blue water between brain preservation research and AI research in the public's mind.'

'True. It's funny, though,' David mused. 'I'm sure a lot of people – perhaps the majority – still don't really get what we're doing here. It's not a hard thing to understand, and hell knows, we had enough publicity on the back of Matt's disappearance. But I think people just don't really understand that – assuming our timeline is roughly right – we may be just two short years away from abolishing unwanted death. You'd think they would be queuing up and pressing their noses against that window there to book an early slot for themselves and their families.' He jabbed a fork towards the massive plate glass window which separated the research building from a superbly landscaped park, with ornamental trees offering up the first buds of spring, and colourful birds dive-bombing the artificial lake, looking for fish to refuel themselves after their migration back from the south.

Vic gave David a searching glance. 'You still think about Matt all the time, don't you? Of course you do – how could you not? It's been a hard couple of years for you. It's great that Sophie has decided to move out here after all, though. Do the two of you have any new ideas about what happened to him?'

'No, not really. We go round and round the same old explanations. We realise that Matt may have quickly ceased to be recognisably human, but we just can't believe that he would have gone off to some other world or dimension without ever contacting us again. You know, when the initial flurry died down. We keep circling back to the conclusion that something must have gone wrong for him.'

'Well, maybe we'll find out one day. I hope so: I miss him too. But at least you have Sophie here now. How is she settling in?'

'She's doing great. Leo thinks he has wangled her a really interesting contract with a medical equipment firm he consults to which has some operations over here. We should know within a week.'

'Good old Leo!' Vic said.

'Yup, good old Leo. I don't know how I would have survived the last couple of years without him, to be honest.'

*

The warriors tied their war canoes to the trees at the edge of the Usumacinta River, and waited. The canoes were long, each carrying up to 50 men. They came from several different cities: the first to arrive were from Palenque, but over the next couple of hours they were followed by boats from Bonampak, Piedras Negras and Yaxchilan – cities linked by the river. As each group arrived they were greeted by those already waiting with grins and raised fists, but no-one said a word. This was the biggest fighting force deployed in the Maya rainforest for generations, and they wanted to retain the advantage of surprise for as long as possible

The air was heavy and humid as they waited for the drums which would let them know that their other allies from the cities of Calakmul and Caracol had also arrived. Mighty Pakal, the ruler of Palenque, had spent months negotiating this alliance with the other chiefs, and today was the day when the alliance would be tested, and sealed in blood.

His elite fighting group the Jaguars, led by Mat-B'alam, squatted, checking their equipment while they waited. Most of them wore short cotton protective jackets packed with rock salt, and tight bindings of leather or cloth on their forearms and legs. A few pulled on elbow, wrist and knee protectors made of copper alloys, worked to fit comfortably and to glance off sword and knife blows.

Many had daubed patterns on their faces with azure blue paint. They ran calloused fingers along the sharp blades of their weapons to check they had not been nicked or blunted during the two-day river journey.

The jungle heat increased. High above them, birds swooped and cawed, commencing their own daily battle for survival and supremacy, food and reproduction. Up and down the chain of life, birds, animals and men all fought the same battles, wrestled with the same imperative to kill or be killed. The larger animals of the jungle floor knew better than to reveal their presence to a group of humans like this, but smaller mammals could be seen, scurrying in and out of holes in trees and the mossy ground. And of course the insects were everywhere, endlessly noisy in the air, on the ground, and on the twisted, gnarly roots and branches of the enormous trees.

The warriors were ready. They waited only for the sound of the drums.

ACKNOWLEDGEMENTS

The idea for this book arose in 1999, at the height of the dotcom bubble, as I drove to Yahoo's office in Palo Alto for a meeting. I had recently finished reading Ray Kurzweil's *The Age of Spiritual Machines*, which had made me consider the astounding possibility that conscious machines could be created within my lifetime.

That book had been recommended by an old friend, Nick Hadlow, and when I returned to England I suggested that we write a novel together based on the premise. We did, and it was awful. Actually Nick's chapters were rather good, but with hindsight I realised that as mere stripling of 40, I was too young to write a novel. I had recently co-authored a best-selling business book (*The Internet Startup Bible*, which featured prominently in Amazon's first ever UK TV advert) but I didn't realise how much harder it is to write a good novel.

A decade or so later I retired from full-time work, and had both the time and (arguably) the more rounded life experience to do a better job. The story arc is the same, but the characters and much else are wholly different.

The book wouldn't exist without the help of my partner Julia. Somehow she manages to provide penetrating critical insight, substantial contributions to plot and character, and buoyant encouragement – all at the same time. I guess it's because she is both an experienced teacher and a highly effective business manager. However she does it, I know that I am a very lucky fellow.

I have also benefited enormously from the generous help of a number of talented first readers. I didn't learn until too late that the first draft of a novel is an execrable thing which you should show to no-one, so some of these first readers had very questionable material to work with. Nevertheless they offered encouragement and invaluable comments with great tact. In particular I should mention (in mostly alphabetical order) Rob Carter, Lauren Chace, William Charlwood, Lesley and Peter Fenton O'Creevy, Leah Eatwell, Giles Harris, Mary Jagger, Adam Jolly, Peter Monk, Jeff Pinsker, Tess Read and Clare Smith (respectively co-author and publisher of the *Startup Bible*), David Roche and David Wood. Collectively they have weeded out many failures of plotting and characterisation, and even more solecisms and inconsistencies. Those which remain are of course entirely my fault.

The cover image was Julia's idea, and we had valuable help realising it from a talented artist named Neftali Carreira. The overall design of the cover and the interior is the handiwork of Rachel Lawston. Finding Rachel was a blessing: she is a very experienced professional designer who combines great skill with great tact. She is also one of life's great enthusiasts, and has made what can sometimes be a difficult process into a real pleasure

I hope you enjoyed *Pandora's Brain*. If you did, please leave a comment on Amazon. A sequel, *Pandora's Oracle*, is in the works, with a target for publication in mid-2015.

Printed in Great Britain
by Amazon